HELL PREVAILS M.C.

THE COMPLETE COLLECTION

PENNY CRANE

NEF HOUSE PUBLISHING

Hell Prevails MC: The Complete Collection
Copyright © 2023 Penny Crane

ISBN: 978-1-958414-98-9

ALSO BY PENNY CRANE

The Dark Nights Chicago Mafia Romance Series
Dark Rivals
Dark Desires
Dark Secrets
Dark Nights Boxset

Penny Crane's Reverse Harem MC Romance
Hell Prevails
Fate Prevails
Love Prevails
Hell Prevails MC Boxset

Erotic Steampunk LitRPG
Steamship Brass Anchor

Billionaire Romance
Theirs

HPMC PLAYLIST

It's Too Late to Love Me Now by Dolly Parton

The Death of Peace of Mind by Bad Omens

Animals by Architects

Drag the Lake by The Amity Affliction

Something in the Orange by Zach Bryan

Burn it Down by Silverstein

Alone by I Prevail

Feel Nothing by The Plot in You

Nerve Endings by Too Close to Touch

God's Going to Cut You Down by Johnny Cash

Sleeptalk by Dayseeker

Low by Wage War

Soak Me in Bleach by The Amity Affliction

My Heart I Surrender by I Prevail

Sex Metal Barbie by In This Moment

Bury a Friend by Billie Eilish

The River by Wage War

Faded Out by Asking Alexandria feat. Within Temptation

So Good by Halsey

Burial Plot by Dayseeker

If Tomorrow Never Comes by Wage War

Bow Down by I Prevail

Limits by Bad Omens

OMNIBUS EXCLUSIVE BONUS CHAPTER

Beau

I'll never love another woman for the rest of my life.

That's what I think as I sit on her bed, watching her on her bedroom floor packing while Dolly Parton plays from her phone. She doesn't have as many clothes or other things as most girls her age. Most of her stuff consists of a huge book collection and some mementos from various dates we've gone on over the past two years. One of those items is a teddy bear I got her for our first Valentine's Day together. She has the dried bouquet of roses from that same year pinned to a cork board above her now empty desk. It might break my heart a little bit more if she just throws them away . . .

"You could move with me in a year, you know?" she says, folding some band tees and flannels. One of the flannels belongs to me, but she can keep it. I like knowing she'll be taking a piece of me with her. "I only have to live in the dorms for a year, and then I can get an apartment with you."

"You know I can't leave," I tell her. I pick up a framed photo of us from our senior prom. It was the best night of my life. I made love for the first time to my beautiful girlfriend. "Can I have this?"

I hold up the frame to show her, and she nods.

"Yeah, I have another copy printed. It's already packed," she says, zipping the giant suitcase full of clothes.

She stands and places her fists on her hips, looking at the packed room with an emotion I can't read. All of her posters and wall art has been down for three months because her parents are selling their home. They've already moved to Florida, and since their daughter turned eighteen the week after graduation, they went ahead and took off for their new life, leaving Christina here for the summer in a mostly empty home. I'm not complaining too much, though. We've played house for most of the summer, but our time is coming to an end. The house is sold, the new owners move in tomorrow morning, and Christina will be staying with me for two days before she also moves onto *her* new life.

"Come here," I say, patting the space beside me. She obliges and lies down beside me, resting her head on my shoulder. I can tell with great certainty that I'll never love another woman for the rest of my life.

"Are you sure I can't sneak you off to college with me?" she asks, placing her small hand on my chest. "I bet no one would notice you shacked up in my dorm."

I chuckle. "No, baby. You've gotta go on your own. You're going to change the world."

She scoffs. "Yeah, right. I'm scared, Beau."

"Baby, you've got nothing to be scared of," I tell her, holding her closer to me and pressing a kiss on her forehead. "I'll be here waiting for you when you're ready to come back. *If* you come back."

She lifts her head up and looks at me. "You promise, Beau Grady?"

I nod my head and push some of her blonde hair behind her ear. "Give college a chance, make some friends, and if you haven't found the man of your dreams, I'll be here waiting for you."

She rests her head back on my shirt and doesn't say anything for a moment. I feel my shirt dampening beneath her face. "I think I already found the man of my dreams."

"I know, sweetheart," I say softly, holding her a little tighter. "I know."

Her body shudders. I know she's breaking just as much as I am, but we've reached the end of our love story—for now. I'm not going to be that boyfriend who holds her back from a better life, who holds her back from becoming the woman she's destined to be. What's painful is knowing that she'll be out there without me to keep watch on her. There's evil in this world, and I'll no longer be able to make sure she gets home safely. College campuses are filled with predators, they just wear shiny masks and drive around in daddy's Porsche. I can't have her rot away here in Lexington with me either.

It's getting dangerous as the population grows and the city expands.

Most people look the other way when they pass the danger on the streets, but some of the predators wear shiny suits and have their hands in the pockets of the government. You can't trust them—that's what I've learned during my time as a Prospect. I need to get Christina as far away from this little city as possible, before she finds out what I've done, who I've pledged my loyalty to.

Christina sits up, avoiding my gaze and wiping her eyes.

"We should probably head out," she tells me. "The realtor is bringing the new owners by at eight for the final walkthrough."

"Okay," I answer. I shove my feet in my boots. I packed most of her stuff into my truck two hours ago and then watched her pack her clothes and other final items. She's leaving her desk and bed here since there's no sense taking them with her to her dorm room. The new owners will probably just throw them out.

I grab her duffle bag and the framed prom picture. She takes her cork board off the wall, being careful with the ticket stubs, dried flowers, and pictures. I smile at the thought of her hanging it up at her dorm with all the pictures of us smiling back at her every day. Some punk might eventually be in her dorm room, and he'll see my face and probably ask who I am. I hope she tells him the truth. I'm the first guy she ever loved, but I guess I won't be the last.

* * *

I park the truck in the garage so Christina's boxed up items are safe until I move them into the little U-Haul trailer she's renting. She opens the truck door and spots the project I've been working on during my downtime.

"When did you get a motorcycle?" she asks, a bright smile on her face as she runs a hand over the handlebars.

"My uncle passed it onto me," I say with a shrug. "It hasn't run in years, and he had no plans on fixing it up. He gave the title over, so I'm fixing it up. Or . . . I'm trying to fix it up."

"Does it run?" she asks.

I shake my head. "Not yet, but it will soon. Just waiting for a part or two to be delivered."

"Aww, man," she says sadly. "I was hoping you would give me a little ride."

"One day, maybe," I tell her, wrapping my arms around her waist and pulling her against me. "I'll take you for a ride one day. Just going to have to get you a helmet and leather jacket."

She smiles and blushes. "Sounds like I could be your old lady or something with a leather jacket."

My heart accelerates. She doesn't realize just how much meaning those two words hold. None of the guys in the MC I'm joining call their wives their wife. They all refer to them as their old ladies, even if they're not exactly old. I'd make Christina my old lady today if she wasn't leaving. I'd be proud to have her perched on the back of my bike—once it's running safely.

"You could be something like that," I assure her, placing a kiss on her forehead. "Let's get inside. I wanna savor our time."

Christina's pupils dilate, and I know she understands exactly what I'm saying. She sticks her tongue out at me and then hauls ass out of the garage, toward the trailer I grew up in. It's very different from the cozy house that Christina's family just sold. Her house was big and decorated to the nines, and the trailer my uncle raised me in was falling apart, but it was still a roof over my head, filled with all the love I could be given by someone who didn't ask to raise a kid but still stepped up when my mom left.

Christina throws open the screen door and jimmies the door open. She glances over her shoulder and squeals, playfully running from me. I'd chase her to the ends of the earth just to hear her laughter and see her smile.

"There's nowhere for you to run, baby," I shout when I walk into the trailer and lock the door behind us. My uncle went on a fishing trip for the weekend, so we get two more days to pretend like we're adults. Honestly, he wouldn't have cared if Christina stayed with us for the weekend. He was always smitten by her, letting her stay all night as long as it wasn't a school night. She'd tell her parents she was sleeping at some friend's house, but they honestly didn't give a shit. They're like my mom was, I guess: didn't ever want to be parents but too stupid to wear condoms. At least Christina's parents were nice enough to wait and leave until she was of legal age. My mom dropped me off on the front porch of my uncle's trailer without even leaving a note before I even hit puberty.

The house is quiet, but I can hear the rustling of fabric coming from down the hall.

"Chris," I sing, sliding off my boots at the front door beside her tiny sandals. "Where are you?"

She doesn't say anything. I get some sort of thrill from her playing games like this with me. I love chasing her, finding her.

When I get to my bedroom, I stop in the doorframe, finding Christina lying on my bed in the hottest bra and matching thong I've ever seen, wearing my leather cut on her small shoulders. I must have forgotten to put away the cut so she wouldn't see it. I don't want her knowing that I'm joining the MC, but the sexy smile on her face tells me she's oblivious to the patches on the back and what they mean.

"Fuck, baby," I say, running a hand through my blonde hair. "This is unexpected."

"You like?" She asks, crossing her legs at her ankles.

"Hell yeah, I do," I whisper, approaching the bed slowly.

"I wanted to make sure it was special," she says softly. "Make sure you wouldn't forget about me."

"Baby, I'll *never* forget you," I say, placing one knee on the bed and running a hand up her smooth thigh. "And right now you will be cemented forever in my mind."

She lets out a shaky breath. "Make me feel good, Beau."

She doesn't have to tell me twice. I carefully separate her legs and lay between them on the bed, placing kisses against her bare thighs as I make my way up to the tiny cloth covering her sweet cunt. I smell her arousal, and it sends the blood straight to my dick.

I carefully push the red fabric of the thong to the side, revealing her pink, swollen slit. My tongue comes out, and I lick from her clit all the way to her tiny little asshole, making her gasp and thrust her hips. She's let me explore her body a little more every time we make love to each other. She even confessed to me one night that she's been curious about anal. I haven't told her that I bought her a new toy for us to try and some lube to go with it. I'm not going to fuck her ass tonight, she's not ready, but I think she'll let me play.

Moving my attention back to her clit, I suck it into my mouth, and she bucks her hips into my face and tugs on my hair. I love how wild she gets when we explore each other's bodies. I love it. I love her.

I slide two of my fingers into her tight pussy and lift my head so I can watch her unravel. Her breasts strain against the bra she's wearing, and she looks so fucking sexy wearing my cut. I think I'm going to make her keep it on when I finally put my cock inside her.

"Baby," I say sweetly, waiting for her to open her eyes. "You wanna try something new tonight?"

She nods quickly. "Anything. Anything for you, Beau."

I smile at her enthusiasm. I'm pretty sure I could convince her of anything when she's on the verge of cumming. It makes me feel powerful. Before I ask her to try something new, I'm going to make her explode.

Leaning back down, I flick my tongue quickly over her clit again and turn my fingers so I can hook them inside her and find that sweet spot she loves so much. Her words are gibberish as she crests her pleasure, and I shove my fingers in and out of her until I feel her pussy clench against them, holding them tightly inside.

"Yes, yes, yes!" she chants loudly, and I smirk against her pussy as I begin licking up her pleasure while she comes down from her orgasm. "God damn, Beau Grady. You're so good at that. How?"

I chuckle, pulling back and licking my fingers clean before licking my lips too. "I lived off of pudding cups and no silverware for a while."

She laughs and rests her head against the pillow. "That's an image right there."

"You good?" I ask, lying beside her.

She nods her head and then reaches down to cup my cock through my shorts. My erection is almost painful at this point, but I want to try putting that toy in her before I get off too.

"You ready for your surprise?" I ask, running my finger over the spot on my cut where my nickname will soon be sewed in once the president figures one out for me. They nickname all the prospects, sometimes the name sticks for your entire membership, but sometimes once you make it out of your prospect duties and become an official member, you get to put your real name on it along with your title.

"I'm ready," she says.

I reach over for the bag on the nightstand, pulling out the bottle of lube and butt plug I bought a few days ago. My eyes find Christina's and her mouth opens on a gasp.

"You wanna try?" I ask her.

She stares at the metal plug, her eyes wide. It's the smallest one that they sold, but I'm sure it'll still get the experience. I hold the plug out for her to examine, and she takes it from me, rolling it around in her fingers. It's got a red heart jewel on the stopper end, and I can't wait to see her holding it in that tight little ass of hers.

"You'll help me put it in?" she asks.

"Of course, baby." My heart races. "I'll be as gentle as I can be, and if it doesn't feel good, just tell me, and we'll stop."

"Okay," she says.

"Flip over, baby," I tell her. "On your knees, ass up."

She's obviously eager to try it out, and it's made even more obvious by how quickly she flips over and shows me her ass. She rocks her hips back and forth. She's got the most perfect ass. I place a kiss on each of her cheeks.

"I'm going to take your thong off," I tell her, reaching for the tiny strings and pulling them over her hips and down her thighs. "But you're going to keep everything else on, okay?"

"You like my outfit?" she asks, glancing over her shoulder and giving me a wicked smile.

"You're damn right I like your outfit," I fire back, putting some lube on the plug. I don't want to traumatize her. I'm not going to be the asshole boyfriend who tries to shove a dry butt plug into my girlfriend's ass. Assholes don't self lubricate, and the amount of idiots who don't realize that drives me nuts. Anal, even just with toys, takes time and preparation if you want it to feel good for everyone involved.

"It might be cold," I tell her, rubbing my hand over her plump ass, spreading her cheeks open a little bit. "Just keep breathing, don't tense up. We'll go slow."

She nods. "I'll try."

"Just stay like this, baby," I whisper, running the plug over her hole to get her used to the feeling. Instead of flinching away, she just sways her hips a little bit, almost like she's trying to chase the sensation.

I place the tip of the plug against its destination, and when she doesn't flinch or pull away, I hold it at an angle and begin pushing against the tiny entrance. She pushes back on it a little bit, and I let her take control.

"You wanna do it, baby?" I ask. "Fuck yourself against it. Get it all the way inside."

"Mmhmm," she moans, glancing over her shoulder again, biting her bottom lip as she smiles.

My voice shakes, mesmerized. "You're my dirty little girl, aren't you? You want this ass and pussy filled?"

"Yes, Beau," she tells me. "Fuck, this is so hot."

I reach my hand out to run my fingers through her pussy lips, and she's drenched. My girl apparently likes the idea of being double penetrated. Shit, just the thought almost has me creaming my pants. I can't wait to be inside her and feel the plug on the other side.

She bucks against the plug, taking it slowly inside her until all I can see is the little heart gem. Her asshole holds it neatly in place. I turn it so the heart jewel is sitting there perfectly between her cheeks, and then sit back to enjoy the view. Her pussy is glistening wet, and the plug looks so fucking hot.

"Beau, this feels so good," she says, wiggling her hips. "Holy shit."

"I should make you walk around with it for the rest of the weekend," I say without even thinking. She's used to my sweet words, not this dirty talk. I think she likes it though—she likes this new side of me. I just wish she wasn't leaving so soon.

"I'd do it for you," she says sweetly. "Anything for you, Beau Grady."

"You're my good girl, my dirty girl," I tell her. "Don't you forget it."

She drops her head and moans, loving the praise. "Fuck me, Beau. Show me that I'm still yours."

Getting back up on my knees, a shift until my cock is notched right up against her. I rub my shaft against her opening, loving how wet I've made her. She's always ready to go for me. It's crazy how sweet and demure she was before we had sex the first time, but as soon as we lost our virginity together, it's like I flipped a switch. She became insatiable, always wanting me inside her. I'm not complaining, of course.

"Beau, stop teasing," Christina gasps, arching her back.

I grip my shaft and slowly slide into her tight, warm cunt, loving the way it grips me so perfectly. However, there's a new sensation that I feel when I pull out and press in. The butt plug feels so hot in her ass, and I'm betting she feels so full right now.

"You like it, baby?" I pant, moving in and out.

She nods quickly. "Yes, I love it. Fuck, I want more."

"Too bad your dildo is already packed up," I tell her, gently smacking her ass as I pump in and out. "I bet I could fuck that little ass with it at the same time."

Her pussy clenches around me, and I smirk.

"You like the idea of two cocks using your body, baby?" I ask her.

"Y-yeah."

I've seen a lot of crazy shit since I started hanging around the clubhouse. I've seen a handful of orgies; two girls going down on each other while some of the Brothers watch; I've seen two of the guys fucking the same girl at the same time. HPMC is filled with horny motherfuckers, but I would never dream of participating in their fuckery. I'm only into my girl, and I don't know if I could ever share her.

"It's okay to get turned on by that, baby," I say, reaching down and gently tugging on the butt plug, but I don't remove it. "Fuck, you would look so good with two cocks in you. You're mine though, you know that?"

"I'm yours," she gasps, pushing back against me, meeting my thrusts. "I've always been yours, Beau Grady. Shiiiit, I think I'm going to cum. Play with my ass, Beau. I like feeling you tug on the plug."

"Yeah, baby?" I speed up my thrusts and tug on the plug until I see her hole expand around it before pushing it back in. I'm going to make myself cum just by watching her ass grip the toy.

"There it is," I say, feeling her pussy throb around my cock. "There's my dirty girl milking my cock. Take it, baby."

She continues pulsing and when I hear her whimper, I release myself deep inside her. I don't pull out until I feel myself soften inside her. We both collapse on my bed next to each other, catching our breath.

"Holy shit, that was intense," she says, laughing a bit.

I smile over at her. "Let's clean up, and then I'll make some popcorn and we can watch a movie."

"That sounds perfect."

"I'll get the shower ready," I tell her, placing a kiss on her forehead. "Take your time. I'll help you remove the toy when you're ready."

She blushes and instantly becomes my sweet girlfriend again as if I didn't just fuck her like a crazed animal. This girl . . . she's the one, just at the wrong time.

* * *

I wake up in the middle of the night to my phone vibrating on my nightstand. Christina is curled up asleep beside me. I try to get out of bed and answer the call without disturbing her. She goes to college later today and doesn't need the stress of poor sleep. Yesterday, we picked up her U-Haul trailer. I attached it to her SUV and loaded the boxes inside. We spent the rest of Saturday making love, eating pizza, and watching all her favorite movies while we cuddled in bed. It was perfect.

I don't answer my phone until I'm able to close the door behind me.

"What's up?" I ask. "Bit early." I check the time. 4:06am.

He chuckles on the other end, but I can tell he's also just as tired as me. "Pres wants everyone at the clubhouse. More prospect hoops to jump through. Not sure how much more of this shit I can handle."

"We've got this, Brother," I tell him, rubbing the sleep from my eyes.

"Want me to pick you up?" he asks. "You're on my way, I can be there in five."

I peek through the crack in my door, checking on Christina. She's still asleep. "Nah, I've got somewhere to be as soon as we're done with the meeting. I'll just see you there."

"Sounds good," he says.

"See you soon, Dan," I tell the other prospect. We've gotten close in the last month.

Dan and I are moving into a house with the Pres's son in a month or so. Griff is alright, not the most agreeable person, but it's best to keep close to him since he'll probably become president one day. And staying on his good side is an added benefit.

I end the phone call and head back into my room. I pull on a pair of jeans, a black shirt that I find lying on the ground, and my cut that I eventually hung up in my closet after having our fun with it. Christina's scent surrounds me when I slip my arms into the cut, and I wish it would smell like her forever. I snag a piece of paper off my desk and write her a note that I have to go run an errand. I'll probably be back before she wakes up, and it won't matter anyway. Before I head out, I place a gentle kiss on her forehead and tell her I love her. She stirs a little but goes back to sleep by the time I grab the keys to my truck off the nightstand.

* * *

The meeting was bullshit.

Pres literally just called us prospects in to clean the clubhouse after they threw a rager the night before—a rager that the prospects weren't even invited to. Danny, Griff, me, and four other guys spent almost five hours cleaning the clubhouse. We scrubbed the floor, picked up trash, cleaned the bar area, and threw away so many empty bottles that it's a miracle anyone in the club is still alive. I didn't want to go home smelling like a dumpster, so I showered in one of the stalls in the gym. I wasn't trying to explain to Christina why I smelled like urine and stale beer.

Finally released, I speed out of the clubhouse, my heart racing as I drive back home, hoping I can make Christina breakfast in bed. Creedence Clearwater Revival plays on the radio, and I tap my fingers to the beat.

It's only nine or so in the morning, so the church crowd isn't on the road yet, making it easier for me to navigate the roads. I steer down the gravel road, but something feels off. I find out what that feeling is a moment later when I pull up to the house and Christina's SUV and U-Haul aren't in the driveway. My heart plummets . . . She wouldn't have left without saying goodbye or something. I toss my truck into park and head straight for the front door. It's locked like I left it, but when I open the door, the house feels empty.

"Chris?" I yell. Her shoes are gone. "Chris, I'm home. Where'd you go?"

I go back to my bedroom, finding the bed unmade and empty. I walk to the bathroom, but she's not in there either. I go to inspect my room, looking for a note or something, but the one I wrote her is still there next to the water bottle I left for her.

I grab my phone and call her. It goes straight to voicemail. I call again, same thing. I hang up, not bothering to leave a voicemail. I spot the picture frame with our prom photo propped up on my bedside table. I wasn't the one who set it there. It's the only sign that she was here other than her smell on my sheets.

* * *

I call Christina everyday for a month straight. I get no response, but at least my calls don't go straight to voicemail. She's disabled all her social media, almost like she's disappeared. I've spent the last month wondering if I did something wrong. Did she think that I ditched her and wasn't coming back? Did something happen? Did I take it too far, too quickly when we used the toy? She could have at least left a note, but she didn't even do that. I know because I flipped my bedroom upside down looking for a goodbye from her, but there was nothing.

"How's that bike coming along?" Griff asks, popping open a beer and sitting down on the bench across from where I'm working on the finishing touches.

"Almost road ready," I answer. "If your dad gave us some slack every now and then, it would be done by now."

"You know him," he says, kicking his legs out. "Hardass on an ego trip. Just likes having someone to push around."

Griff, Danny, and I moved in together a week ago. It's been an adjustment, but it's nice living with people who are working toward the same goal in life—much better than living at the clubhouse that never sleeps. It's a constant party, and not always in a good way.

"Today's the day," he tells me. "You ready to pledge your allegiance to the patch?"

"I guess so." I wipe my greased hands on a cloth. "You?"

"I was literally born ready," Griff says, almost sadly. I think he believes his dad actually wanted to have a son to pass the Pres patch down to. "I'll go get Danny, and then we can head out."

"Cool." Griff heads back in the house, and I slip my cut back onto my shoulders. Christina's scent is long gone from it, like that night she wore it never existed. I've been walking around as an empty shell of a human since she left. The club noticed my personality change. They tried to make me snap out of it by offering up various women, but I've turned down every single one. They aren't Christina. She's the only one I want, but she scrubbed me from her life.

And the worst part? I don't even know why.

* * *

"We did it," Danny says, plopping down on the barstool beside me. He pats me on the back and then stares out at the party unraveling in front of us. I glance at the patch on my chest with the nickname they gave me: 'Saint.'

Danny got 'Lover Boy' because he's constantly swooning over the sweet butts that come around the club. Mine is for the opposite. I don't swoon over anyone, I'm a Saint. The guys think I'm a virgin, too. So be it. I've already decided none of these women will make me happy, so I guess I'm celibate now. A pious monk in a motorcycle club. We only have to keep the nicknames for a year, and then we can get our real name on a patch.

"You okay, man?" Danny asks. "You should be celebrating."

I shrug my shoulders and check my phone for a message that I know I'm not going to get. "I'm alright. Just not sure if it was worth it."

"Don't let Pres hear you say that," Dan whispers. "He lives, breathes, and bleeds for this club."

I look at Danny, a flash of fear in his eyes. As prospects, we didn't really get to see what the club was truly about, we just did all the bitch work. We cooked, cleaned, went on runs that the official members didn't want to do, and so on. Starting tomorrow, we'll be diving deeper into the work of Hell Prevails MC. Tonight we're supposed to enjoy ourselves, but I'm not sure I can with the veil of mystery hanging over me. The specter of the unknown. Another variable in my tumultuous life.

I take a swig of my beer and turn back to the party. Griff is making a beeline over to us, a huge, wicked grin on his face. A girl with jet black hair and huge tits follows close behind him, looking blitzed out of her mind.

"Gentlemen," Griff says when he gets to us. He slings his arm around the woman and holds her tightly against him. "Josie here told me she'd love to christen our new patches by fucking us. Who wants in?"

"I'm in," Danny announces, not missing a beat. He finishes his beer and stands on the other side of Josie. She licks her lips like a cheap beer commercial floozie and looks him up and down.

Then she turns her head to me. "What about you, handsome? You wanna join us? I've got room for three."

I bet she does.

"Nah, Sugar," Danny says so I don't have to speak to the girl. "This here is Saint. Ain't no way you can convince him to touch you with a ten-foot pole."

I laugh and take a swig of my beer as the woman gives me the nastiest look. Danny's not wrong. He may be totally fine about sticking his dick in crazy, but this girl isn't my type. Not even if Christina didn't exist somewhere out there in the world. This woman is probably thirty something, but she's got some extra years on her in all the wrong places. I'm kind of shocked that Griff is going for her, he's usually fairly picky too, but I guess he's looking for someone easy to celebrate his patching in. What better person to go with than an eager patch bunny?

"Have fun," I tell the guys, but they're already sauntering away.

* * *

This is bullshit.

It's been over two years since I joined the 'club,' and it's the exact opposite of what I was told it would be. What I thought it would be. If I could go back in time, I would have never attended my patching ceremony. I would rather still be a prospect than see the shit I've seen. Not only am I dodging patch bunnies left and right, but I've also killed too many times to count. Pres swears they're all bad men and we're just protecting the community, but I'm starting to feel like we've been lied to.

Griff and Danny know I've had enough of the murder. They've noticed me self-medicating more and more with alcohol. They told me they'll try their best to step up and take my spot if they know we're going on a kill—like right now. I'm on getaway duty. They met Pres and some of the others at the end of an alley next to Big Jon's bar downtown. I'm sitting at a meter waiting for word to come cleanup.

Animals by Architects plays low on the stereo, and I act as relaxed as I can. It's the fifth time we've had to do it in three weeks. Something big is happening, but Pres refuses to disclose all the information. Something needs to be done, but I can't do it alone.

One of the guys waves me down the alley, and I toss the van into gear so I can back it up and collect the body. This thing doesn't have a backup cam, so I have to watch in the side mirrors. Danny's got his mouth over someone's face, but I can't tell much about them. Whatever. Just more of the job, I suppose.

By the time I'm backed up all the way, they've got a pillowcase over the person's head and their hands tied in front of them. I breathe a sigh of relief that for once we didn't kill the person, but no—looks like this is just a witness. They're rolling up the dead guy and tossing him into the van. I stay seated, drumming my fingers on the steering wheel and trying not to think too much.

Danny and Griff hop into the cab with me once the witness and dead guy are secured in the back, and I put the van in drive to head to the lake, same as usual. Griff and Danny are quiet as can be, and the longer they keep their mouths shut, the more irritated I become.

"It wasn't supposed to be this way," I say through clenched teeth, one hand on the steering wheel. I should have never agreed to join this stupid club with Danny. I thought it would be fun rebuilding my uncle's motorcycle and joining a group of guys to ride with on the weekends. No, I was so wrong, and now I have no idea how to get out.

HELL PREVAILS

CHAPTER 1

It wasn't supposed to be this way.

It really wasn't. I was supposed to go off to college after graduating high school. Hell, I was the valedictorian. I had my college acceptance letter framed; it still is framed, just sitting in one of the boxes in the back of my closet that I never unpacked when I left my sorority to move back home.

You see, I did go to college. I was in my second year when I threw my sorority sisters under the bus over a bout of intense physical hazing. If there was one thing I hated in life, it was bullying, and there was plenty in that house. The problem is, once the ladies finished up their community service, they made it their duty to turn the majority of the Greek system at our college against me. They turned my world upside down. The only thing I could do was leave the school that spring and never come back. So that's exactly what I did.

I loaded up my little black Yaris and headed back home to Kentucky. The only issue with that was my parents had sold my childhood home and ran off to Florida. I had no choice but to get a job at a small local bar, find a tiny studio apartment in bum-fuck nowhere, and live out the rest of my days as a failure. I was on track to finish my degree in social work and graduate top of my class, but that all got taken away when I became known as a college narc.

Yes, I could have applied to another college to finish my degree, but my name was all over the news and who knows how many states had reported on my 'good behavior.'

"Christina," my boss, Big Jon, yells from the end of the bar. "Can you take out the trash?"

"Sure thing," I say, tossing my bar rag into the sink and wiping my hands on my dark jeans. I grab the trash from behind the bar and also go to change out the trash next to the front door. I hold them up and away from my body, hoping to God that they don't rip open like they did the last time I took out the trash. Yesterday they spilled to the floor and some of the liquid contents ended up on me. *Fucking disgusting.* I felt like I would never get clean. I swear my jeans still smell like stale beer despite a thorough wash, but I don't really have spare money lying around for a shopping spree. I'm already paying on student loans since I dropped out.

Just as I push open the back door that leads to the alley our dumpster is in, the door bangs shut behind me, but that's not the only bang that I hear. Simultaneously, the loud crack of a gunshot breaks through the alleyway. I drop the trash bags at my feet, where they do indeed rip open on the rough concrete, and my eyes make contact with four men standing around a lifeless body on the ground, one of them holding a handgun. Two of their motorcycles lean on kickstands nearby.

"Shit," one of the men curses, looking up at me and pulling a knife from a leather sheath on his hip.

I've seen two of the men before. It's a small town, after all. They come into Big Jon's bar every weekend. People talk about them, I've heard stories, but small towns are full of gossip, and I take everything with a grain of salt. Or at least I used to.

"Griff," says the man with the gun. "Handle the body. Danny, get the girl. Alive, you dumb fuck."

The second the man with the knife starts advancing on me, I begin walking away slowly, but he speeds up his steps and I turn away to run but I'm not quick enough. My morning runs didn't train me to get away from men with weapons. And despite all the adrenaline, I'm too panicked to think straight and go full speed.

The guy is behind me in an instant, placing his hand over my mouth to muffle the scream that I was just about to let out, using his other hand to wrap around my waist. He leans in to whisper in my ear, yanking me against his chest.

"I won't hurt you," he says. "Pres just needs to figure out what he's going to do with you. Don't worry."

I whimper against him and try my best to remain calm, doing an exercise that I try to do when I'm running and thinking about giving up. I name two things I can see: some cars passing by on Main Street and a barber cutting someone's hair in a storefront. Two things I can smell: the man must have recently washed his hands or showered using Old Spice and the spilled beer at our feet. Two things I can hear: I close my eyes and listen to Dolly Parton's muffled music playing in the bar and the church bells ringing down the street. Must be exactly six.

"Griff is going to put some tape over your mouth, tie some rope around your wrists, a pillowcase over your head, and then we're going to put you in that van right over there," he says softly, nodding as a white van with tinted windows backs down the alley, a van perfect for kidnapping. Everything just happens too fucking fast. "We're just going to go for a little ride. Dispose of the bad guy over there and then we'll all sit down for a chat. Can you cooperate?"

He turns me to Griff, who somehow managed to get the dead body rolled up in a tarp fairly quickly. He's got some rope in one hand and the duct tape in the other, already pulling off a piece to cover my mouth.

"You going to be a good girl?" the man holding me against his chest asks, and even though I'm crying, I nod my head, praying that Big Jon comes looking for me before these men toss me into their van.

Griff places the duct tape over my mouth and then forces me to put my hands in a praying position as the other guy comes over to tie my hands together. I'm mesmerized by the intricate knots they tie to secure my hands together, and suddenly the promised pillowcase is placed over my head, making everything go dark.

"Toss the girl in the back of the van with the body," demands the man I assume to be their leader. "You three go in the van to get rid of the body, we'll meet you back at the clubhouse. Do *not* hurt the girl, scare her if you want, but she better be alive when you get back. And unharmed, too."

I whimper as two strong arms lift me up and put me in the van. I scoot as far away from them as possible until my back hits what I think is a seat. I can't see a thing, but I jump when I hear something else get tossed into the van and the doors close behind it. I try not to think about the fact that there's a dead body next to me, blood probably seeping through the tarp.

Two more doors open and close, and the van begins to move. I pull my knees up to my chest and wrap my arms around my legs, rocking myself back and forth.

"It wasn't supposed to be this way," a new voice says right behind me. I assume the new speaker to be the driver. "You said this was just a motorcycle club, not a freaking gang. What the fuck have you gotten me into, Danny?"

"I screwed up," says the other guy from the front seat. "I just wanted us to be close again. I thought being prospects was going to get us somewhere."

A third guy chuckles. "You thought wrong. Now we're burying bodies, kidnapping innocent women, and running whatever the hell the Pres puts in this van."

"Who is the chick anyway?" the other guy asks. His voice sends a familiar shiver down my spine. I stop whimpering and turn my head, hoping to put a face to the voice.

"Don't know," says Danny. "She saw us shoot the guy in the alley, not sure what she was doing there. Way too pretty to be on this side of the tracks. What do you think Pres is going to do to her?"

"Who knows? Maybe we should let her go, give her a fighting chance. Release her in the woods," says the driver.

"Yeah right," answers one of the other men. "Pres will hunt her down and kill all four of us for something like that."

"We can say she got away," Danny offers. "I've noticed her running around town, she's pretty fast."

"She's not getting out of those knots," says the other guy. "Trust me. I tend to toil in shibari."

"God, you're a freak," mutters the driver.

I feel something pooling at my left thigh, thinking maybe I've pissed myself, but then I remember the bloody body next to me, and I flip out. I squeal and try to stand up to move further away from my dead backseat companion, but end up slipping on what I assume is his blood. There's zero traction in the back of the van. I can't help but wonder how many dead bodies have been inside it before this one.

"The fuck?" one of the guys says. I feel the seat move behind me as the guy turns around. "Shit, Griff! Dude is bleeding all over the back!"

"We'll wash it out, calm down!" he says back as we turn onto a bumpy gravel road.

"It's getting all over this chick's clothes!" he says, gagging. "What are we going to do with her clothes?"

"Burn them?" retorts the other guy.

I try to scream as I thrash my head back and forth, but the tape silences me.

"Jesus Christ!" says the driver. "First we kidnap her, now you're talking about burning her?"

"Burning her clothes!" shouts the guy. "Not her. You have a change of clothes in that duffle?"

"Yeah, but I doubt they will fit her," the driver says. We haven't gone far, and he's already pulling the van to a stop. That doesn't seem good.

"Whatever, here's the plan," the guy in the middle says. "You go take her to the pond, burn the clothes, and change her into yours. Make sure there's no blood on her. I'll clean the van out, Danny can bury the body."

The guys open their doors to get out of the van, slamming them behind before coming around to open the back doors. I feel some weight leave the van, but then feel someone crawling toward me, yanking my legs to pull me out of the van.

I resist a little, trying to kick my legs, but it's no use. His grip tightens on my ankles and I fall to the ground, knocking my head on the bumper. There's no way I can fight them off. Even if I somehow got free of the duct tape, I wouldn't stand a chance.

"Sorry," the guy whispers. "I'm going to stand you up now. Don't run, or you'll trip and hurt yourself. There are trees and roots everywhere. Even a giant cliff." Well, that at least tells me where I am. There aren't many cliffs near town, after all. I'm in a park maybe five or six miles from the bar. But still, five or six miles is *a lot*.

The two other guys chuckle as they watch me get pulled to my feet. My kidnapper rubs a gentle hand over my head where I knocked it on the bumper. I pull away from him and he sighs, holding me by the elbow and forcing me to walk into the unknown.

He doesn't talk as we go, and I stumble a few times over tree roots, just like he told me I would, but he holds onto my arm, making sure that I don't fall on my face. I try to concentrate on the crickets and frogs singing their nightly song, trying to keep my breathing steady. In the back of mind, I plan an escape route back to civilization should the opportunity arise.

"Here we are," he says, letting go of my elbow. "Don't move. We're right next to the water. Now, I'm going to take your clothes off so you're not covered in blood. I'll have to untie those ridiculous knots, but you're going to keep the pillowcase and duct tape on, understood?"

I nod my head and cry, thinking about this stranger removing my clothes—as if being kidnapped wasn't humiliating enough.

He must sense my fear because he places a gentle hand on my chin. "Hey, you're okay with me. I promise," he whispers. "I know you're probably imagining the worst, but I've never hurt a woman and I'm not starting tonight."

I nod my head but continue to cry as he unbuttons my jeans and pulls them down my legs, removing my boots as well, then standing back up to pull off my top. Just as he has my shirt halfway off, he stops and gasps. When he yanks the pillowcase off my head, I've got my eyes squeezed shut, tears running down my cheeks. I'm fairly certain I've just pissed myself.

"Christina?" he asks, ripping the duct tape from my lips.

When I open my eyes, it takes them a minute to adjust before I realize I know this boy—this man standing in front of me. I've loved this man before, years ago.

I sag to the ground, cowering at Beau's dirty black boots, crying silently.

"Shit," he says, kneeling down next to me, pushing my hair away from the face. "This can't be fucking happening. Christina?"

"Please," I whisper. "Please don't hurt me, Beau. Please. Don't let them hurt me."

My body shakes with fear as I let Beau pull me into his lap. The smell of blood and piss mingling with dirt.

"I swear I'm not going to hurt you, bab—" he begins to say, calling me by my pet name like he used to when we were high school sweethearts. "Christina. I'm not going to hurt you. Let's get you cleaned up and dressed. I don't want Danny or Griff coming to look for us while you're in this state."

Beau begins untying my hands and once they're free, I yank my shirt back down and wrap my arms around myself, turning away from him. He sighs behind me and places a gentle hand on my shoulder.

"I need that shirt, Chris," he says. "If you want, I'll turn around while you clean yourself off in the pond, but I need that shirt. It needs to be burned. It's covered in the blood you fell in."

I glance down at the shirt and realize it's indeed covered in their victim's blood. I pull it off and toss it behind my head, but I still reek of blood. It's on my bra and underwear too, though not as badly.

"Go on and get in the water, Chris," Beau says gently, but when I don't move, he raises his voice, startling me. "Get in the water, Christina!"

I begin another silent cry and walk toward the embankment of the pond. It's filled with green moss, and I try to push it away from me as I walk just far enough to be shoulder deep. I begin scrubbing the blood off my arms and legs with my hands, but without any soap it is a slow process. I feel small fish at my ankles and kick them away. After five minutes, I think I've gotten the blood off of me. Almost all of it, at least.

Beau is waiting for me with a small gym towel. I wrap my arms around myself as he begins wiping the pond water off of me. At least he's being sure not to cross any boundaries.

"How'd you know it was me?" I ask as he kneels down in front of me to dry off my legs. "Before you took the blindfold off, how'd you know it was me?"

His face is right at my crotch and I hope the pond water washed off the smell of my piss. "Birthmark," he says simply. "You have three in the shape of a triangle on your stomach."

"I do?" I ask. Honestly, I've never spent too much time looking at myself in a mirror. I hate looking at my body, and I *certainly* hate others looking at my body. Beau takes his pointer finger and pokes three small dots onto my skin, right below my breasts. Which explains why I can't see them—my tits block the view.

He finishes drying my legs and turns to grab some clothes out of his duffle bag. He hands over a pair of black gym shorts and a plain black t-shirt. I take them from him and yank the shorts on as quickly as possible and slide the shirt over my wet bra. Beau puts the towel in his bag and grabs the rope and pillowcase.

"Beau," I say pleadingly as he walks toward me.

He glances at the items in his hand, like he's reluctant to do what he's about to do, but he places the pillowcase over his shoulder and reaches for my hands.

"I'm sorry," he says. "You just have to wear this stuff until we get to the clubhouse. I promise I'm not going to let anything happen to you. You can trust me, remember?"

When I don't comply, he snatches my hands and starts tying them together, albeit loosely. He doesn't tie them the way the other guy did, it's kind of sloppy to be honest, and I think his reluctance is preventing him from doing it correctly. Nevertheless, I'm crying again as he places the pillowcase over my head.

Before he begins walking me back to the van, he places a hand on my pillowcase covered cheek and I think I hear him curse right before he picks up his duffle bag to walk us to the other guys.

I smell fire as we walk through the woods, and I try not to wonder if the fire is to burn the body because another scent fills the air and I think it's the smell of smoldering flesh. But hell, how would I know what that smells like?

"Bout damn time," one of the other guys says, I'm thinking it's Danny. "Toss the clothes into the fire so we can get out of here. These woods freak me the fuck out."

"Beau, what the hell man?" says the other, definitely Griff. "Don't you know how to tie a woman up properly?"

Beau scoffs beside me, keeping his palm on the small of my back. "Sorry I don't spend my alone time watching BDSM pornos."

"I don't watch," Griff says. "I do. Bring her here, I'll fix her up good."

When Beau doesn't move us toward Griff, I hear the other man's footsteps approach over the gravel. He removes the loose rope from my hands quickly before tying them tighter and in the same praying position.

"Sorry my friend here doesn't know how to properly bind you," Griff says. "He's never been with a woman before."

"Griff," Beau growls next to me. "Don't get any ideas."

"Please," I whisper, pulling my hands to my chest once they've been tied. "Don't hurt me."

Griff laughs and removes the pillowcase. "Sweetheart, we're not the ones who get to make that decision."

He removes a piece of the duct tape from the roll around his tattooed wrist and places it over my lips before sliding the hood back over my eyes.

"Stop scaring her," Beau says, a bit of edge to his voice. He places his hand back on me to show me to the van.

"I'm not trying to scare her," Griff replies as someone opens the back doors. "Just being honest. What do you think Pres is going to do? Let her go? She just watched us murder someone."

"Fuck," Beau says, his tone angry, scared even.

"Ready to get going?" asks a calmer, kinder voice.

"Danny, I need your help," Beau whispers.

It feels like Danny comes closer to us, and I assume Griff has walked away.

"What's up?" Danny whispers.

"It's Christina," Beau says quietly, as if Danny should make a connection. After a long pause between the guys, Danny pulls off the pillowcase to show my face.

"Oh, shit. This is *your* Christina?" he asks, looking at me with huge eyes. "I thought you said she moved away. What's she doing back in Lexington?"

Beau runs a hand through his shaggy black hair and blows out a slow breath. "I don't know. I just need you to help me out. We've got to make sure Pres doesn't hurt her. We've got to make sure she can get back to living a normal civilian life. She doesn't need to be messed up with all this shit."

"Beau, you know that's slim," Danny says. "I want to help you, but you know we have no say, we're just prospects. Our opinions mean nothing. We just do all the grunt work. Nobody pays us to think."

"Fuck!" Beau curses, kicking the rear tire on the van. I flinch and close my eyes as more tears fall down my cheeks.

"Get in the van, you ass wipes!" Griff barks from the front.

When Beau goes to place the pillowcase over my head, all I can think about is some motorcycle club president having his way with me. Locking me in his clubhouse for all the gang members to take turns with my body until I'm no longer wanted. Then I'll be the corpse in the next body bag, and my clothes will get burned once more. I can't help but panic, my breaths coming in jagged bursts through my nostrils, and I pass out before I can do anything else.

CHAPTER 2

When I come to, I'm in a room with no windows. The rope has been removed from my wrists, and there's not a pillowcase in sight. At least that part of my situation has improved. I'm still in the clothes Beau gave me to change into, but I notice a familiar bag next to the cot I woke up on. It's one of my bags, and when I pick it up to go through it, I find at least a week's worth of *my* clothes. From *my* house.

They know where I live. The clothes were inside my apartment. They even took a hairbrush from my bathroom.

How?

I toss the bag against the wall and run over to the door, even though I know it's probably locked, I still try it. To my surprise, it opens the second I turn the knob, but not because I'm getting out. Instead, two strong hands push me back into the room and no matter how hard I thrash, I can't break free.

"Hey, hey, it's me," says Beau, as if that means anything. He's not the guy I knew back in high school, he's not the guy I was in love with. He's working for my captor. "Calm down. Please."

I notice Danny standing in front of the closed door, so even if I break free from Beau, I'd still have to get around him as well. Before giving up, I give Beau one swift knee to the balls. I don't feel an ounce of guilt as he collapses to the floor.

"You sure she's worth all the trouble, Beau?" Danny asks from the door, not moving to help his friend up. Wise choice. The second he moves from the door, I'm going to make a run for it. I don't care if I die trying.

Beau is still on his knees, holding his hands on his jeans. "I'm trying to help you, damnit!"

"Fuck you, Beau Grady!" I yell, pointing a finger at him before moving my gaze to the man blocking my escape. "And fuck you, Danny whatever your last name is!"

"It would be my pleasure," Danny responds, winking at me as he leans against the door. He crosses his arms over his chest and props one foot up against the doorframe. The way he's looking at me isn't predatorial like I would expect from a guy in a motorcycle club, it's flirtier and more boyish. I clench my fists at my sides and try not to fall for his witchy charm. It won't be hard considering what he's done.

Beau is now curled up in a ball on the floor, his eyes squeezed tightly shut as he cries out in pain. Turns out I'm a bit stronger than I thought. Seems like those morning runs have paid off. I almost feel bad that I did that. Almost.

"Should I give the two of you some privacy?" Danny asks from behind him. "You've probably got some catching up to do."

I give my escape one final shot and charge the door. Right before I go to punch my fists against him, he's instantly grabbing them, twisting me around and holding my arms against my chest with his mouth to my ear.

"Easy there, sugar," he says, holding me tightly against him. "Beau and I are all you've got. If you try to escape right now, Pres will hunt you down and put your body in the ground without a blink of an eye."

I struggle to get out of his grip, but it only tightens more, his arms feeling like a boa constrictor around my small body. Beau finally pulls himself off the ground, and once he's standing on his feet again, he hobbles over to where Danny is holding me. He doesn't get too close at first, probably afraid I'm going to kick or knee him in his balls again. He should be afraid. I'm afraid.

"Christina," he says softly. "Please, stop fighting us. Danny and I want to get you back to your normal life, but we can't help you if you're going to fight us. We have to come up with a plan, we need your cooperation. Can you please help us help you?"

"Why are you doing this?" I ask him, staring into his deep blue eyes. "You can just let me go. I'll leave town. I won't say anything to anyone!"

Beau shakes his head quickly, running both his hands through his hair. "We can't do that. We have to make sure we can trust you first. We have to convince Pres to trust you."

"Trust me?" I ask, baffled. "Trust me? I'm not the one who shot an innocent guy in the middle of an alley!"

"Sugar," Danny says into my ear. "If you think that man was innocent, you're in for a treat."

Beau nods in agreement. "That man is part of a ring of child predators in town. Believe it or not, this town isn't what you remember it to be. It's not all horses and bourbon anymore. It actually hasn't been like that for a long time."

"So you what?" I ask. "Kill people who hurt other people like some kind of superhero? That doesn't even make sense! How does that solve anything?"

I feel Danny shrug his shoulders behind me. "One less pedophile walking around town."

"And you just act like you're innocent in the matter?" I shout, trying to turn around in Danny's arms, but he's too strong. "You're still killing someone! Why not just tell the police? Let them handle it!"

"Chris," Beau says. "If we waited for the police, nothing would ever be done. You'd be surprised by the number of dirty cops out there.

Half the shit that goes on happens right under their noses. But a few thousand bucks in the right palm makes all the charges go away along with the evidence. Cops aren't paid shit, so they're easy to bribe."

When I shake my head, Danny pipes up from behind me. "It's true. Do you know how many of them actually work for the bad guys? More than you know. And a few of 'em are on the take from the club, too. The whole system runs on backdoor deals and political leverage."

I begin shaking from my sobs and drop my weight, forcing Danny to hold me up. I'm honestly surprised he doesn't drop me to the ground. Instead, he holds me up as if I'm light as a feather. He walks us around Beau and places me on the cot where I woke up not long ago, laying my limp body down where I curl up into a ball and cry. I don't want to believe it. I grew up in a world that made sense. A world of laws and rules and punishments for people who did the wrong thing.

Beau walks over to kneel in front of me, Danny standing quietly behind him just in case.

"We're going to get you out of here, Christina," he says. "We just need time to figure out how. Pres wants to speak to you tomorrow, and I need you to follow my lead. Do not fight him, do not talk back, do not disrespect him. If you want to get out of here alive, you need to be good, okay?"

Even though I'm crying, I nod my head. The two men exchange a look before Beau gets up to leave me here in this room. I reach out for his hand, pulling him to a stop, squeezing tightly.

"Don't leave me alone, please . . ." I plead. He ponders something in his head before going over to whisper to Danny who gives him a small nod before leaving the two of us in the room alone together.

Once the door closes behind Danny, Beau takes a seat on the recliner near my cot. I finally take a moment to look around the room and figure out where I am. Other than the old recliner, the cot, and my bag filled with clothes, there's not much else to see. There's a toilet in the corner that looks like something you would see on a prison TV show with a pedestal sink next to it. The walls are just studs with no drywall covering them, and the floor is cement with a drain in the center. I must be in a basement somewhere. *Home, sweet home.* I shiver at the stain around the drain, hoping it's not the blood of one of the motorcycle club's enemies that died down here.

"Why can't you just let me go, Beau?" I ask, not looking at him. I know if I look him in the eyes I'm going to cry again.

"Because, Pres needs to make sure you can be trusted," he says matter-of-factly.

I honestly can't believe this is the same Beau Grady that I knew back in high school. He was the love of my life, the perfect gentleman. He held every door open for me, walked me to my door when he dropped me off at home, always getting me back at least ten minutes before my curfew. He used to hold my hand the whole ride to and from school in his big diesel truck. He would kiss me on the cheek at every stoplight.

And just like any high school stereotype, prom was a big deal for us, and that was the night we lost our virginity to each other. I wore a skintight white dress that honestly looked like it should have been worn to a wedding, and he looked so handsome in his black tuxedo; black shirt, black tie, black shoes, black pants, and black jacket. Only his cufflinks were white. He turned the bed of his truck into a bed of comfy blankets and pillows with twinkle lights strung around the side, parked us in the back of a secluded field, and it was perfect.

But things can't be perfect forever. I broke Beau's heart when I decided I wanted to go away for college. I cut him off completely, disabling my social media, and disappearing into the world of sororities and college. I never went a day without thinking about Beau and where he might be, who he might be with, what he was doing. I never stopped loving Beau Grady. I only stopped being there for him.

"Do you remember that time we rented a bed and breakfast in

Berea and pretended that we were on our honeymoon?" Beau asks, snapping me out of my reverie.

I do remember that. I still have the cheap ring he bought from Walmart, though it's tarnished now. I still keep it in my jewelry box . . .

"The owners kept fawning over me, asking me if we were expecting, because why else would we get married so young?" I say. In reality, I was just bloated because I had so many carbs that day. I swear that old lady asked me at least five times if she could place her hand on my belly to feel the baby.

Beau laughs, but it's sort of sad. "Because they were in love."

I sit up on the cot and back myself against the wall, pulling my legs up to my chest and wrapping my arms around them.

"What if he doesn't want to let me free?" I ask, and I know I don't need to clarify who I'm asking about. He knows.

"He's going to," Beau says, finally catching my eyes. "Danny and I are going to make sure of it. I promise. We're not going to let anything bad happen to you."

"You really promise?" I ask, knowing that Beau takes his promises seriously. That's always been his quirk.

He stands up from the recliner, coming over me, offering his pinky. "I promise you, Christina."

I reach my hand out slowly, wrapping my pinky around Beau's, and for some reason I believe him. Beau has always been my safety net, my protector. He just needs to come through one last time.

CHAPTER 3

There's a knock on the door. I jump at the sound, scolding myself for letting my guard down. I'm a prisoner. I should always be on alert. Beau gets up from the recliner where he must have dozed off as well. Just then the door opens and Danny walks in. I notice Beau stiffen when Griff follows behind him, an annoyed scowl on his face.

"What's he doing here?" Beau spits, clearly asking Danny. I sit back in the corner, trying to pretend like I'm invisible. I don't like Griff and I don't think that Beau likes him either.

Danny puts a hand up to calm the situation. "He's here to help," he says. "He agreed to help us convince Pres to release her."

"He's his son!" Beau retorts, obviously disgusted by the thought of Griff helping us. "You really think he's going to be helpful? Fucking bastard . . ."

Griff crosses his arms over his chest. His massive, tattooed biceps stretch out the sleeves of his t-shirt. While Beau and Danny are almost just as muscular, they're also lankier. Griff is built like a brick house with a scruffy red beard and buzzed red hair. He's the kind of guy I wouldn't want to meet in a dark alley . . . oh, wait.

"The way I see it," Griff huffs, "I'm your only hope. You really think my father is going to listen to the two of you shitheads? You may want to be the heroes, but I share the same blood with the boss. He's going to listen to me before he listens to either of you."

"So what do we do?" Danny asks him, shoving his hands in his pockets and leaning back against the closed door.

"He's going to expect a price to pay for her release," Griff answers, looking right at me.

Beau steps in front of him, cutting off my view of Griff. "I'll pay whatever price it costs to save her."

Griff shakes his head and shoves Beau out of the way, walking right to me. "It's not their price to pay, princess, it's yours. You willing to save yourself?"

I stare up at Griff's body, the other two flanking him, watching and waiting for my answer. I nod my head quickly. "Yes," I whisper. "Anything."

* * *

After an hour of coming up with a game plan, the three men escort me to their president. We're standing right outside a large oak door, Danny and Beau at my sides and Griff standing in front of me, putting his fist against the door to knock three times.

Someone opens on the other side, and he's got a gun strapped to his hip. I follow Griff inside, glancing back as the door is closed on Danny and Beau; the only two people here that I feel like I can sort of trust. They told me that this is how it had to be: only one member can be in the president's office at a time unless it's a scheduled club meeting. What I'm not prepared for is the man sitting behind a large, well-kept oak desk.

The president, who is apparently Griff's father, is wearing a royal blue suit with a white dress shirt underneath it and a blood red tie. His face matches the man I saw murder the guy in the alley last night, but his clothing aesthetic has changed completely. I never pictured a motorcycle club president wearing a clean cut suit. He looks like he should be running in the next presidential election, not murdering people in back alleys behind dingy bars.

He's just finishing up a phone call when we walk in, and I glance at Griff who is now beside me, trying to compare his features with his father's. They look damn near identical, except for the fact that his father's red beard is beginning to turn gray. They're both monsters though—I don't let that thought pass me by.

"This the girl?" his father asks when he hangs up the phone. "You actually think she's capable of proving her worth, son?"

I stand up a little taller, wishing I had some clothes edgier than the pink and black polka dot blouse and blue jeans I chose to wear. I'm not attending a brunch for God's sake; I need some leather pants and a cut off tank top.

"This is her," Griff confirms, glancing down at me. "She says she's willing to cooperate."

"I'll do whatever it takes, sir," I add, trying to sound polite, but it just ends with the president and his bodyguard laughing at me.

"We'll see," he says, folding his hands in front of him. "You'll be staying here for three more days and then I'll give you your assignment. Griff will make sure you do what you're told, but if you fail, you'll disappear just like our friend did the other night."

"Three days?" I gulp, but before I can get an answer, Griff is grabbing me by the arm and hauling me out of the office. I guess the meeting is finished.

Griff walks me back to the basement, Danny and Beau on our heels. No one says a word until the door is closed behind us.

"I have to sit here for three more days?" I ask, staring up at Griff. "Why three days? Why not tonight?"

Griff gets in my face, and I try not to shrink away from him. "You don't get to ask questions. You'll be a good girl, sit here for three days, and then when he makes his decision we'll move forward."

Beau pulls Griff away from me and shoves him on the shoulders. "Get out of her face, Griffin! You're scaring her."

Griff gives him a wicked smile and then turns his attention back to me. He leans over, placing his hands on his thighs. I force myself to hold his gaze, even though it's breaking me inside. He brings one of his hands up to my cheek, and I'm surprised by the current that explodes in my body.

"Do I scare you, princess?" he whispers. "You know, there's another option to get you out of here sooner, guaranteed safety."

"Griff!" Beau says, but Danny shushes him.

"She deserves to know her options," Danny says. "Even if they suck."

Griff's eyes never leave mine, and his smile never falters. "What do you say? Want to know what's behind door number three?"

I bite my lip and squeeze my thighs together, hating the throbbing between them that Griff is somehow creating. I haven't felt that sensation since Beau and I dated in high school.

When I nod, Griff's grin gets even wider. I think I liked him better when he was scowling.

"You can become my old lady," he says, like I'm supposed to know what that even means. "We can walk out of here right now, head to the courthouse, file for a marriage license. Guarantees you automatic safety from the club . . ."

I don't let him finish the sentence. I slap him hard right across his cheek, wiping that disgusting smile from his face.

"I would never marry you in a million years," I say between gritted teeth.

Danny laughs behind me, and I glance up to see Beau looking proud. Shocked, but proud, I think. The same look he gave me as he dropped me off at college even though I broke his heart.

"You little bitch," Griff spits, turning back around. I'm surprised to see a smile on his face again. "Looks like you can fight for yourself, princess."

"Let's go get dinner," Danny says, tugging on the back of Griff's shirt to pull him away from me. "What would Miss. Christina like?"

"Chinese?" Beau pipes up, knowing that was always my go-to cuisine when stressed. "Your usual?"

I nod and go over to the cot to sit, folding my legs under me.

The guys file out of the door, locking it shut once they're all out, leaving me to ponder what their president has in mind for me to do to show my loyalty and get out of this horrible situation. But I wonder, am I actually willing to do *anything?* Am I capable of doing whatever sinister thing the club comes up with?

CHAPTER 4

Time passes at an excruciatingly slow pace. The three men alternate keeping me company during, bringing me a deck of cards to keep me busy, food to keep me from starving, but by day three, I never want to play another game of poker or eat another bite of takeout food.

Griff storms in the room on the night of day three while Beau and I were sitting on the cot watching an episode of How to Get Away with Murder on his cell phone.

"Time to go, losers," he says, tossing an outfit on my lap. I pick it up to see what he's brought. Black leggings, black long sleeve shirt, black ski mask. "Put your boots on with that, and you're good to go. Get dressed quickly, we leave in five minutes. Beau, I need you to get the van ready."

"There's not much to get ready," Beau says, standing up and pocketing his phone. "Danny got the gas cans filled earlier, they're already good."

"Just go fucking double check!" Griff roars. Something has really pissed him off, and I have no idea what it might be. Not a lot of info coming into my cell these days. Reluctantly, Beau leaves the room, leaving me to get ready.

When I stand up to put the clothes on, Griff just hovers with his arms across his chest. "Uh, can a girl get some privacy?" I ask.

"Ya know," Griff says, smirking a bit. "I'm going to miss having you around. Maybe I should just convince my father to keep you around as the MC's little whore."

I pick up one of my boots and chuck it right at Griff's head as hard as I can. "Fuck you, Griff!" I yell as it hits him square in the face. I thought for sure his reflexes would have been just a little quicker. In all honesty, I didn't mean to *actually* hit him.

He takes a few steps closer, part of me wishing he'd place his hand on my cheek like he did on day one, but he doesn't, he just picks up the ski mask and tugs it over my head, reminding me of the pillowcase he first put on me. "You wish, princess."

I shove him on his shoulder, but he doesn't budge from the impact, giving me one final smirk before he turns around to leave the room. This time, no one locks it as they leave, which makes me feel less safe because now I have to change. Who knows how many people are actually walking by the basement dungeon?

Once I pull on the black leggings, shirt, and my boots, I grab my duffle bag from the floor, tugging the ski mask off and holding it in my other hand. I pause at the door, sort of afraid to open it. Once I move past this door, I have to follow through with whatever task the president has come up with. I'll probably be committing some horrible crime.

I take a deep breath as I turn the handle and find Danny waiting for me on the other side of the door. He reaches out to take my duffle bag for me, and I'm shocked by the gentlemanly act.

"You ready?" he asks.

I nod and follow him up the stairs. "I guess so."

When we're up in the main part of the clubhouse and walking toward the garage, I try not to let my eyes linger on some of the sinful activities going on around us. They make the things in frat houses look tame. There's a naked girl in the corner getting screwed by a man

double her age and a few guys doing lines of coke on a weathered coffee table. I wonder how deep Beau is in the club. Does he take part in
any of these extracurriculars? What's it matter to me, though? Once
I finish my task, I'm staying the hell away from this MC. I might call
my mom and see if I can move down to Florida with her and Dad. I
just need *out*.

Griff appears out of nowhere, following alongside us. He has a stupid grin on his face, his eyes shining. "Like what you see, princess?" he
says, nodding toward the man and woman hooking up in the corner.
"Want to stay a little longer? You can take me for a ride."

"I would rather burn in a fire than ever let you touch me," I spew at
him as he opens the door to the garage, not to let me walk through, but
for himself. Danny motions for me to follow behind him.

"That could be arranged tonight," Griff adds over his shoulder.

A shudder runs down my spine. I know he's telling the truth.

This time when the guys make me get in the van, they let me take
the middle seat in the front and I don't have to wear a pillowcase.
Part of me is relieved, the other part is scared because this means
they're not worried about me seeing where the club house is or where
we're going.

Griff takes the driver's seat and Danny sits on my other side. I
watch as Beau hops on a black motorcycle in front of the van.

"He's not coming with us?" I ask, worried about being alone with
two people I barely know.

"He's going to make a distraction on the other side of town," Griff
says, starting up the van and following Beau out of the garage. "That
way we have time to get things heated up."

When we exit a set of iron gates at the end of a long driveway, Beau
heads right and we go left. I try not to think about never seeing him
again, but hopefully, I *won't* have to ever see him again. Hopefully,
after tonight, I never have to see another member of Hell Prevails MC
ever again.

* * *

When Danny, Griff, and I pull into the empty parking lot, I sit in the middle staring at a dark house someone turned into a daycare business years ago. I've seen this place fill up with kids under the age of seven every morning and then get picked up by their parents after work. I'm not sure why we're here. Actually, I have no idea.

We sit in silence for what feels like eternity. Finally, Griff's phone rings. He answers it and holds it to his ear, but he doesn't say a word.

"Go," commands the voice on the other line, sirens blasting in the background.

Griff and Danny open their doors, and I follow quickly behind, pulling on my ski mask just like they do.

We go to the back of the van and they grab the gas cans, each of them carrying two, and they begin dumping them around the daycare. I stare at them wide-eyed as they come back for the final two jerry-cans. They douse some of the gasoline on the windows, making sure to get the wooden front door.

"What the hell are you guys going to do?" I ask, though the answer is painfully obvious. I follow them around the back of the building where they finish covering the daycare in pungent fuel.

"Just assisting you," Danny says, as if I should know what that means. "Come on."

Griff lights up a cigarette with a match and once he shakes it out, he hands me the rest of the matchbook.

"Strike 'em and watch it burn," he says when I take it from him.

I shake my head and stare back and forth between the two men. I know I have two options; do as I'm told and I'm set free, or don't do it and I die.

"There's got to be another way," I say, clutching the matchbook in my hand. "Kids come here. This is their safe place while their parents work. We can't do this."

Griff leans down to get in my face, blowing some of his smoke in my eyes. "This ain't no sanctuary, princess, this is hell. The owners of this place have done some awful, awful things to these kids. We're punishing them for what they've done."

"No . . ." I grit my teeth and shake my head. "That's not true. There's no way."

"Don't be a sheep, Christina," Danny says, leaning against the van. "We can show you proof if you'd like. It's not pretty though."

"Pedophiles run this daycare. We need to send them a message," Griff says, gripping my hand to take the matchbook. He tears out one of the matches and holds it in front of my face. "Light. It. Up."

I don't reach out to take the match from Griff, and when I stall, his patience wears thin and he grabs me by the wrist. He forces me to hold the match and strike it against the matchbox. When it ignites, I think about blowing it out to piss off Griff even more, but I know that I won't ever be released from them until I do what I'm told. Just as the flame reaches my fingertips, I chuck it into the gasoline and light up another match. The fire doesn't mix with the gas immediately, so Danny goes to the back of the van to grab a bottle with some cloth, setting the cloth on fire with a lighter from his pocket.

Once he tosses the flaming bottle through a window in the daycare, it catches immediately and the place lights up like someone turned on a spotlight inside. I hope to God no one is actually in there right now. Even if they are crappy humans, it doesn't give me or Griff the right to decide their fates. It doesn't give us the right to play God.

"Let's get out of here," Griff says, shoving my shoulder to get me to walk back to the van. "Time to get you home before your carriage turns into a pumpkin, princess."

Griff opens the door for me and I climb up into the van, sitting between the two men. I hope to God that this is the last night I see them. The last time I ever encounter Hell Prevails MC, but I know I won't be that lucky.

CHAPTER 5

For the last seventy-two hours, I've barricaded myself in my apartment. I've checked my door to make sure that the lock and deadbolt haven't been tampered with or outright destroyed. I've closed my blinds and my curtains, only peeking outside when I hear a noise, which is constantly because my mind keeps playing tricks on me. Every little honk or bark has me on edge. I've probably only slept a single hour since Griff and Danny escorted me back to my apartment. They didn't say a word as I jumped out of the van, grabbing my duffle bag and darting up the steps to my door. However, the van didn't leave until I made it inside, as if they wanted to make sure I made it in safely. Ha, as though they really cared about my safety.

Needless to say, I'm still on edge though.

There's a motorcycle rally in town this weekend, so every time I hear one go by, my heart feels like it's going to punch right through my chest. I swear I might end up being one of the youngest people to have a heart attack. I need to get out of here.

I do the only thing I can right now, even though I would rather not ask for my parents' help. My mom answers her phone just as I think I'm going to need to leave a voicemail. She sounds calm as ever, quite the opposite of how I'm feeling. I picture her laying by her in-ground pool, sipping on some fruity cocktail, living the perfect stay-at-home trophy wife lifestyle.

"Sweetheart," she says as a hello. "How are you?"

"I'm fine," I say softly, peering out my window as more motorcycles tear down Main Street. "I was just thinking, I haven't seen you guys in a while. Maybe I could come down for a few days?"

"Oh, honey," Mom says, "I don't know if that will work. We're having part of the house remodeled right now. Everything is out of place. It's really not a good time. Maybe in a few weeks?"

Tears threaten to invade my eyes as my heart begins racing again, thinking about being stuck here alone. "Mom, please. I swear I won't be a burden. You won't even know I'm there. Maybe I could stay in the guest house?"

"We're renting that out on Air B&B, darling," she says, not sounding sorry at all.

My parents moved into a mansion on the beach with six bedrooms and seven bathrooms—they literally won't even know I'm there. "Mom," I beg. "Please. Just for a couple of days. You don't need to worry about entertaining me, feeding me, or anything."

The line goes quiet, and I hope for my sake that my mom isn't as cold-hearted as I grew up thinking she was. She was never the kindest or warmest person, but her maternal instinct has to hear my distraught tone and want to protect me, right?

"Okay," she huffs. "But you need to pay for your own flight and your own food. I swear if you disturb any of our guests, you're out of there."

I sigh with relief. "Thank you, mother," I say, already going over to my closet to pull out my duffle bag again to start packing. "You won't hear a peep out of me, I promise."

After another five minutes of my mom trying to scare me out of not coming down to Florida, I assure her that I'll be there, but I plan on driving. It's late in the day, so I'll be driving through the night, but until I get hundreds of miles between me and Hell Prevails, I'm not going to sleep a wink. I'll totally need to stop for caffeine. A small price to pay for my sanity.

I toss my phone in my purse and start grabbing t-shirts, shorts, and my one and only bikini from my dresser drawers, shoving them haphazardly into the duffle. I take one last look around my apartment, making sure I have everything I need. I grab the novel I'm currently reading off my nightstand and slide it into my tote before grabbing my keys off the wall and going to the door to leave.

The moment I open the door, my body freezes. Three figures are standing in the doorway clad in leather jackets and ripped jeans. Before I get a chance to scream, Griff is placing a hand over my mouth and walking me backward into my apartment, Danny and Beau following and closing the door behind them.

"Don't scream, princess," Griff says as he starts to remove his hand. I shock him and myself by biting his hand before he moves away. He shakes it out and smirks at me. "Damn, baby. Didn't peg you as a biter. Lucky for you, I'm into that."

"Back off, Griff," Beau says, moving about my apartment and obviously looking for something. Once he's satisfied with my tiny studio apartment, he turns to me, glancing at my duffle and purse hanging off my slender shoulder. "Going somewhere?"

"That's none of your business," I spit back, holding my bags a little tighter and backing away from Griff only to find body making contact with Danny. I move away from him too, suddenly feeling like a caged animal. "Why are you here? How did you know I was leaving?"

Griff picks up a ceramic cat from my bookshelf and chuckles to himself. "You think we haven't been watching you the last few days? We had to make sure you weren't going to narc on us. I mean, you do have a history with that. Pledge class hazing ring a bell?"

"How'd you find out about that?" I ask, my heart racing.

"Quick Google search," Danny says. "We're very surprised you didn't go to the cops. You made Griff and I lose a decent chunk of money on a bet."

"My money was on you," Beau says, eyes still darting about the room. "We've got to go. Now."

"You know where the door is," I say sternly. "Please leave. My boyfriend is going to be here any moment, and he's a marine."

"Hoo-rah," Danny laughs, pacing around me. "But I think you're lying."

Beau turns and looks at me, making my eye twitch—my signature tell. "She's lying," he says, turning against me. "Stop lying to us, we're here to protect you, Christina."

I can't help but burst into hysterical laughter. I bend over and try to catch my breath as the three men make a half circle around me and block my exit.

"You guys—protect me?" I ask as my giggles subside. "You kidnapped me! You forced me into a van with a dead guy, made me set fire to a daycare, and now you claim that you're trying to protect me?"

The three of them exchange some silent conversation, and I take that as my moment to dodge around them and open the door.

"Out you go," I say, holding the door wide open, but the only one who makes a move is Danny who comes over and closes the door, standing in front of it. Always the door-blocker.

He looks down at me and crosses his hands over his chest, just like he did when I was locked in the basement of the clubhouse. "No can do, sugar" he says.

I drop my bags at my feet and give Danny a shove with both arms, but he doesn't budge at all. Which makes me even more furious. I slap his crossed, tatted arms until Beau comes over and wraps me in a strong embrace, pinning my arms at my side. I know I should hate him for getting me wrapped up in this mess, but I never realized just how much I had missed him.

"Chris," he says, breathing against my neck. He smells like artificial fruit, sugary sweet. I bet if I turned around in his arms and kissed him, I could taste whatever it is he's been eating. "We're not going to do that. Stop fighting the people who are trying to help you."

"I don't know," Griff says, circling around us with admiration in his eyes. "I kind of like her feisty. Let her have a few swings on me."

Griff reaches a hand out to brush some hair from my mouth, and I snap my teeth at his fingers, but the tactic backfires on me because his fingers just graze my lips and it sends an electric jolt through my body. The same jolt I still get whenever Beau's skin makes contact with any part of my body, even through the cloth barrier of my clothes.

For a moment, I imagine what it would be like to experience that same jolt of pleasure from all of the men standing in my apartment. However, Griff's cocky grin is a major lady boner killer.

"Where were you going, princess?" Griff asks, continuing his circle around Beau and I.

"To my parents," I say. "I don't feel safe in this town. Not with a lunatic motorcycle gang like you idiots driving by my apartment at all hours. You got me fired from my job by the way."

"Club," Beau says as I struggle against his strong arms. "Motorcycle club. And we're the least of your worries right now."

"Word is out that there's a price for you," Griff says, looking my body up and down. "We're not sure who it is that's after you or how they even know, but we need to make sure you disappear from town for a little bit."

"That's what I was trying to do until you assholes showed up!" I yell through gritted teeth.

I don't take my eyes off Griff as Beau walks me over to my futon and forces me to sit. I plop down on the cushion, crossing my arms over my chest and pouting. The three men stand in front of me, and the only thing between us is my old pink ottoman from my college dorm. Honestly, it's kind of embarrassing that my adult apartment still consists of stuff from my short time as a college co-ed. I'm sure these three probably couldn't care less about my décor. They probably sleep in whatever room is open at the clubhouse, falling into bed with whomever—a different girl every night. My heart breaks thinking about Beau being so infatuated with that kind of lifestyle. Where did he go so wrong?

"Here's the plan," Griff says, shoving his hands into the pockets of his jeans that are already hanging dangerously low on his hips. I try not to stare at the Glock strapped to his waist. "Danny and Beau here will be joining you at your parents. I don't need to know where you're going, I just need you to get the hell out of Lexington until I give you the all clear."

I stand up, but when Griff gives me a nasty look, I flop back down—but not without protest. "They can't go with me! My parents don't even want me around. What am I supposed to say when I show up with two tattooed thugs at their front door?"

"First off," Griff says. "We're not thugs. We're modern-day Robin Hoods, if you will, or maybe you could call us vigilantes. Second, I don't care what you have to tell your parents. Tell them they're your lovers. Who the fuck cares? Just get out of here. Now!"

"Ready?" Beau asks as Danny reaches to grab my bags off the floor. Griff moves over and takes some reusable grocery bags from my kitchen counter and then walks to my dresser where he starts tossing in even more clothing.

"What does he think he's doing?" I ask Beau instead of answering his question.

Once the bags are full, Griff places them on the ottoman. "Who knows when you'll be able to come back. You've got to be prepared for the long haul."

I get up and grab the extra bags from the ottoman. Beau helps me with what I can't carry. "How am I supposed to trust you?" I ask Griff. "You've done nothing but ruin my life, and I hardly know you."

Griff reaches for my chin, and I shock myself by not jerking from his grasp this time. "Princess, it's a cruel world out there, I'm only trying to take out the bad guys. I'm trying to protect the good ones. Are you going to be a good girl and do what we say?"

My lady parts betray me, making my panties wet from excitement. I swear if I open my mouth, I'll drool all over the floor. Instead, I play it safe and nod my head, which seems to please Griff.

He gives me a smile. "Good girl, now do everything that Danny and Beau tell you to do. They may be just a pair of tatted thugs, but if I find out you disobey, you will be punished when you get back home."

"Cut out your weird dom shit," Beau tells Griff from behind me, cutting off whatever spell Griff had put on me. I pull away from him and follow dutifully out the front door with my bags.

"I'll drive," Danny says, and Griff tosses him the keys from my purse after he closes and locks my apartment door.

Danny catches them effortlessly where they collide with his tattooed fingers and make a jingle as they hit his rings. He has a unique ring on every single finger, I notice, except for his pinkies and the wedding band on his left hand.

"Keep me up to date on your route," Griff says as the four of us shuffle down the stairs. "Remember, this is only between us. I don't want my father to get involved."

"What are you going to say when he realizes we're gone?" Danny asks. We make it to my car. We all stop dead in our tracks when we see that all four of the tires on my Yaris have been slashed.

"Fuck," Beau yells, dropping the bags at his feet and going to check on the tires to confirm that they've been slashed. I notice Griff and Danny move in closer to me, looking around the street for whoever might be the culprit. Sadly, the sidewalks and streets are way too busy with the motorcycle rally going on all over town. "We need to get out of here. Fast."

Griff pulls out a set of keys from his pocket. "Take my truck, I'll walk back to the clubhouse. Don't worry about my dad, I'll keep him occupied while you're gone. We'll get the other prospects to do whatever jobs he would have assigned to you guys."

Danny swaps my keys with Griff's, and I follow them around the bar where I no longer work. Without even realizing it, I move closer to Beau and keep glancing over my shoulder.

"It'll be okay," Beau says, staying alert. "I'm not going to let anyone hurt you, Christina."

My eyes stop darting, and I settle on looking ahead—not saying another word, but knowing that Beau means it when he promises to never let anyone hurt me. Beau has always made sure I'm safe. It's the other two men that I'm unsure of.

CHAPTER 6

Danny and Beau don't stop glancing over their shoulders until we cross the Kentucky state line and enter Tennessee. After that, I'm not sure what happens because I finally manage to fall asleep between the two of them. I don't wake up until I hear one of the truck doors slam. I jerk alert, finding that my head was resting on Danny's shoulder. He gives me a soft smile when he glances down at his leather cut. I'm mortified to find a small patch of drool. I wipe at my mouth and glance around the parking lot. We've stopped for gas.

"No worries," Danny says, grabbing a napkin from the glove box. I notice a pistol next to the stack of napkins, and I cringe away as he closes the box and wipes his shoulder. "Have a good nap?"

I ignore his question. "Where are we?"

"Almost out of Georgia," he says, placing the wet napkin in the cupholder, brushing my leg but I don't think it was an accident. "Griff said he ran into some trouble, but it doesn't seem like anyone has noticed we've skipped town."

"That's good then?" I ask, brushing my hair from my face. "Maybe you guys can head back after we get to Florida? I can schedule a flight home if you just want to head back."

"No can do, baby girl," Danny says, placing an arm on the seat rest behind me, I shiver as his arm almost wraps around my shoulders. "We're not leaving your side."

Beau finishes filling up the tank and climbs back into the truck. I have to scoot back over and I'm once again sandwiched between the two men. Beau hands me a plastic bag and cranks the engine, putting the truck into drive.

I peek into the bag and find three bottles of water, some energy drinks, and some snacks.

"Favorite candy bar still Kit Kat?" Beau asks as my eyes spot a king-sized Kit Kat at the bottom of the bag.

"You remembered?" I ask, pulling the candy from the bag.

"Of course," he says. We head in the direction of the interstate. "You would bribe me at Halloween, telling me I could have all of your candy as long as I gave you all the Kit Kats I got."

"That doesn't sound like a fair trade," Danny comments, taking a water and a bag of Fritos.

"You underestimate my love for Kit Kats," I explain, opening up the candy and breaking off a piece. It's been way too long since I've had a candy bar. I had to watch my figure when I was rushing a sorority. The president had all these bogus rules about sizes.

"I, myself, also enjoy Kit Kats," Danny says seductively and takes the candy bar from my hands. He bites off a piece and then moves the other half slowly to my mouth. "Open," he commands.

My heart races and I do as I say, allowing Danny to feed me the other bite of the candy bar. The tip of his finger touches my lip, and my body buzzes with pleasure. How the hell is this guy feeding me a candy bar and making it seem like a sexual act?

"Dan," Beau scolds. "Cool it."

I can't take my eyes off Danny, and he chuckles as he returns my gaze. "I think I'm making him jealous."

"We need to keep her safe," Beau says, carefully merging onto the interstate. "Keep your dick in your pants."

I feel my cheeks blush at Beau's crass language, but then I find myself glancing down at Danny's black jeans, as if his dick might actually be out of his pants.

"I'll only get it out if you ask, baby girl," Danny says when I draw my eyes back to his.

I spend the rest of our drive with my hands under my thighs, keeping my legs closed so they don't brush against Beau or Danny's knees. I don't dare to look at either of them, only staring straight ahead while scolding myself for the fantasies I come up with in my mind of the three of us together in a bed.

* * *

When we arrive at my parents' massive house, Danny walks around back like I ask him to, and Beau escorts me to the front door. He gives me a quizzical look when I ring the doorbell instead of pulling out my own key or walking right in.

My mom answers the door with a martini in hand, full hair and makeup, and it looks like she's hosting a book club of sorts in her living room. I've never known my mother to read a day in her life. But there are five women sitting there, laughing and sipping on cocktails with the same book in their laps or on the coffee table. I bet none of them actually read the book, they probably just come over to gossip.

"Christina," my mother says, leaning in to place a kiss on both of my cheeks, like she's a fancy French woman or something. When she notices Beau standing next to me, the edge that's always in her voice when we talk evaporates. "Well, look who it is! Is that Beau?" I'm surprised she remembers him so easily.

"Yes, ma'am," Beau says. "It's good to see you again."

"You as well," my mom says, and I cringe when she pulls down the front of her shirt to reveal more cleavage. My mom always liked when I had Beau over. She was constantly fawning over him like some teenage girl trying to steal her sister's man. "Christina didn't tell me she was bringing a friend along. Or are the two of you seeing each other again? I always told her that her biggest mistake was letting a boy like you go." She tsks.

I feign a yawn and over exaggerate a stretch, and then wrap my arm through Beau's. "Sorry, mother, we're really tired from the drive. I think we're going to go take a nap."

"Beau doesn't look tired," she says, placing a hand on his other arm. "You though, you look like you could use a nap and some under eye coverage. Did you not put on makeup today?"

I grit my teeth. "No mom," I say. "Didn't really have the time. Enjoy your book club."

I pull Beau down the staircase with me, and we open the back door for Danny to come in. He follows quietly behind me as we head for the room furthest away from my dad's bar. I've only been to their Florida house once, during spring break my second semester of college, so I take the same room I stayed in then. The room is so large that there's a full sitting room and private bathroom with a soaking tub.

The guys follow me through the door, and I sit on the edge of the four-poster bed as the two of them look around the room.

"Aw, baby," Danny says with a smile. "You didn't tell me you got us the honeymoon suite."

I roll my eyes and flop down on the bed. "Why did I even bother coming all the way down here?"

I feel the bed slant down next to me and look up to see Beau sitting beside me. "It's the best place to be. No one is going to come looking for you down here. We didn't leave a trail."

"Have you heard from Griff?" I ask. "Maybe we can just come back early. I'm already sick of being here."

Beau shakes his head. "Can't go back yet. We'll stay here for a few days like planned, and then we'll find somewhere else."

"What if my mom tries to bang you by then?" I ask, staring up at the high ceiling.

"She's not my type," Beau says honestly. I *mostly* believe him.

Danny hops on the bed on my other side. "Beau only has one type, and it's you. Honestly, I didn't understand why he was so hung up on the girl who broke his heart in high school, but now that I've met you . . ."

"We broke each other's hearts," I add, trying not to choke on my honesty. "I was never okay after I left for college. Let's get that straight. I wanted him to come after me, but he never did, and that broke me even more."

When I look at the boys, they're both staring down at me. I feel this odd tension in the room. It's almost visible in the air. Something inside pulls me into a sitting position, and I'm turning my body into Beau's.

"Why didn't you fight for me?" I demand. "Why didn't you come with me? Or at least try?"

Beau's mouth falls open at a loss for words, and I take that as my chance to shock him even more. I climb onto him, straddling his lap, and lean in to kiss him, darting my tongue out to lick across his bottom lip. It doesn't take much convincing to get him to kiss me back.

"I'll give you two some privacy," Danny says awkwardly. He gets up from the bed, and I pull my mouth away from Beau's to see a look of defeat on Danny's face.

Before he can walk behind me and out the door, I reach for his hand to stop him, shaking my head. "You can't go out there. You can't leave this room. No one knows you're here, and we need to keep it that way."

He looks at me confused, his brows knitting together. "Do you want me to hide out in the bathroom while the two of you have a reunion?"

I shake my head again and pull him to sit right next to Beau—who hasn't stopped kissing me, my neck, my cheek, my chin. The world could be on fire, and I don't think Beau would care right now. I know exactly what I want, and I'm just shocked by the fact that it feels like I'm going to get it. However, if Griff were here instead of Danny, I doubt any of this would be happening. Mostly because Griff's intensity scares me. He looks at me like he wants to tear me apart all by himself. What scares me more is that I might let him.

"What do you want?" Danny asks, watching as Beau trails some kisses down my neck, nibbling at the top of my chest. I bite my lip as a rush of pleasure pools between my legs. God, I've missed him so much. I tried hooking up with some random guy at a party once, but the second he took my shirt off, I couldn't follow through. Beau was it for me. Until Danny. Now they're both mine.

I open my eyes and lean over to grab one of Danny's hands, urging him to touch me. "I want you both to make me forget you turned my world upside down."

"What's that even mean?" Danny asks, his eyebrows pulled together.

I reluctantly climb off Beau's lap and climb over onto Danny's. The second my hips rest against his, I feel that he wants the same things I do, and I haven't even done anything to him yet.

"I want you to fuck me to forget," I whisper, placing one of his large, tattooed hands on my chest. "Please don't let me down."

Danny glances over at Beau, and I do as well, seeing Beau's pupils dilated, his chest rising rapidly. "You okay with this?" Danny asks him breathlessly.

Beau moves his gaze to me, and to my surprise, he looks hopeful, happy even.

"If this is what I have to do to have her back in my life," Beau says, "I'll do whatever she tells me to. I'm not losing her again, Dan. Don't make me lose her."

Danny shakes his head and then turns his attention to me. "You know there's no turning back, right? If you want this, you're our girl. He's not going to let you go again, and I don't give up either."

I nod my head and reach down to pull off my shirt. The bra I have on is nothing special, but you'd think it was some crazy lingerie from a sex shop with the way the two men stare at me and my chest.

"Griff is going to be really jealous that he missed out," Danny remarks, sliding both his calloused hands up my smooth torso.

I push him back on the bed and grind my hips against his, making him dig his fingers into my body to urge me on. Motioning for Beau to come over so I can remove his vest and shirt, I continue kissing him as I work myself up against the massive bulge behind Danny's zipper.

"Holy fuck," Danny hisses, looking up at the two of us. "Why the fuck am I so turned on right now?"

I remove my hands from Beau's chest and find my way to Danny's pants, unbuttoning them and pulling down the zipper. I'm shocked to find that he's commando.

I arch a brow at him.

He shrugs his shoulders. "I hate underwear. Always bunches up in the wrong places."

I lift my hips up so he can slide his pants down his butt where they stay.

"Have you been tested recently?" I ask, but he seems confused by my question. "STDs. No one knows what sorts of things are being passed around the clubhouse and all your slutty conquests."

I shiver thinking about the woman I saw being passed around amongst the members of Hell Prevails. Is that what I'm currently allowing to be done? Or asking for? Being passed between Danny and Beau? I tell myself that this isn't the same. I really want both of these men. I want to feel sexy having both of them. They make me feel safe. Powerful even. Erotic.

Danny reaches down between my legs and even though I still have my pants on, the brush of his finger against my core has me getting wet. I'm begging for them, and they don't even know it yet. Danny's hand finds its way to his pants where he pulls out a wallet and retrieves a condom.

"I get tested frequently and haven't caught a thing. I also wear condoms every time. I don't need a Danny Jr. running around town making me a nervous wreck," he says with a wink. "Not just yet."

"And you," I say over my shoulder to Beau even though I already believe that he hasn't been with anyone else. I just want to hear him say it again. "You don't have anything for me to worry about?"

Beau shakes his head quickly. "Nothing to worry about. It's always been you. Only you, Christina."

My heart swells, and I try not to dwell on his words too long. This isn't me trying to make love to my ex, this is me trying to get them out of my system and get rid of all this sexual tension.

"Just so you know, I'm on birth control," I say, looking at Beau as his face falls. "Not necessarily for pregnancy prevention, more so for cramps. I haven't been with anyone either."

"You haven't?" Beau asks, relief obvious in his voice.

I shake my head and breathe in deeply and then turn my attention back to Danny. "So don't expect stripper quality sex. You can leave right now if you expect insane, mind-blowing sex. I'm very rusty. But you'll still have to hide in the bathroom. Can't have you running around the house."

Danny gives me a sincere smile, reaching down to my zipper. "I saw those romance books on your bookshelf. I'm sure you can make do."

I roll my eyes but try to conjure up some of the confidence from the women in the romance novels I've read. The only issue is, I've only read romance with one man and one woman—this is unchartered territory for me.

Danny seems to notice my unease. "Play with us however you want, we'll take it from there," he urges.

I stand up off the bed, making sure the bedroom door is locked before I remove my pants. I go over to the Bluetooth speaker on the nightstand and connect my phone to it. I've got my back to the boys, but I practically feel their eyes on me. They're being very patient. I take a breath to calm my hammering heart as I select my favorite play-list and turn up the volume enough to muffle whatever noises might be heard through the door.

Walking back around the bed, I crawl up the end of it, pulling Danny's pants off the rest of the way. The dark hair on his legs tickles my wrists as I move back up and place kisses around his hips. I glance up at him just as my tongue makes contact with the underside of his thick cock.

His head falls back against the pillows and he whispers a low, "fuck."

His pleasure only urges me on, making me confident enough to take his whole member into my mouth. Just as I'm finding a good pace, I feel a light whisper across my underwear and a gentle finger pulls the thin fabric out of the way.

Beau pulls my ass further in the air, making my mouth come down even more on Danny's length, and I moan the second Beau plunges his tongue into my core. The moan sends a vibration against Danny's cock, causing his hips to thrust up and his cock to hit the back of my throat. He reaches down and wraps my ponytail around his hand and grabs onto the back of my head to show me the pace he wants.

I let out another moan as Beau continues to suck on my clit, add-ing a finger into my core, and I instinctively tighten around his finger when he tries to remove it. I pick up the pace on Danny, moving my whole body, trying to get Beau to use more force.

"You've got to tell him what you want, baby girl," Danny says, brushing hair out of my face and pulling my head up so I can speak. "What do you want?"

Beau thrusts a second finger inside me, all the way to his knuckles, and I know that's not deep enough to make me forget about the trou-ble they've put me in. Not enough to make me forget that my mom doesn't want me here. Beau pulls out his fingers and places his mouth over my cunt, lapping up all my juices.

"I want him to fuck me," I tell Danny.

Danny gives me a smile. "Clean his mouth off and then let me taste you."

Danny doesn't have to ask me twice. I pull away from him to turn around and kiss Beau deeply. I kiss him like I'm begging for him to save my life, as if cleaning myself from his lips is what it will take to save all of our lives.

I pull away breathlessly and move up to straddle Danny, kissing him the way I was kissing Beau. Beau doesn't waste any time lining himself up with my hips. He knows I loved when we made love that way. He was able to get so deep, making me scream in pleasure.

"Holy shit, Chris," Beau says, placing his hands on my narrow hips. "I forgot how much I enjoyed this. Enjoy you. I've missed you so much, baby."

Just as Beau says the words, I'm cumming around his cock. Danny's there to catch my moans with his mouth, holding me against him as Beau keeps thrusting into me from behind. Once I relax, Beau moves away, not finishing himself, but not seeming to be bothered anyway.

I collapse on top of Danny, but he moves out from under me, and I frown at his departure.

"You're not done yet," Danny says instead, ripping open the condom packet and rolling it down his rock-hard cock.

Beau climbs up the bed to sit behind me, letting me rest my head in his lap, I lazily reach my arm behind me so I can stroke his cock. I smile up at him as he reaches down to cup my breasts in his hands.

Danny brings my legs to rest on his forearms and scoots between them, staring down at my underwear that's still in place but drenched with my pleasure.

"This won't do," Dan says, reaching his hands down and ripping a hole in my underwear. "Much better."

I'd be mad if it wasn't for the fact that I'm floating on a cloud right now. Luckily, I packed a couple extra pairs of underwear. Or maybe I'll make the boys buy something new with money from the club.

Danny lets my legs fall to his thighs as he enters me slowly, savoring every tight inch of me. Once he's all the way in, he opens his eyes and looks right at me and then looks up at Beau.

"Dude," he breathes out. "This is not going to be a onetime thing—I'm telling you both right now."

I lift myself on my elbows to get closer to Danny. "As long as it's just me you're fucking, we can do this forever," I promise.

"You got it, baby girl," Danny says without argument. He starts thrusting into me harder. I lean back onto Beau and tug his cock at the same pace Danny penetrates me.

It takes three songs before both men are cumming. Danny grunts as he releases into the condom while still inside me, and I turn to take Beau into my mouth just as I hear a faint curse come from his lips—the sign that I know he's close to orgasm.

Danny pulls out and collapses, and I smile up at Beau and swallow his seed as he lays on my other side, bringing the blanket up from the bottom of the bed to cover the three of us. Though I don't think I really need a blanket, the body heat radiating off of the two of them is enough to keep me warm.

"Wow," I laugh, wrapping my arm around Beau's waist. Danny spoons me from behind, placing soft kisses and nibbles along my shoulder.

"Griff's going to lose his damn mind if he finds out," Danny whispers.

"Why?" I ask, trying to turn over to look at him.

Beau speaks up, running his fingers through my tangled hair. "Because you've distracted us. How are we supposed to keep you safe when you're such a vixen? Griffin is very no nonsense."

"So, is this our secret then?" I ask, tracing one of the tattoos on Beau's chest.

"You will never be a secret," Beau says.

"But on the other hand," Dan interrupts, "we can't let anyone know you're of importance to us. Once an enemy knows we have someone we care about, they try to attack us at our weakest point."

"I basically have a bigger target on my back now?" I ask.

Beau places a kiss on my forehead. "Yeah, but I've told you. I'm not going to let anything bad happen to you. I lost you once, and I'm not going to let it happen again."

I give a small nod and let myself relax into the comfort of the two men, finally finding the first restful sleep I've had in a long time.

CHAPTER 7

When I wake up, I'm naked and alone in the bed, but I glance over at the sitting area and see Beau talking quietly on the phone and peering out the window. The sun is starting to set, so it must be way after dinner. Only one day into my makeshift vacation and my sleep schedule is already destroyed.

I wrap the sheet around me, too lazy to pull some clean clothes from my duffle, and I walk over to Beau. He smiles, and I sit down on his lap, leaning against him and resting my head on his shoulder. The voice on the other line sounds like Griff, but I can't make out what he's saying. There's a bit of static obscuring his words.

"Sounds fine," Beau tells him. "We're good on our end. Might ditch this place in a few days. Her mom is kind of a royal bitch and very judgmental."

I roll my eyes, but I know Beau's description of my mother is correct. I want to leave here as soon as possible. It just doesn't seem like the safest thing to do right now.

"Alright," Beau says. "Let us know when we can move. Later."

Beau hangs up the phone and places it on the table next to us, wrapping his arms around me.

"Where'd Dan go?" I ask.

"He went to grab dinner," Beau answers, rubbing circles on my arm. "Your mother woke us up earlier and requested you and I join her for dinner, but I told her you weren't feeling well."

I smile at that. "I'm feeling better than I've felt in years."

"Yeah?" he asks. "No regrets?"

I shake my head. "No regrets—well, maybe one."

Beau's Adam's apple bobs up and down as he swallows. "What is it?" He's obviously scared of what I could say next.

I lean in and kiss him on the nose. "I wish I hadn't fallen asleep because I could have gone for round two—or would it be rounds three and four since there are two of you?"

Beau rests his forehead against mine and shakes his head ever so slightly. "You scared me."

"Was that Griff?" I ask for confirmation, leaning against Beau once again.

"Yeah," Beau says. "He wants us to stay here for a few more days, just to make sure things are safe."

"Has he figured out who is looking for me?" I ask, swallowing a lump in my throat.

Beau shakes his head and slides a hand under the sheet to stroke my bare thigh. "No, but he's trying to figure it out. It's just tough because we don't know who we can trust right now. His dad is pointing fingers at the daycare owners, but I don't think they have the balls to actually follow through with a rebuttal attack. It could be someone on the inside for all we know."

"What if—" I begin to say, choking on fear. "What if it's never safe to go home?"

Beau doesn't have a chance to answer my question, because Danny returns at that moment, carrying two armfuls of takeout bags. He closes the door with his boot and sets the food down on the table next to us.

"I didn't know what you liked," Danny starts, peering up at me from a pair of glasses that I didn't even know he owned. Does he wear contacts? Honestly, the glasses make him even more attractive. "I ended up stopping at a few places. We've got Chinese, Italian, and American fare, then I saw this dope taco food truck, so I bought some stuff there too. Kinda went overboard. I hope everyone's hungry."

I get up from Beau's lap and start pulling containers from the bags. "Thanks for getting dinner. I'm starving."

The three of us make our dinner plates, mixing and matching various foods like college kids at a cafeteria, and we put a blanket on the floor and pretend like we're having a picnic inside since we can't eat outside together. My parents still don't know that Danny's here in the house with us. I'm impressed he was able to sneak in and out undetected.

I glance at the two men sitting on the blanket across from me, their legs crossed, eating takeout food. I chuckle, thinking about having a real picnic with these two tattooed men in a park in the middle of summer. They would look so out of place. They would probably scare off all the parents and children.

"What's so funny?" Danny asks, tossing a crumpled napkin at me.

I'm still wrapped up in the bedsheets, feeling like a Greek goddess. All I need is to be fed grapes by my two strapping clones of Adonis.

"I was just thinking about how funny the two of you would look having a picnic in a park," I admit. "You'd scare away all the jogging wives. Women would be hauling their children off the playground equipment and packing them in their minivans to drive away."

Danny gives me a sinister smile. "You wouldn't believe the number of housewives who actually want to take a walk on the wild side. They're so bored with their lawyer or doctor husbands they practically come up to me begging for a ride on my bike. And I'll have you know, bike is a metaphor for my dick."

I throw a French fry at his head, but he deftly catches it in his mouth.

"You're a pig. That's something I would expect Griff to say, not you." I'm surprised by the jealousy I feel, thinking about someone else on Danny's bike, metaphor or not. I hardly know him, but somehow after what happened earlier, I feel like I have a claim on him. Like he belongs to me. Or at least his body does.

I get up from the floor, taking my garbage and putting it into one of the empty to-go bags and tying it up to take to the trash later. I wordlessly walk to the bathroom and slam the door shut behind me. Before I turn on the shower, I hear Beau mutter something to Danny and then footsteps fall in front of the bathroom door, followed by a knock.

I'm not sure if it's Beau or Danny, or which one I *want* it to be, but I ignore the knock. I drop the sheet on the tile floor and turn on the shower. There's no doubt I probably should have showered after our sexcapade earlier, or at least gotten up to use the restroom instead of falling asleep, but I didn't care. I was lost in the moment. I take my time in the shower, using the expensive coconut shampoo and conditioner my mom stocks in all the bathrooms here, exhausting a decent bit of hot water in the process. The shower at my apartment doesn't produce hot water for more than eight or ten minutes, so I take full advantage of the amenities. Just like a proper vacation.

Once I'm out of the shower, I don't bother drying my hair, and I realize I didn't bring any clothes in the bathroom with me. Now I'll have to go back to the room with only the sheet to grab them, exposing myself to Danny who I would rather not be around at the moment.

The issue is, the second I open the door, an outfit is being thrusted into my arms by the man of the hour.

"What the hell, Danny?" I demand.

"Get dressed," he shouts back, returning to my bag to put everything away. "We gotta go."

My heart starts racing. Any safety I felt is now gone. "Go where? What happened?"

"They fucking destroyed your apartment," he says, throwing his hands in the air. "They blew it up! Boom! Gone!"

What? I stand frozen in place, completely unable to process what I'm hearing. I must be like that for longer than Danny's liking because he grabs the t-shirt from my hands and begins dressing me, and then he takes the gym shorts and helps me get into those as well.

"Was—was anyone hurt?" I ask quietly as Danny tosses the sheet on the bed.

He shakes his head and grabs our bags. "No. Griff was on his way to check on it and the fire department was already there. No casualties."

Danny takes my arm, tossing my duffle over his shoulder, and he walks out back and around to the front to get in Griff's pickup truck. The three of us pile in with Danny behind the wheel.

"Let's go," Beau says. He pulls the passenger door closed behind him. Danny already has the truck in drive, leaving some skid marks on my parents' pristine driveway as we peel out. Part of me feels bad, but the other part wishes Danny would have done some permanent damage.

"What did you say to my parents?" I ask, knowing I'll probably get a snotty call from my mother for not really staying to have family time. Then again, probably not. Actually, she's very likely thrilled we left.

"I was honest," Beau says, constantly checking the side mirror. "Said there was an emergency."

I accept that answer. It'll work. It has to. "Where are we going?" I ask. "I obviously can't go back to my apartment. Everything I own is gone!"

The tears begin rolling down my cheeks. I've never been so scared in my life. Maybe they should have just killed me in the alley with that man.

Beau pulls me into his lap and awkwardly wraps the seatbelt around us and holds me tightly. "We're going to Griff's cabin," he says. "He's going to meet us there, and then we'll figure out what to do. I told you . . . I'm not going to let anything happen to you."

I shake my head and wipe my running nose on the edge of my t-shirt. "You should have just killed me. Hell, let Griff do it. I'm sure he doesn't want to risk his life protecting me."

"Hey!" Danny shouts, startling me. "Don't talk like that. No one is going to kill you, certainly not Griffin."

I shiver at his words, but I don't say anything in response. I lean into Beau and listen to his heart beating rapidly in his chest, trying in vain to fall asleep and forget everything.

* * *

I'm not sure how far we've driven or where we even are when we come to a stop. All I can see are trees and a dark cabin illuminated by the headlights of the truck. When Danny cuts the engine, the cabin disappears into the dark trees, leaving me with nothing but my reflection in the windshield. There aren't any lights for miles. The inside of the truck is quiet, none of the men saying a word. Just as I'm about to interrupt the silence, there's a knock on the driver's side and Danny's opening the door.

I jump at the sound, but I guess Danny and Beau were both expecting it because neither of them seems worried about who is on the other side. I find some sort of relief that it's only Griff.

"Hey, princess," he says to me, but the normal arrogance is no longer in his voice. It sounds like he hasn't slept in a while, but I guess none of us really have.

I climb out of the truck, and a soft breeze passes through the trees, chilling my body. That's when I realize I never put on a bra or underwear before we left Florida. I'm only wearing the shorts and t-shirt that Danny gave me. My nipples harden and I cover my chest, feeling like Griff can see right through my shirt and right through me.

He looks between the three of us, cocking his head to the side, but then just shakes it and walks toward the front door of the cabin, me and the guys following behind.

"I already checked the perimeter and inside," Griff says as he opens the door. "I also rebooted the cameras so we can see if anyone heads down the driveway."

Inside, all the lights are already on in the main area, and I notice that there are black-out curtains on all the windows, which explains why the cabin appears dark and deserted from the driveway. Griff locks the door behind us and goes over to a computer in the corner with various live feeds from security cameras on the screen. There's nothing to be seen but a deer casually eating something from the grass.

"Who wants the first watch?" Griff asks, glancing up at Beau and Danny.

"I'll do it," Danny says.

He takes a seat at the computer as Griff gives him a run through of his security setup. Beau goes out to the truck to grab our bags and shows me to a room down the hall. I'm not even tired, but I still let Beau get me set up in the bedroom. I climb in the bed and let him pull the covers up to my chin.

"I'll just be across the hall," he says. "If you need anything, let me know."

I give him a nod, tempted to ask him to stay, but I know he needs his rest. If he stays in here with me, we won't do much sleeping. I'll convince him to make up for lost time and that won't be good for us. Besides, Griff doesn't need to know that Beau and I have history, or that Beau, Danny, and I were intimate earlier today—well, I guess that was yesterday now. Still, he doesn't need to know.

"Good night," I tell Beau as he turns off the overhead light and exits the room, leaving the door cracked a little.

I listen intently as the three men talk in the other room, their voices hushed. After about twenty minutes I hear Griff and Beau head off to bed, and I'm wondering how many rooms the small cabin has. Maybe I was given the master? If that's the case, and this is Griff's cabin, then I've got to be in Griff's room. Where's he sleeping then? Maybe tomorrow I can sate my curiosity and get a tour of the rest of the cabin. It seems like we might end up being here for a little bit.

I can't shut off my mind or body for the next couple of hours, so I toss and turn and jump at any creak in the cabin, any noise from outside the window. Maybe I should have asked Beau to sleep in here with me after all. After what feels like forever, I glance at the illuminated alarm clock on the nightstand and find that it's five in the morning.

Normally, I would be waking up and getting ready for my morning jog around town, trying to get in at least five miles before the sun comes up. Not today. No one knows when I'll be able to get back into my normal routine. Maybe if I hadn't narced on my sorority sisters about hazing, I wouldn't be in a life-or-death situation. No, it's not a maybe—I *wouldn't* be in this situation. I'd still be in college, earning my degree, and I would have never returned to my hometown. I would have probably never seen Beau again.

My heart aches at the thought. If one good thing comes from this situation, it's that I get to be reunited with Beau one more time. If I could change one thing, I would have pleaded with him to come to college with me, even if he didn't get in. We could have gotten an apartment together, he could have gone to a trade school . . . something so we wouldn't be here right now. He could have been with me.

Then again, I wouldn't have met Danny. Yes, I'm still mad at him for his comment earlier even though I really have no right to be upset. What he did before me is none of my business, but I can't control the acidic taste that comes into my mouth when I think about him fucking one of those housewives. Of him fucking anyone that's not me.

I toss off the bedding, angry with myself for not being able to fall asleep, and open the bedroom door to go make some coffee or something. I can't sit in this bed with nothing to do any longer.

Danny is spinning around in the office chair in front of the computer when I get into the living room. He tosses a pen up in the air and catches it, obviously just as bored as I am.

"Hey," I say, not meeting his eyes as I go over to the coffee pot, hoping there are some filters and coffee grounds readily available. It doesn't seem like Griff is the type of guy to escape to his cabin all that often which means his pantry probably isn't stocked.

"Can't sleep?" Danny asks, stopping his spins.

I shake my head. "No, figured I might as well get up and do something Though to be honest, there's not much to do."

After I go through a few cabinets, coming up empty for the coffee, Danny goes over to the refrigerator and opens it. He pulls out a huge tub of Folgers and hands it over to me.

"Would have never looked there," I say, putting some of the coffee into the filter and starting the coffee maker. "Want some?"

Danny nods, and I grab two coffee mugs off the cute mug tree sitting on the counter. It looks like one of those crafty kind of wooden items a housewife would buy at a summer festival. I lean against the counter as I wait for the coffee to start its slow drip, trying to will it with my mind to brew faster so I have something to do. It's too quiet in this cabin.

"I'm sorry about what I said," Danny whispers, pacing in front of the fridge. "It was dumb. Honestly, I've never had to worry about what I say to a woman because all they want is a one-nighter with a bad boy."

I cringe and cross my arms against my chest.

Danny sighs and comes over to stand in front of me, using one finger to urge my chin up so I'll look at him. "Seriously," he adds. "I'm sorry. It's been a while since I've needed to use manners. If it weren't for Beau, I'd probably be a goner like Griff. That man doesn't know how to have a vanilla encounter at all. I'll try to be better . . . for you."

"You don't have to," I say stubbornly. "I get it. You're a member of a dangerous motorcycle *gang*. You've got an image that you need to keep up with."

"Club," Danny says with a bemused smile, rubbing the dimple in my chin. "Motorcycle club, baby girl. Don't ever let Griff hear you call Hell Prevails a gang or he'll tie you up and make you beg for mercy."

I shiver at the thought of Griff tying me up, but I also have another urge, a craving.

"But that's what you guys are," I push forward, speaking a little louder. "You're a gang. I'm in a gang war right now."

Danny covers my mouth with the palm of his hand and places his other on the back of my head to keep me quiet. "You have a death wish or something?"

I shrug my shoulders.

Danny bends down so we're eye to eye. I glance at his pitch-black beard and reach out to pull my fingers through it, tugging on some of the hair when I get to the end of it.

"Don't tease me," he says through gritted teeth.

I close my eyes and let out a soft moan, trying to get a rise out of him. It works.

The second he removes his hand, his mouth is covering mine in a frenzy. Just as he starts to pull away, I bite his bottom lip, holding him in place for a second before letting it go.

"Mine," I say once I release his lip.

He lifts me and places me on the counter, but before his lips can connect with mine again, we both jolt at the sound of a door opening at the end of the hall.

Danny backs away and begins pouring the two mugs of coffee, just as I turn to see Griff walking down the hall only wearing a pair of low hanging sweatpants, wiping some sleep from his eyes.

"Hey man," Danny says. "Just in time for some coffee, want me to pour you a cup?"

Griff grumbles something and comes over to lean against the counter next to me.

"I'll take that as a yes," Danny says, grabbing another mug. "Nothing on the security cameras."

"Not really expecting much," Griff replies. "We're just here as a precaution. No one knows about this place but you guys."

"Not even your dad?" I ask. Griff turns to me like he's just now noticing that I'm in the kitchen with them.

He chuckles. "Not even my dad. Also, has anyone ever told you that tables are for glasses, not asses?"

"This isn't a table," I say, but the stern look Griffin gives me has me hopping down from the island before he has to tell me again. "Sorry."

"You probably shouldn't be drinking coffee when it's your turn for a break," Griff says, turning to Danny.

Danny just shrugs and takes a sip of his black coffee as he goes to get the creamer from the fridge. "I'll sleep when Beau takes over watch. No worries."

Griffin doesn't like it. I notice his shoulder blades fill with tension for a moment. However, I'm glad that Danny doesn't seem to want to leave me alone with Griff; I'm still kind of afraid of the man.

Danny hands me the creamer and my mug of coffee, watching as I pour just a little of the cream in and take a spoonful of the sugar sitting on the counter, mixing it with a spoon. My cheeks flush when my eyes find his face. His lip is a little swollen. He takes his middle finger and rubs at it, like he knows that I'm thinking about how I claimed him a few seconds ago.

"Do you have cable?" I ask, turning to Griffin.

"Does this look like a high-end hotel to you, princess?" he shoots back, walking over to sit in front of the computer and checking all the cameras.

"Well, what else is there to do?" I ask. "You probably won't let me go for a jog. I didn't bring anything to do. You abducted me from my normal life."

"Forgive me for trying to save your life," Griff snarls through gritted teeth. He takes a sip of his coffee without moving his eyes off the security footage. He's watching the cameras better than Danny was when I walked in here.

I roll my eyes and head over to the couch, pulling my legs up and literally staring at the wall because there's nothing else to do.

"I've got some cards," Danny says, joining me on the couch. "We can play Go Fish or something."

We both ignore Griff's snarky chuckle. I decide that if I'm being forced to follow Griff's rules, I'm going to at least have some fun.

"Let's play poker instead," I say. "We can make it fun. You've got hours before you have to be back on babysitting duty."

"Strip poker?" Danny asks, an eyebrow raised.

I laugh when I hear Griff choke on his coffee. "No," I say, rolling my eyes. "Let's play for shots. You've got to at least have some alcohol here, right? I miss bartending. Loser of each round has to take a shot of the winner's choice."

Danny hops off the couch and goes over to dig through the cabinet above the microwave.

"Don't you dare use my good bourbon for your childish game!" Griff calls.

Danny comes back over with an assortment of liquor, sans any bourbon. I start making up shots in my head, shots that will knock any of these guys on their asses.

"You're going down," Danny says wickedly. "I usually win our poker run every year."

I shrug my shoulders and start shuffling the cards. "I think this will be a win-win situation for the both of us. Maybe Griff will even get to reap some of the reward."

Danny gives me a suggestive wink, and I begin dealing out the cards.

* * *

My idea sort of backfires on me. I managed to literally drink Danny under the table because I've won, but now I have no one to entertain my tipsy ass. Beau isn't supposed to be up for his watch shift for another hour, and Danny's conked out on the couch.

"You proud of yourself?" Griff asks from behind me.

I stick out my chest and walk over to the pantry for a snack. I should have known playing a drinking game before lunch time—on an empty stomach—would do a lot of damage.

"Are you going to answer me?" Griff demands, watching me search for something to eat. "Do you realize that we're trying to keep you safe but you're doing everything in your power to screw with Danny's head?"

"I'm not screwing with anyone's head," I say, turning around with a silver foil package of Pop-Tarts. I rip open the packaging and start eating them because I don't feel like looking for the toaster or asking Griff where it is. "I'm just trying to have some fun because I'm bored."

"Back off my guys," Griff says, getting right in my face.

I smile up at him, wavering on my feet a little. I place my hands on Griff's stone chest to steady myself. "Your guys? More like *my* guys."

Griff stops me, grabbing my wrists when I try to duck under his arm. "What's *that* supposed to mean?"

I bite my lip and look innocently at Griff. "I mean what I said. They're my guys. What do you think happened when you sequestered me in a room with two very attractive men? One of which used to be the love of my life, by the way."

There. I said it! Now he knows.

Griff's eyebrows pinch together. "You're drunk. You're not making any sense."

I laugh and pull my wrist from his grasp. "I'll prove it. Just watch me."

Griff stares in confusion but allows me to strut over to the couch where Danny is sleeping. He has an arm on the armrest holding his head, just barely keeping him upright. I remove the shot glass that he was somehow still holding and place it on the table before straddling Danny's lap.

"Dan," I whisper, placing a soft fingertip on his cheek. "Dan, wake up."

He stirs— somewhat to my surprise—and his hands move to my waist, tugging me closer to him. His lips twitch in a lazy smile.

"Whatcha want, baby girl?" he asks, keeping his eyes closed.

I lean my head on his shoulder and pout. "You fell asleep on me. We didn't get to . . ."

Danny doesn't let me finish. He moves quicker than I expected, laying me down on the couch and covering his body with mine.

His sleepy eyes finally find my gaze. "I was just resting. Did Griff go to sleep? I can be quiet if you can."

In an instant, Danny is yanked off of me, shock coloring his face.

Griff shoves him out of the living room. "What the fuck, man?" Griff roars. "You can't go a day without getting your dick wet? Our lives are all on the line! Not just hers."

"Live a little," Danny says groggily, holding up his hands. "If I'm going to die, I at least want to do it while pleasing her. Dude, she is one *hell* of a woman."

I blush at his compliment. I've never heard him talk like that to someone else. He's never made me feel so attractive before in my life.

"Go to your room!" Griff yells like he's the father of our group. Honestly, I wouldn't mind calling him daddy.

Danny laughs and stumbles forward drunkenly. "You're not the boss of me," he says. "I can fuck who I want, when I want."

Griff squeezes his temples in frustration. "Just go to bed. *Please*. I don't need your drunk ass keeping watch. You need to rest so your awareness is at max. We have a job to do here. Don't forget that."

Danny gives me a smile. "Oh, I'm very aware. Aware of that beautiful woman who I want to devour."

Griff shoves Danny down the hall before turning back to me. If looks could kill, I'd be in my grave right now.

"You," Griff says. "I don't know what kind of game you're playing, but you need to go to your room too. I don't want to see your face for the rest of the day."

"I don't have a room," I say, nibbling on my Pop-Tart.

Griff punches a hole in the dry wall. His fist comes out covered in white dust. "Go to my room, damn it!"

I jump at the violence, but my lady bits celebrate. "Yes, sir," I say with a mischievous grin.

CHAPTER 8

Miraculously, I finally fell asleep, though I have no idea when. The issue is, the amount of alcohol in my blood made me pass out for hours, and then it also woke me up. I toss the covers off and run over to a door that I hope is the bathroom. I get lucky. I kneel down and pray to the porcelain gods as my stomach lurches from my body, and I empty its contents into the bowl. *Been a long time since I was this drunk*, I silently muse.

I'm never mixing vodka and coconut rum ever again.

I rest my head against the toilet seat and hope that Griffin cleans the bathroom every time he's down here. Thinking about how dirty this place could be makes me vomit once again. I remove the hair tie from my wrist and throw my hair into a messy bun. I sit there another five minutes, making sure I'm not going to hurl again. My head just spins and spins.

Getting myself off the floor, I brace my body on the sink and flush the toilet before washing my hands and rinsing my mouth out with mouthwash. After retrieving my toothbrush and toothpaste from my suitcase, I brush the horrible taste from my mouth and head to the living room, hoping Griff isn't around.

To my surprise, I find only Beau and Danny. Beau's sitting at the computer watching the cameras and eating a slice of pizza while Danny is sprawled on the couch with an ice pack pressed up against his left eye.

"What happened to you?" I ask, hovering over Danny.

He lifts the ice pack, revealing a fresh black eye. A stinger, as my mom would have called it. I drop to my knees instinctively and gently touch the bruised skin around his eye.

"Griff punched me," he says, placing the ice back on his eye. He sits up on the couch. "He demanded that I tell him everything that happened between the three of us, and then he gave me a blow to my eye. Jealous fuck."

"Shit," I say, letting out a breath. "Where is he now?"

Beau spins around in the chair to look at us, wiping his hands on a napkin. "He's out back letting out some aggression. Come and see if you'd like."

I walk over to the computer screen and find one of the cameras pointing at a wood pile. Griff lifts up an axe and uses all his strength to split a log in half. The cameras have amazing resolution, and I can see all of Griff's muscles moving in his torso, flexing like tight fibers beneath a rushing stream.

Beau pulls me down in his lap, and I lean back against him but continue to stare at the screen as Griff slays another piece of wood.

"He's jealous," Beau whispers into my ear. "I've never seen him this jealous before. Kinda crazy."

"He's an asshole," Danny adds from his spot on the couch. "A pouty little asshole."

Beau kisses my shoulder blade as I keep watching Griff chop out his aggression. I could probably watch him all day. The way the sweat glistens on his muscles and covers his tattoos . . .

"You hungry?" Beau asks. "We got some pizza."

My reverie broken, I nod my head and extricate myself from Beau's warm lap. "Hungry and hungover. Pizza sounds perfect."

"And dangerous," Danny says with a smirk. "This lady out drank me! She outdrank a biker! How is that possible?"

I give him a small smile. "I was a sorority girl for a little bit, remember? And then I was a bartender."

"Probably doesn't help that I used to steal my uncle's scotch for us," Beau says. "Remember that time we hiked out to that field behind my house and shared a bottle of it?"

I cringe at the memory. "That's one of my best *and* worst memories. Loved being out in that field with you, but it was the worst hangover. I swear, every time I see a bottle of that scotch or have to pour some for a customer, I want to vomit. The smell still wrecks me. Your uncle drank shitty scotch."

Beau gets up and grabs a paper plate and puts two slices of cheesy, greasy pizza on it for me. My stomach rumbles at the sight, craving the carbs, wanting it to soak up any of the liquor still inside.

I hop up on one of the barstools at the kitchen island and dig into the pizza. I'm so hungry I devour the two pieces in no time. I feel like the Cookie Monster being unleashed in a bakery, and the thought makes me laugh.

Sadly, my cheeriness doesn't last.

"He's coming," warns Danny. He gets up from the couch to watch the security cameras.

My eyes go wide, and I start to go back to the bedroom, remembering Griff's words that he didn't want me to come out until he said otherwise. Instead, Beau places a hand on my shoulder, keeping me in place.

"If he's got a problem, he can talk to me," Beau states defiantly. He gently massages my shoulders. I stay seated and pick at my pizza crust, suddenly losing my appetite.

The three of us stare at the door as Griff enters. He's still shirtless. I take back what I thought about the cameras earlier—they don't do real life Griff any justice. His six pack is chiseled to perfection, and his shorts are riding dangerously low, revealing the perfect v-taper or whatever that muscle is called. Tattoos cover his entire torso, and when my eyes meet his, I want to crawl under a rock.

"Stay out of my room," he says, storming down the hall. "I'm sure you'll be more comfortable sleeping in the same room as your fuck boys."

With that last crass comment, he slams his bedroom door shut. A couple seconds later, I hear the shower.

Beau clears his throat and drops his hands from my shoulders. "Well, I guess that's as much of a blessing as we'll be getting from him."

* * *

Griff doesn't leave his room for hours.

Danny and Beau take turns watching the security cameras, and I flip through some motorcycle magazines from beneath the coffee table. A lot of them have pictures of female models straddling Harley Davidson bikes and various other models. Most of the women hardly have any clothes on. I stop on one image of a blonde wearing only fishnet stockings with black leather booty shorts and a very cropped Ducati shirt. You can definitely tell that she's not wearing a bra by the amount of under boob showing. Not to mention her nipples.

Danny plops down beside me and leans over to check out what I'm reading.

He wiggles his eyebrows. "You would look so hot wearing that."

I roll my eyes at him and flip the page. "In your dreams."

He nods approvingly. "Yeah, you're right, in my dreams. You wanna make them a reality?"

"Pig," I scold, but I smile anyway, flipping the page. Honestly, I could pull it off. I kind of *want* to pull it off. To be the hot piece of biker ass everyone stares at when I walk into a bar.

Danny leans in and kisses me on my neck. I giggle as his beard tickles my skin, and I try and shrug him off, but he urges me down onto the couch.

"Call me whatever you want," he says, his breathing hitched. "As long as you keep calling me something."

"Asshole," I tease, testing to see if he's serious. His grin only encourages me. "Dumbass. Freak. Cocksu—"

He places a finger on my lips. "Shh. We both know that the only cocksucker here is you, baby girl."

I bite the tip of his finger, and he closes his eyes in response.

When he opens them again, his eyes find mine and his mouth covers my own in an instant. I can't help but moan into him, my tongue dancing around his. I know I should probably feel weird making out with Danny while my ex is still in the room, but my carnal needs take over, and suddenly it's just Danny and I in the room. I don't even care if Griff comes storming in and yelling at us. Hell, a tornado could touch down and I wouldn't notice.

We make out like teenagers long enough for my lips to feel like they're numb, and we grind against each other so long that I've soaked through my underwear and my leggings. I glance down between us and see that I've even managed to spatter Danny's jeans with my pleasure. It's almost embarrassing.

"Baby girl, you're so wet for me," Danny breathes, a triumphant smile plastered on his handsome face. "I haven't even really touched you yet."

I shove him away from me, knocking the smile from his face, but quickly bringing it back when I straddle his lap, grinding my wet core against the hard shaft below his pants.

"Don't be an ass," I scold, bending down and biting him on his neck until he grips my hips.

I pull away from him, and the two of us immediately start removing each other's clothes. I swear I'm going to explode from the anticipation. I glance over to Beau sitting quietly at the computer, and our eyes meet in the reflection of the screen. He gives me an encouraging nod, and I notice his arm moving in a gentle rhythm. He's touching himself while watching us.

Holy. Shit.

That's all the encouragement I need.

I don't even bother pulling down Danny's pants after I unzip his jeans. I grab his cock and take it out. I stand up only long enough to slide down my leggings, deciding I might just start wearing dresses and skirts for easier access around these two men.

The second I straddle Danny's lap, I impale my cunt on his rock hard dick and toss my head back with pleasure. Danny lifts my hips up and has me slamming down on him again. After my body takes on the pace he wants, he moves one of his hands to the small bundle of nerves at my clit and uses his wet fingers to rub insistent circles that send wave after wave vibrating through my body.

All of a sudden, I'm hit with the urge to pee, but Danny doesn't let me leave his lap and he doesn't let up on his circles. In the blink of an eye, a rush of pleasure leaves my body and I look down just in time to see that pleasure squirt all over Danny's cock and torso. Some of it splashes on his chin.

"Fuck, baby girl," Danny says, clearly both surprised and pleased with himself. "I had a feeling that was going to happen. You didn't tell me you're a squirter."

"That's never happened before," I whisper.

Danny smiles and moves himself to a sitting position. "Let's see if you can do it again, but this time, we're doing it in my favorite position and we're going to ruin this couch."

I don't have a chance to deny him, but I wouldn't even if I could.

Danny moves us flawlessly and has me on my knees on the couch, pressing my hands into the back of the sofa. He's thrusting inside me from behind, and the second his hand reaches around my body to find my clit again, I already feel the buildup beginning. I'm going to squirt all over his cock.

He takes his other hand and places it over my mouth to cover my moans as he pounds away inside me. My body convulses and gushes again. I'm like a fountain, and Danny was right—the couch is pretty much ruined.

"Baby girl, where have you been all of my life?" he whispers in my ear.

A towel gets tossed in our faces while Danny is still inside me, and we both flinch.

"Get dressed and clean up this fucking mess," Griffin growls. "We're going home."

Danny slides out of me and uses the towel to cover me up as Griffin stomps back down the hall. Once Griff is gone, I sit down on the couch and Danny begins cleaning me off. I glance around him to where Beau is sitting.

"Hey," I whisper when he turns around in the chair, his face flushed. "You okay?"

Beau stands up and slowly walks over to us. I stare up at him from where I'm sitting, and he bends down in front of me, placing a soft hand on my cheek. I'm surprised he's smiling.

"As long as you're okay, I'm okay," he answers. He leans in to place a kiss on my lips. My heart soars. I was worried he was going to be jealous or uncomfortable with the fact that he just witnessed another man pleasuring me. Another man getting soaked by me.

"Let's get you cleaned up and presentable before Griff comes out here again," Danny says. The two of them help me up on my shaky legs.

When my post-orgasm knees give out, but Beau is there to catch me, picking me up and carrying me like a bride. I lean my head on his shoulder as he takes me to the bathroom. I savor his touch, and I never want it to end.

CHAPTER 9

"I'm not getting on that thing with you!" I shout, crossing my arms. "No way in hell."

Danny and Beau pause at the truck after they toss our bags in the back, but I'm not talking to them. My anger is aimed at Griffin who is holding a helmet for me.

"Get on the damn bike, Princess," he says through gritted teeth. "I've had enough of your shit. Now."

I cross my arms. "Then let me ride in the truck with Beau and Danny."

"No," he growls, shoving the helmet toward me. I have no choice but to take it. "You will ride with me since those two fuckers don't know how to keep their dicks in their pants."

I pull the helmet over my head and fumble with the chin strap. "You're disgusting."

He pushes my hands away and buckles the chin strap, tightening it and then patting the top of the helmet. "Why, thank you! I'll take that as a compliment." His voice drips with sarcasm.

Griff straddles the bike and offers a hand to me. "Your chariot awaits, Princess."

I groan, ignore his hand, and climb onto the back of the bike, holding onto the sides instead of wrapping my arms around his torso. He flicks the kickstand back with his foot and chuckles. "You're going to want to hold onto me."

Sure enough, he revs the bike and tosses up some gravel as we head down the unpaved drive. I squeal and grab onto his waist, holding so tightly I wonder if he can even breathe. Danny and Beau follow behind us in the truck, and I know for a fact that I would give anything to be sitting in the middle of the two of them again instead of on the back of this stupid bike with Griffin.

As we head back toward home, I stare at the landscapes to either side. Even though I'm on the bike with my least favorite person, I can still admit that there's something freeing about feeling my hair whipping in the wind beneath my helmet. Instead of fighting it, I relax against Griff and let him give me the ride of my lifetime.

Hopefully, once I'm back home, I'll never have to get back on a bike with Griff ever again. I'm not afraid to admit I wouldn't mind riding on the back of Beau's bike though. Actually, that sounds pretty nice.

* * *

"I just want to go home!" I say, crossing my arms over my chest and stomping my foot, practically pouting like a child.

"I've told you," Griff shouts, slamming the front door closed. "You have no home to go to! It no longer exists! The people who want you dead are still out there looking for you!"

"This is bullshit!" I shout right back, picking up a glass ashtray from the coffee table and chucking it at Griff. I have horrible aim, so it hits the wall behind him just as Danny and Beau walk through the door. They both look at me with fear in their eyes, but Griffin is anything but afraid. He crosses the room to me in three steps and places two strong hands on my arms, gripping me almost painfully.

"Did you just throw something at me?" he growls through clenched teeth. "One more stunt like that and your ass will be tossed out of my home for good. I won't be protecting you anymore. Hell! I'll put you out like bait for the bad guys that want you dead, and then I'll *help* them kill you."

Danny pulls Griff away, but he quickly turns and grips Danny by the throat.

"Don't," Griff says. "You and Beau are going to get all of us killed if you keep letting the girl get between us."

Griff lets go, and Danny instantly rubs his hand over the spot that Griff just wrapped his hand around. I move to stand beside him, wanting to check and make sure he's okay. My old girlfriend instincts must be kicking in.

Griff turns his back to us. "Get that glass cleaned up. I'm going to call my dad and let him know we're back in town. No one interrupt me for the rest of the night."

He storms up the stairs and slams his door. A moment later I hear the rumbling cacophony of metal music barely muffled by the door and distance. I shake my heard and turn my attention back to Danny.

"Are you okay?" I ask. Looking at the red skin, I can see imprints of Griff's fingers. I wonder if I'll have a matching bruise on my arms. The man is too strong for his own good.

He gives me a small smile. "I'm fine. Griff loses his temper sometimes. He means well, he just doesn't want anything bad to happen to this fucked up little family he has."

Beau begins carefully picking up the broken glass from the floor and walks over to put the shards in the trash.

"Want a tour of the place?" he asks from the kitchen. "Since you'll be staying for a while."

I shrug my shoulders and glance around the house. It's surprisingly clean for a place inhabited by three young motorcycle gang—no, club—members.

"Kitchen, living room," Beau says, pointing out the obvious. "There's a bathroom behind that door over there, and all the bedrooms are upstairs."

Danny wraps an arm around my shoulder and pulls me against him, giving me a quick peck on my forehead. Once he releases me, I follow Beau up the stairs.

"That's the master," Beau whispers. He points toward the door where the music has ceased, but there's a muffled phone conversation replacing it. "Griff gets the master since he owns the place and is technically in line to take over the MC. Kind of patriarchal like that, I guess. Like an old monarchy or something."

I nod as our tour continues. There's a lot to take in on the walls. Signed vinyl records from bands I don't recognize, old leather cuts from what I presume are past club members, and so much more. The entire hallway reminds me of a museum.

"This is the guest bathroom," Beau says, leaning in and flicking on a light. "If you need us to stock it with something, just let us know. Dan—he used to have girls over often and tries to keep the bathroom stocked with things a female might need to be comfortable."

I try not to think about Danny entertaining other girls. More than the past, I try not to think about him starting that up again with me in the house. I want to own him now.

We arrive at another door. "This one is Danny's room," he explains, but I don't cross the threshold. If Danny wants me in his room, he can invite me. We stop our tour in front of the next door. It sports a full-length poster of the club's fiery logo. "And this one is mine."

I follow Beau into his room and notice there's another door leading to the guest bathroom as well, and it opens up on the other side of the wall to reveal Danny's room. A Jack and Jill guest bathroom. It strikes me as a bit odd for a motorcycle club, but whatever.

Beau leans against his desk and watches me as I take in his

bedroom. It's nothing like the room he had in high school. There aren't any posters up, only blank walls. He's got a bookshelf with some old mementos and books, and I go to browse it, finding a picture of us on our prom night. I pick it up and smile at the stiff pose the photographer had us do, my back to Beau's stomach and his hands on my hips. I wore a white dress. It basically looked like a wedding dress. Beau wore a pitch-black tux, and I thought he was the most handsome boy in our town. He still is.

"You kept this?" I ask him, turning and holding the picture.

He smiles at me from across the room. "Of course. You were my high school sweetheart. You think I was just going to toss that in a box to never be opened again? I like seeing it up there."

I shrug my shoulders and place the frame back down next to Beau's dried-out boutonniere from prom. I kept all my stuff after our breakup as well. I just put mine in a plastic storage bin under my bed and only got it out on nights when I was wine drunk in college. I put that bin along with some of my other things in a storage unit that I pay on monthly, thank God. None of it was lost. My apartment was way too small to put anything that wasn't a necessity inside, forcing me to purge some items and buy the smallest storage unit available. I don't know what I would have done had I lost everything I own.

Maybe one of the guys can take me by the unit this week so I can have some of my personal items here, or maybe I should just leave them in the unit. I feel like nothing and no one is safe in this house. The bad guys burned down my apartment, who's to say they won't burn down Griff's house?

I walk over to Beau's bed and sit on the edge. He's still got the same bedding from high school. I'm not sure if I should be grossed out or feel nostalgic.

He stands from his spot at the desk and walks over to sit next to me.

"So, where am I going to sleep?" I ask after taking in a deep breath.

"If you'd like, you can have my room and I'll take the couch," he says softly. "Or there's the other option."

"What's that?" I ask as my heart sprints.

"You could stay in here with me," he says, lifting his gaze to find my eyes. "It's kind of convenient if you ask me. You can stay here or cross through the bathroom to Danny. You never have to leave the room and see Griff if you don't want to."

I don't answer his proposition. Not directly. Instead, I climb onto his lap and push him back on his bed, straddling him as I crash our lips together. My kiss is urgent. Passionate. He comes back with just as much urgency.

I'm not sure how much time we spend tangled in each other, groping one another through our clothes, but it's long enough for my stomach to protest between us.

Beau carefully sits us both up and slows the kiss down to a complete stop, punctuated with a smile.

"Let's get you something to eat," he says.

I don't move to get off his lap. "I'm not hungry for food."

He arches an eyebrow. "Your stomach says otherwise. I need you to have some sustenance."

"Someone called for sustenance?" Danny says from the doorway. When I turn around, I see he's carrying a large tray covered with breakfast items, even though it's supper time. I also notice he's wearing an apron like he's some innocent house wife or something. I grin at his appearance as he sets the food down in the middle of the floor and pats the spot next to him for me to sit.

"I'm not good at cooking much," he adds. Beau and I join him on the floor. He passes each of us a paper plate and plastic fork. "But I can make a fantastic breakfast. And eggs are pretty easy."

"Is that where you've been?" I ask, picking up a homemade scone from the platter. My stomach growls even louder, demanding the scone at once. I wonder how long Beau and I had been making out. How long do scones take to make from scratch?

"He stress bakes," Beau says, taking a few pieces of bacon and a blueberry pancake onto his plate.

Danny nods, leaning onto his side and nibbling on his own scone. "It's true. When I first joined the MC, I was baking so much I had to donate some of the stuff to a church nearby."

"That's nice of you," I say with a smile.

"I was donating it everyday for over a month," he deadpans. "I would get up early and start baking, then I'd report to the president for my assignments and when I was done, I would bake again."

"Oh," I say through a mouthful of scone. It sounds rough.

"Don't give me that pitiful look," Danny says with a sad smile. "I knew what I was getting myself into. I chose the life."

I shrug my shoulders. "Did you though? Did you know you would have to kill people?"

Danny and Beau both flinch at my words, but I refuse to retract them. Yeah, I've been enjoying this little sexual fantasy we've been acting out, but when it comes down to it, they're still murderers. They've still done more bad things than I ever want to know. If I could go back in time, I would have asked Beau to go with me to college. I hate that I left him and now his life is so far off track now.

"We kill bad guys, Princess," Griff says from the open bedroom door. He doesn't cross the barrier, just leans against the door frame with a half-eaten egg and bacon biscuit in his hand. "We kill bad guys, and we try our best to protect the innocent. I don't know how many times I have to tell you that to get it through that pretty, naïve little brain of yours."

My heart races at the thought of him thinking I'm pretty, but I know Griffin is the most dangerous of them all. I can't get close to him, but that doesn't mean I don't want to though. *Of course* I do.

"She's going to need some more clothes," Griff says to Danny and Beau. "The two of you can run to the store and buy some stuff since you're more acquainted with her body. I'm sure you know what sizes to get."

"I can go buy my own clothes—" I begin to protest, but Griff turns his gaze to me, cutting me off.

"No, you're not leaving this house," he states in no uncertain terms. "You and I have some discussing to do, and I don't want these two trying to ruin the plan. They will be going shopping, and you and I will be discussing how long or short you intend your life to be."

To my surprise, my guys stand from the floor without a glance at me or a protest to Griff. I assume Griff gave them some silent command I didn't catch that they couldn't argue with. I know that if Beau truly thought I was in danger by being alone with Griff, he would have done something to stay with me.

* * *

Griff paces back and forth across the kitchen floor. I watch him from my spot at the table. He ordered me to sit in this chair after the guys left, and he hasn't stopped pacing for a good five minutes. I cross my arms over my chest and roll my eyes at him, but apparently that's the wrong thing to do.

"Did you just roll your eyes at me, Princess?" Griff demands, getting right in my face. He smells like tobacco and mint. Like he chews on a piece of gum after every cancer stick he smokes. I wonder if the gum covers up the taste of cigarettes when he's fucking someone.

I shrug my shoulders in lieu of answering him.

He balls up his fist and punches the table, making me jump in my chair.

"Can't you see I'm trying to keep you alive?" he yells.

I put my hands under my thighs, sitting on them. "I guess the phone call with your dad didn't go well?"

He shoves away from me, and the table legs squeal on the tile floor. "You know what he wants me to do?" I shake my head, and Griff continues. "He wants me to hand you over to him so he can give up your life to the people who want you dead. He doesn't think your life is worth it. He thinks you're worthless to us."

My heart thunders in my chest. "What do you think?" My voice comes out so quietly it can barely be heard.

Griff stops in his tracks and stares at me, his eyes flashing. It feels like he's looking right into my soul. I can practically touch him in there trying to figure out everything I've done in my life, and if I am truly worthy of trying to keep alive.

"I think . . ." he pauses. "I think that Beau and Dan would murder me themselves if I let my father have his way or let anyone kill you."

"What if they weren't part of the equation?" I ask, wanting to know Griff's true motives. "What if Beau didn't know me and I was nothing to any of you? What would you do then?"

He pulls out the chair next to me and sits down, lacing his fingers together in front of him. "I want to do the right thing."

I give a subtle nod. "What will happen if you refuse to let your dad handle things?"

"I'll lose everything that I've been working my whole life for," he says, staring me directly in the eyes. "I'll lose my position as vice president and will be removed from inheriting the MC. My father will surely disown me—if he doesn't kill me first."

I want to ask if he's joking, but it's painfully obvious that he's not.

CHAPTER 10

"What are we going to do?" Beau asks, pulling on his hair with both of his hands.

Griff just updated him and Danny on the conversation with his father when they returned from shopping. They brought back six bags full of clothes from various stores in the mall, but I haven't bothered to go peek at the goodies. Who knows if I'll be alive long enough to enjoy them.

Griff rests his head on his arms and grunts. "I don't know. I've been going over options all evening."

No one says a thing. Griff hasn't lifted his head since he told the guys what's happening. Danny's sitting across from me swirling a glass of bourbon and staring at me, and Beau looks like he's going to have a mental breakdown.

"Maybe you should just hand me over," I suggest softly. It feels like someone else is speaking. It isn't me.

All three men jerk their heads up in disbelief. Danny actually drops his glass where it shatters to the floor.

"Fuck no," Griff spits. I'm shocked by his reaction. I expected him to drive me right over to the clubhouse and hand deliver me to his father. "You're staying with us. That's the only option. Either we all live or we all die."

Beau and Danny exchange a look, and I let Griff's words sink in. He doesn't want to hand me over to his father who wants to hand me over to the people that want me dead. He would rather die than sacrifice me.

What. The. Hell.

"Fuck!" Griff suddenly shouts. He shoves up from the table and storms across the room to retreat upstairs. "I'm going to bed. Make sure no one breaks in to kill us all tonight."

I quickly stand and run over to the stairs, but Griff is already half way up them. "Wait . . . it's only eight."

"Princess, I've had enough feelings today," Griff says over his shoulder. "I'm calling up a sweet butt to fuck me into oblivion."

"Sweet butt?" I whisper, pondering what exactly that is. It sounds . . . well, I don't know.

Danny comes up behind me and wraps his arms around my waist. "It's basically a girl who you can booty call. Usually they're trying to climb the ladder to be someone's old lady in the MC. Looks like you got to Griff."

"I—I didn't mean to upset him," I say softly. Griff shuts his door, and metal blasts behind it a moment later. I recognize the song from the bar at least, and it's one I mostly enjoy: *Walk* by Pantera. "Maybe I should—"

Danny spins me around in his arms. "Griff is going to call on one of his lady friends, she's going to come over and fuck him while they get high, then she's going to go home and everything will be fine."

I shake my head. "It won't be fine. I'm going to get us all killed."

"Shh," Danny whispers. "Why don't you go change into some of the pajamas we bought for you and then the three of us will watch a movie?"

He gently urges me to go grab the shopping bags, giving me a soft pat on my ass in the process. Beau beats me to the shopping bags and starts carrying them up the stairs like a proper gentleman, and I follow him to the bedroom. I feel like I'm just going through the motions as I look through the bags of clothes on Beau's bed. He begins folding the ones that I toss his way and placing them on the top of the dresser.

I finally find a black pajama set lined with white around the edges. I go to the bathroom where a fresh toothbrush has been placed next to a toothbrush holder on the sink that is already occupied by two others. I remove my clothes, pull on the shorts and button-up shirt, and then brush my teeth. The tasks feel so normal, but my life is currently anything but.

When Beau and I leave the bedroom maybe ten minutes later, I catch a glimpse of Griff pulling a girl into his room and shutting the door before I can get a good look at her. That was quick. I try my best not to feel jealous.

* * *

I've reached for the remote control about ten times to turn up the TV volume. I can't drown out the sound of whips against skin, moans, grunting, and screaming pleasure. I've got my legs in Danny's lap where he's massaging my calves, and my head is in Beau's lap and he's running his hand through my hair. The two of them have been at it for an hour now. Aren't they bored? Tired?

"Jesus," I shout. "Are they fucking or killing each other with their genitals up there?"

Danny laughs and moves his hand up to my thigh, gently massaging. "Probably both? Griff likes to be a dom. He's into some real kinky shit."

"He's a sadist if you ask me," Beau mumbles. "I don't think I could ever do half the shit I've heard him do. Or half the shit I've *seen* him do."

I give up on the movie we're trying to watch and turn off the TV, rolling over so I'm looking at Beau. "You've never even thought about it?" I ask.

He stops playing with my hair. "Not really. I've only been with you, and I've never fantasized about hurting you, even if it was for pleasure. Whether it be yours or mine."

I direct my attention to Danny, whose hand is getting dangerously close to the hem of my pajama shorts. "What about you?"

"I've tried some stuff here and there," he admits. "But I wouldn't consider bondage to be my number one kink."

"What *is* your number one kink?" I ask, letting his fingers dip into my panties as Beau moves his right hand to the buttons of my shirt, opening the top two.

Danny's fingers glide over my center with ease. "Sugar, I think we've already achieved my number one kink."

Danny plunges two fingers deep inside me, and I arch my back up from the couch as I feel Beau slide his hand to my breast.

"You think we can be louder than the two upstairs?" Danny challenges Beau.

Instead of answering him, Beau pinches one of my nipples in his fingers, making me scream out in pleasure.

"I'll take that as a yes," Danny says, dipping a third finger into me and leaning down to plunge his tongue into my mouth.

Beau continues to play with my breasts, alternating soft strokes with aggressive tweaks of my nipples as Danny moves down my body where his mouth joins his hand to bring me to a quick climax.

"Let's take this upstairs," Beau suggested. Danny removes his tongue and fingers from me, I open my eyes just in time to see him sucking my orgasm off his fingers and savoring the taste.

Beau pulls me from the couch and makes me wrap my shaking legs around his waist so he can carry me up the steps. I trail kisses and love bites all over his neck until he tosses my limp body on the bed.

Danny appears at his side, and the two of them take off their shirts and pants, both standing in front of me without an ounce of embarrassment.

"How do you want us this time, little one?" Danny asks.

I smile and sit up in the bed, crawling to the edge. "I want . . . double penetration. Both of you at once. My ass and my pussy."

I may look sweet and innocent with my doe eyes, sandy hair, and sundresses, but I've watched a porno here and there—for research, of course, in my Women's Studies course in college. I wrote a paper on the effects of pornography on an individual. I'm not a prude.

Danny arches an eyebrow at me with a smile and then takes my hand, kissing it softly. "Not sure I would call it that. Sounds a bit clinical," he laughs. "But rest assured. It would be our pleasure, mademoiselle."

Once I'm standing, Beau squats down enough to lift me up so I'm wrapping my legs around his waist, and Danny is there to catch some of my weight so Beau isn't doing all the work.

"You're going to need some lube . . ." Beau begins to say, looking over my shoulder at Danny.

"No, I'm not," Dan says, sliding a hand between my legs and taking some of my juices from my warm core. I toss my head back in pleasure, and he kisses my neck. "We've got all the natural lube here, my friend."

"Fuck me already!" I beg, bucking my hips against Beau, whose erection has slipped free from his boxers.

Both of the men jump into action. Beau enters me immediately with a groan, and Dan uses two fingers to get me ready. I know it's probably going to hurt, but I want it anyway.

"Hurry up, Dan. I *want* you," I whisper.

"Baby girl, I'm trying to make sure I don't hurt you," he says, thrusting his fingers inside me, making sure there's going to be enough room.

"I'm good," I promise. "Just go slow to start."

Danny removes his fingers, and I feel him line up his cock with my ass. I can't help but tense up a little. Beau's still inside me, but he's stopped his movements to allow Dan to get situated.

"Breathe," Dan says sweetly. "Breathe and relax. If it hurts, tell me and I'll stop."

I nod my head, and Danny penetrates me from behind. He moves so slowly I wonder if he's even moving at all. I squeeze my eyes shut and grit my teeth at the pain.

"Open your eyes," Beau says. "Look at me, babe."

I open my eyes to find Beau smiling at me sweetly as Danny moves in another inch.

"Fuck, babe," Beau smiles. "You're doing so good."

His praise has me relaxing a little more onto his cock. I push down enough that Dan manages to sink the rest of the way into me.

"Oh fuuuuuuck," he moans into my ear. "I'm not going to move until you tell me too. But damn, this feels so fucking good."

I take a deep breath in and let it out slowly, nodding at Beau. "I'm good. Continue, please."

The boys begin lifting me up and moving in and out of me, Danny being a little more cautious of his speed. It doesn't take any of us too long before we're all finding our release. I ask the guys to put me down just as I feel them both shuddering and about to cum. I drop to my knees on the floor, looking up at the two men as they both stoke their cocks. Beau rests his hand gently on the back of my head, and I place a hand on the back of Danny's muscular calf, urging him closer.

Both men release their loads directly on my chest. I smile up at them, proud of myself for bringing them both to climax. I don't move until their aftershocks of pleasure appear to be done. Beau moves over to his door where he has a towel hanging up.

He kneels down in front of me and begins wiping off the mess the two of them made.

"We should shower," Dan says. "It'll be tight in there—"

"That's what she said," I cut in, getting up from the ground and heading toward the shower.

Dan smiles at me and shakes his head. "You're going to fit in with us just fine."

* * *

It's around one in the morning when I wake up restless. The two men are lying to either side of me on their backs, so I try my best to slide out of bed without waking them.

I pick up one of their t-shirts from our pile of clothes on the floor, not caring whose it is, but relishing that I have their scent covering me. I tiptoe across the floor to the door. It's still closed, and it's quiet on the other side. I'm not sure when we finally drowned out the sounds coming from Griff's room.

Once I'm downstairs, I go to the fridge and grab a beer. I hop onto the counter and just listen to the silence of the house. This is probably the first time I've been able to be alone since the whole ordeal started. I don't think I like it. My body is practically begging me to go back upstairs and crawl into bed with my lovers. To feel their warmth and security enveloping me.

I'm just about to jump off the counter and head back to bed when a light comes on and Griff's voice sounds along with a girl giggling.

I watch, enjoying my IPA as they descend the stairs. Griff walks her to the door like he's some sort of gentleman. Yeah, right! He closes the door behind her and locks it. Instead of going back upstairs he starts walking toward me.

"Did you make sure to wrap it up?" I ask him when he enters the dark kitchen and opens the fridge. Though, if I'm being honest with myself, the question is a little hypocritical. We didn't wrap it. But I trust Beau was honest that I've been his only. Danny on the other hand . . .

It wouldn't be a bad idea for all of us to get tested, just to be safe. Besides, my birth control prescription is almost out, and I'm going to be getting an exam soon anyway. Might as well get everything checked.

Apparently, Griff didn't notice me, and he jumps at my voice, grabbing a butcher's knife from the block before realizing who I am.

"Fuck, Christina!" he shouts, dropping the knife to the counter. "I could have hurt you! You're lucky I wasn't packing heat."

I take a swig of my beer and glance at his boxers, not sure where he would have carried a gun. "You would have been doing yourself a favor. Wouldn't have to worry about giving up your position in the MC and your life."

He shakes his head and clutches his chest, probably just trying to get the adrenaline out of his body.

"So did you?" I ask after another sip of beer. "Did you wrap it up? I'm sure you're not the only guy that girl is hooking up with. Is she a stripper? Prostitute?"

"Jealousy doesn't look cute on you, Princess," Griff says, taking a beer from the fridge and twisting it open. "But yeah, I did use protection. I'm not trying to catch crabs."

"I'm not jealous," I tell him with a chuckle. "I've got plenty of attention. And I think you can still get crabs even with a condom."

"I heard some of that attention," Griff throws back, taking a swig from his bottle. "Sounded like the three of you were trying to make *me* jealous."

"If we were, did it work?" I ask, arching a brow.

Griff sets his bottle on the counter and slowly approaches me like a cheetah on the hunt. I can see his muscles rippling under his skin. He stops right in front of me, placing his hands on either side of my thighs. He leans in, staring into my eyes.

"Bad girls get punished for that kind of behavior, but I'm betting you would love to be punished. Wouldn't you, little girl?"

My breath catches in my throat, but I don't get the chance to respond.

Beau's voice comes from the top of the stairs. "Christina? Come back to bed."

"Tell him you'll be up in a minute," Griff whispers into my ear.

I clear my throat. "I'll be up in a minute!" I say, but my voice sounds off, half of it cracked.

"You okay?" he asks. Beau can always tell when something is wrong. He knows my voice so well.

"Tell him you're just thirsty, you'll be up soon," Griff commands, running a finger across my bare thigh.

"I was thirsty, just getting a drink of water," I say. "I'll be up soon."

It's quiet on the stairs, but then Beau speaks again, believing me, though reluctantly. "Okay."

When we both hear the door close, Griff pulls back to look at me again. "Good girl. I'm surprised you can take orders. You've been fairly defiant before tonight."

I push him away and slide off the counter. "I need to go to bed. Good night, Griff."

"Good night, Princess," he says with a grin, his voice eerily quiet and seductive.

When I get back to bed, I crawl between Danny and Beau, and they both instantly wrap their bodies into mine. I try not to think about what it would be like to add Griff into our equation, but he doesn't seem to be the sharing type.

CHAPTER 11

"Where are you going?" I ask Danny as I enter the kitchen the following morning. He and Griff are both dressed in their club gear, wearing their cuts over their t-shirts and sipping on coffee.

Griff looks up and answers for Danny, or maybe he thought I was actually asking him. Maybe I was. But it doesn't matter.

"We have to go to a meeting with my dad," Griff says, rinsing his empty coffee mug in the sink and placing it into the open dishwasher. "I need to figure out a different plan because this isn't going to work."

"When will you be back?" I ask. My heart races in my chest. I woke up from a nightmare, and I haven't been able to shake an awful feeling of tragedy. Something bad is going to happen—I can feel it in my bones.

"Couple of hours," Danny replies. "Beau's going to stay here with you. Don't worry, we're going to figure something out."

Danny places his cup in the dishwasher and then comes over to place a kiss on my forehead.

"Don't worry," he says again. "We're just going to talk to the boss and see what we can do to fix everything. We'll be home by dinner time. Nothing bad is going to happen."

"You don't know that," I whisper. He walks over to the front door and grabs his helmet.

Griff approaches me and pulls something from his back pocket. "Do me a favor, Princess?"

I nod.

"Wear these today. Show me you know how to follow my rules," he commands, handing over a piece of fabric. "I'll give you a reward if you're a good girl."

"What are they?" I ask, though I have an idea.

"Just a little something for me to tell you that I'll be thinking about you today."

Once he's out the door, I finally open my palm to inspect what he's given me. In an instant, the fabric starts vibrating, and I drop it to the floor. He's out of his damn mind leaving vibrating underwear for me to wear. Fine! I'll play his game. If anything, it'll backfire on him because I'll be spending so much time with Beau today.

I pick up the panties once they stop vibrating and go to the powder room to put them on under my shorts. My cheeks blush at the thought of wearing them when he won't be here to see me orgasm, but he'll know. He's Griff. He'll get his own form of pleasure knowing I'm obeying his command.

* * *

For most of the day, I spend my time organizing clothes in Beau's closet. He cleaned it up a little and even cleared out a couple of drawers in his dresser for me. It's almost as if we're playing house today and it's just the two of us. When I get nervous about something, I go into housewife mode and start cleaning everything. Our sorority was always super clean any time I had a test looming on the horizon.

I have to stop halfway through putting my clothes away when Griff cranks up his toy a bit too much. I have an orgasm on the floor of the closet while Beau takes a shower. It barely takes anything. Just a few strategically placed fingers on my clit, and my body is off to the races.

I have my second one at the kitchen table while Beau and I are eating lunch and listening to the news. Luckily it gets cut short as the vibrations halt before Beau notices anything is up.

"Kind of weird that we haven't heard from Griff at all," Beau says, popping a piece of Kung Pao chicken into his mouth.

I bite my lip. "I've heard from him . . . sort of. Does he normally keep you updated?"

Beau looks at me quizzically. "Griff contacted you?"

I shrug my shoulders as another random vibration comes through but quickly stops. "Yeah. Sort of." Maybe he's too far away for the remote to get a solid connection.

Beau looks at me and then pushes around some rice on his plate. "Something going on with you and Griff? It's okay if there is, you know? I'm honestly just glad that we found each other again . . ."

"No!" I blurt. "Nothing is going on. I think. Honestly, I don't know. He's intense, right? Not really my style."

Beau gives me a soft smile, drops his fork on his plate, and reaches across the table for my hand. "You don't have to tell me anything, but just be careful. Griff does some pretty crazy shit, and I don't want him to hurt you."

"I don't think he would intentionally try to hurt me," I say, staring down at our hands on the table. "Right? I mean, he was scary as hell when we first met, but last night . . ."

"Last night?" Beau's ears perk.

I clamp my hand over my mouth. *Shit.*

"Is that where you went last night?" Beau asks, and even though he said it was okay, I can hear the sadness in his voice, like he thinks he's going to lose me. It breaks my heart.

"I was getting a beer, and he let his friend out, and we both had a drink down here. We just talked," I explain. "But then this morning when he left, he gave me an order. A command. It sounded like a fun game to play, I guess. I don't think anything is going to come from it. I'm not Griff's type, obviously."

"What was the command?" Beau asks, curiosity written all over his face.

I'm almost too embarrassed to tell him, so instead, I go over to him and sit on his lap, leaning in to kiss his lips softly. As if Griff knows we're discussing him, he uses the remote to send one of the heaviest vibrations right into my clit. I dig my ass into Beau's lap and moan into his mouth.

He pulls away from my lips. "Oh, that type of game. Griff has the remote?"

The vibration keeps going. "Yes!" I gasp. I'm glad I finally don't have to keep it a secret. It was getting rough keeping quiet during the orgasms.

Beau captures my lips with his, letting me thrash my pelvis into him as I ride out the orgasm. The issue is, the vibrator keeps going, and going, and going . . .

It keeps shaking for another thirty minutes after I take off the underwear and hop in the shower. When I get out, I find Beau pacing back and forth in the bedroom with his phone against his ear.

He stops when I place my hand on his shoulder.

"Something's not right," Beau says. "Griff isn't answering my phone calls or texts, and neither is Danny."

"Maybe their meeting is taking a while?" I ask. "Would they shut their phones off during something like that?"

Beau shakes his head and pockets his phone. "No, they always keep their phones on. Something isn't right."

The vibrator suddenly ceases, and the two of us glance over at it.

"Must've run out of battery," I say. If I weren't so worried about Danny and Griff, I'd probably be laughing at the fact that my vibrating panties have issued us a warning.

"Get dressed," Beau says. "We need to get out—"

He stops mid-sentence, his phone screeching.

"Hello?" he asks, turning away from me. "Hey, boss! Is Griff with you?"

I go to the closet and pull on some leather pants and a cheetah print sweater. Not my typical style, and I'm sure it is an outfit Danny picked out. Beau seemed to get me mostly sundresses and sandals from their shopping trip. When I join Beau in his room again, his face has gone pale.

"That's your son!" Beau says through clenched teeth. "What the hell is wrong with you?"

I freeze in place at Beau's tone. I've never heard him so angry. I try to listen to what the other person is saying, but they're speaking way too softly. Beau hangs up the phone and throws it against the wall where it smashes into pieces and falls to the floor.

"Fuck!" he yells, running his hands through his hair and tugging it. "Fuck! Fuck! Fuck!"

Beau storms down the hall and opens what I thought was a linen closet, but when I peek from behind him, it's actually a gun safe. A huge gun safe.

"Do you remember how to shoot?" he asks me, not looking to see if I followed him. I hate the detachment in his voice.

When Beau and I were in high school, he lived with his uncle and I would go over there all the time to shoot in his massive backyard with him. He was always so proud of how good my aim was; he could put a paper target, clay pigeon, empty soda can, or pretty much anything in front of me, and I would always hit it. I haven't picked up a gun since then, but not much changes.

"I think I can figure it out," I answer as he hands me a pistol. "Hand on the trigger and pull."

"It's loaded," he states flatly. He grabs two guns for himself. "Even if it wasn't, always assume that any gun is loaded and ready to go."

"Are Danny and Griff okay?" I ask, even though I know damn well that I wouldn't be holding a gun if that was the case.

Beau stops in his tracks and turns to place both of his hands on my cheeks. "I am so sorry that you've been dragged into this fucked up life we're living, but I swear this isn't how things were supposed to be. I'm going to try and get Danny and Griff out alive, and when I do, we're getting the hell out of here. All of us."

I nod, but I can't help the tiny tear that slips from my eye. It slides down my cheek and lands on Beau's hand.

"I love you," I say as more tears follow. "I never stopped loving you, I just want you to know that. I wish we would have left this town together a long time ago."

Beau leans in to place a kiss on my forehead. "I've never stopped loving you either, and I will love you until my heart stops beating."

I pull away from him. "Don't let tonight be that night."

FATE PREVAILS

CHAPTER 1

"I'm going with you!" I shout at Beau as we both stand at the front door.

We're wasting time arguing. Time we don't really have. I know. But there's no way in hell I'm staying here alone while the three of them are risking their lives for me. If something bad happens, I don't want to be a sitting duck in their home. And I *certainly* don't want their blood on my hands. We need to work together. I need Beau to see me as an asset to him and the guys—not some pretty little damsel in distress.

"You need to stay here, you're safe if you stay here," Beau says, his hand on the door knob. "You've got your gun for protection. I'm going to go and try to get Danny and Griff. Lock the door behind me."

I stomp my foot in anger. "Your president wants *me!* He doesn't care about you guys. Use me as bait—we can do this. The second you hand me over, I'll shoot Griff's dad and you guys can escape."

Beau cackles the most wicked laugh I've ever heard from him and shakes his head, obviously not thinking this is funny at all. "I'm not letting that man get near you, Christina. I just got you back in my life, I'm not giving him the opportunity to take you from me. I— I can't lose you again."

Griff's dad wants me dead. That's what Beau told me when he got off the phone. Apparently, it's been Griff's father all along. Yeah, the child traffickers were pissed after we— well, after I lit one of their properties on fire—but they got the message and have been silent since. They're still a threat, but they aren't *the* current threat. It was Griff's father and his loyal lackeys who slashed my tires and blew up my apartment. Once his father realized I was with the guys, he purposefully lured us home by telling us that the threat had been dealt with. He wants me out of the picture. And it seems he'll do anything, including harming his own flesh and blood, in order to get rid of me. Now I know he was never planning on letting me live from the moment he kidnapped me in the alley.

"He's going to kill you all if you don't hand me over," I say. "And then he's going to find me, and we'll all be dead. At least if you hand me over, he'll probably let the three of you go and take me instead. That is . . . if I don't succeed at putting a bullet through his brain."

Beau drops his hand from the door and moves so he's towering over me. I think he's trying to intimidate me, but I've never felt threatened by Beau; even when I met his eyes at the lake after being taken captive. Beau has always been my protector, and now it's my turn to step up and protect him. I'll do what must be done to keep him safe.

"Do you actually think you'll be able pull the trigger?" he asks me, stepping even closer so we're toe to toe. "Do you think you'll actually be able to pull the trigger on a human? I've done it, Christina. It *changes* you. With Pres, you can't hesitate. The second he sees that you're backing down, he'll strike like a snake, no questions asked. Do you really think you won't stumble when it comes to actually killing a man?"

I puff up my chest, trying to be as brave as possible. Trying to ignore the fact that he just told me that he has killed someone. My high school sweetheart, the gentlest man I've met, has killed someone. "I can do it. What I *can't* do is lose you again. I can't lose Danny either, or Griff, I guess. The three of you, I can do it for the three of you."

Beau looks like he's somewhere between locking me in a room forever and patting me on the back.

He hands me his helmet as he shakes his head. "I swear, if I lose you today, I'll kill every single traitor in this MC with my bare hands."

I wrap my arms around him. "You're not going to lose me. We're going to succeed. We're going to get the guys and get the hell out of here. You owe me a happily ever after, Beau Grady."

Beau squeezes me one last time before we leave the house. We don't speak a word to one another until we approach the clubhouse.

* * *

The plan is simple.

Beau will escort me into the president's office. Hopefully that's where Danny and Griff are. We're going to pretend like I'm about to put up a fight until I'm right in front of Griff's dad . . . and then I'm going to execute him. After that, Beau said I'm supposed to take cover because it's probably going to be utter chaos. Beau's going to try to lock the door the moment we get in the office, and we're hoping only two other club members are in the room with us.

Beau parks his bike right out front instead of in the line of bikes on the side, making for an easier getaway if need be. What he doesn't know terrifies me: if we need to make a getaway, it's just going to be him. I'm not leaving Danny and Griff in that office. I've got nothing to lose but the guys, so if it comes down to it, I'll die with them in the clubhouse.

Beau helps me off the bike and then places a hand around my arm, leading me in and making it look like I'm his prisoner.

The clubhouse is kind of quiet tonight. There are a few guys playing a round of pool in the corner and two others watching a Lex

Mustangs' hockey game, but that's all. Something feels wrong in my gut. The last time I was here, there were way more bikers. "Where is everyone?" I try to whisper, but my voice is small that no one else can hear me.

One guy stands guard at the president's door. He'll have to be locked out of the office in order for our plan to work. I make a show of struggling against Beau's hold, hoping the man thinks I've really been captured.

"Beau," the man says with a nod. "Glad to see you came to your senses. The Pres will be pleased."

The man knocks on the door, and it's opened from the inside by two other men strapped with guns. I try to count the firearms I've seen since we've walked in. Every guy has at least two guns hanging from his hips. That's a lot of firepower. Hopefully they can't tell that I'm armed like them, though I've only brought half the heat that everyone else seems to need.

The door closes behind us, and the two men move to stand behind their president.

My eyes scan the room, finding Danny and Griff sitting in two chairs, bikers with guns behind them as well. Danny is shaking his head, his face showing defeat, and Griff looks furious to see us. I want to go over and wrap my arms around Danny and tell him how much I've worried about him, but I can't. Beau's grip tightens on me, as if he knows I want to move over to the two of them.

"Well, well, well," the president says, leaning back in his leather chair. "Long time no see, Ms. Christina. Glad you stopped in. I was beginning to think I would have to kill my own son. What a pity that would have been, murdering the club's next in line."

"Let them go," Beau demands as I try to pull away from him, trying to act like I'm struggling. "I brought you the girl."

The president gives us both a sinister smile, and it sets me on high alert. Something isn't right. It's not going to be as easy as I hoped. I knew this guy was a snake, and it feels like we've walked into his den. Someone is going to die here today. Please don't let it be my men.

"The four of you have caused a lot of trouble recently," the president explains like he's giving a college lecture, propping his feet up on his desk all relaxed and cocky. He has his leather cut on tonight and his motorcycle boots. I prefer him like that as opposed to his pristine suit that made him look like a wealthy business man. It's easier for me to believe he's done wicked things when he's clad in leather. "We all know there's only one way for all this to go."

"And how's that?" Beau asks, loosening his grip on me, signaling it's almost my time.

"You all die," he says simply, and my heart races with adrenaline. "Clearly you're all rats, and I don't have rats in my club."

Beau jerks away from me, a strong hand on his shoulder, and one of the bikers hauls him to the execution line. Beau, Griff, and Danny—everything I care about in the world—each have guns trained to the backs of their heads.

My eyes go wide, but I don't hesitate. I don't let Griff's father say another word. I pull the pistol from my waist band, point the barrel . . . and squeeze. The crack of primer igniting powder is deafening in such a small room, but I squeeze the trigger again, and the revolver's cylinder rotates a new round into position a split second before sending the bullet deep into the president's chest. Screams erupt from everywhere at once, and I swing my arm to the execution line. In the blink of an eye, I fire three more rounds.

Beau told me to count when I shoot, something about an old Clint Eastwood movie, and I know I only have one round left before empty. The smoke from the end of the barrel clears, and all three guards are lying on the ground. Two blood splatters adorn the wall behind my lovers, and I can barely . . . *wait* . . . only two. I wrench open my eyes and level the gun at the third biker, but his hands are on the back of his head.

"Please . . ." he mutters. "I—I didn't want to kill 'em anyway. I give up." He shoves his own gun across the room in the direction of my feet. Instead of a blood splatter where he was standing, there's a fairly large bullet hole. I missed.

Three lives taken with the squeeze of the trigger. My heart pounds in my chest, and I can hear it in my ears. I didn't hesitate like Beau thought I would.

My gun still trained on the final threat, Beau slowly walks over to me and grabs the weapon by the barrel, aiming it at the ceiling before it can accidentally go off.

"Hey, hey," he says, placing a hand on my cheek. "It's okay. We're done. He surrendered. Let him live."

I notice the guy is staring at me, shocked and frightened. As if he's not a blood-thirsty murderer himself. Beau checks the revolver's chamber before stuffing it into his pants and then going to untie the other guys. When Danny and Griff are free, Danny checks the final guard for any more weapons, but all he had was a knife.

Griff gets up from his chair and quietly walks over to his dead father. I turn and realize I can see the blood pooling from his head. I immediately lean over and vomit on the concrete floor as the weight of the last half a minute crushes down on my shoulders. *What have I done? Who am I?*

"Shit," Beau says, leaning down to hold my hair. I heave and heave between sobs and saying that I'm sorry. I feel like I'm partially apologizing for vomiting on a dead man's floor and apologizing for murdering Griff's father, even if it was in self-defense. I stand up, wiping the vomit from my mouth and onto my arm, my legs still shaking.

Griff is just silently staring at his father's bleeding corpse.

"Griff?" I whimper, placing my hand on his shoulder. "I am so sorry."

He shakes my hand from his shoulder and turns on me in a flash. "Don't touch me, Princess!"

I flinch back from him and wrap my arms around my body, step-ping away and into the corner of the room where I drop down to the ground and sob.

* * *

"I killed him, I killed him, I killed him," I repeat over and over as I rock myself in the corner of the room. Danny and Beau have both tried, unsuccessfully, to pick me up and escort me outside. Any time one of them reaches out to touch me, I flinch away. I can't help it.

Griff won't even speak to me, and I don't blame him. He won't look away from his father's dead body.

"Griff," Beau says softly. "You need to get up. The longer you sit in here, the more chaos is out there. The guys need to see you, you're their president now."

"We'll take care of things in here," Danny says, coming out of the bathroom with a bucket and a mop, ready to clean up my vomit and all the blood. So much blood.

Finally, Griff speaks. "Whose idea was it for Christina to kill my father?"

Beau's jaw drops at the question, but he just shakes his head. "That was the only option. He would have killed the four of us."

"So it was your idea?" Griff demands, walking over to be toe-to-toe with Beau. I think he's going to punch him. Wild images of an all-out brawl explode through my mind.

I can't let them kill each other. There's already been so much vi-olence. "It was my idea," I say, standing up from my corner and still shaking from my adrenaline. I feel like my back is going to break, so much adrenaline courses through my veins. "I told Beau to act like we were surrendering. I told him to let me hand myself over. It was my idea to . . . kill him. I did it to save you."

Griff turns to me and I'm expecting anger to cover his face, but instead it's shock.

"This was your idea?" he asks. I nod my head. "You're an idiot, Princess. He could have killed you! Beau should have never let you come here!"

"He would have killed *you*!" I cry out, forming tight fists with my hands at my sides. "He would have killed you both had I not used myself as bait, and we all know that. I was protecting us all!"

"Stop worrying about us, Christina!" Griff screams, slamming a fist on his father's desk. "What you did could have ruined everything!"

"You're just mad she saved our asses!" Beau yells, defending me.

Griff moves over to Beau and shoves his chest. "You could have gotten her killed!"

"What's it matter to you, huh?" Beau shouts back, cocking his head to the side. "You can't stand her. You hate that Danny and I would lay down our lives for her."

"Shut up!" Griff roars. "Luis, clean up this mess. I need to fucking deal with this shit."

The other man moves in an instant and starts dragging the bodies from the room, out a back door that I didn't even notice until he propped it open. Griff takes one last look at his bleeding father and then comes over to me, grabbing me by the wrist and pulling me out the other door into the main area of the clubhouse, his gun in his other hand now. For the first time today, I feel fear instead of anger. I think Griff might actually have it in him to kill me, and he wouldn't even think twice.

And I probably deserve it.

"Alright! Listen up," Griff yells as everyone in the room takes a step back. Some of them stare daggers at me. There are way more men in here now than when we first walked in. Someone must have called the whole MC to the clubhouse while I had my meltdown. "Who here wants to kill this woman?"

One man takes five steps toward us, a scowl on his face. Griff holds up his gun and shoots the random member of the club in the chest like it's nothing. I jump and scream as the shot rings through my ears. The man falls to the floor without a sound.

"Anyone else?" Griff yells, but everyone shakes their heads. "Good! Now if I ever find out that any of you have plans on harming her, you're dead. Ya hear? She's under my protection now. No one lays a hand on her!"

They all mumble agreements, but everyone is too afraid to look at the two of us.

"I'm your new president now," Griff says with authority. "My father is dead, so it's my duty to step up."

"You're not the president yet, kid," a man says who has been leaning against the wall casually. "We have to follow club protocol. We have to put it to a vote. Right now, you're just a placeholder. Any of us could dethrone you."

No one else can probably hear it, but I do— a faint growl coming from Griff's throat.

"Good luck trying," Griff says through gritted teeth.

CHAPTER 2

I've been sitting on a grungy couch at the clubhouse for over an hour. All the members of Hell Prevails were called in for an emergency club meeting by Griff; you know, after I murdered their president and a couple other members. It was only supposed to be the president. One person. Instead, I ended up killing a handful of men today, and Griff killed another. So many lives gone with a squeeze of a trigger.

Beau set me up with some tea and snacks and told me not to leave this couch until he comes back. Other than two women sitting at the bar chatting, it's just me. They keep glancing over their shoulders and giggling, but I try to ignore them. I'm almost certain that one of them is the girl Griff banged at the house, which means they're both just toys to the men here. I wonder who they think I am. Do they think I'm a club toy too? Am I? Is that what Beau and Danny think of me?

The clubhouse door opens, and I jerk at the sound of squeaking metal. I see a woman who appears to be a little older than me walk in with a toddler on her hip.

"Ladies," she says as she moves her sunglasses to perch on the top of her head, looking at the girls at the bar, not noticing me. "Where are the men?"

"Oh, hey, Bon Bon!" one of the girls says, chewing obnoxiously on some bubble gum. "Team meeting, some crazy shit went down while you were being the perfect little housewife."

"What happened?" the woman asks, holding onto her toddler a little tighter.

The girl from Griff's house spins around on her stool. "The Pres was assassinated."

"Is Luis okay?" the woman they called Bon Bon asks, panic suddenly in her voice.

"He's fine," the girl answers. One reaches over the bar and grabs a bottle of tequila and two shot glasses. "Griff called them all for a meeting since he's temporarily president."

"Oh, God," she gasps, placing her hand over her mouth in shock. "Did they catch who did it? Was it an enemy club?"

The girls don't say anything as they nod toward me. I dip my head because I don't want to see this woman look at me in disgust or fear. I've never done anything bad before tonight. Never in my life. Instead, the woman bursts into a fit of laughter and walks over to where I'm sitting in the lounge and sits down across from me. She doesn't let her kid out of her lap, but she does pull a toy out from her bag for him to play with.

"I'm Bonnie," the woman says. "This is Carlos. I'm Luis' wife. Who do you belong to? You don't look like the type of girl who is coming around here for drugs or sex."

She whispers the last part, but it doesn't really matter because those girls are now doing tequila shots. They wouldn't hear anything short of more gunshots.

"Um," I say, not really sure what to say to that question. "I guess Beau." *But also Danny.*

The girl gives me a sweet smile. "Ah, Beau, he's a sweetheart. So do you know what actually happened tonight? I haven't been able to contact Luis all afternoon. He was supposed to be home for dinner two hours ago."

"I killed the leader," I whisper, not even believing my own words, staring into my tea. "I shot him. He's dead."

Bonnie's smile fades, but luckily, she doesn't have time to say anything because the meeting is released. Danny and Beau are the first out of the door and they walk quickly over to me. Danny places a hand on my shoulder protectively, and Bonnie cocks her head to the side.

"Hey, Bonnie," Beau says, sitting beside me, reaching down to lace our hands together. "Luis will be out in a minute, he's gotta talk to Griff for a little longer."

Bonnie lets her son scramble down from her lap, and he stumbles over to Beau, putting his fist up.

Beau gives him a fist bump and musses up his hair. "Hey, buddy. How are you doing?"

"Good!" the little boy responds to Beau. "Mommy took me to the park today!"

"Is it true?" Bonnie asks, staring at Beau with a frown on her face. "Is your president dead?"

Beau's smile falls and nods his head.

"She did it?" Bonnie asks, nodding at me. Danny rubs small circles on my back, feeling the tension crushing my shoulders.

"She was protecting us. He wanted her dead, he would have killed me, Danny, and Griff for her."

Bonnie drops her head in her hands and I think she's crying, but when she lifts her head, she's smiling. "Thank God. He was dragging you guys down a dark path. I was so worried for Luis and our growing family. Griff needs to set you guys on a better path before it's too late. I think you can turn this group around, Beau. Someone has to."

I notice her small baby bump then and my heart hammers in my chest. It drops when I see the remaining guy I almost shot walk out the door with Griff, *Luis*. They're both looking at me with grim expressions until the guy notices the little boy standing at Beau's feet.

"Hey, hijo!" he says, opening his arms for the kid to run into. He scoops him up and places a kiss on his forehead, coming over to do the same to Bonnie.

"Luis," I whisper to myself, looking from him to Bonnie, to Carlos, and Bonnie's baby bump. "Luis."

Danny must hear me because he leans down to whisper in my ear. "You didn't know. It's okay."

He must sense that I'm on the edge of another breakdown. I almost killed this man. I almost made his wife a widow. I almost killed the father of two kids. I did kill a father, I killed Griff's father.

"I just wanted to protect them—" I begin, but Griff holds up a hand.

"Danny, Beau, get Christina home," Griff says sternly. "I'll meet you guys there."

Beau helps me up from my spot on the couch, but I can't take my eyes off Bonnie and her baby bump.

"I am so sorry," I say, shaking my head. "I didn't know he had a family. Oh, God. They all probably had families. Oh God. Oh God. Oh God. Beau, what did I do?"

I begin sobbing and notice Bonnie's concerned face, but she doesn't have time to respond to me because my guys are ushering me out the door of the clubhouse and Danny helps me climb on the back of Beau's bike.

"I'll be right behind you," he says, placing his hands on both sides of my face, forcing me to look him in the eyes. "It's going to be okay. I need you to hang on tight, and don't let go of Beau."

My arms feel numb. My whole body feels numb, but I manage to slip my arms around Beau's waist as he starts up his bike. Danny places the helmet over my head, buckles the strap, and walks down the row of motorcycles to get on his own. We can't get away from here quick enough, but no matter how far away we get, I can't stop seeing puddles of blood on the floor.

* * *

Griff gets home late that night—or early morning if I'm being technical. Danny and Beau both went up to bed, though reluctantly. I told them I just wanted to be alone tonight, so I've had the TV on mute for hours now, not really interested in watching anything.

When Griff walks in the door, he puts his keys on the hook and turns to look at me.

"What are you still doing up?" he asks.

I turn off the TV and the room goes pitch black. I wait for my eyes to adjust before I speak again.

"Every time I close my eyes, I see blood."

Griff sits down next to me on the couch, propping his feet on the coffee table. "I'm so mad at you, Christina."

A tear slides down my cheek, and I wipe it away as quickly as possible. "I understand. I'm so sorry. I shouldn't have shot him. I don't know if I'll ever be able to unhear that gunshot or unsee the blood."

"I'm not mad about that," Griff says, flicking his gaze up to me.

"You're not?" I ask, astonished. "I killed your father. You have every right to be mad at me."

He removes his feet from the coffee table and turns to me, some anger returning to his voice. "My dad was a *monster* when it came down to it, his days were numbered. What I'm mad about is the fact that you showed up to the clubhouse and risked your life to save us tonight. We're monsters too. We don't deserve to be rescued. None of us do."

"Don't say that," I whisper, turning to him. "You're not monsters—"

Griff smiles wickedly. "But we are. I can count every person I've killed or tortured, and I'm betting Danny and Beau can also do the same."

"I could have killed that woman's husband," I say softly. "I could have killed those babies' father."

Griff begins to reach a hand out to touch me, but he retracts it. "Why did you hesitate with him, with Luis?"

I shrug my shoulders. "He didn't seem like a threat. I noticed him when we came in. He looked scared, scared of your father."

Griff nods. "You're right. He wasn't a threat. If I'm being honest, you've killed more people than Luis has, and I'd like for it to remain that way."

I turn to him in confusion. "What do you mean?"

"I'm going to try to get voted in as permanent president of the club, and I'm going to turn things around before we get too deep into serious shit. My father was turning our club into a gang, and I don't want that for us. I want us to be a brotherhood. I just need to make sure I can get everyone else on board."

Some of it is starting to make a little more sense, but not much.

"I want to put an end to the bad things this club has done," Griff says. "I've just got one issue."

"What's that?" I ask, pulling at a loose thread on my shirt.

"The president has to be married within a certain amount of time after the election," he says. The way he says, married, sounds like a vulgar word, like even he doesn't want to say it. "I can still be president, but I have a year to find a wife."

"Your mother—" I start to say, panicking that I took a wife's husband from her.

"She passed away years ago," Griff says sadly. "That's when things went downhill with my father and the club. I think he lost every decent part of himself when my mother died."

"So what are you going to do?" I ask. "You're not seeing anyone . . . except for that sugar tit the other night."

Griff laughs. "Sweet butt," he corrects me. "We call play things like her sweet butts. I'm not interested in making her the First Lady of HPMC though. She doesn't have the qualities for that position."

"Then who?" I ask, just in time to see Griff pulling a small box from his leather vest pocket. The air leaves the room as he cracks it open.

CHAPTER 3

"Are you fucking kidding me?"

I jolt out of my sleep and squint as the sunlight streams through the windows of Beau's room. I'm alone though. I shrug on Beau's Hell Prevails hoodie that's hanging on the hook behind the door. It reaches all the way to my knees, and I tip-toe toward the commotion downstairs.

"You can't be serious!" Beau says, pacing back and forth in the kitchen. "You don't even love her. You're doing this because you're jealous of what *we* have with her."

I can't see Griff's face from where he's sitting at the table, but his voice is calm. "I'm doing this because I need to do what's best for the MC, what's best for us. Hell, we have a year, maybe in the meantime we can find a loophole out of this shit. Believe it or not, I'm not too happy with this situation either. I'd rather not get married."

Beau shakes his head and runs a hand through his hair. "You could pick any woman. Any woman, Griff. Why does it have to be my Christina?"

My heart breaks at the sadness Beau must be feeling. Beau and I talked about getting married when we dated in high school. We talked about how many kids we would have, what type of house we'd live in. We'd have a little boy, and he'd become a big brother to our baby girl. I'd stay home and take care of the kids while Beau went out to provide for our family. On the weekends, we'd go to t-ball games and gymnastic meets. We'd have family dinner at six every night and read bedtime stories at eight on the dot. But we were naive kids—we didn't get happily ever after, and we probably never will. I also think Beau understands that this is what's best for the group, I just think he's as frightened as I am. We just got each other back, and now we're losing each other again. It isn't fair.

"You're right," Griff says. "I could have any woman, but you know damn well that this will be what's best for her. No one can harm her if she's the wife of an MC president. It would mean the extinction of a chapter, members and their families, if someone harmed the president's old lady. You should be thanking me for choosing Christina and trying to work as quickly as possible."

Danny notices me from his spot at the kitchen table. He's stayed silent this whole time. I wonder if that means he doesn't care if I marry Griff or if he just knows it's the right thing to do.

"Hey, sugar," Dan says, standing from the table. "Want me to make you a cup of coffee?"

I nod as I enter the kitchen and sit at the open spot. I don't even have to tell Dan how I like my coffee—he remembers from the cabin. I notice Beau's staring at me as I take the mug from Dan and blow on the steaming liquid, stalling because I don't know what to say.

Griff places the ring box in the center of the table, offering it up to me once again.

"Guessing you didn't get any sleep last night," Griff says, crossing his arms and leaning back in his chair. "But that means you had plenty of time to think about your decision."

I nod my head but don't dare to look any of these men in the eyes.

I could be called a coward, but I think I proved that wrong last night when I pulled the trigger. I close my eyes and try to push away the images of blood.

"If I marry you," I begin to say, staring into my coffee. "What happens with Beau and Danny?"

Griff chuckles. "They dick you that well?" I don't respond to his crude language. "You can still play with your boy toys if you're my wife, but I expect you to behave like you're mine in public. Because that's what you will be: *mine*."

"What do you mean by that?"

"You're going to need to act like you enjoy being my old lady," he says, leaning forward and placing his elbows on the table. "What you guys do at home is no one's business, but if we're at the clubhouse or around other members, you're mine once we're married."

The way he says mine sends a shiver through me, but suddenly the thought of being claimed by Griff isn't so unsettling. He exudes protection, safety, strength, dominance. All the things that I desperately need right now.

"I think I can do that," I say softly. "That doesn't seem too hard."

"You can't be serious, Christina!" Beau shouts. He begins pacing again. "I can't stand by and watch you marry a guy like Griff."

"I'm doing it to protect us, Beau," I say gently. "You can still have me. I'll just be Griff's wife on paper and for MC purposes."

Beau shakes his head and stares at me, his eyes watering. "I can't. I can handle sharing you with Danny, he's my best friend, but I'm not going to sit back and watch you marry Griffin. I've seen how he uses women for his pleasure and discards them like a used toothbrush. Fuck that. You're better than that, or I thought you were."

My stomach drops, my throat tightens. "Are you breaking up with me?"

"No, I think you're breaking up with me," he finally says, brushing away a tear from his cheek with his fist. "You're choosing to marry him . . . when all I've ever wanted was to marry you. I wanted to be your husband."

"I'm doing this for you! For us!" I practically scream, standing up from the table, my chair screeching across the linoleum.

Beau shakes his head again and walks away from me when I reach for him. "I'm leaving. I can't sit here while you two plan your magical day."

"Beau, Griff still has to win the election first. We have time!" I shoot back. I take a step to chase him, but Danny grabs my hoodie and holds me back. Beau's hoodie.

"Give him some time," Dan says, dropping his hand from me.

I use my sleeves to wipe away my tears. "Are you going to break up with me too?"

"Hell no, sugar," he says, pulling me into his chest and hugging me. "And I've got a feeling Beau will change his mind."

Griff pushes back from the table and joins us, bringing the ring box with him.

I'm shocked when he drops down to one knee in front of me, opening the box and pulling the ring out.

"I can't promise that you won't hate me, but I can promise that I will protect you," Griff states with determination. "I'll make sure you don't have to fear for your life ever again. I've already put you through enough. You will be my queen. You will stand beside me and the club."

He slides the ring on my finger, and it fits perfectly. "It was my mom's," Griff says proudly. "It's the only thing I have left of her, so I want you to take extra good care of it."

I nod at him because I'm not sure how to respond to this side of Griff that I'm experiencing. He's never been so . . . caring before. Not that I have ever seen. He stands up and brushes some hair from my face, and I flinch at his touch.

"I think I'm supposed to kiss you now to seal the deal," he says. "Is that okay?"

I glance at Danny but he just gives me a small smile.

"Sure," I say shyly.

Griff grips the back of my neck and pulls me toward him. I have to stand up on my tippy toes and he has to bend down quite a bit, but our lips connect like magnets. I whimper against his kiss, shocked by the satisfaction I'm feeling, but also torn between having my heart ripped out of my chest by Beau only moments ago.

"Damn, Princess," Griff says, pulling away. "You taste like peppermint."

"Thank you?" I ask, taking a few steps away from him so I don't have to crane my neck to look up into his eyes. It's probably the peppermint from the coffee Danny has started buying. He only changed because I mentioned I like the flavored stuff and not regular Folger's.

Griff glances at my chest, and I follow his gaze, looking down at the embroidered name on the left side of the hoodie: *Grady*. The last name that I dreamt of having when I was a girl. Beau's last name. Instead, I'll be Mrs. Griffin Thomas. Christina Thomas.

"I need to head to the clubhouse," Griff says, moving away from me to grab his wallet and cut from the entryway. "Danny, why don't you and Christina stay home today and relax. Maybe see if Beau shows up so you can talk some sense into him. We've got to stick together. We're a family."

"Sure thing," Danny says. "Keep me updated on things at the club, alright?"

"Of course," Griff answers with a nod.

My throat tightens. I was just proposed to and now Griff is leaving? Just like that? No celebration? Nothing? I cross the floor and reach for Griff's hand. "Wait!"

He glances down at my hand and then back up at my face, confused. "What?"

I shrug my shoulders and drop my hand. "That's it? You propose and now you're just leaving to go to work?"

Griff rolls his eyes. "Sorry, Princess, I can't stay to celebrate. I need to work on covering up the mess you've made. What did you expect?"

"I—" I'm not sure what I expected actually. Maybe some sign that Griff actually likes the woman he just proposed to? Maybe he would take the morning off to hang out with me?

Griff runs a finger over the dimple in my chin. "Tell you what," he says. "Why don't you have Danny help you move all your stuff to my room. That's where you will be sleeping from now on."

"How about . . . no . . ." I say, fury filling my bloodstream, he said things could stay the same with Beau and Danny while we're in the privacy of our home, and I still have a year before I'm his wife. "I'm not moving into your BDSM lair. I'll continue sleeping—"

"In Beau's room?" Griff asks with a chuckle. "Newsflash, babe, he probably wants you out of his space. You will sleep in my room. You're going to be my wife. You can visit Danny's room whenever, but at night, you sleep with me."

I grit my teeth and clench my fists. "I'm not fucking you if you think that's what's going to happen."

"You're right about that," Griff says. "I only fuck well behaved women who can obey my commands, and you're being a little brat. Being fucked by me is a reward."

His words catch me off guard, and Griff uses my shock as a way for him to slip out the door and head to the clubhouse. I turn around to look at Danny who is leaning against the doorframe by the kitchen. He just shrugs his shoulders in a 'what can I do' sort of way. He pushes off the frame, and I follow him up the stairs where we spend the day moving my new clothes and few possessions into Griff's room. But I never take off Beau's hoodie.

The rest of the day I spend getting drunk so I don't have to think about sharing a space with Griff, waiting for him and Beau to return home.

* * *

I'm lying on the couch, my head in Danny's lap, when I hear a key in the door. Griff steps inside a second later. I lift my head just in time to see a stumbling Beau practically fall through the open door. Griff catches him by the waist, right before he face-plants on the floor. I sit up on the couch too quickly, and my head spins from the movement.

"I got it, man!" Beau says, shoving Griff away. "I'm fine." He certainly doesn't look fine.

Griff puts his hands up and walks away, plopping down in the recliner to take off his boots.

"What happened to him?" Danny asks Griff.

"Asshole almost drank the club bar dry," Griff says. "Bonnie gave us a lift home. I need a ride back later to get my bike."

Danny gives him a nod.

"What did you two do today?" Griff asks.

I cut Danny off with a grin. "I got fucked up, just like Beau!"

"Danny, what the hell?" Griff scolds. "You let her get wasted?"

I stand on shaky legs and try to stroll over to Griff, stumbling a little.

"Aww," I say, sitting down in Griff's lap. "Don't be mad at Danny. It's not his fault."

"You're right," Griff says. "It's your fault, and if you keep acting like a spoiled brat who can do whatever she wants, you're going to get punished."

My smile dissipates, but my stomach tightens with interest.

Griff notices me shifting uncomfortably on his lap, and when I try to move away, he holds me in his lap. "You would like that, wouldn't you?" he asks, his voice practically a demand. "You're just waiting for me to offer to punish you, waiting for me to take charge? Have you ever heard of a brat tamer?"

"Griff, don't push it," Danny warns. "She's wasted."

"I'm not going to take advantage of her when she's drunk, asshole,"

Griff barks back, releasing his grip on me—but he holds onto my hand before I can walk away. His gaze penetrates mine. "Listen here, Princess, if you expect me to want you, you're not going to play games with me. You think you were being cute tonight, sitting down on my lap while you're drunk, but that does nothing to my sex drive. I won't be fucking you until you learn to obey, and even then, I won't be doing it until you're on your knees begging me, drenched between your legs."

With that, Griff rises from the recliner and stomps up the stairs where he slams his bedroom door shut. Suddenly, I feel the most sober I have felt in my whole life. A giggle comes from the couch, and I look over to find a drunken Beau lying down with a smile on his face.

"Can you believe that guy?" he asks no one in particular. "The love of my life is going to marry that asshole. God must really hate me."

"Come on, buddy," Danny says, pulling Beau up from the couch. "Let's get you to bed. Boss gave you one day off, tomorrow you have to be on point and back in the saddle."

I start to say something, but Danny shakes his head and dismisses me. I follow the two of them up the stairs and watch from the door of Beau's room as Danny puts him to bed like an older frat brother taking care of a pledge. He drunkenly moans something before rolling over and beginning to snore. Danny comes out of his room, shuts off the light, and closes the door behind him.

Both of us glance at Griff's closed door, and Danny shrugs. "You know the rule, baby girl," Danny says. "He might be pissed, but he said you are to sleep in his room."

A tear slides down my cheek. I wipe it away before he can notice.

"Can I—" I begin to say. "Can you just let me cuddle with you in your bed for a couple of minutes?"

He smiles sadly and pulls me in for a hug. "You know we'll both end up falling asleep for the night, and that will just give Griff something else to be pissed about."

"Maybe we can compromise?" I ask. "Maybe you can see if he'll let you sleep in the bed with us tonight? Just tonight! I promise. I just—I don't want to be alone with him yet. I'll have a nightmare, and he won't know how to whisper me back to sleep."

"Okay, okay," Danny says as I ramble off. "I will, but you're going to need to be the one to make such an insane request."

* * *

Griff stares down at me, his massive arms crossed against his chest, grey sweatpants hanging on his hips, all the tattoos covering his torso on full display. I try not to crumble under his gaze.

"Yes, Princess?" he asks, waiting for me to ask my question.

"I'd like to make a compromise," I say, looking down at my feet. "Since you requested I sleep in your room, I would like some normalcy for my first night. I was wondering if it would be okay if Danny joined us. Just for one night."

Griff laughs and places his arms over his head, holding on the top of the door frame. "You guys are not going to do any of your harem shit in my bed."

"We're not," I say, agreeing. "I'm just—"

"Scared?" he asks, leaning down to be eye level with me. "Good. You should be scared."

"Griff," warns Danny. "Give her a break. She's having nightmares . . ."

I look up to see the two of them staring at each other like boxers at a weigh-in before Griff finally nods and motions us to follow him into his room. I veer off into the bathroom, walking to the master closet where I put my clothes earlier to grab a pair of pajamas. When I turn around, Griff is standing at the sink brushing his teeth. I close the closet door and change in privacy, also trying to cool down the blush that's covering my cheeks. With Griff turned to the side, there was no hiding the shape of his cock behind his thin pants. I toss my clothes from today into the hamper and trot out of the closet to brush my own teeth. Griff doesn't say a word to me as he finishes up and wipes his mouth on his hand towel.

When I'm finished, I find the spot between Griff and Danny invitingly open. I crawl into the bed between the two of them, sliding under the blankets. Danny leans over and places a soft kiss on my forehead before he flips over to face away from me. I lie on my back and try not to glance over at Griff. He starts some white noise on his phone before turning off his bedside light.

"Thanks for letting Dan stay, Griff," I whisper into the darkness, closing my eyes, hoping to not see blood in my dreams.

He flips onto his side, away from me. "Just for tonight. Get some rest, Christina."

* * *

Something doesn't feel right.

My vision feels blurry. I can't recall the drive to the clubhouse, yet here I am, standing at the front door. What I find odd is, there isn't a line of motorcycles out front, not even a car. How did I get here? Did I go for a run and black out or something? Beau wouldn't have let me go for a run alone, he always jogs with me. It reminds me of the feeling when I'm driving on autopilot and can't recall stopping at stop signs or traffic lights, yet somehow I know I made it to my destination safely . . . Whatever that is, some kind of blind mental processing I guess, that's what it feels like. I somehow made it to the MC's clubhouse without realizing it.

I open the heavy steel door, my Keds squeaking on the concrete. No one's inside. It's a complete ghost town. Maybe everyone is at home. Maybe Griff requested I come here today to go over our wedding plans.

A man stands up from where he was kneeling behind the bar, but his back is turned away from me. He's got a rag in his hand, wiping down the counter.

"Excuse me," I say to him across the empty room. "Where is everyone?"

The man doesn't respond, he just keeps cleaning the bar. I take a few steps toward him, trying to see if he's maybe got some earbuds in or something, but I don't see any. I sit at the bar and clear my throat to get the guy's attention, but still nothing. He's wearing a black suit, clearly not a new prospect of Griff's. I've only ever seen one member wearing a suit before, I just can't remember who it was. My memory is so fuzzy.

"Hello?" I ask again, sitting right behind him. "Have you seen Griff? I think I'm supposed to meet him here. We're engaged. I'm his future wife."

The man turns around slowly, and it takes me a minute to realize something is very wrong with him. My mind is going into overdrive trying to process the fact that he has a bullet hole in his head, fresh blood seeping from the wound, and a sinister smile on his face. A line of crimson rolls down his nose, across his lips, bleeding onto his pristine white collared shirt.

"Mr. Thom—" I try to say.

"I've been waiting for you, little girl," he snarls, blood flowing from his mouth as he speaks, turning his white teeth red.

"This isn't real," I whisper, trying to move from my bar stool, but it's like someone has glued me down. I glance and see it's not glue, it's ropes. Ropes tying me to the stool. "This isn't real, this isn't real, this isn't real . . ."

I let out a scream as the bloodied form of Mr. Thomas lunges at me.

"This isn't real! This isn't real!" I scream, trying to remove my body from the tight bindings. They bite into my wrists, rubbing them raw like the jaws of a hungry animal shredding its prey.

Hands grip my arms, shaking me, a voice urging me to open my eyes.

"Don't touch me!" I scream at my captor.

"Chris, it's me," says a soothing voice, pulling my body in tight. "It's me. You're okay. I'm not going to hurt you. We're not going to hurt you."

I open my eyes to find Griff looking down at me, fear on his face. It is the first time I've ever seen him scared. Not even when he was sitting in that office with a gun to his head... He's holding me in his lap, smoothing a hand over my arms. I relax against him and let out a tiny whimper.

"It was just a bad dream," he assures me. "You're safe."

"Everything okay?" asks Beau from the door of the bedroom. I must have woken him up with my screams. Somehow, even drunk, Beau woke up to come protect me.

"I'm sorry," I whisper, a tear sliding down my face. "I'm such a spaz, I just had a nightmare."

"Do you need me to get you anything?" Beau asks, hesitating in the doorway, running a hand through his blonde bedhead.

The bathroom door opens, and Danny comes out with a glass of water, offering it to me. I take it with a shaky hand and swallow a quick sip before handing it back to Danny to put on the nightstand.

I look at Griff. "Can you guys just stay here until I fall back to sleep? All of you?"

He glances over at Beau and motions for him to come in the room with a nod of his chin. Beau climbs in bed next to me. I'm thankful that Griff has a king, but even then, four people take up a lot of room. There's isn't much left. I untangle myself from Griff and lay down beside him, my back pressed into Beau who drapes an arm around me, placing a soft kiss on my shoulder. Griff gently holds my hand. I hesitate before closing my eyes. I just . . . I want the nightmares to end. I'm rapidly approaching my limit.

"It's okay," Griff whispers. "We're here, no one is going to hurt you, I promise you that."

I nod and hold our clasped hands closer to my chest, trying to not think about blood flowing from a corpse.

CHAPTER 4

"You want to tell me what spooked you last night?" Griff asks. I open my eyes to sunlight streaming in the bedroom. Griff must have gotten out of bed at some point to open the curtains as this is the brightest I've ever seen his room. The dark walls only seem to cast shadows. Last night, I noticed there was zero light in his room, thanks to the blackout curtains, and that might have made my nightmares worse. Maybe he'll let me open the curtains tonight.

I stretch my back and glance over my shoulder, finding Beau fast asleep, but his arm is still wrapped around me. Like he's afraid of letting go. I hear some music playing downstairs and smell bacon. Danny must be cooking breakfast. I wonder how I could explain my nightmare. Griff hasn't really spoken of his father. Would he mock me for having dreams about the dead? Would it upset him if I mentioned Mr. Thomas?

Finally, I decide to just tell him the truth. "I had a dream I was at the clubhouse, alone, but I wasn't alone," I say softly, not looking him in the eyes. "Your dad was behind the bar, and when he turned around, I could see so much blood. I couldn't get away from him. I was tied to the barstool. Like when he commanded you guys to tie me up in the van."

He doesn't speak for a moment. I expect him to laugh, to call me a pussy, but he doesn't. "You know what my mom always recommended I do when I was afraid of something?" he asks, but I shake my head. "She told me that the only way to get over my fear is if I face it head on."

"And how do you propose I face the trauma of killing your father?" I ask bluntly, feeling defensive. His advice seems so ridiculous. Downright absurd.

"Maybe you should try coming to the office with me today," he says. "It might help."

"News flash, I've been there," I fire back. The clubhouse is filled with negative memories for me; being held captive, murdering Griff's dad and the others—I don't think I can face this fear. I doubt Griff's mother had to face a fear as big as mine.

He shakes his head. "I mean, come into the office with me. We can even go check out the basement. I think it'll do you some good."

"No girls allowed, remember?" I ask. "I'm not supposed to go in there."

"I make the rules now," he says flatly. "You're welcome there whenever you please. Especially if it will help you get over your fear. We need to announce our engagement anyway."

My heart starts racing. I'm not ready to go into the clubhouse office. It's too soon, it probably still smells like the chemicals Danny and Luis used to clean up the blood.

"Are you going to have a funeral?" I ask.

He shakes his head and rolls onto his back. "No, we're just having a wake to honor him, not that he was an honorable man."

"When are you having that?" I ask, hoping I don't have to go. I'm sure the rest of the MC would be livid if I were to show up to the wake for a man I killed, a wake for *all* the men I killed.

"This weekend," Griff answers, getting out of bed and pulling on a t-shirt. "Don't worry, I'm not going to make you go to that."

"What happens at a wake for an MC member?" I ask. All I really know is what I've seen on TV shows, and I'm sure those are all exaggerated.

Griff turns around and grins at me. "Well, a lot of drinking. It's basically a huge party. There will be some girls there to ease the pain of our members from losing their beloved president."

"'Ease the pain?'" I ask, my throat tightening.

"Ya know, fuck us while we mourn the dead," Griff says slyly, arching an eyebrow at me. "Don't worry, Princess. I'll keep an eye on Danny boy for you."

"What about—" I start to ask, but I can hear the clinginess in my voice. Why should I care if Griff fucks one of the sweet butts at the wake? He's not truly mine—yet.

Griff leans down, pressing his hands against the king size mattress and staring me right in my eyes. "Just say it, Princess. You want to make sure that I'm not going to fuck any whores. You're a greedy little thing, aren't you? Want all three of your boys all to yourself? Don't want me to have any fun unless it involves you?"

He reaches out a finger to stroke my bottom lip, but I flinch away from him.

"All you have to do is tell me that you're mine," Griff whispers. "And I'll be yours. Only yours. Just admit it."

It's on the tip of my tongue. Somewhere deep down, I want to claim him as mine. But there's a part of me that wants to make Griff earn my attention, earn my affection. We're both equally stubborn, and it's obvious he wants to be the dominant in everything he does, but I'm not sure I have it in me to submit to him. I also don't want him to sleep with any woman who walks into that MC. Danny and Beau have both agreed to only keep this thing we have going between the three of us, but what about Griff? Could he give up the bachelor lifestyle he lives . . . for me?

He's about five inches from my face when he speaks again. "I'll give you until Friday to decide if you want to stop playing this game with me, Christina. You either admit you're mine, or you have to watch your future husband fuck any leather-clad woman with tits who walks into the club. It's an easy decision. You just need to tell me. Am I yours?"

Without waiting for my response, he heads downstairs. I let out an annoyed grunt, stirring Beau from his sleep. He must have forgotten where he was sleeping because he looks confused for a moment before he realizes how mad at me he is. I watch as his usually kind face morphs into disappointment.

He stands from the bed and glances back at me as I sit up. "You okay? That seemed like an intense dream you had."

I give him a shrug. "It was. I think I'm having some PTSD. I can't unsee the . . . blood. I can't stop hearing the gun."

Beau gives me a sad nod and crosses his arms over her chest. "Yeah, that happened to me my first time too. I would say you get used to it . . . but it's almost impossible."

"Griff wants me to go with you guys to the clubhouse today," I say, glancing down at the covers and pulling at a loose thread. "He thinks I should try and face my fears. He wants me to try and go into the office today."

"Don't let him push you too fast, Christina," Beau says. I notice his fists clench. "Griff isn't used to people telling him no."

I nod in understanding. "If I do go today, can you go with me to the office? I trust you."

Something softens in Beau's expression. Something familiar, like the time he taught me how to drive a stick shift when I was sixteen. Like he had all the patience and love to spend the rest of our lives helping me. The anger he's been holding onto since Griff asked me to be his wife appears to dissolve.

"Of course, baby," he says with a soft voice. "You know you can always count on me for the tough stuff. That will never change."

I bite my lip and nod. "I know. Well, I guess I should get ready.

Looks like it's 'take your girlfriend to work' day. And in this case, I have three of you to show me off—that is, as long as you'll still have me?"

Beau sits down on the edge of the bed, and this time it's his turn to look down at the rumpled covers. "I'm sorry for what I said. I'll take you however I can have you in my life, and if that means I can just be your boyfriend for the rest of our lives while Griff gets to marry you, I guess I'll deal with it. I don't want to lose you again. I've never stopped loving you, and I never will."

I'm scrambling across the bed on my hands and knees in an instant, wrapping my arms around Beau. His arms snake around me, hugging me closely. He nestles his face into my neck, placing a kiss on the delicate skin above my shoulder, sending a spark of electricity through my spine. "I'll always be yours, Beau Grady," I whisper. "I've always been yours."

We sit like that for a few more seconds before pulling apart. Beau places a gentle kiss on my forehead and slides away with a smile.

"Will you wear a sundress today?" he asks me. "Don't get me wrong, you were super hot in those leather pants the other day, but I want to see *my* Christina. You're so beautiful in those little dresses. Heart-stoppingly beautiful."

I give him a smile and nod my head. "I'll see you downstairs."

* * *

Me and the guys ride together in Danny's vintage muscle car, me in the back with Beau sitting in the middle seat. Griff's been on the phone with someone for the entire ride talking MC business, and I don't pay attention to much of it. Beau's hand hasn't left my thigh. It keeps rubbing circles along my bare skin. I'm so glad he told me to wear a sundress today. I giggle as his hand slides further beneath the hem of my dress, and I bite my lip when I feel myself grow aroused. Danny and Griff are in the front seats, unable to participate in my secret playtime, but I notice Danny's eyes keep flickering up to look at us in the rear-view mirror. He's got a smile on his face as our eyes meet. Griff is completely unaware of what's happening in the back seat. His ignorance adds a bit of deceptive excitement that turns me on even more.

I nibble on my lip as Beau's fingers dip into my panties, but I don't take my eyes off the mirror. Danny must get lost in the pleasure of my eyes because he takes his own off the road for too long.

Griff punches him in the shoulder. "Watch the road, ass hat!" he growls, and then he's back to his phone conversation.

I let out a laugh that morphs into a soft moan as Beau's fingers run along my slick folds before finding my clit and rubbing gentle, teasing circles. I clamp my hand over my mouth so whoever is on the phone with Griff can't hear me. Just as we pull into the clubhouse parking lot, Beau plunges a finger inside of me with three thrusts before removing his hand as Danny puts the car in park. Griff exits the car without a glance to the backseat, slamming the door behind him.

I watch in awe as Beau puts his finger in his mouth, licking my flavor off his skin. I'm so glad what tension was between us is finally gone.

"Mmm," he whispers. "So good. I could eat you all up."

I drop my head back against the headrest. "And you think I'm the tease? Now I have to sit in drenched panties all day!"

Danny turns around and smiles at me. "You don't have to. You can hand them over to me. I'll keep them safe for you."

I shake my head at him and roll my eyes. "You have some fetish for stealing panties from women?"

He chuckles. "Only your panties, sugar."

"Are you guys coming or not?" I hear Griff's muffled yell from the parking lot. "We've got work to do!"

That's when I realize that Beau must have been trying to distract me from the memories that were bound to flood my system when we arrived here. My heart starts pounding as I look at the building. All at once, everything comes rushing back.

"It's okay, I'm here," Beau says, reaching out to hold my hand and give it a squeeze. "I'm not going to let anything bad happen to you."

"Me either," Danny adds. "Hell, if things get too bad in there, you can help me work on some bikes outside."

I laugh. "I don't know anything about motorcycle servicing."

Dan shrugs. "Well, you can just perch that cute little ass on a chair and watch me at work then. Or I can take you home around lunch and finish what this guy started."

I scoff playfully and get out of the car before the two of them can tease me any longer. I don't look at Griff or the building as I march inside, my guys flanking me for support.

CHAPTER 5

The guys had to go right to a club meeting when we walked in, which was a good and a bad thing. Good because it saved me from facing my demons right away, bad because I'm now stuck sitting in the multipurpose area with the sweet butts of the club. The girls are posted at the bar once again, helping themselves to liquor, while I pretend like I'm scrolling through my phone on the couch. Beau had the MC's personal chef cook me some lunch, but I finished that off over an hour ago, so now I'm just watching the clock until one of the guys comes to get me. I feel like an abandoned puppy at a county shelter waiting to be rescued, surrounded by strange and violent creatures.

Every now and then, shouts from the office draw my attention, but it just sounds like typical club disagreements. Griff said they're going to do nominations for club president today, I assumed he wouldn't have to worry about not winning the presidency, but he seems unsure. It worries me what will happen if someone else wins—what will happen to me? Will the guys be able to keep me safe if Griff doesn't win?

The girls at the bar say Griff's name, and I turn to look at them just in time to catch them laughing in my direction.

"What?" I ask, recrossing my legs and smoothing the fabric of my dress over my thighs.

"Oh, nothing, honey," says the brunette with highlights. She needs a touchup badly. I can see three inches of her roots. "Candy and I were just talking about the party we'll be attending in honor of Griff's father and the other men that the club lost. We can't wait to talk him into a threesome with us. What do you think? He's joined us before, and it was the best night of my life! He really knows how to please a woman."

My stomach drops. It shouldn't, I know. I haven't claimed Griff as my own. He told me all I have to do is say the words, but I'm not sure I can. What the hell is wrong with me? I shouldn't be jealous of some club whores wanting to fuck a guy who isn't mine. Danny and Beau should be enough, they *are* enough, but something in my gut tells me that it has to be all three of them or none at all. I want the four of us to be a unit, a team. I don't want Griff to bring any trash home to our house, and certainly not to our bed.

"Hey, I asked you a question," says the girl again, raising her voice. "You think I can fuck Griff with my sister? Me and his dad used to fool around all the time until you killed him, you crazy bitch. Now I'll just have to settle for his son."

I see red, but not the same blood red from my nightmares. I see fury. But I was raised to be a lady. I smile sweetly at the girls, showing all my teeth, baring them wickedly.

"No, I don't think that you can fuck him," I say, standing up from the couch, trying to keep my feet in place. I've seen cat fights during my short time as a sorority sister, I've watched girls fight over guys, I've made fun of those girls; but something tells me Griff is worth fighting for.

"Excuse me?" laughs the girl, standing up from her bar stool on drunken, wobbly legs. "You don't think Griff wants a piece of our ass? Candy's real good with her mouth. She brought Griff to his knees begging for more last time."

I shake my head. "Why would Griff want you two whores when he can have me? I'm sure you've probably been wrung out and hung up to dry a few too many times, if you know what I mean."

"The fuck did you say?" she snaps, her smile gone.

"Ah, so not only are you a whore, but you're also dumb and don't understand simple sentences," I taunt. Okay, so my mom didn't raise me to speak like this at all, but maybe that's why she took off to Florida and abandoned me in Kentucky when I was old enough to shove to the side. Maybe she couldn't handle my no-nonsense personality.

"You fucking bitch!" she screams, kicking off her heels and darting across the room at me. Her friend, Candy, is so wasted she just laughs until she falls to the floor. Good, one on one works for me.

Just as she's about to collide with me, I step out of the way like a matador toying with a bull. As predicted, she crashes onto the couch. I flip her over onto her back and pin her to the fabric, smacking her hard across her face.

"Don't you ever talk to me like that again!" I yell, smacking her a second time while she's still stunned. "And don't you ever put your whore hands on Griff ever again! Don't even fucking look at him, and don't fucking look at Danny and Beau while you're at it! They're mine!"

A splatter of blood distorts her face, and she lets out a sinister laugh. "And you call me a whore? You're letting three guys run a train on you. Sounds like you're no different than me, sweetheart. They'll get bored of you, sooner or later." Her voice is flat, all the passion suddenly gone.

I let out a banshee scream and wrap my tiny hands around her throat. She goes from stoic to frantic in seconds. She flails her hands, trying to get me to release my grip, but it just makes me press down harder. For a second, a flash of me shooting Griff's father pops into my head. Maybe this MC has awoken a murderer inside me. Maybe this is who I am now, someone who will kill anyone who dares to threaten the men in my life. *Someone who will kill.*

I don't even notice the office door fly open, but strong hands are pulling me off of her and she's gasping for breath, coughing and rubbing at her red throat. I hope it bruises in the shape of my slender fingers.

"I'll fucking kill you if you ever touch them again!" I scream at her. "I've done it before, I can do it again!"

The whole MC is standing behind her, some of them stunned, some of them laughing to themselves as Danny tries to keep a grip on me so I don't lunge at her again.

"You're fucking crazy!" the woman chokes out, struggling to stand. But between her intoxicated state and my attack, she collapses back onto the couch.

"Candy, Sissy," Griff says sternly, crossing his arms across his broad chest. "Get the fuck out of my club. I never want to see you here again."

"But Griffy," the one called Sissy pouts. "She attacked us! You can't be serious, I'm not the problem here."

He shakes his head and turns from her. "If my girl has a problem with you, then I have a problem with you. So . . . get the fuck out, and don't come back."

She shrieks and goes over to pick her sister off the floor, tugging her out of the club. The members clap and jeer as the girls leave. I realize that I probably wasn't the only one in the club who hated those whores.

Danny releases his hold on me and rubs my arms gently. I'm still shaking with anger. I turn to Griff, adrenaline slowly leaving my body. He must notice.

"Beau, why don't you take her home for the day?" Griff asks. "I think she's had a bit too much excitement today."

Beau takes the car keys from Danny and tells him to call when they're ready to be picked up. Right as I'm about to walk out with Beau, Griff calls out to me. I turn around and he summons me over to him.

"I'm sorry I got out of hand," I say, looking down at my sandals.

He places a tattooed finger under my chin, lifting it so I'll look at him. "Can I take that little scene as you are claiming me as yours?"

My heart rate kicks up again, the relentless cardiac rollercoaster of the past few days probably giving me serious medical problems. I'm probably going to pass out the second we leave. "Mine," I say sternly.

"Good girl," Griff answers with a smile. "That's all I needed to know. Go home and wait for me, Princess."

My body craves for a kiss to seal the deal, but Griff turns around, casually dismissing me. Now I wonder if he's just plotting a punishment for my actions or if he's going to make me sit and wait until I'm on my hands and knees, begging for him to take me.

* * *

"That was fucking crazy," Beau says proudly as we pull up at the house. "Absolutely insane. Where did you learn to fight like that?"

I shrug my shoulders, trying not to shake too much. "Watched one of the girls in my old sorority take down another for eating her pint of ice cream. Never mess with a girl while she's PMSing."

He laughs at my joke, and we both climb out of the car.

I glance at the road and back at the house.

"What's wrong?" he asks, suddenly concerned.

"Can I change and go for a run?" I ask. "My body won't stop shaking. I need to get this energy out as quickly as possible."

"Yeah, sure," he says. "But I'm coming with you. We're still on watch for potential threats. I know you handled your own back at the clubhouse, but there are bigger monsters out there than a couple boozed-up whores."

I nod in agreement, and we both go inside to change before heading out on a mile jog. It's been weeks since I've been able to go on a run, and my body protests at first, but it quickly finds a rhythm it's used to. Beau runs beside me, keeping my pace, his breathing even. We used to run together all the time in the mornings before school. Sometimes, if I couldn't sleep, I could call Beau and he would meet me for a run around the block. Maybe he was even protecting me back then, maybe he was aware of the things that go bump in the night.

When we make it back to the house, I'm covered in sweat, but I love it. I released the tension, and now I feel like I could use a nice bubble bath. Maybe I could get a quick one in Griff's massive soaking tub before he gets home. Beau doesn't even seem fazed by our run, no heavy breathing, hardly any sweat on his red shirt. He's certainly kept up with his physique while I've been less than diligent.

"How are you not panting right now?" I ask him, bent over at the waist and bracing my hands on my knees.

I glance up just in time to catch a smile from the man I've always loved. "I workout every day," he answers with a shrug. "And there's a decent bit of manual labor I do at the clubhouse."

"You work out everyday?" I ask, and he nods his head. "But I haven't noticed since I've been around you. I've never seen you heading to the gym."

He nods his head to the garage. "We've got a weight bench in there, sometimes I'll take a run, but only when I know you're safe and the other guys are here."

I stand up and wipe the sweat from my forehead with the neck of my t-shirt. "Think we could start running together again? Like we used to in the mornings?"

He smiles, remembering the good ol' days. "I would love to, Christina."

He's about to wrap me up in a hug, but I place a hand on his chest and push him away. "Ew, no. I'm so gross and sweaty. I think I'm going to go take a bath if that's okay."

"Of course," he says, unlocking the front door for me. "This is basically your home now. You can do what you want here. I'm going to start working on dinner before the guys get back."

"Family dinner?" I tease, arching a brow at him.

"More like a dysfunctional family meeting where we eat dinner together," he replies, though it doesn't sound as grim as I would imagine.

"Did everything go okay at the meeting?" I ask. I know today was important for Griff and the club's future, but he hasn't said anything about it yet.

He runs his hand across the top of my hair and pulls gently on my ponytail once. "It was better than I had hoped, we've just got a lot to discuss as a unit, the four of us."

The four of us? Better than Beau hoped? That's gotta be good news, right?

Now I'm really interested. I quickly head up the stairs and change my mind at the last minute about the bath to hop in the shower instead. I can't get clean fast enough. I try to slow down when I'm drying my hair, but when I turn off the bathroom fan, I hear Griff and Danny's voices downstairs talking to Beau. *My guys are home!* I yank on another dress, sans underwear because I don't feel like waiting any longer, and I'm curious to see how the guys would react to finding me without panties—or which one would figure it out first.

I take the stairs in stride, and all three guys look my way as I enter the kitchen.

"Hi!" I say to the three of them and then direct my attention to Beau. "Is dinner almost done? I'm starved."

"It'll be ready in about five minutes," Beau answers, smiling at me. It's the happiest I've seen him since before Griff mentioned marrying me, wanting to make me the queen of the MC.

"Good! I'll set the table," I say, already reaching into the cabinets on my tiptoes to grab some plates. I feel my dress rise up a little, maybe not enough to reveal my bare ass to the guys, but I can still feel their gazes on me. Sure enough, when I turn around, all three of them are looking at my legs. They quickly turn their gazes anywhere else in the room, trying to pretend like they weren't staring at my ass.

I begin setting plates for the four of us around the small kitchen table, nibbling on my lower lip. "You guys *are* allowed to look," I say, going over to grab some silverware from the drawer. "I don't mind."

Griff sits down at the table as I finish, and he pulls me into his lap. I gasp, surprised by his assertiveness. It's the first time I give into the butterflies he causes.

"What came over you at the clubhouse?" he asks, looking into my eyes.

I look down, but not at him, my mood falling a bit. "Are you mad?"

He shakes his head. "Just surprised. Sissy and Candy have been coming around for a long time."

"Well, they're . . . stupid," I say, embarrassingly childlike. I scold myself for not finding the right words to describe them. Actually, I know what I want to call them, I did that earlier.

Griff's chest rumbles with laughter, and I look at him, my eyebrows pulling together, trying to give him my best pissed off look.

"I agree, but why did you beat the shit out of Sissy?" But we all know that he knows exactly why I attacked her. He just wants me to admit it. I try to climb out of his lap, but he holds me in place, gripping my hips.

"I didn't like how she was talking about you!" I yell. "Are you happy now? I don't want you fucking anyone else, only me! She got what was coming to her! She kept running her mouth about fucking you, and I made her shut up. Someone had to."

Griff smiles and glances at the two other guys.

I shove him, and he finally releases me. "You're an asshole," I say, pointing a finger at his chest and turning around to cross my arms. Now I'm actually pouting.

The room is quiet, aside from the sizzling coming from the pan on the stove that Beau is mixing around. I glance back at Griff to find that he's leaning back in his chair with a huge smile on his face. Like he's proud of himself.

"Well, boys, looks like I'm officially part of your fun little arrangement."

I scoff and roll my eyes. "Is this what the 'family meeting' is about? You finally getting your way and me admitting that I don't want you screwing around with other women?"

"No, actually," Griff begins. "I had assumed that Beau would have already told you the news."

I glance at Beau, and he shakes his head. "Nope, I figured we'd all tell her together."

Beau places a hot pad on the center of the table and puts the frying pan on top, filled with chicken and chopped veggies. He goes over to the counter and grabs the bag of tortillas for fajitas and tosses them on the table.

"Dig in," he says, and we all take our seats at the table. He knows I'm a sucker for his homemade fajitas, or any Mexican cuisine he makes, really. Beau's grandpa took him to Mexico for vacation one summer, and he came back with amazing cooking skills, which was fantastic for me since my mom hated to cook.

My annoyance with Griffin subsides as I take a tortilla, pass the bag, and load up my plate. I'm practically salivating for the meal. Between the adrenaline from my cat fight and my run with Beau, I didn't real-ize just how hungry I was. The guys and I eat in silence, which gives me time to think. Mostly about what it means now that I've admitted that I don't want anyone's grimy hands on Griff. Does that mean he's officially part of the sexcapade that we have going? Does he think that I'm going to be his submissive to his BDSM fetish? Would he be will-ing to give that up if I'm not interested?

"That was fantastic, Beau," Danny says, tossing his napkin on his plate and leaning back in his chair to rub his belly. "Great meal."

"So good." I close my eyes and moan as I finish my last bite. When

I open my eyes, all three men are staring at me with similar expressions of . . . lust? If I were wearing panties, I'm sure the looks of hunger they're giving me would be making my own lust seep through. "What?" I ask, feigning innocence.

"Anyway," Danny says with a wink, moving his attention to Beau and Griff. "Who is going to break the news to her?"

"What news?" I demand. "Tell me! Did something bad happen?"

"Actually, something really good happened," Griff says. "Well, good for Beau. Two people were nominated for the MC election. Me, of course, being one of them."

"Who else?" I ask, my patience wearing thin. Some panic rises up inside of me. I'm not sure if I trust any of the other men in the MC. I've only met Luis, but he might be an enemy with the way I pulled a gun on him.

Danny clears his throat across the table from me, lacing his fingers together in front of him. "Looks like Griffin will be running against Beau."

I stare back and forth between Beau and Griff, waiting for a fight to break out, but the two of them seem fine with the outcome of the meeting. Smiles tug at their lips, and I find myself smiling too.

"I feel like we should be celebrating!" I say, standing up and taking each of the guys' empty plates and setting them in the sink. One of us will get to the dishes eventually, but it's time for a drink right now.

"What do you have in mind, Princess?" Griff asks.

I reach into a cabinet and grab four glasses, bringing them over to the table, and I go over to the pantry to retrieve a bottle of whiskey. "Let's have a toast," I say. "Drink a little."

"That sounds like a great idea," Dan adds as he cleans off the leftovers from our dinner and puts them in a plastic bowl to go into the fridge.

I fill each of the glasses with some cubes of ice before pouring two fingers of Glenlivet into them and going to the fridge to pour some

Coke into my glass. I know the guys prefer their liquor straight, but I still can't manage the burn.

Handing the boys their glasses, I move to sit in Beau's lap instead of my own chair. He wraps an arm around my stomach and places a kiss on my bare shoulder. I'm so glad that we made up this morning, it feels good to be in his arms again.

Me and the guys raise our glasses toward the middle of the table.

"To Beau and Griff," I say. "It doesn't matter who wins, as long as we stick together."

"To us," Griff corrects. "To a new beginning."

"To us," Beau and Danny say in unison as we clink our glasses together.

We all sit at the table for over an hour. At some point we abandon our glasses and begin passing the bottle around to drink straight from it. We're all laughing and planning what's going to happen between now and the election. Griff decides for the four of us to take a vacation to his cabin two weekends from now, because things are going to get real busy at the clubhouse. They've got some shipments coming in to handle, and I'm not sure what the shipments are, but it sounds important. I'm excited to see how the election is going to go though.

Danny takes the last swig of the whiskey and tosses the empty bottle into the garbage. A silence settles over us, and Griff mutters something about getting to bed for an early morning, to which Beau reluctantly agrees. I, however, have a desire forming in my belly . . . I don't want the night to end just yet. Kind of like Sunday nights when you're a little kid, and you don't want to go to bed to return to school on Monday. I don't want this night to end, the four of us finally just getting on the same page.

Beau moves to try and stand up, but I turn around in the chair to straddle him, forcing him back into place. I lean in and urgently press a kiss against his lips, and my tongue comes out, licking at the seam of his lips, asking for entrance into his mouth.

He moans against my lips and opens so I can run my tongue against his. I take his hands and move them along my thighs under my dress. I keep moving them until they push my dress up to my hips to reveal my bare ass to the rest of the guys. Beau pulls back to look at me, but then I see only urgency in his eyes. I release his hands, and they find their way to my ass, and he palms my cheeks. I grind against him, wanting friction.

"Fuck . . ." I hear Danny mutter beside us. I turn my head to look at him, and Beau moves to trail kisses along my neck, sucking the skin. I'm already drunk on the sensations—and tipsy from the whiskey.

"Touch yourself, Danny," I command breathlessly.

"Are you giving out orders tonight, Princess?" Griff asks from across the table. He's probably got the best view of my ass as I grind my hips against Beau's jean-covered crotch.

"I am," I say, not able to turn around enough to look at Griff. "And you're going to watch."

Griff chuckles. "Putting on a show for me then?"

Instead of speaking, I answer him by pulling my dress the rest of the way over my head, leaving me completely naked.

Beau drinks in the sight and then looks into my eyes, moving some hair behind my ear. "You're so beautiful, baby."

I press my finger to his lips and he kisses it. "Shh," I say. "Stop trying to swoon me. You've already got me."

He shakes his head. "I'll never stop trying, and I'll always fight for you."

My heart races, and I place my palm over Beau's mouth to shut him up. "Stop talking!"

I grind down harder on him, and he lets out a muffled moan behind my palm.

"I've got a gag in the bedroom if you want to ensure he's quiet," Griff says calmly. "That would be pretty entertaining for me."

Though the thought of Beau being at my mercy sounds tempting,

I just want him to worship my body right now and that's not going to happen in a kitchen chair. I stand and tug on his arm to pull him up.

"Let's go upstairs," I whisper, looking over to Danny who is gripping his cock in his hand. I almost fall to my knees at the sight. I want to lick the bead of pre-cum that's on the tip before he wipes it away. *Mine.*

Griff stands and rubs his hands together. "Does my little Princess have a bit of a dom inside her?"

I stand in front of him, bare naked, and place my hand on his chest. As much as he's pretending to act unaffected by me, his heart is racing in his chest. His smile falters a little as he stares down at my body. I press my bare chest against him.

"The only way I'm going to have any dom inside me is if you fuck me tonight," I tell him, a playful smile on my lips.

Without another word, I make my way to the stairs and climb up. I can hear at least one of the boys hot on my heels, making me pick up my pace, my breasts bouncing as I jog quicker to the bedroom. By the time I get to Griff's room, I'm breathless and Beau is spinning me around to face him, assaulting me with kisses, urging me backward until I fall onto the bed. Beau pulls back long enough to remove his shirt, and I watch as the other two men strut into the room behind him.

I crawl up until I get to the top of the bed and lean back on the pillows, beckoning Beau to lay over my body.

Before he gets a chance, Griff is pulling him off the bed, leaving me alone and pouting.

"Uh uh," Griff commands. "I've got an idea."

He smiles at me and I smile back, getting on my knees and coming over to him. "What's your idea?" I ask.

"Go to my closet, open the trunk, and grab the ropes," Griff says.

My smile falters. I'm not sure how I feel about being tied up after the kidnapping his father orchestrated. "Griff, I don't think I'm ready for—"

He smirks and runs a finger over my cheek. "They're not for you, Princess."

I gulp and scurry off into his closet, following his directions and coming back as quickly as possible. Beau and Danny are both sitting toward the top of the bed, one on either side. They don't look too happy, but I don't think they're going to argue.

"Good girl," Griff tells me, taking some of the rope from me. "You're going to watch me tie Beau first, and then you're going to do the same to Dan."

"But why?" I ask, my brows furrowing.

"To let you know what control feels like, to let you experience the power," Griff explains. "One day, I would like you to let me bind you, but I want you to get to top first. I want you to understand what it feels like. Now watch."

I follow Griff up to Beau and sit on the bed while watching him intricately tie the ropes on Beau's wrists. Griff tosses out some knot terms and shows me how to safely but securely tie my boyfriend.

"Your turn," Griff says, nodding toward Dan.

I cross the bed on my hands and knees, and Dan holds his wrists out for me, smiling broadly, whereas Beau looks a little put out. Like he wants to punch Griff for cockblocking him.

"Hey there, sugar," Danny says as I begin wrapping the rope around his wrists.

Griff watches and corrects me when I tie the knot wrong, telling me how to correct my mistake. Once I'm done, Griff pulls at the rope to see if it's possible for Dan to get out, and he smiles at me proudly.

"Well done," he says. "Now, what were you saying about having a dom inside you?"

My stomach flutters with nerves, but I tug Griff to the bed, gripping a fistful of his shirt. My lips crash against his, and the mattress dips down as he climbs onto the bed. Instead of pushing me to lie down between the guys, Griff lies on the bed and pulls me onto his lap where I come into contact with his rock-hard cock beneath his pants.

I bite my lip and grind down on him, pulling a groan from his lips, making him rock up against me. I move down his body so I can unzip his jeans and pull them down, finding that he's gone commando, but that's not the only thing I find—he's huge. Beau and Danny are above average, but they don't measure up to Griff. I'm not sure he'll fit, and I know damn sure he won't get to take me at the same time as one of the other guys. I'm not ready for that, and I'm not sure I'll ever be.

"Are you going to keep staring?" Griff asks, his arms behind his head. "Didn't your mom tell you that staring is rude?"

I roll my eyes and grip his thick member in my hand, my fingertips an inch short from being able to wrap around him completely. Then it hits me. Griff's past. I feel my face pale.

"What's wrong?" Beau asks, trying to reach his bound hands toward me.

I look back at Griff who is now propped up on his elbows, concern pulling his eyebrows together.

"Are you—" I start to ask, not sure how to phrase the question without sounding rude or judgmental. I release my grip on him. "Are you clean? Beau and Dan are. Can I trust that you are? I don't want to have to worry about what those . . . bitches at the club have given out recklessly."

Griff grabs for his jeans that are resting next to me, and I think he's going to push me off of him and put his clothes back on, but instead, he pulls out a folded piece of paper and hands it to me.

"It's my results," he says, nodding to the paper as I unfold it. "I would never do anything to harm you, Princess. I got tested last week just to be safe. I haven't touched anyone since the last girl you saw in this house, and we never actually had penetrating sex that night, we just played, and I plan on you being the only one I touch now."

My eyes move over the print out. It looks like he got tested for everything possible when it comes to STDs and came back completely clean.

"Not quite the man-whore that you expected?" Griff asks as I fold the paper back up and sit it on the bed by his jeans. "Guess the condoms I used every time actually worked to prevent me from catching anything."

"Well, that's good," I say, nodding over and over. Honestly, I'm shocked that Griff thought ahead and got tested. "Why though? You've hated me since you met me."

He shrugs and reaches out, his hands caressing the curves of my torso. "I guess if you can't beat 'em, join 'em."

I roll my eyes.

"But also," he says, his hands squeezing my hips and tugging me against him so my already slick folds find some friction. "It really helped watching you claim me as yours. You will never know just how fucking hot that was, maybe I should bring in some more girls to the clubhouse . . ."

I grind hard against his hips and reach a hand up to wrap around his throat, just for the threat, not the actual act because my hands are so small. "Don't. You. Dare."

Griff bites his lower lip and grins up at me. "I wouldn't dream of doing such a thing when I've got a pretty little lady like you in my bed."

I grind against Griff again, moaning in pleasure, my head falling back in ecstasy.

"Stop teasing," Griff says, and for the first time, it sounds like he's pleading with me.

Lifting my hips, I reach down and grab his cock to line up with my entrance, and slowly slide down his length. When he bottoms out, I grind down, letting my body adjust to his impressive size. We're both breathing heavily, none of us speaking for a moment. Just as Griff's eyes fall closed, I lean forward on him, pressing my hands against his tattooed chest, and begin moving up and down on his cock urgently.

"Oh, fuck," Griff groans, his eyes popping open. He looks up at me with wonder in his eyes, letting me take him the way I want. "Fuck, Princess. You're so goddamn tight!"

I smile down at him as I keep up my tempo, finding even more pleasure by catching Griff off guard with how good it feels to be inside me.

"Say that you're mine," I tell him, pressing him deeper into the mattress. "Say you're mine!"

He lifts his upper body off the bed and presses a searing kiss to my lips. "I'm yours, Princess. Let me feel you cum all over my cock."

He lies back down and I fall off tempo, my hips grinding and pumping, trying to find a release. Griff watches me intently as I chase down my orgasm, my walls clenching him tightly.

"Good girl," Griff praises, brushing my wild hair out of my face and flipping us over effortlessly so he can be on top. "It's my turn to have some fun."

Griff pulls all the way out before thrusting back in, and I scream from the impact.

He stops halfway out, panic in his voice. "You okay?"

I nod my head quickly. "Yes, just don't stop. I think I'm going to cum again!"

Griff grins and continues thrusting, but not as deeply. Instead, he places his thumb over my clit and begins rubbing circles until I'm writhing beneath him, gasping for more, harder, deeper.

He chuckles and shakes his head. "I don't think you go that deep, Princess. I don't want to hurt you."

Concerned about hurting me? I never thought Griff would ever be concerned about me, yet here he is. I can tell he's holding back—a vein in his tattooed neck bulges with every beat of his heart. I don't want him to hold back, I want to feel all of him, I want to know what he's like unrestrained. But am I ready for it?

I wrap my legs as far around his waist as possible, pulling him against me. I reach my arms out, reaching for Beau and Danny's hard, thick cocks, stroking them quickly, thankful that they were naked before we tied them up.

They both groan, but I don't look at either of them—my eyes are on Griff's.

"Fuck me, Griff," I say through gritted teeth. "Don't hold back. I want to see what you look like when you give in to your own desire."

Something in Griff snaps, something primal. He grips one hand onto my hip and places the other one over one of my breasts. He pumps in and out of me, unapologetically this time, taking what he wants from my body, grunting as my pussy tightens around him even more as another orgasm barrels its way through me. I stroke Beau and Danny's cocks, feeling both of them getting closer as I stroke up and down. Beau is the first one to spill his cum all over my hand, and I slow my strokes, letting him come down from his pleasure. Danny's not too far behind, my name on his lips as I feel him pulse in my hand.

I remove my hands from them and use one to rub circles on my clit, and the other to squeeze the nipple that Griff isn't tugging on, not at all concerned about smearing their cum all over my skin.

"Oh, shit," Griff says, watching as I touch myself. "Keep doing that! Keep rubbing their cum all over you. Fuck that's hot."

"You like me dirty?" I ask, arching my back.

"Fuck yes," Griff grinds out. "You're going to make me cum, Princess. You're so fucking dirty."

Griff thrusts one, two, three more times into me before I feel him spilling his cum inside me. He collapses halfway on top of me, both of our chests rising and falling as we come down from the pleasure. He only gets up to untie the ropes from around the other guys before falling back onto the bed next to me.

"We're never letting you go, Christina," Griff says as the

four of us lie together on the giant California King bed. "I hope you're happy."

I smile and snuggle against him, his sticky cum starting to seep from between my quivering legs. "I'm very happy."

CHAPTER 6

I'm sitting at the kitchen table eating a bowl of cereal when the guys finally emerge from upstairs. They're all dressed in matching memorial t-shirts under their vests, and Griff's already got his sunglasses on, a grim expression on his face. Quite the opposite from his smile last night when he delicately cleaned me in the shower. Beau comes over and places a kiss on my forehead, and Danny's hand brushes some hair over my shoulder as he passes me on the way to the fridge.

"Can I trust you to not do anything stupid while we're at the memorial?" Griff asks, bracing his hands on the kitchen chair opposite of me. I can't see his eyes behind his sunglasses.

"Yes, daddy," I say, rolling my eyes and taking a bite of my cereal.

One corner of Griff's lips pull up in a smile. "If that's what you want to continue calling me, I'm perfectly fine with it, Princess."

"Hell no," Beau mutters under his breath. "So weird."

For some reason, I find it the opposite of weird. I rub my thighs together as heat starts to spread. Griff must be able to see right through me, and my poker face slips as he pokes his tongue out to lick his bottom lip.

"Well, well, well," he says. "You do want to continue calling me that, don't you, Princess?"

I lift my middle finger and turn my attention to Beau. "Can we go for our jog when you get home? Since we missed it this morning."

Beau smiles down at me. "You're the one who insisted we stay in bed for fifteen more minutes. But yes, we'll jog when I get home."

"How long will you . . . be gone?" I ask no one in particular.

"Should be home by nine," Danny says, handing the guys their helmets. "We'll all have our phones though if you need us."

I nod and stare into my cereal bowl, using the spoon to swirl around the final piece of soggy processed sugar. It's only ten in the morning. I'm going to get so bored sitting in this house by myself. Griff gave me strict orders that I'm not allowed to leave the house by myself until further notice because it's still too dangerous. I've hardly got anything from my life before the boys to keep me busy, just a few of my paperback romances that I've already read cover to cover. I guess there's always a Netflix marathon of some sort, or maybe I can workout in the garage gym. Still, that won't occupy my mind for a full eleven hours.

Beau and Danny head outside, and Griff lingers in the doorway before turning around and coming to kneel beside me, removing his sunglasses so his eyes aren't shielded from me.

"It won't always have to be like this," he says. "One day you'll be—"

"Free?" I ask abruptly. "You know, you keeping me holed up in this house is almost just as bad as your father keeping me in that basement."

"Don't be so dramatic," he says, shaking his head. "You were a prisoner when my father had you, I'm just trying to keep you safe now. Beau and Danny would murder me if anything happened to you."

I lean my forehead against his. "Sorry, I just . . . I worry every time one of you leaves."

He pulls away from me and cups my cheek with his calloused fingers. "Try not to worry. We're going to get through this. It's just going to take a little bit longer. You have my word though, one day you'll be able to go about your day normally, just not right now. We need you safe."

Griff surprises me by placing a soft kiss to my forehead. Without anyone else around, he's so much softer. So much nicer.

"Are you sore this morning?" he asks, glancing down at my lap.

I shrug my shoulders, but I am sore. Last night was so worth it though.

"Take some Tylenol, Princess," Griff says. "I'll try to be gentle next time."

My lips lift in a smirk and I shake my head. "Don't you dare. I loved every minute of last night."

He smiles at me. "Good, but we're going to have to come up with a safe word too. Maybe think about one while we're gone today, I don't want to hurt you at all."

I nod my head and watch Griff as he stands back up and heads out the door.

* * *

Six episodes of some baking show, three scandalous texts to the boys in our group chat, and one hour of weight lifting in the garage later, the boredom sets in. I'm literally pacing the floor when I hear my phone ring from its spot on the charger in the kitchen. I ran the battery down mindlessly scrolling through Instagram and TikTok. Somehow I ended up in the rabbit hole of KinkTok, which hasn't helped curb my sexual desire at all. I've watched about a hundred different videos on how to be a sub, and I've got about a hundred more questions for Griffin.

I snatch my cell phone from the charger and smile when I see Beau's picture flash across the screen. I swipe to answer. "Hey, are you guys on your way home?" I ask.

"Not yet," he says, and I hear some motorcycles rumbling in the background. "Griff actually wanted me to give you a call to ask you to go upstairs and look out the window in the next ten minutes."

"Um, okay?" I ask, my heart falling because I miss my guys. "That's an odd request."

"It'll make sense," he says. "He wants to show you what a community we have. He wants you to see that our MC isn't just a bunch of scary men who aren't afraid of anything."

I let out a sigh and head up for Griff's bedroom. "Okay, I'll be watching. Come home soon?"

"I will, baby," Beau says quietly. "As soon as I can."

We say goodbye and end the call. I open the curtains in Griff's room and peer out the window, giving me the perfect view of the road in front of the house. They live in a decent neighborhood, nothing like the fancy one I grew up in, but it feels safe. Whether that feeling of safety is from the guys protecting me or that we're not in a neighborhood I would have expected three bachelor, motorcycle club members to live in—all that matters is that I feel safe here. I do miss my space and my apartment, but it was starting to get lonely.

I just worry that I'm going to wear out my welcome here and that I can't actually settle and call this place home. My stomach clenches at the thought. Could I survive another heartbreak from Beau? Could I let him go again? Just as my thoughts begin to spiral, I hear the muffled sounds of engines in the distance. I open the window, letting in the gentle summer breeze as the noise becomes louder.

Motorcycles.

And it sounds like a bunch of them. Way more than the three I would normally hear.

Sure enough, one side of the road is taken up by lines of black motorcycles passing by. It's not just Hell Prevails MC though, it's multiple clubs. I can tell by the different patches on their backs: some with skulls, other with snakes or birds, and one that catches my eye featuring a large white upside down cross. I climb through the open window to perch on the roof and get a better view as they all drive by. They acquire a decent audience as other people come out of their houses to watch all of them drive down the street. It must be a memorial ride for Griff's father and the other fallen members. It reminds me of a Fourth of July parade or something from when I was little.

I try to find my guys in the crowd of bikers, but it's hard to tell them apart when there's so many of them and most are wearing helmets. That is, until one of them breaks from the group and looks up toward the window to give me a wave and a thumbs up. Beau smiles and eases back into the procession of bikes just as the end of it appears. I wonder if they do this sort of thing anytime a member dies or if it's only for the presidents of clubs. I wonder if any of the other clubs know they were driving by the woman who murdered the man this memorial ride was for. I watch until I don't see any more motorcycles, and then carefully go back into the bedroom to wait—forever the helpless Princess trapped in her ivory tower.

* * *

My guys get home at nine on the dot just like they promised. Each of them sit their helmets on the bench by the garage door and stash their cuts on the hanger above. The fourth hook now holds my purse. I smile at the domestic feel of it, but the smile falters when I think again about how this isn't my home. One day they're probably going to send me back out on my own, and I don't know if that's what I want. Maybe a month ago, but not now. Now I can't imagine not having these guys come home to me.

On the other hand, I'm going stir crazy. I would love to get my bartending job back. I feel useless sitting at home while they're off doing all their vigilante justice and whatever else it is that they do. I feel like

I need to be pulling my weight around here. Maybe bringing in some income to help cover the expenses.

"What's on your mind, baby girl?" Danny asks, coming over and scooping me up into his arms. I wrap my legs around his torso, my hands on his shoulders for balance. I'm amazed at his strength. Not many people would be able to casually lift a grown adult with such ease. I close my eyes and breathe him in.

"Just had a lot of time to think today," I say with a shrug.

"Uh oh," he says, wincing. "Do you want to talk?"

I nod my head and look over Danny's shoulder at the two other guys who have all eyes on me. Danny carries me to the living room and sits us on the couch, me in his lap, and Griff takes the recliner like usual. Beau sits next to us and gives me a small smile.

"What's on your mind, Princess?" Griff asks, and I can see his guard is up. Like he's waiting for me to say that all of this is too much for me. He's looking at me like I've already got one foot out the door.

I take a deep breath. "I'm worried about what's going to happen if any of you get sick of me being here . . . worried about what's going to happen if you want me to leave your house. I'm worried about getting my heart broken, getting too attached, getting hurt. I'm also worried I'll be losing who I am by being stuck in this house all day. I'd like to go back to work. I kind of miss bartending. I loved people watching and listening to customers tell me interesting stories. I like when you call me Princess, but I don't want to be a damsel. I want to carry some of the weight in this . . . relationship." The words more or less tumble out of my mouth, but they needed to be said. Already, it feels like a weight being lifted from my shoulders.

"As long as you want us," Beau says, reaching for my hand, "you can stay here. You're ours, and it's okay to be scared. You've been through so many scary things in the last couple of weeks, but we're here for you."

Danny brushes my blonde hair behind my ear, and his hand runs down my back soothingly. "Beau's right. We want you here with us, but if you want to leave once the threat is gone, we're not going to hold you here as a prisoner. It would hurt like a bitch to let you go, to lose you, but your happiness is what matters."

I give him a quick peck on the cheek and run my hand over his thick black beard.

"But what about the marriage thing?" I ask, looking over to Griff. "Whichever one of you becomes the official president will have to get married . . ."

"We'll cross that bridge when we get there," Beau answers, drawing my attention back to him. "Rules are made to be bent."

I glance over toward Griff. Instead of his closed-off look, it appears he's sorting through the options in his head. He scratches his chin and finally nods.

"Come here," he says, beckoning me to come sit on his lap by patting his thigh. I think back to those sensual dom TikToks I watched earlier. I obey and sit on Griff's lap. "Good girl."

I blush at the praise and look away from him, but he draws my attention back to his eyes by gently placing one finger under my chin.

"I don't want you to go back to working at any bar," he says, and my shoulders sag in defeat. "How about we compromise, Princess? You can bartend at the clubhouse. You'll still get paid, and we can also keep an eye on you, keep you safe. Granted, almost everyone just drinks beer or straight whiskey, so the work isn't extremely exciting, but you'll be out of the house."

My heart rate picks up, and I shake my head. "I can't go into the office. I can't."

He softly shushes me, somehow slowing my heart rate with the soft look in his eyes. "You don't have to step foot in the office, I promise. Just the bar area. I'd rather you stick close to home, but I understand that you want to work, so I'm not going to keep you cooped up like some sexy 1950's housewife."

I bite my bottom lip and nod. "Will I work while you guys are there?"

"Of course," he says. "We won't leave you in the clubhouse without one of us there with you. And if any of the other guys give you shit, I'll put my boot up their ass."

I laugh, earning the biggest smile I've ever seen from Griff. My heart swells. "So you want me here as well?" I ask. "I can stay with you in your home, even after the danger settles?"

He nods. "I don't think the danger will ever completely settle, but yes, I do want you to stay, even after. As long as you're happy."

"So, when do I start, boss?" I ask with a smile, finally feeling like I'll be getting part of my life back on track.

CHAPTER 7

Getting back into a bartending gig felt good. I finished my first week working at the clubhouse with a smile on my face. It started out a little weary, but I ended up earning some respect from the other members of the MC fairly quickly. By Saturday evening, I even had some of the big burly regulars laughing as I cleaned up the bar.

To my surprise, the bartending gig was only from noon to nine in the evening. Griff closes the clubhouse at night to make sure all the men who have families get home at a reasonable hour to see their wives and children, and they close the clubhouse altogether on Sundays. It surprises me how much of a family-friendly man Griff is turning out to be. I even caught him giving Luis' and Bonnie's kid a piggyback ride earlier today. What surprises me ever more is how much I like seeing him with a kid in his arms.

Moose, one of my new MC pals, has been telling me a story about the dog he just adopted last week. This big, intimidating man went to the shelter and adopted the tiniest dog they had available.

He lifts his phone up to show me a picture of the scrappy dog. "I named him Rocky. His name was Bruce, but that's the name of my brother-in-law, and I can't stand the guy. Had to change the name, obviously."

I rest my chin on the mop handle and look at the photos of Rocky. "Oh my God, Moose! He's adorable. You've got to bring him by to see me next week!"

Moose gives me a smile, showing his crooked teeth. Rocky also has crooked teeth. I read somewhere that dogs usually resemble their owners, and that might be the case with Moose and Rocky, though they're probably three hundred pounds apart in weight.

"Of course, sugar," he says. "Anything for you."

Griff takes that moment to come over and lean on the bar, playfully nudging Moose's shoulder as he pockets his phone.

"You trying to steal my girl, Moose?" Griff jokes to the man who is clearly past his sixties.

Moose laughs and pushes his empty beer stein to me to put in the dishwasher. "Can't help but give her some company while you're running the show, boss."

"Just no funny business," Griff says, turning to wink at me. I can't help but love this side of Griff, but I also love when he puts on his dominant persona at home. I'm not sure which one I like more. Lucky for me, I don't have to choose.

"You almost ready to head home, Princess?" Griff asks, taking a seat at the bar.

I nod. "Almost. Let me finish mopping."

"I'll see you Monday, Miss Christina," Moose says, hobbling from his customary barstool. I'm not sure how he holds up his motorcycle. Beau told me yesterday that Moose is probably going to sell his two wheeler soon and get a three wheeler, he's just getting way too old for the current bike.

"See you and Rocky then!" I call back as he disappears out the door.

"Can I help you with the barware?" Griff asks, already making his way around the bar. It's just the two of us now.

"Thanks." I toss him a dry rag to wipe the water from the glasses.

We clean up in silence for a moment, and I go over to start shutting off some of the lights, only leaving the bar illuminated.

"Bonnie invited me for a girls day next week," I say quietly as I help Griff put the glasses away. We haven't broached the topic of if I can go out with anyone other than him and the guys, only that it's not safe for me to go alone.

"Yeah?" Griff asks. "Bonnie is good company, I'm glad you two are getting along. It's good to have a friend in our group."

I nod. "She said she wants me to meet two of the other wives. Maybe go get a pedi and some margaritas during lunchtime. She's obviously passing on the margs since she's got a baby on the way."

"I think that would do you some good," Griff agrees. "I'd like Danny to go with you though—you ladies need someone to keep an eye on you."

I roll my eyes and cross my arms across my chest. "I don't need a babysitter. It's girls day. It'll be so embarrassing to bring my boy-friend along to creep on us."

As much as I like Danny, I really need some girl time. I haven't had a solid girl gang since before I lost my spot in my sorority. Clearly those girls weren't my real friends, though. I'd like to have some girls that I can talk to about the MC.

"If you want to go out, you need someone to keep you safe," Griff says sternly. "That's final."

Suddenly, a burst of hot rage fills my chest. "That's not fair!"

Griff turns to stare me down. "Princess," he warns through clenched teeth.

My body betrays me as a rush of heat quickly follows the rage.

I move to shove Griff in the chest, trying to regain some sort of high ground, but he easily catches my wrists in his hands before I make contact.

"Do *not* shove me, Princess," he says. "And talking back will only get you punishments, and not the fun kind."

I swallow and stop fighting against Griff's superior hold. "What kind of punishments?"

He grins, realizing I've simmered down. He bends to whisper in my ear. "You're not going to find out, because you're going to be a good girl. Now, finalize your plans with Bonnie when we get home, and let Danny know as well."

I nod my head, my heart racing.

"Princess," Griff says, holding my chin between his thumb and a finger. "Daddy needs to hear you say it."

My cheeks blush, and I swear I would let Griff fuck me over this bar right now if he asked.

"Yes," I whisper.

"Yes, what?"

"Yes, daddy," I say softly. "I understand."

Griff smiles and runs his calloused hand down my neck. "I love when you call me that," he says. "Who knew I would be so into it?"

I glance down between us and notice the outline of Griff's cock pressing against his jeans. "Has no one called you that before?" I ask, looking back up at him.

He shakes his head. "You're the first."

I try to conceal my smile, knowing that I was able to be one of Griff's firsts for something. He rolls his eyes and turns me around to walk around the bar, grabbing our helmets on the way out.

"Don't let it go to your head," he says, slinging an arm over my shoulder.

* * *

Before bed, I send a quick message to Bonnie, asking her if next Friday works for our girls day, but not before I ask Griff if I could have that afternoon off. He said he would have one of the prospects cover my shift, and I could have the whole day to get to know some of the wives in the club. A little positive reinforcement for following his rules. It just feels good to have some sort of routine again.

Bonnie says she'll get a sitter for little Carlos and adds me to her group chat with the ladies.

"What's that smile for?" Beau asks, climbing into the bed next to me.

Griff is in the shower, and Danny's still in the garage tuning up his vintage muscle car. It's just Beau and I in Griff's massive bed, where we've all been sleeping since we became a foursome. I thought Griff would want his space, but he kept insisting we all sleep here, as long as he gets to keep his side of the bed and I'm beside him. At first, he didn't want to share me at night with the guys, but I think he realized that I need the other two there to help keep the nightmares at bay.

I lean over and place my phone on the nightstand.

"Just feels like things are finally getting back to normal," I say, lying on my side to face Beau as he pulls the covers over us. He's shirtless, only wearing boxers. I trail my fingers over his chest. "I get to hang out with Bonnie next week. I love bartending at the clubhouse, and I'm just happy. It's been awhile since I've felt this happy."

Beau smiles at me, fiddling with the color of his shirt that I'm wearing. I always steal his shirts to wear to bed.

"I'm glad you're happy," he says.

"Are you happy?" I ask, praying that he says yes.

He nods his head. "I'm very happy. I'm a little worried about the future, but happy. I've got you back in my life . . . it's what I've always wanted."

My smile falters. "Why are you worried about the future?"

He runs a finger over my lips, tracing them delicately, before moving his hand to rest on my hip. "I'm worried about the future of the club, if I've got it in me to be the president if I win the election. I'm worried that if I do, will Griff resent me for it? He's always had his heart set on becoming president. I don't want to take that away from him. But—"

He pauses. Behind the bathroom door, I hear Griff rinsing off in the shower. We've probably got five minutes before he gets out of the shower to join us.

"But what?" I ask.

"Part of me hopes to God that he doesn't win the election because I want to be your husband and I want you to be my wife. I've wanted it since we were in high school. I know you're the one for me, Christina. You're my world, you always have been."

"Oh, Beau," I say, pulling him against me, wrapping my body around his. "Even if I'm married to Griff on paper when all of this is over, I'm still yours. I've always been yours."

"It won't be the same, Chris," he whispers. His voice sounds like regret, and he rolls onto his back. Maybe we're not as okay as I thought we were.

I pull back from him. "Do you . . . do you think this is too much? The four of us. Hurting you is the last thing I want, Beau. If you want this to end, we'll end it!"

The shower shuts off. The vent fan is still on, but we're running out of time.

"No!" Beau says quickly. "Hell no, I don't want this to end. As fucked up as this relationship looks on the outside, I love what we have. Part of me loves watching my best friends savor and tease your body. I don't think I can let that go. But . . . I don't know if something like this can continue into marriage. I wanted you to be the mother of my children, but if there are three of us, how do we explain to a five year old why they have three daddies? And there's just something about you taking my last name that I crave. Maybe I'm old fashioned, but that feels like the best way to claim you as mine."

I'm not sure what to say. Then an idea hits me right in the chest.

"What if I take your last name? No matter the outcome? I could take all of your last names . . ."

Beau laughs at the ceiling. "You would be Christina Grady Thomas Blackford?"

I shrug my shoulders. "We can figure out an order later."

"I like Christina Thomas Blackford Grady," says a voice standing in the doorway of the bathroom—Griff.

Neither of us noticed the vent fan turn off in the bathroom or the door open. That's what happens when I'm caught up with one of my guys—I don't notice anything else in the world.

I sit up in bed as Griff confidently walks over to the bed, bare naked.

He leans over Beau and places a kiss on my lips.

"Our queen gets the last decision though," he says, pulling away from me and looking at Beau.

"How much did you hear?" Beau asks, making sure he keeps eye contact. As confident as the guys are in their bodies and with each other, if we're not in the middle of an intimate moment, I think Beau gets slightly weirded out.

Griff shrugs. "Enough. You know I won't be mad if you win the election right? My world was thrown for a loop when I met Christina, well, when I opened up to our little Princess. I'm not sure the election is a concern for me any longer. I just want to know that the club is in good hands and we're going to get it back on track from the shitstorm my father put HPMC in. I think you would make a good president, bro."

Beau smiles, and we all turn to the bedroom doorway as Danny enters, slow clapping, his fingers still stained with grime from his car.

"Aww, why don't you boys kiss to seal the deal?" Danny mocks.

I smile at him. "I'm not opposed to that."

"Oh, fuck off," Griff shoots back, walking around to his side of the bed. "You wish you could see that."

Danny shrugs and rips his black muscle tank over his head, tossing it on the floor before hopping in the bed. "Don't knock it till you try it, boys!" He leans over Beau and plants a wet kiss on my lips. "Hey, sugar."

I smile and kiss him back. "Hi, Dan."

Griff pulls me down against him, spooning my body, breathing in the scent of my hair. "Mine."

"Ours," Beau and Dan growl at the same time. The four of us break out in a fit of laughter. I giggle until my belly hurts, and then I snuggle into Griff and Beau as I let sleep take over.

CHAPTER 8

A small black blur sprints across the concrete floor of the clubhouse as I'm pouring a stout from the tap. I only see it in the bar mirror's reflection, and when I turn around, it has completely disappeared. The bar is pretty quiet right now with everyone in Griff's office getting ready to start a meeting. I hand one of the members his beer, and he heads in to join the crew.

I wipe my hands on the bar towel and toss it over my shoulder. In my peripheral vision, I see the blur again, but it darts behind the couch. What the hell? Are there rats in the clubhouse?

I come around the bar carefully, trying not to make a noise. Griff mentioned that one of the stray cats that lives around the property sometimes finds its way in, and it's not a big deal, the cat keeps the mouse population under control. So it shouldn't be a rat.

When I make it to the side of the couch, I quietly peek around the top of it, and I'm met with gnashing teeth as a tiny dog jumps up in a very violent attempt to greet me. I chuckle at his extreme underbite and come around the couch the rest of the way to pick him up.

"You must be Rocky!" I say in a baby voice as the dog tries to lick my face right off. "Such a good boy, and so handsome!"

"Just like his pops," Moose adds. He comes hobbling into the open door of the clubhouse, the sunlight streaming in behind him. "You mind watching him for me while I'm in the meeting?"

"I don't mind!" I say, not taking my eyes off of the scraggly dog. "He can keep me company since all my patrons are apparently too busy to drink!"

Moose hands Rocky's leash over to me and ruffles both mine and the dog's hair. "Thanks, darlin.'"

Rocky follows me all around the clubhouse as I tidy things up. Anytime I stop, he sniffs the ground at my feet. I grab my packed lunch from the refrigerator and split my string cheese with my new furry friend. He eventually loses interest in being my shadow and hops up on one of the couches to rest. I have no doubt that his tiny legs are exhausted from following me around for the last hour.

I'm wiping down the bar top when the clubhouse door opens, startling Rocky from his sleep—which makes him go absolutely insane. He starts barking and running to the intruder, nipping at the man's ankles, not playing like he was with me earlier. I quickly race over and pick him up, but he's trying to wiggle out of my arms. He's furiously squirming and barking.

"Sorry!" I say, brushing my blonde hair from my mouth and finally meeting the man's eyes. "Guess this little one is pretty territorial."

"Most bitches are," the man says, not looking too happy. He brushes some fuzz from his suit jacket. I don't correct him that Rocky is not a female dog and therefore his statement doesn't punch like it should.

I take two steps back from the man, Rocky stops wiggling, and the little beast lets out an angry growl at the man.

"I'm sorry, but this is a private bar," I tell the stranger, hugging Rocky to my chest. "Are you here for business?"

The man pulls his sunglasses off and places them on top of his bald head, looking around the clubhouse. "Sort of," he says. "Where is everyone?"

Something isn't right. Rocky and I both have racing hearts. Rocky lets out another loud bark, making me jump.

"They're in a meeting," I tell the man. "You can leave a business card, and I'll get it to the owner."

The man's eyes move back to mine and he scoffs. "'Owner,'" he mutters. "You mean the presumptive president."

I stammer, not sure what to say to this man. I don't have any idea how much the public knows about HPMC or what I'm allowed to disclose to anyone who asks. The hair stands up on the back of my neck. I don't think this man accidentally walked into the clubhouse looking for a beer from our bar. Something tells me I need to get myself out of this situation, even Rocky is acting like he wants to either bite this man or run away.

"You're Christina, right?" the man asks, smiling at me now, looking me up and down with his slimy gaze. Thank God I wore jeans and an HPMC hoodie today, covering my skin from his intrusive stare.

"Yes," I say, and Rocky wiggles in my arms, but I hold him tightly. "Why don't you just leave your card so I can get it to my boss?"

The man scratches his chin and laughs. "Boss? Does he make you call him that in bed?"

My body freezes. How does he know about my relationship with Griff? We don't advertise it. The only people who see us together are the members of the club. I don't have the chance to respond to the stranger's vulgar statement.

Beau suddenly appears and steps between us, blocking the man's view.

"You need to leave," he tells the stranger. "This is private property."

"I've got a message for Griffin Thomas," the stranger calmly replies.

Beau crosses his arms over his chest. "Well, he's busy. Either give the message to me or fuck off, and don't ever speak to or look at Christina again."

The man turns on his heel and walks to the door, but glances over his shoulder before stepping outside. "I'll be back. Tell Griff we're watching."

He leaves, letting the door slam behind him. Rocky turns in my arms and begins licking my cheek as if he knows the man has unsettled me. Beau places a hand on my shoulder.

"You okay?" he asks.

I nod, even though I'm shaking. "Yeah, he just spooked me. I told him to leave! He wouldn't listen to me."

"Shh, it's okay." He scratches Rocky's chin in my arms. "Looks like you've got a guard dog."

I nod. "Rocky's a good boy. He didn't want that man anywhere near me."

"I'll tell Moose that Rocky's welcome to hang out here with you all the time if it makes you feel better," Beau says, using both of his hands to brush my hair away from my face. "Maybe we can convince Griff to get a dog at home."

I shake my head. "I don't think that's necessary. When we're home I usually have you guys, and here I wouldn't mind having Rocky around."

Beau looks at me like he wants to argue, but he lets the subject go. Danny and Griff come to stand beside us, and I put Rocky down on the ground to run after his owner who just emerged from the meeting room.

"What was that about?" Griff asks, looking between the two of us.

"Some guy is looking for you," Beau says, crossing his arms over his chest. "Says he'll be back to deliver his message. Sounds like we need to get some prospects on security watch."

Griff curses under his breath and then looks at me, noticing my body shivering from nerves. "You okay, Princess? Did he touch you?"

I shake my head. "I'm fine, he just . . . I told him my 'boss' was in a meeting, and he somehow knew that I was sleeping with you. He asked if I call you 'boss' when we're together. It just—it surprised me, and

Rocky kept barking at the guy, and I was worried how much longer you were going to be because the guy wasn't budging on leaving . . ."

Griff pulls me against his chest, wrapping his strong arms around me. "It's okay, Chris. The meeting went way over, and I shouldn't have left you alone out here so long. From now on, we'll have someone at the door. This was my fault. You did everything right."

I melt into Griff's embrace, breathing in the tobacco and soap scent that always sticks to him. I concentrate on his heartbeat against my ear as I lean on his chest, letting it soothe me as my own heart slows to an acceptable pace. The man didn't look threatening at all, but the way he spoke to me left me with an ominous feeling. I hope I never have to see that man again, but something tells me that I will.

Something isn't right.

CHAPTER 9

As much as I hated the idea of Danny tagging along with me on my first girls' day with the wives of the MC, after my run in with the stranger, I'm all for having my own personal security guard for the day. And honestly, having a bodyguard as big and strapping as Danny feels nice. I like to imagine I'm some kind of celebrity out for a day on the town with my friends, and I simply cannot go out in public without being mobbed by adoring fans.

Bonnie seems to find it highly entertaining to talk about her sex life with Luis while Danny sits across from us at the nail salon. Me and the three wives are getting pedicures, and the nail artists are cracking up as Bonnie recounts the first time she had sex after giving birth.

"Luis was trying to be so gentle," Bonnie says. "Finally, I grabbed him by the ear and told him that if he didn't show me what I had been missing for the last few months, I was going to kick him out of the bedroom and screw one of my toys."

"Sometimes a girl just has to use a toy," agrees one of the wives, Marnie, scrolling through her phone. "You should have seen the look on Cam's face when he discovered my ten inch beauty. I swear he looked like a little pug puppy, his eyes were so bugged out. I think I traumatized the poor guy."

"What about you, Christina?" Bonnie smirks. "Ever broke into the fun of sex toys?"

I blush and look down at my toes as the nail artist does the first coat of red. Danny picked the color solely based on the name: 'Ravenous Rouge.' I steal a quick glance at Danny, and he arches a brow at me, waiting for me to answer the ladies.

"Actually, I can't say that I have," I say, moving my gaze back to Bonnie, Marnie, and Erica. "I was pretty sheltered growing up."

Erica snorts and giggles. "And now look at you," she says, wiggling her eyebrows at me. "Got yourself more boys than you know what to do with."

Marnie pockets her phone and leans in to whisper, suddenly very interested in the conversation. "So tell us, who has the biggest dick? Who's packin' the best toy?"

It didn't take long for the MC family to figure out that I was dating all three of the men, and now the girls are nothing but curious. Just as I'm thinking about answering their question, I'm interrupted.

"My bet is on Griff," says Sissy, strutting into the nail salon. She sits down across from us, right next to my boyfriend. She's dressed nicer than the last time I saw her—when I was punching her—and she sits what appears to be a Birkin bag on her lap. I can guarantee she doesn't have the money to pay for it herself. She must be dating a sugar daddy or something. "Mmm, that was one fine cock. Does he still do that cool trick with his tongue when he goes down on you?"

She's probably lying, trying to get a rise out of me. My relationship with Griff is still new. We haven't branched out into much else beyond sex, and it's only been the one time. I stare at her, feeling my cheeks flame.

"What the hell are you doing here, Sissy?" Bonnie demands.

"Getting my nails done, duh," she says and then pouts. "Why didn't any of you ladies invite me to girls' day?"

"Because you're not our friend," Erica spits. "You don't belong to this crew. You never did."

Sissy just smiles. "Yeah, I've moved onto bigger and better things, ladies. They put your motorcycle manwhores to shame."

"You should leave," Danny says quietly. His body is tense like a cobra ready to strike.

She turns her head and smirks at him. "I think I'll stay here, thank you very much. What are you going to do? Call Griff and tattle on me for upsetting your little whore?"

Danny starts to stand up from his chair, but I stop him with my voice.

"It's okay, we're leaving soon," I say, only looking at Danny. "I'm ready to go get a drink. Right, girls?"

I turn to look at my new friends, and they all nod their heads. Collecting their purses once they're toes are finished.

"Good call, Chris," Marnie says. "It was starting to smell in here anyway. Kinda smells like trash. Old, used up trash."

The girls snicker and file out of the salon, Danny and I right behind them. He places his hand on the small of my back, handing over a couple hundred dollar bills to the host at the front on our way out. The wad of cash is enough for all the girls' pedicures and a decent tip for the employees.

* * *

Something about the interaction with Sissy has me on edge. Between that and the stranger who visited, something feels off. I don't want to bring it up in front of the girls while we're trying to have a laid back afternoon, so I sit back quietly and sip from my oversized margarita. I try my best to laugh when the girls laugh, to try and keep up with their conversations. My gaze meets Danny's twice before I start avoiding his eyes, so I don't let him see the paranoia in my own.

I'm scared.

More scared than when they tossed me into the back of the van. More scared than when I pulled the trigger on Griff's dad.

We pay our tab with the sound of motorcycles approaching from down the street. The husbands are picking up their wives, and Danny is taking me home on his bike. With the nail salon and Mexican restaurant in the same strip mall, I was constantly glancing around, looking for Sissy to make another unwanted appearance.

I hug each of the girls goodbye, and they hop on the back of their husbands' bikes. Danny hands me my helmet, and I buckle it while he puts on his own.

"You okay, sugar?" he asks before straddling the bike and holding a hand out to help me climb on the back.

"I've just got a theory," I say. "I think we need to talk to Griff and Beau immediately."

He gives me a nod. "They're still at the clubhouse. Shall we?"

I nod, placing my arms around his torso as he cranks up the bike and backs out of the parking space. My mind races with possible scenarios. I could be wrong, but isn't it best to be vigilant when we've got a target on our backs? The situation with Sissy and the stranger showing up a couple of days ago rubs me the wrong way. Something seems sketchy. My mind continues to wander as we pull into the clubhouse and only gets worse as I hold Danny's hand all the way into the office.

The office.

I hadn't even had time to think about how much I feared being in here.

Griff has his legs propped up on his desk, leaning back in his chair with his arms behind his head, but he quickly stands when he notices me and Danny coming in. Beau's across from him in an armchair, and he stands at attention and turns around to stare at me. I've come to a complete stop.

I close my eyes and take three deep breaths, hoping to calm a panic attack that's threatening to break through. I don't want to open my eyes for fear that I'll see an imaginary bullet hole in Griff's head—like the one I put in his father. I can't look at Griff sitting in the same chair, resembling his dead father way more than I noticed before.

"Why don't we go over here and sit?" Danny asks, wrapping an arm around me and pulling me toward a sitting area on the opposite side of the room. It's just the four of us here. I should feel fine, but my mind tells me I can still smell the cleaning products they used to get rid of the blood I spilled. Maybe I should request that the prospects use a new cleaning product from now on. It's silly, but maybe it would help.

I don't open my eyes again until I'm sitting on the couch facing away from Griff's desk.

"Here you go, Princess," Griff says softly, holding a water bottle out for me and stroking a gentle hand across my cheek. "You just took a big step. I'm proud of you."

Even though my heart is racing, I smile from being able to make Griff proud. Moments like this make him seem less intimidating. I wasn't sure I would be able to break through his scary exterior, but here we are.

"Thanks," I tell him, opening the bottle and taking a sip of it.

Danny hasn't left my side.

"Christina has a theory she wants to share with us," Dan says, rubbing my shoulder. "Something interesting happened while we were at the nail salon."

Beau's forehead crinkles with concern. "Everything okay?"

I shrug my shoulders and lean into Danny. "So, while me and the girls were getting our nails done, we ran into Sissy. The weird thing was, she wasn't dressed like she was when she hung around here. It looked like she did a complete one-eighty with her clothes, and she was carrying this designer bag. Like, I'm talking you could pay multiple mortgages with the price of one of those purses. She was probably just trying to get a rise out of me by butting into our conversation and talking about Griff and her new sugar daddy, but . . ."

Griff leans forward in his chair, listening intently. "But what?"

"It just seems like too big of a coincidence," I tell the three of them. "Earlier this week that guy showed up, and then I ran into a completely different version of Sissy. They must be connected, right?" The three men look at me but don't say a word. I pull at a loose thread on my shirt. "Forget I said anything. It's probably nothing. I guess I'm just getting a little paranoid."

Griff leans back in his chair, propping his legs up on the coffee table. "What exactly did she say?"

"She started talking about how good you were in bed," I mutter. "And then she started talking about how she's so much better than us because now she's got a new man in her life. The man that was here was wearing an expensive looking suit, and she shows up with a freaking Birkin bag? I've only ever seen one other Birkin bag in my life, and it was owned by the president of my sorority who had a senator for a father. It's not something someone like Sissy would just happen to own."

"It did seem really strange," Danny agrees. "Though I don't know shit about purses."

"Did you notice anything else out of the ordinary?" Griff asks, nodding.

Danny shakes his head. "No, I kept my eyes peeled after that. No one followed us here."

Griff stands up. "Okay, we'll have Luis look into this. I'll give him a call, and then we'll go home. Christina, why don't you go treat yourself to a drink at the bar? You look like you could use one."

Danny helps me up from the couch. I don't look away from the floor until I'm out of that room again. Beau goes behind the bar to grab a pint glass for me and fills it to the brim with my favorite beer that we have on tap, Shotgun Wedding. Its dark but not too dark. Just enough bitter stout flavor to give it some kick without requiring a fork and knife like the imperial stout we also have on tap.

"Drink up, lady," Beau says, handing me the glass and leaning against the bar on his forearms. "I'm sure it's just a weird coincidence and the two aren't connected, but we'll keep you safe."

I give him a small smile. "I trust you."

A dimpled grin spreads across Beau's face. My favorite dimples.

"What do you say we introduce Griff and Danny to one of our old traditions?" Beau asks.

"Which tradition?" I ask after taking a gulp of my beer. The dark flavor mixes poorly with the remnants of sweet margarita still on my tongue.

Beau and I used to have so many traditions. Some of them I still kept up with when I went away for college, and when I had to return home to Lexington after getting bullied out of the school by my sorority sisters, girls I thought were my friends. The traditions made me feel less lonely. Morning runs, weekend long marathons of shitty movies, reading by candlelight whenever it stormed, late night Taco Bell runs when I had a really bad day, ice cream Sundaes on Sundays, stargazing in the bed of his truck with tons of blankets and pillows . . .

I miss what the two of us had in high school, but I know we had to grow up. Now that we've found each other again, we can continue our traditions; we get to share them with my two new boyfriends as well. I may not have grown out of my love for Beau, but I do need to let go of what we had in high school. Things are different now, more real, and there's more at stake.

"I'm thinking of a nice little picnic at the park for dinner," Beau suggests. "We can pick up some of that wine you love."

"The cheap stuff from Target?" I ask, grinning.

"Hell yeah, I've got five bucks," he says. "What do you think?"

I smile. "That sounds very adorable and romantic. Not like something three tatted up motorcyclists would be interested in doing."

Griff locks his office as he finishes his phone call. I chug the rest of my beer and wipe my mouth with the back of my hand.

"Pretty sure these three motorcyclists would do anything for you," Beau admits.

I hop off the bar stool and meet the three of them at the door. Danny and Beau both wrap an arm around my shoulder, and I catch Griff rolling his eyes at us as he holds the door open.

CHAPTER 10

Luis couldn't find anything on the stranger who came into the clubhouse. We haven't seen Sissy since the nail salon two weeks ago. Everything has been rather quiet, even Rocky hasn't made a peep while he hangs out with me during the day. Moose was ecstatic that Griff allowed him to bring his dog to work everyday. Moose's wife works long shifts as a nurse at the university hospital downtown, so if he were at home, Rocky would be cooped up all day. At least he gets some exercise following me around the clubhouse and taking the trash out with me.

I toss the garbage into the dumpster behind the building and turn around to head back in. Rocky runs ahead of me, and I watch as he disappears back into the building. I'm almost to the entrance when someone comes up from behind, making me startle. They clasp a hand over my mouth before I have a chance to scream. I stumble as the person drags me back around the building and pulls me against their body.

"Princess . . ." whispers a voice in my ear. I relax when Griff wraps his arm around me. "You look delicious today."

I smile against the hand that he still has over my mouth and lean my head back against his chest.

He keeps me pinned against his sculpted body and trails a hand down my hip and under my flowy black skater skirt. His fingers trail over the edge of my lace panties, and I instantly feel myself become aroused. I'd be lying if I didn't say Griff scaring me didn't turn me on. Something about how dangerous he is, how unpredictable, drives me wild. And he knows it.

He chuckles softly and slips a finger under my panties.

"God, you're always so eager," he whispers and then licks a line up my neck. A breeze tickles the wet trail, making me shiver. "I want to fuck you right here. All by myself."

I whimper against his hand and grind my ass back against him, agreeing.

Without missing a beat, he spins me around and pins me against the back of the building. He lets his eyes linger all over my body, taking his time, his hand still over my mouth. I don't want him to move that hand, but I still think about the things he could replace it with: his mouth, his cock, some sort of gag . . .

"I think you like this," he says, staring me in the eyes. "I think you get off on me taking you prisoner. Maybe I should go inside and get some duck tape to put over that pretty mouth of yours. Remember when you stumbled into our lives? Didn't I promise to tie you up really well?"

I nod my head. If he didn't have me pressed up against the cold cement of the building, I would be on my knees begging.

Griff smiles. "You *do* like it," he says smugly. "Sadly, I don't have any of my special rope here right now. Would you let me tie you up later, Princess?"

I nod my head and jutt my hips forward, trying to rub myself against him for some friction.

"Have you ever been fucked in public?" he asks, leaning in and nibbling on my neck. He sucks at the delicate skin above my collarbone, marking me.

He moves his hand from my mouth and places it over my neck, lightly choking me. I shake my head no. He tightens his hand around me.

"Speak," he commands. "I asked you a question, Princess. Speak your answer. Use your words."

"No," I say.

"Have you ever been fucked outdoors? Outside where anyone could stumble upon you?"

I bite my lip. "Yes. Beau and I did it in the back of his pickup truck in a field when we were in high school."

Griff growls. "Did he make you scream?"

I shrug my shoulders. We were young, and neither of us really knew what we were doing. "Not really."

Griff smiles again, rewarding me with a kiss.

"As much as I would love to make you scream right now," he says, "I'm going to need you to stay quiet. We don't want you drawing attention to what we're doing and someone coming back here to try and be a hero. I want you for myself right now."

"Please," I say, moving my hands up to grasp Griff's leather cut in my hands.

I don't have to say more. Griff places his hands under my thighs, lifts me up to wrap my legs around his waist, and shifts his hips in line with mine. He braces me against the wall, and moves my skirt up, and then unzips his pants to pull out his hard erection. He yanks my panties to the side and thrusts into my ready and waiting pussy. I gasp at the connection, and Griff covers my moan with a deep kiss.

He thrusts in and out of me effortlessly, and I hold on tightly for the ride of my life. A motorcycle revs from the front of the building, but it hardly registers. Griff grips my thighs and pounds harder into me.

"You're so tight, Princess," he grunts in my ear. "So fucking good. I want to only be inside you for the rest of my life. You're so fucking perfect."

"You mean that?" I ask, trying to get him deeper inside me, grinding against him.

He looks at me with passion in his eyes and doesn't slow his thrusts. "Fuck yes, I mean it. You're ours. You will always be ours. Don't you dare forget that."

He's right. They've made a mark on me forever. I don't think I could ever be happy away from them. Nothing else can compare. I want the four of us to survive and thrive together. Forever.

"Griff," I say, closing my eyes. "You're going to make me cum. I don't think I can be quiet."

He adjusts his hold on me, moving one of his hands to cover my mouth again, and I moan against it, practically screaming against his warm flesh with my entire body.

"Tonight, I'm going to tie you up and put duct tape over your mouth and introduce you to rope play," he promises. "I'm going to make you cum over and over and over. Just you wait, Princess. You're going to be my filthy little rope bunny. Let daddy take care of you right now. Cum all over my cock. I want to feel that pussy throbbing on my cock. *My* pussy."

I squeeze my eyes shut as my orgasm takes over. My walls squeeze against Griff's shaft, and he lets out a curse as he follows me into bliss with his own orgasm. He doesn't pull out until our breathing returns to normal. He slides out and places me on the ground. My legs wobble, and he places my hands on his shoulders for support.

Griff pulls a bandana from his back pocket and kneels down in front of me, lifting my skirt as some of his cum begins to run down my thighs. He gently wipes it off of my legs, folds the bandana, and places my skirt back into place. I lean down and place a kiss on his cheek. For a man who gets off on choking his partner, he excels at aftercare. If someone told me that Griff was such a gentleman after sex, I'd probably laugh in their face before punching them out of jealousy like I did with Sissy.

"After you, my Princess," Griff says, standing up and shoving his messy bandana into his back pocket.

"Not yet," I say, batting my eyelashes like a good girl. "You cleaned me up. Now I need to clean you up."

I don't wait for his reply. I kneel in front of his still bulging cock and take it deep into my mouth, sucking every last ounce of his warm cum onto my tongue. There isn't much left—just enough to show off a little. I gaze up at him, my eyes big, and show him my prize.

He looks like he might faint. "I—"

I swallow his cum and smile before he can stammer out whatever it was he wanted to say. "Thank you, daddy." I run my tongue along the rest of his cock to clean up all my own juices before stuffing it back inside his pants.

Griff is speechless. I stand and place a kiss on his cheek. "There. All clean," I say, spinning quickly so my skirt flutters up for one last tease.

Finally feeling proud of myself, I stretch my back and head around the building, but come to an abrupt stop, making Griff bump into me.

CHAPTER 11

"Good to see you again, Christina," says the stranger that walked right into the clubhouse last week. "Sorry for interrupting your afternoon activities."

I glance at the woman who has her arm looped through his: Sissy. I was right that the two are connected, however, I'm shocked to also see her sister Candy on his other arm. Both of the women are dressed in designer clothes, a huge transformation from their ratty tube tops and mini skirts.

"Who the fuck are you?" Griff demands, standing stiff as a board in front of me.

The man reaches a hand out to shake Griff's, but he doesn't accept it.

"Name's Stanford Williams, I'm the president of an MC in Louisville, Demon Rebirth," says our stranger, placing one of his hands in the pocket of his slacks. On reflex, Griff reaches his hand to the holster at his hip, ready to pull his gun in the blink of an eye.

Stanford chuckles and puts his hands in the air. "Woah there, buddy. I'm just here to talk. Me and your pops had some unfinished business, and I hear he's dead and gone, so I need to take up my business with his heir."

Griff nods in the direction behind the man. "Well, why don't we go out in the open and you can talk to me and my men together."

We're blocked back here. The building on one side of us, a tall, barbed wire fence on the other. There aren't any doors at the back of the building for re-entry, no exit for us back here. Griff wants to remove us from the situation. I place a gentle hand to his hip, letting him know I'm still with him, that I trust him.

The man rolls his eyes. "Of course. Ladies, after you."

Sissy and Candy walk ahead of us, followed by Stanford. His name sounds like a law firm, not a person. I reach for one of Griff's hands, and he gives it a gentle squeeze as we follow the man to the front of the clubhouse.

"Go inside," Griff whispers to me. "Get the guys. Tell them to be on alert."

I scurry inside, my heart racing in fear. Most of the members are just hanging out, playing cards in small groups, or drinking at the bar.

"Griff needs everyone outside," I yell into the room. "The president from another MC is here. He said be on high alert."

Chairs scratch against the floor. The men don't even ask questions. Beau and Danny come out of the office hearing the commotion, and all the men file out of the building, guns in hand.

"You okay?" Beau asks, coming up and placing a hand on my flushed cheek.

I nod. "He's got Sissy and Candy with him. I'm not sure if his MC members are nearby. Griff wants backup just in case. I'm worried."

"We got it, sugar," Danny says as we head outside.

The whole MC is standing behind Griff when we come out. Stanford paces back and forth. Sissy and Candy are standing to the side, their eyes watching Griff. I try to control my emotions. Now's not the time to have a cat fight with Griff's ex-hookup.

"You scared?" Stanford asks, laughing like a cocky asshole. "I just came to bargain with you. No need to gather your crew for a show of force."

"What makes you think we want to bargain with you?" Griff asks. I want so badly to be by his side, but the rest of the MC is blocking my way to him. Protecting me. Backing up Griff.

I try to peek over one of their shoulders, and Stanford's gaze meets mine. He gives me a wink. It makes my stomach twist.

"I know you guys burned down the daycare," Stanford says. "Every club in Kentucky knows it, actually, including the owners of the building. Word on the street is, they're cooking up an attack on your whole MC . . . and those that you love."

"Why should we believe you?" Beau demands, taking his place right next to Griff. Danny flanks him on his other side.

"Because I've got connections, and I can end the war with a snap of my fingers," Stanford replies, snapping his fingers for effect. "It's just going to cost you."

"What do you want?" Griff asks, his voice betraying boredom. Almost like he doesn't believe a word coming out of this man's mouth. But why should he? None of us have a clue who he really is.

I'm standing right behind Luis, and he's got his phone out. I notice him type out the plate number on the black G-Wagon idling in front of the clubhouse. He plugs it into a database where it pulls up a mugshot of Stanford Williams along with some other information that looks useful. He takes a screenshot and texts the info to Griff.

"I want the girl," Stanford says, nodding his head toward me. Everyone turns to look—everyone except Griff. "Christina. Hand her over, and I'll make sure all your troubles disappear. She was promised to me by a Mr. Thomas who I believe was your father."

My heart sinks in my chest. I can't believe what I'm hearing.

"Fuck no!" Griff roars. "She stays with us. She's ours."

"I do believe the girl can speak for herself," Stanford says, and then he turns his icy attention to me. "What do you say, Christina? Want to come be my queen? Believe me when I say I can give you way more than three of these men combined. Their MC is going to crumble. It will burn just as that daycare burned. Mine is thriving. Flush with money and everything else you could ever desire."

"What the fuck, Stan?" Sissy asks, smacking him on the arm. "I thought we were good enough for you!"

"Do not *ever* touch me like that again!" Stanford yells. He places a hand around Sissy's throat, choking her, hurting her. It's not playful or sexy like Griff was with me moments ago behind the clubhouse. Candy screams from beside them and takes off running.

Sissy falls to the ground when Stanford releases his grip, gasping for air. As much as I hate her, I need someone to go check on her. A man gets out from the G-Wagon, scoops up Sissy like she weighs nothing, and tosses her into the back seat.

"Christina," Stanford says again, cracking his knuckles. "All you have to do is walk away from here. I can give you whatever you want. I can promise you safety. Why don't you come with me?"

I squeeze past Moose and Luis and pause next to Griff.

I reach down and twine my fingers with his, he gives my hand a squeeze.

"You're a lunatic," I tell the man in front of us. "What makes you think I would betray these men? I've got all I need here."

Stanford laughs. "Silly girl, someone needs to show you some manners," he turns his attention over to Griff. "You should have just handed her over to me. You sentenced your whole club to death. She's going to be mine, one way or another, and your little club of misfits will be no more."

Weapons are raised by the men standing at our sides, and Griff drops my hands and pulls the pistol from his waistband.

Stanford doesn't even flinch.

"Get. The. Fuck. Away from my property," Griff says through

clenched teeth. I'm not sure if he's referring to the clubhouse or me. Either way, I share the sentiment.

The man turns away from us, heading back to the waiting car. When he gets to the door, he turns around and addresses me.

"I'll be seeing you soon, Christina," he says before climbing in the car and shutting the door.

Luis comes up next to Griff and places a gentle hand on his shoulder.

"I sent some info to your phone about Stanford Williams," Luis says. "I can look deeper now that we have more to go off of."

Griff turns to him, putting away his gun. "Good job, Luis. I think we're going to disappear for a little bit. I don't think it's safe here."

Luis nods. "What do I need to do?"

"Tell everyone to get their families, leave town, go to your designated safe houses until I give word," Griff says. "No one is to return to the clubhouse until Beau or I say."

"What about the election?" Danny asks.

Griff shakes his head. "We'll figure it out. Our priority right now is our families and our brothers. Keep your phone on you, Luis, just in case."

"Yes, sir," Luis says, speaking to Griff like he's the older, wiser man, but Luis is about fifteen years older than Griff. "Good luck."

Griff doesn't let go of my hand as we walk back into the clubhouse to grab his backpack from the office. I try to be brave for Griff when we enter the office, but tears come to my eyes, and I start shaking when I see a drop of blood on the corner of his desk.

"Hey, hey," he says, placing his hands on either side of my face. "What's wrong, Chris?"

"Bl—" I stutter and point to the spot. "Blood. It's not clean. Luis missed a spot. Fuck, why isn't it gone?"

Griff glances down and uses his thumb nail to scratch at the spot of blood. It doesn't smear. Why would it? It's dried. It's been weeks since I murdered his father and the others.

"Baby," Griff says. "It's just paint, I spilled some paint the other day."

I shake my head. "No, you're lying, it's blood! It's his fucking blood!"

Griff pulls me against him as the panic attack starts to erupt full force. There's just too much happening. The election, some unknown threat supposedly coming from everywhere all at once, and I just *cannot* go into hiding again. Not after I finally feel like I'm getting some sort of normal routine back in my life.

"Christina, I have never lied to you. It's not his blood, baby. I need you to be brave for me right now, I need you to relax and breathe. We've got to go."

I quickly nod and try to match my breathing to Griff's. I hear someone enter the room, but I'm not sure who it is. Griff won't let go of his hold on me. He just keeps telling me to breathe in, breathe out.

When I finally calm down, he bends over and lifts his backpack from the ground.

"Can you ride on the back of the bike, or do we need to get Danny's car?" Griff whispers.

I shake my head and cling to him. "I can ride on the bike. I'll be okay."

"Why don't you guys go get some clothes for us," Griff asks, and I turn in his arms to see a worried Beau and concerned Danny. "Act fast. Chris and I will meet you at the safe house. Grab the package on top of my dresser."

They both head out the door. From the look on Beau's face, I can tell it took all his strength to just walk away and follow Griff's orders. I know he wanted to come over here and make sure I was okay and safe.

"Come on," Griff says, grabbing my hand and pulling me out the door.

Once outside, he swipes my helmet off of Beau's bike and walks over to his. I put it over my head, and we wait on his motorcycle until the last member leaves the property.

* * *

The drive to the safe house is odd this time: less scary because I can see the scenery around us, the beautiful mountains and trees we pass as we go down the back roads, and Griff keeps reaching down with his left hand to rub my thigh. Everytime he reaches back to touch my flesh, it feels like a promise. A promise to always keep me safe.

We come to a stop in front of the cabin, and it's completely quiet out here once Griff cuts the engine. I climb off the bike and remove my helmet, smoothing my skirt back into place, and stretch my legs. Griff removes his helmet and takes mine from his hands, pulling the cabin key out of his pocket and going to unlock the door. I close the door behind us and watch as he takes a walkthrough of the cabin, making sure that nothing has been disturbed.

He comes from the back room, his room, and places our helmets on the island.

"All clear," he says.

"How far behind do you think Beau and Danny are?" I ask softly, going over to look out one of the windows as if they'll pull up right behind us, but there's nothing but forest.

"Probably forty five minutes," Griff says, coming up behind me. I catch sight of his reflection in the glass. Even though I know I should be scared right now—Griff would never make a full evacuation of the MC without feeling scared himself—my body aches in a familiar way that only happens when my guys are around.

I realize this is the first time I've been alone with Griffin.

He notices me draw in a ragged breath.

He places a hand over my heart and I lean back against him, closing my eyes at the sensation.

"Your heart is racing," he whispers against my ear. "You're safe. Try to relax, Chris. We're going to keep you safe."

My heart doesn't slow. I turn around in his arms and look up at him through my lashes.

"I'm not scared," I say shyly, placing both my hands on his chest. It is a lie, or least part of a lie. "I'm—"

"What's wrong, Princess?" he asks, placing a gentle hand on my cheek. "Tell me."

I bite my bottom lip, not sure how to tell him what I want. My mom always told me that if I didn't feel comfortable talking about sex, I probably shouldn't be having it, because if I can't talk about it, how can a man give me what I want?

"I know I should be scared right now," I tell him, staring at my hands on his chest. "But all I want is for you to take me to your bedroom and play with me. I wanna shut out the world."

"Play with y—" he says, and then it hits him. "What about Beau and Danny?"

I look up at him, ignoring his question. "Do you have toys here?" I ask softly.

He shakes his head. "I've never had a reason to have toys here. You're the only woman who has been in this safe house."

I run my hands down his torso and lift his t-shirt over his head. He removed his MC cut before we left town, trying to hide his identity on the road just in case we ran into trouble. I hook my finger in his belt loop and urge him to follow me down the hall.

"Guess I'll have to be the only toy you get to play with then," I say with a smile.

Something changes in his eyes, and I release his belt loop and let out a shriek as I run toward his bedroom.

"On the bed, Princess," he commands as he unbuckles his belt and slides it out of the loops. I crawl up the bed and lie my head on the pillows. "Now, are you going to be a good little girl?"

I nod my head but flinch when Griff cracks the belt.

"Use your words," he says.

I stare at him, letting my eyes trail from where his jeans are hanging on his hips, up his tattooed torso, and to his face. He looks at me like he could eat me up.

"Yes," I sigh. "I'll be a good girl."

Griff crawls up the bed and hovers over my body, the belt still gripped in his hand. He drags it over my cheek, and I close my eyes, sort of expecting him to slap my face with it, but he doesn't.

"Who do you belong to?" he asks me.

"You," I whisper, but he shakes his head, and I try again. "Daddy."

He smirks and places a kiss on my cheek. "Good girl. Now, daddy's going to take care of you, okay?"

A quiver of anticipation glides through my body. "Okay."

"Did you think of a safe word for when we're playing?" he asks, straddling my torso with his powerful legs.

I nod. "Yes." I wiggle underneath him. I want to play—he's taking too long.

"What's your safe word? When you want me to stop completely, what will you say?"

"Mercy," I tell him, moving my hands to unbuckle his jeans, but he grabs my wrists.

"And what about when it becomes too much, but you don't want me to stop, you just want me to back off a little?"

I didn't know I was going to need two safe words. I sit there and ponder for a moment, trying to think of something sexy that wouldn't ruin the moment but also wouldn't come up during play time.

"Trigger?" I ask.

"Perfect," he says, and then has me repeat my safe words and what they mean two more times before taking both of my wrists and binding them together with his belt. I didn't even realize that the notches went all the way around his belt. He's literally been wearing a belt that he could tie me up with forever.

He shrugs his shoulders, noticing my surprise. "I said I didn't have any toys here, not that I didn't bring any with me."

He pads down the hall and comes back with his backpack, tossing it on the bed, and pulls out two items from the small pocket. He brings them up to show me, and I blush.

"Have you ever worn one of these, Princess?" he asks, holding up a black butt plug.

I shake my head as he opens the cap on the bottle of lube. "Why did you happen to have that in your backpack?"

He grins and applies some lube to it. "I was waiting for the perfect opportunity to make you wear this. Think you can be a good girl and wear this all evening?"

I shiver as he holds the plug in front of my face. Yeah, I've done anal now, but this is different. I've got zero experience with toys. Does it feel good? What pleasure will Griff get out of it?

"Princess, you've got to answer me," Griff says sternly. "Do you want to wear this butt plug for daddy?"

"Yes," I say. "How do I put it in?"

He places the plug on the bedside table and grins. "First I'm going to fuck you, and when you're ready to cum, I'm going to fuck your tight little ass with that plug. Only I can remove it, got it?"

"I understand," I tell him.

In an instant, he pushes up my shirt and bra, exposing my breasts. He sucks on one of my nipples as he slides my skirt up to my hips. His hands are unapologetic, taking what he wants, and I don't dare move my hands that are bound above my head. Griff pushes his jeans and boxers down his legs and moves his mouth to my other nipple, making it unbearably hard. I thrust my hips skyward, begging for his cock inside my body.

He rips my panties down my legs. "I don't think you're going to have much use for your underwear around here," he says with a smile, licking a line from my breasts up to my neck.

"Griff," I beg. "Please."

"Aww, is my Princess going to beg?" he mocks.

My cheeks flame. I'm mad at him for taunting me. I pull at my wrists, but he reaches one hand up and holds them where they are, thrusting into my waiting pussy hard. I let out a scream, and he praises me.

"Good girl," he says, and thrusts harder and faster into me. He moves his hand from my wrists and uses his thumb to rub circles on my clit. It feels so good that I almost beg him to stop. There's something about this cabin that's sexually liberating for me. I don't have to worry about anyone hearing me scream. I'm safe, I'm happy. For a little bit, I can forget about the outside world threatening to hurt us.

"You ready to cum, Princess?" Griff asks, his voice low and labored.

"Yes," I moan.

I feel something poke at my back hole, and I freeze. I was so lost in my pleasure that I forgot what Griff promised to do to me. The toy.

"Relax," he says, continuing to rub gentle circles on my clit. "You can cum when you let me put this in that pretty, tight asshole of yours. I want it to be mine."

"It's yours," I promise, trying to calm down. I faintly hear the sound of motorcycles in the distance. My guys.

"Better hurry," Griff says, pushing the toy a little more. "I'm not sharing you right now, and I don't want your boyfriends getting jealous."

I bite my lip and relax, sinking down onto the plug as Griff pushes it the rest of the way. I gasp as he makes sure it's still in place, and then he's back to pumping into me and rubbing my clit faster.

"Cum for me, Princess," he demands. "Squeeze my cock with that pussy."

"You're so fucking crude," I fire back just as my walls clench around him.

"And you fucking love it, you dirty girl," he says, leaning down to cover my scream with his mouth. I feel him release himself inside me.

Griff places kisses all over my face before pulling out of me and grabbing a wet cloth from the attached bathroom to clean between my thighs. He unbuckles the belt from my wrists and places kisses where the leather was biting my skin. Someone calls our names from the front of the house, but I'm too high on my pleasure to respond.

"Good girl," Griff says again, smiling at me and tossing the wet rag into the empty hamper.

I squirm a little, waiting for him to remove the butt plug, but he just leans down and picks up my skirt, sliding it up to my hips.

"Griff, the plug," I wine. "We need to get out there and make sure everything is okay."

He brushes some hair behind my ear. "We will, but you're keeping the toy in place. Can you follow those orders?"

I shrug my shoulders, and he helps me sit up in bed. It feels odd, but I think I can do what he's asking of me.

Griff pulls on his jeans and t-shirt and tosses my panties into the hamper. He comes over and reaches out a hand to help me off the bed, and I follow him carefully down the hall where the other guys are waiting for us.

CHAPTER 12

Griff takes a video call from Luis with the guys in the living room. I excused myself and went to the kitchen to make myself useful, but now I'm sort of just standing in front of the cupboards without a plan. I'm craving brownies so badly, and I find all the ingredients I need in the small pantry and fridge, thankful that Danny stress bakes, or else half the stuff I needed probably wouldn't be stocked in the safe house. I take the apron from the pantry hook and put it around my neck, double wrapping it around my waist and securing it with a bow.

Luis tells the guys about the new dirt he managed to dig up, and I stand at the edge of the kitchen. Griff glances toward me, obviously seeing the worry on my face.

"What's wrong?" he asks, putting up a finger to stop Luis mid sentence.

I wring out my hands. "I just wanted to know if Bonnie and Carlos are okay."

The side of Griff's lips lift in a smile, and he turns to Luis. "Christina wants to know that you're keeping Bonnie and Carlos safe."

I hear Luis let out a sad chuckle. "They're fine. Carlos just went to sleep, and Bonnie is taking a bubble bath. I should be attending to her soon."

"And you, Luis?" I ask, peeking around to see him on the laptop screen. "Are you okay?"

He raises his voice, not sure where I am in our house since he can't see me on screen. "I'm going to be okay. Keep my boys safe, Chris."

"I will!" I say back. "Night, Luis. Give Carlos a hug for me."

I go back to the kitchen to start hand mixing my ingredients together, letting the guys finish their meeting. I'm moving slower than I normally would, being careful to keep the toy inside my body. It's surprisingly not that uncomfortable, and every time I feel it in my ass it sends a shiver of pleasure up my spine.

"Whatcha making?" Danny asks, coming up to stand behind me, gently brushing his fingertips over the skin on my arms.

"Brownies," I answer, nudging him away when he tries to suck on the delicate skin of my neck. He wraps his arms around me and grinds us against the kitchen counter, making me spill some of the flour I was getting ready to pour into my bowl. "Dan! I'm trying to bake!"

I can hear the smile in his voice. "Let me help you crack the eggs. I've got a little trick for you."

He takes an egg in each of his large hands and cracks them on the side of the bowl at the same time. He somehow manages to not break any shells into the bowl. Usually, I have to dig my fingers in and try to pull out broken bits of shell. Though if I'm being honest . . . I've totally just left a little bit of shell in an omelet before.

"Your hands are bigger than mine," I grumble. "Of course you can easily crack two eggs at once."

"I'll show you how at breakfast tomorrow," Danny whispers his promise into my ear before backing away and smacking my ass.

I yelp at the contact and squeeze my muscles so the plug doesn't move.

"Someone's jumpy," Beau remarks, pulling a beer from the fridge and cracking the top. "You okay?"

I shrug my shoulders. "I mean, I think I have good enough reason to be jumpy. We had to evacuate the whole clubhouse and scatter the members across the safe houses. We have no idea what exactly Stanford is plotting to do. First Griff's father kidnaps me, and now we've got another threat. When will it stop?"

I'm breathless when I finish, and I lean my hands on the counter, gripping hard for support. Beau comes over and stands beside me, placing a kiss on my forehead.

"It's going to be okay," he says. "Luis is still learning more stuff about Stanford and Demon Rebirth. Once he thinks he's dug up enough, we're going to come up with a game plan. In the meantime, you're safe here with us."

Griff stands in front of the island behind us, and the kitchen suddenly feels small with all my guys in it.

"Take off your skirt, Princess," Griff commands.

Beau scoffs. "Griff, buddy, I don't think this is the time. She's scared. Keep your dick in your pants for once."

I look over my shoulder at Griff and wipe my hands on my apron. I know exactly what he's doing.

"I'm trying to take her mind off of the situation," Griff says as though it is such an obvious explanation. "And show her she has nothing to fear, we'll take care of everything for her. That's what a dom is for: safety, security. Now, take your skirt off, Princess. I don't want you chancing getting it dirty. You can keep the apron and shirt on."

I nod politely and slide the skirt down my legs, carefully bending over to pick it up and hand it to Griff who folds it and places it on the counter behind him.

"Oh," Danny says from behind me as I finish putting the ingredients in the glass bowl and start whisking them together. "Looks like someone brought a toy with them."

"What?" Beau asks, confused, looking me over, but he can't see the butt plug from where he stands.

"You're going to need a pan, Princess," Griff says. "Those are in the bottom cabinet on your left."

"I'll get it—" Beau starts to say, but Griff cuts him off.

"She'll get it," he commands, not taking his eyes off of me.

I finish whisking and walk over to the cabinet, bending over for the pan, but it's not there. I turn just in time to see Griff's wicked smile.

"Sorry, wrong cabinet," he says, shrugging his shoulders. "I think it's the one up above. My mistake."

I roll my eyes, opening the cabinet above and pulling out a rectangular glass pan.

When I turn back around, I find the gazes of three hungry men eyeing me. It makes me smile and blush at the same time. It also kind of makes me feel powerful, like I can use my sexuality as a super power or something.

"See something you like, Beau?" Griff asks, but when I turn to Beau, he just nods his head. "Don't forget the cooking spray, Princess. We don't want the brownies sticking to the pan. We learned about proper lubrication earlier, remember?"

"How could I forget?" I answer with a smile, reaching next to the stove to grab the spray.

I hear Griff walk over behind me. He rubs his hands over my ass and grinds himself into me before sticking his finger in the brownie batter. He tugs on my pony tail and tells me to open my mouth. I suck the sweet batter off his finger like a good girl.

"Is it nice?" he whispers against my lips.

I nod, and he places his finger back into the batter, putting another small amount into my mouth.

"Let me taste it," he says, moving his lips to my mouth and darting his tongue in to take the batter from me that I just licked off of his finger. "Mmm, that tastes good. Can't wait for them to be done,

Princess. Why don't you finish up and meet us in the living room. I've got a gift for you."

The oven pings that it's done preheating just as the guys leave the kitchen. I smile and bend over to put the brownie pan into the oven, setting the timer. I hear Danny groan as he walks out of the kitchen behind Griff and Beau. I put the dirty dishes in the sink, clean off the counters, put the unused ingredients away in the pantry, and wash my hands, all while having a shit-eating grin on my face. Griff is driving me insane with his toy, but I also get to drive the other guys inane as well. I didn't realize being a submissive for Griff was also going to feel this empowering for me.

I dry my hands on a towel and head into the living room. The guys are all three sitting on the couch—the only place to sit because there's no other furniture besides the coffee table in here. My pulse races thinking about what I did on this couch with Danny the last time I was here. I glance at him and he winks at me, probably thinking the exact same thing.

"Open your gift, Princess," Griff says, motioning to the wrapped box on the coffee table. It's wrapped in newspaper, and I smile when I pick it up. "We don't really do gifts in this fucked up family. I didn't have any gift wrapping paper."

"That's okay," I say, sticking a finger under the wrapping paper to rip it off the box.

I crumble the paper and drop it on the table, opening up the white box. There's black leather inside. It smells like genuine leather too, which means this was probably a pricey gift.

I stare at it in the box and then lift my eyes to Griff's. "This isn't something you want me to wear in the bedroom right? You don't have a leather fetish?"

He rolls his eyes. "Just pull it out of the box."

I lift up the leather and discard the box. It is a leather jacket in my size. It has a little patch on the front, like Griff's 'president' patch, except mine says 'First Lady.' I smile and spin it around, looking at the back. There's a matching patch like everyone in HPMC has: a skull with flames burning in the background.

"You got me a matching leather jacket?" I ask.

"Do you like it?"

I nod, sliding it on over my shirt and apron. It fits like a glove. "I love it. Thank you."

"Figure you're a part of us now, might as well start looking the part as the future First Lady of this MC," he says with a smile. He pats his lap, requesting me to come sit.

I obey him, and when I sit, I feel the plug get a little more snug inside me. Griff unties the bow of my apron and removes it over my head, tossing it to Danny to get rid of.

"Damn, Princess," Griff says, looking at me without under-wear, in only my white tee and the black leather jacket. "You look so fucking hot."

I squirm in his lap, crossing my legs because I feel like I'm about to drip some of my excitement all over his jeans. When will I ever stop being turned on by the things these three men do and say to me?

Griff reaches under my shirt, pulling the cup of my bra to tweak one of my nipples.

"Please—" I start to say, closing my eyes and dropping my head back.

"Please what, baby?" Griff asks in his husky bedroom voice that I love to death. I want to hear that voice every day for the rest of my life.

I whine and push my chest into Griff's hand, but he pulls it out of my shirt completely.

"Use your words, Princess," Griff says. "Or did you forget how?"

"Please touch me more," I answer, lifting my head to stare him in the eyes. "Please, Griff."

He chuckles and instead of moving his hand back up to tease my tits, he pushes me over his knee so my head rests in Beau's lap. Beau moves my hair out of my face, playing with some of the stands as

I relax into his lap. Griff runs his calloused hand over my bare ass cheeks. He moves down to where my ass meets my thigh and grips it, pushing the butt plug up a little. I begin to squirm on his knee, so he uses his other hand to hold me in place.

His fingers graze over my ass until they reach the butt plug, and then he tugs on it a little. I whimper, and he lets go of the plug to spank me.

"Princess, trust that we'll take care of you," Griff says. "Relax."

I try to calm my body as best as possible, and Griff moves back to the butt plug, slowly pulling it out and pushing it back in, playing with my tight hole, teasing it. He and Danny probably have the best view of my ass right now. Griff pulls me up, using my hair to drag me where he wants me. He sits me between Beau and Danny, where he was just sitting, and kneels in front of me.

"Hold her legs open for me," he tells the other guys as he spreads my thighs wide, and the guys do as he commands. "Look at that pretty pussy. So fucking wet."

I whimper and try to close my legs, but Beau and Danny have them secured.

"Don't be embarrassed, baby," Griff says, running his tattooed fingers up my inner thighs. "It's hot. I remember when you made a mess of this couch thanks to Dan. You think I can make you squirt just the same?"

"I—I don't know," I stutter, closing my eyes, dropping my head back against the couch.

"You don't know?" Griff mocks. I let out a scream as I feel his hand smack my bare pussy. "I'm telling you I can."

Griff leans forward and sucks my clit into his mouth. He shoves two fingers into my dripping cunt, and I scream with pleasure. I feel that same sensation in my belly as Griff curls his fingers inside me and flicks his tongue quickly over my clit. It's the feeling like I'm going to pee myself, and I try to hold it back as best as I can. I try to close my legs, I try to wiggle away, but the guys have me secured. I could use a safe word to get out of this, but I don't want to. I like it.

I like being controlled.

"Come on, darlin'," Danny says in my ear as Beau leans over and kisses my neck. "Cum on Griff's face. Squirt all over him. You can do it. Make a mess for us."

I moan and whimper as Griff's mouth continues it's torture on my most sensitive spot. When I can't handle the feeling of holding it in any longer, I let go. Griff pulls his mouth from me and moves his hand to rub my clit as the liquid gushes out. His mouth is dripping when I look down at him, and he pulls his shirt off to wipe himself dry before standing up and flipping me over to straddle Danny.

"Take his pants off, Christina," Griff says, but I'm so wracked with ecstasy that I only barely hear him. The oven beeps signaling that the brownies are done. I start to push up to go take them out of the oven, but Griff forces me back down. "I'll get them out to cool, you take Danny's pants off."

I unbutton Danny's jeans, and he helps me shove them down his legs. I straddle his hips again as Griff comes back and stands beside me.

"Take what you want, Princess," Griff says, leaning over me.

Danny holds his hard shaft for me, and I sink down on it. Another groan escapes my lips. I can feel his pelvis against my legs, and I know he's completely inside me. I place my hands on his shoulders for support as I rise up and down on his cock. His hands are on my hips, giving me some assistance until I get the rhythm just right. Danny tugs me down to place a kiss on his lips, and I tense as I feel someone's hand on the butt plug.

"Relax, baby," Griff says softly. "You've been a good girl, so we're going to reward you by having all of our cocks inside you."

I rest my head on Danny's chest, stopping my thrusts as Griff slowly removes the toy from my tight hole. When it's gone, I whimper from the loss of being full, but also relief.

"Who do you want to fill this pretty hole?" Griff asks, his finger rubbing the entrance.

"You, please," I answer meekly, wiggling my ass to entice him. I reach my hand out for Beau's cock as I feel the pressure of Griff's trying to push into my ass. Beau undoes his jeans and lets them fall down his muscular legs before he slides off his boxers in similar fashion and allows me to take his member into my small hand.

I bite my lips so I don't scream as Griff slides in an inch. It stings a little, but not as much since he prepared me with the toy. Danny reaches up and urges me to stop biting my lip.

"Make all the noise you need to, baby," he says. "No one can hear you out here, only us."

For anyone else, those words should be a red flag. Hell, if this were two months ago, I'd be scared to death at those words. I trust these men though—I trust them with my life now. And not just because I don't have much of a choice. I trust them because I *want* to trust them. They're my guys, and I need them.

I glance over my shoulder at Griff who is laser-focused on not hurting me. "Let me do it," I say. "Let me take you in."

Griff looks me in the eyes and gives me a nod as I slowly sink back against him, taking him inch by inch. When I finally have Griff and Danny all the way inside me, I give Beau a stroke with my hand.

"I'm ready," I tell the guys. *My* guys. Waiting for them to take over the movements, to use my body for their pleasure. Griff pulls out, and as he pushes back in, Danny pulls out. I hover over them, and they quickly find a rhythm. I try my best to concentrate on stroking Beau, but it's hard when each of the men are so distracting.

I look at Beau sitting right next to us, and he watches me with awe.

"I want your cock in my mouth when you cum," I tell him, and he groans at my dirty words. "I want each of you to cum inside me."

"We can do that, Princess," Griff says with a rough grunt. I've still got the leather jacket on, and it squeaks as the guys thrust in and out of me. The smell of leather and each of the guy's signature scents starts to mingle together. Leather, tobacco, mint, the brownies cooling on the oven, the cologne that Beau has worn since junior year of high school; I want to turn this scent into a candle and light it anytime I feel lonely.

Danny reaches between us and starts rubbing slow circles over the little nub there. It's sensitive from my first orgasm, but that's just going to make the next one so much easier. The question is, just how many orgasms are the guys going to try and pull out of me before they let my body rest?

"Please," I beg, not sure what exactly I'm asking for.

"Aw, what, baby?" Griff asks, leaning over my body. "We can feel you holding back. Stop."

"I want you to cum too," I beg. Beau takes his cock from my reach, and I watch as he slowly strokes it next to me.

"We will," Griff promises. "But first you're going to cum two more times, once for each of us in total. From now on, that's what you're giving us. You want three boyfriends, you have to have three orgasms. Can you be a good girl and do that?"

I whimper. Before I fell for these guys, I had never cum from sex with a guy. I always had to have the assistance of my vibrator. I haven't needed to get it out since I met these guys.

Griff smacks my ass, the sting making me jerk in Danny's lap. "Answer me, Princess."

"Yes, daddy," I gasp. "I can cum three times for my boyfriends."

"Mmm," he growls. "I think I can get used to that pet name, baby. Give us our second."

Danny circles my clit harder and leans forward to suck one of my tits into his mouth, and Beau uses his other hand to play with my tit. Griff rams into me from behind and it's suddenly sensation overload. The dam between my thighs bursts.

I cum again with a scream.

"Good girl," Danny says, releasing my breast from his mouth and looking up at me with hooded eyes. "Only one more to go."

* * *

I'm absolutely spent by the time the guys make me cum once more. I'm cuddled up in bed with all three, only wearing a long baggy shirt, when Griff's phone rings. We're in the middle of a movie, and I was almost out cold from tiredness, but the phone has my skin pebbling with goosebumps. It's nearly one in the morning—this can't be good.

"Luis," Griff says after swiping his phone to answer and putting it on speaker so the guys can hear.

"Turn on the news," Luis says. "Lex18. We're fucked."

Griff grabs the remote and quickly changes the channel past several screens of static until he reaches the correct one. There's a reporter standing in front of a firetruck. All four of us bolt upright in the bed to watch, and Griff turns up the volume.

"No one was in the club building at the time," the blonde woman with a microphone says calmly. "It appears it was an act of arson. Local police are saying that it's a possible turf war between two rival motorcycle gangs."

"Motorcycle club!" Griff corrects through gritted teeth.

"Oh, fuck my dick!" Danny shouts at the screen. If I weren't completely terrified, I would make a joke with Danny that I already fucked his dick tonight. A chill runs down my spine. The camera pans to a wide-angle shot of the debris. There's basically nothing left.

"Fuck," Griff mutters. "Have you found out any more information on Stanford?"

"Right before I saw the news," Luis answers. The service out here in the woods isn't great, and his voice is garbled with a veil of static. "I think Stanford and your father were trying to merge their clubs at one point, but then Stanford wouldn't let your father take on some of the business and your father retaliated by burning down the daycare. Stanford owned that building.

"One of our guys called me," Luis continues. "He's freaking the hell out. He told me about some stuff that your old man was getting into right before his death. He thinks that your dad was planning on handing over Christina in order to get more of their business. He thinks your dad wanted to start getting into human trafficking."

Griff turns and looks at me and the boys, his eyes bloodshot from exhaustion. "Who gave you this info?"

"Randy," Luis says. "He's scared shitless, boss."

Griff sighs. "I'll give him a call. Stay alert, and keep your phone near you for further instructions. And I'm sure it goes without saying, but stay armed. We don't know what's coming next."

The other line is silent for a moment before Luis speaks again. "What are we going to do, boss?"

"I don't know," Griff answers after a pause of his own. "Just keep your head low and keep researching. I know you're probably exhausted, but we can't rest right now. We need to stay on our toes."

"Of course, boss." The phone line goes silent.

Griff stands up and pulls on his boxers and sweatpants. The other two guys follow his actions. I pull the blankets to my chin, wishing the world would stop being so chaotic for just one minute, and worried about asking the wrong question. Worried that if I speak, it'll make this more real.

"I'm going to call Randy," Griff says. "Danny, see if you can remote access the cameras and catch anything. Beau, start the phone tree, let everyone know to prepare for the worst. I believe Stanford just declared war."

"What can I do?" I croak from the middle of the bed.

He glances over at me and gives me a sad smile. "Going to need you to pack, Princess. We're going to be on the move again."

"Where to?" Danny asks before I can.

"Everyone needs to meet at the warehouse," he replied, nodding to Beau. "Let them know to report there in twenty-four hours unless told otherwise."

Danny and Beau jump into action. I follow suit by picking up all our discarded clothes and putting them into the correct backpack to whom they belong. Griff is talking on his phone in the corner of the room as I pull on a pair of leggings, one of my shirts, and the leather jacket he got me. Griff raises his voice at whoever is on the phone, making me flinch. He notices and comes over to place a gentle kiss on my forehead.

"You should have come to me sooner with this information," he tells the person on the other line. "Now we're in the middle of a gang war because of my father, and the enemy has the upperhand."

I can hear the man's muffled begs of forgiveness on the phone, and I shiver.

"Look, brother," Griff growls, "I'm not my father. I'm not going to torture you for fucking up. Just don't screw us again. Get your head on straight and meet at the warehouse in twenty-four hours."

Griff hangs up the phone, and I stand there quietly, wrapping my arms around myself like I'm trying to hold my body together. I'm still a little sore from earlier, but the nerves have taken away some of the pain. I love the life I have with these guys, but when is everything going to relax? It's been nothing but hell since I met these men; the kidnapping, murdering Mr. Thomas, and now this issue with the other MC and Stanford. Stanford who owns the human trafficking group. Was he planning on selling me?

Griff wraps his arms around me, and I try to relax into him.

"We'll keep you safe, Princess," he says. "It's not going to be easy, but we're going to get out of this mess that my father created."

CHAPTER 13

I've been quiet since we got the call from Luis. I've been thinking non-stop. While the men have been plotting a plan on how to take out Stanford and his MC before they try and take out Hell Prevails, I've come up with another plan—something I think will work better, but the guys aren't going to like it.

Luis finally confirmed that Stanford is the Louisville MC's president, which will work for the plan I have up my sleeve.

I ride on the back of Beau's motorcycle on the way to the warehouse. He occasionally reaches one hand back to rub my thigh, and I smile at the touch. I wish we could live in this bubble forever, riding on the back of Beau's bike with the other two men flanking our sides.

We get to our exit and drive down a country road, passing the occasional church, cemetery, a couple of hoarder houses or double wides, and farms. Beau turns on his right turn signal and we ease onto a gravel road with a couple old 'no trespassing' signs. One of them has what appears to be a bullet hole, though if it is, it's obviously ancient. The headlights of the bikes hardly give off enough light to read the faded letters. I get a sense of déjà vu as we drive. Yes, I've been here before. This is where they burned my bloodied clothes that first day. This time we don't stop at the small lake where I bathed. We continue on another mile down the dirt road.

Beau slows down and comes to a stop at the end of the gravel lane. He shuts off the bike and props us up on the kickstand as the guys do the same behind us. When the headlights go off, we're in complete darkness. Someone helps me off the bike and holds my hand after I take off my helmet. I can't see a damn thing out here in the country, so I follow along blindly with the guys, their boots crunching on the gravel until we reach a heavy steel door large enough for two cars to pass side by side.

"Welcome to the warehouse," Griff announces. He unlocks the door and ushers me in before turning on some lights. I blink a couple times, trying to adjust to the fluorescent brightness. There are some folded tables sitting against a wall and two racks of folding chairs. On another wall are some cots lined up. They don't look comfy, but I'm sure they serve their purpose.

"You hungry?" Danny asks me. "We've got a full kitchen we keep stocked here, though everything is canned or powdered, of course."

I shake my head. I couldn't eat right now even if I wanted to. My stomach is in knots.

"Where is everyone?" I ask.

"They'll come in waves," Griff tells me. "Help Beau set up the cots. He'll show you where we keep the linens."

I follow Beau to a storage closet and take a stack of sheets from him. We quietly make all the beds. There's about thirty of them, so the task takes us a little bit. None of us are really saying much. The guys must be just as scared as I am.

Griff paces back and forth on the hard concrete floor. "Can I talk to you?" I ask. Danny has been working on a laptop in the corner going over security footage with Luis. A few other club members arrived right after us, and the tension in the air is severe.

Griff runs a hand over his face. "Yeah, sure thing."

I follow him out of the room and down a hall to where the bathrooms are. Beau's right outside one of the industrial windows keeping guard. He's holding a large rifle with a scope, and he has at least one pistol on his hip.

"I have an idea," I tell Griff as we come to a stop. He leans against the wall opposite of me.

"It's not as stupid as your idea to rescue me and Danny, is it?" he asks. "Because if so, that'll be a giant fuck no for me, Princess. You're not risking anymore for me and the guys of this club."

"Griff, just . . ."

"No!" he shouts. "I will not risk your life, Christina."

"I don't want to be your damsel in distress!" I fire back, half whispering and half yelling. "I want to help protect your family, *my* family! Please, just listen to what I have to say."

He laughs wickedly and crosses his arms over his chest before looking back at me. "Fine, what's your plan?"

* * *

"The guys are going to kill me . . ." Griff mumbles.

"That's the best part," I tell him. "You get to pretend like you didn't let me run off. I'll leave a note on my cot saying that I can't live in this constant fear of danger. That I'm going to take Stanford up on his offer because he seems like he's willing to keep me safe."

A tear slides down Griff's face, but he quickly brushes it away. "*We* can keep you safe."

I press my hand to his cheek. "I know you can, but I want to keep our MC safe, too. I'm part of you now. Let me do my duty."

"You're so fucking reckless, Christina," he says, his brows pinched with rage. "If you get yourself killed, I'll fucking . . . I don't know. But it will be bad."

I give him a sad smile. "Just follow the plan. I've taken out a president before, I think I can do it again."

"But at what cost?" Griff asks. "The nightmares—"

I shake my head. "It'll be okay."

I lift the duffle over my shoulder and hand Griff my leather jacket. "Will you hold onto that for me?"

He takes it and hugs the leather to his chest.

I pull the engagement ring off my finger and hand that to him as well. "Save this for me too, please. I'm going to be back for it. I promise."

The plan is simple. I'm going to pretend like I've ran away from my guys. I'm going to make Stanford think that I want to be his. As soon as I gain his trust, I'm going to let Griff know, and he's going to have Hell Prevails retaliate the moment Stanford is least expecting it.

"Good luck at the election," I tell Griff. "Don't let Beau beat himself up, and keep Danny in line."

I swallow, hoping that the guys don't spiral out of control in my absence. I hope Danny doesn't believe that I'm gone forever, and I hope Beau knows that I'm still going to love him no matter what happens over the next few weeks.

Griff gives me a nod. "If Stanford lays one hand on you, I'll fucking kill him."

I stand on my tiptoes and press my hand on his chest, speaking right against his lips so our breath mingles. "If Stanford touches me, I'll stab him in his chest until he takes his final breath."

"That's my girl," he whispers.

I place a kiss on his lips and hand him the letter he helped me write to the guys. He gives me a set of keys to a car he keeps at the warehouse, and I push the backdoor open as quietly as I can.

I don't look back at Griff. I don't linger to see Danny and Beau sleeping on their cots with the rest of the MC because I know that if I do, I won't be able to follow through with the plan. I'm not only breaking one heart as I leave this time, I'm breaking four. I just hope they can forgive me.

EPILOGUE

Beau

The sound of birds chirping brings me out of my sleep. I lift my watch to look at the time. It's not even seven yet. My back aches from the lack of support. The cots are fucking awful. It's quiet in the warehouse, everyone is still sleeping. I turn to my side, expecting to see Christina sleeping peacefully, but her cot is empty. Danny is passed out on the cot beside her abandoned one. She must have gotten up to go keep Griff company or to use the restroom.

I sit up on the cot and rub the sleep from my eyes before taking a drink. My water bottle is just about empty. When I look at the bed again, I see a folded piece of paper and Christina's leather jacket lying on top of the rumpled sheets.

I quickly pick up the paper, unfolding it with shaking hands. A sinking feeling in my chest tells me that I know what it is before I can read the first line.

To the men who I'll never forget,

I can't stay here with you. I have to leave. If I don't, we're all dead. Please don't come after me. I don't want you to rescue me. I'm stronger than you think I am, and I don't need the three of you risking your lives for me.

I'm going to give Stanford what he wants. After all, I was apparently always meant to be his thanks to Mr. Thomas. Maybe that's how it should be, just me and one man. A woman isn't meant to love three men at the same time. That was just make believe. We were fooling ourselves if we actually thought this was going to last forever. You guys would have eventually gotten bored of me, bored of what we started.

Maybe Stanford will get bored of me as well, and if that's the case, I'll be getting as far away from Kentucky as possible after my plan is complete. Don't wait for me. I'm not coming back.

It was fun while it lasted,

Christina

My heart shatters.

LOVE PREVAILS

CHAPTER 1

It's cold. My skimpy outfit does nothing to keep the wind at bay as I stand outside the gentleman's club waiting for him to show up. I check my watch again. He's ten minutes late. He's never late, maybe he's given up on me—I wouldn't blame him. I hold my hoodie tighter over my body, trying to cover as much skin as possible. A set of headlights glaze over my hiding spot behind the building, and they flash twice before I dart across the sketchy parking lot and hop into the passenger seat of the familiar car. This has been my only safety for the last few weeks. Sneaking away to be with him for a few moments here and there.

He drives us over to the corner of the lot and backs into a parking spot before he says a word to me. It's been two long weeks since I've seen him, but it's been four weeks since he lost his spot as president of Hell Prevails Motorcycle Club. It's been six weeks since I've seen the other two men.

Griff's tatted fingers squeeze the steering wheel after he turns off the car. "He's got you working at his strip club now?" Griff asks through clenched teeth. "What's next? Is he going to start pimping you out?"

"It could be worse," I say, shivering at the thought of him selling me in his human trafficking ring. It certainly *could* be worse, that is not something I enjoy thinking about.

I found out a little over a week ago that the president of Demon Rebirth is the same monster that's running one of the biggest sex trafficking rings in Kentucky. I just need to figure out where he's keeping all the girls. Griff keeps insisting on pulling me out of this place, but I want to shut this shit down and free the women and children before I even consider my own safety. I could probably escape, but what would it mean if I left all those people to suffer?

Griff finally turns to me and blanches as his eyes find my face. "Who did that to you? Did he fucking touch you, Princess?"

He's referring to the giant purple bruise on my eye. I thought I covered it well enough with makeup, but I guess I sweated it off while dancing on stage. I've got absolutely no experience with stripping, but one of the other girls just said to wiggle my ass, push out my tits, and circle the pole. None of us get to keep the money we make here. It goes straight to Demon Rebirth's MC. I found one of the girls crying about not being able to afford formula for her baby this week, so I handed her some cash I had stashed, cash that Griff had given me the last time he checked in. One of Stanford's goons saw the exchange and told Stanford, who then stormed out of his office and backhanded me a couple of days ago. His temper has gradually gotten worse. I'll either end up sold or in a shallow, unmarked grave somewhere out in the woods. At least it would be a pretty resting place.

"Griff," I say, trying not to cry. "You were ten minutes late. I only have ten minutes left before I need to get my ass back in there. Don't waste it."

He pulls me across the console and into his arms, holding me tightly. "We could leave right now, you and I, Princess. I can get you out of here. We can go where no one will find us."

I shake my head. "No! It'll ruin the whole plan! I'm not ready to finish the job yet."

He lets out a breath and softens his hold on me. I pull back and run my fingers over his beard. It looks like he's neglecting self-care, his beard could use a good trim. It's almost as unkempt as Danny's was the last time I saw him. He closes his eyes and gives a sad smile. I stroke his scruffy chin.

"How are they?" I ask, obviously referring to Danny and Beau.

He shakes his head. "Danny is a fucking mess. He's been drinking himself stupid. And Beau . . . he's pissed as hell still; he's not going to stop until you're back on our turf, whether it's by your choice or if he has to force you to come home. I can't hold him off much longer, Princess."

"It won't be much longer," I promise. "Think we can take a vacation once this shitshow is over?"

"Anywhere you want," Griff answers, running his hands up and down my torso. "I'll buy you a plane ticket wherever you want to go, and we'll stay there as long as you want. You deserve whatever you want."

I pull Griff to me and crash my mouth into his, sucking on his bottom lip. My tongue flicks out to run across the seam of his lips and he lets me in. For a moment, it's just Griff and I, a normal couple savoring a private moment together. I let all our woes drift away for the time being. I've noticed a change in Griff since the last time I saw him. He's become closer to me, more protective than before. I think losing his spot as president might be the reason. He's letting go of all the high expectations his father and the club had for him, and that's a painful transition to make.

Beau won the election by a landslide when the MC voted. I guess after HPMC's clubhouse was burned down and Mr. Thomas' connections to the rivals came out, no one wanted the heir to the MC to take the throne. It's made it easier for Griff to sneak off and visit with me, but Beau has him on a tight leash. I know he's probably getting suspicious. It's understandable. I wish he was able to sneak away more often to give me updates and help me plot the takedown of DRMC from the inside out.

"I miss you so much," Griff says softly, the kiss quickly going from hungry to something new with him. Dare I say . . . love, affection? "I miss waking up next to you, I miss this bratty little attitude of yours, I miss you at the kitchen table drinking your morning coffee, I miss watching the way my brothers care for you. You belong with us at home."

Just then, his phone lights up in the cupholder, the vibration making me flinch, and we both look at the screen.

"Answer it," I tell him when I see the name on the screen. "Please, I want to hear his voice."

I pick up the ringing phone and hand it to Griff who answers and puts it on speaker.

"Hey man," Griff says, hitting his head on the headrest. "I'll be back in like forty-five minutes. I had to go buy some smokes and needed to get away."

He's lying, of course. Griff hasn't smoked in weeks. Not since I asked him to quit because I'm not a fan of kissing an ashtray. I guess Beau hasn't noticed that Griff no longer smells like smoke, but why *would* he notice? They're probably all back to sleeping in their own bedrooms now that their shared girlfriend is gone. We only shared a bed because of me.

"You can't just leave like that, Griffin," Beau scolds, his voice holding more authority than I remember. "First she leaves, and now you're running off all the time? We're on high alert. I can't babysit you and Danny both. Just get your ass back home as soon as possible. Club meeting in thirty. If you're not here, I'll rip the patches off your cut myself."

Before I can stop myself, I let out a soft cry. The other end of the phone is silent for a moment, before Beau's voice becomes urgent, panicked.

"What was that, Griff?" Beau asks. "Griff, who the fuck are you with?"

"No one," Griff mutters, holding me tighter as I begin to quietly sob into his neck. "I gotta go. See you soon."

"Griff," Beau yells. "If she's with you, you need to bring her home where she belongs! I swear to Go—"

Griff ends the call and tosses his phone back into the cupholder where it immediately starts ringing again. Neither of us touch or look at it.

"He's going to be so pissed, Princess," Griff mumbles, running his hands through my tangled hair. "I hate sneaking behind his back. He's like a brother to me. You know that."

I place my hand softly on his cheek. "It won't be much longer, Griff. For once, just do what I say, and you'll have me home soon. I swear, I'll come back home to you."

He chuckles. "I'll try my best, but just so you know, the second the three of us get you back home, you're never leaving again. You're grounded for the rest of your life, Princess."

I give him a sad smile and brush another kiss on his lips. His beard tickles my chin. "Yes, *Daddy*. I'll never leave again, I promise. I just need to get the information we need to take these fucks down."

"That's my girl," he says, his hand wrapping around the back of my neck and pulling me in for an earth-shattering kiss. I have to end it too soon. If I don't get back inside in the next fifty seconds, who knows how many more bruises Stanford will put on my body?

* * *

"Girl, where have you been?"

I almost jump out of my hand-me-down stripper heels at the voice, but it's not angry, just one of the other dancers worried about the repercussions of my actions. When one of us steps out of line, we're all punished.

"Sorry," I tell her, looking in the mirror to fix my makeup. "I got sidetracked in the parking lot."

"Lucky for you," she says, adjusting her C cups in the too-small lace bra she's wearing. "Stanford had to step out for a meeting. Surprised you didn't cross paths out there."

My spine goes ramrod straight. *Shit!* What if Stanford saw me get in the car with Griff? Hopefully the windows are so tinted he would never have the chance to see me. Thank God Griff drove a car here and not his bike. The car is way more subtle. Still, the hairs on the back of my neck stand straight.

"There was also someone here asking for you," Mercedes says. I know that it's a fake name—we all have fake names here. There was no way in hell I was going to let some creep call me by my real name. I decided to go with Kitty. I'm not sure why I picked it, but I've kind of grown to like it.

"Someone asking for me?" I arch an eyebrow at her and turn from the mirror.

She leans in and whispers: "Not Kitty, he was asking for Christina."

My eyes go wide. "What the fuck. How did he know my real name?"

She shrugs her shoulders. "I don't know, but he's in private suite six waiting for you. Said he wants a *private* dance." She puts the word "private" in air quotes which is basically our signal that a client is being extra weird.

My body crawls with shivers. I've only been asked for two other private dances, and I hate them. At least when I'm on stage, the bodyguards are there to kick out anyone who tries to touch me without paying. On stage I can pretend like it's just me and no one else exists. When I'm in a private room, I have to actually interact with the customer, I have to speak, I have to pretend like I'm interested in fucking them—even though Stanford says we're not to fuck the customers.

That's what his prostitutes are for, and they don't work on the stage. Griff might be right . . . pimping me out could be the next phase if I don't get out of here soon.

"Good luck, Christina," Mercedes whispers, placing a gentle hand on my shoulder.

On the walk to the private suite, I draw up my walls that I let down when Griff visited. I push thoughts of my men out of my mind, I stand up straight, and I prepare myself for the private dance. When I get to the door, the green light is on, and I flip the switch beside it to change it to red as a signal that the room is in use.

I scold myself. My hand shakes on the door handle.

I straighten up and push through the door, closing it behind me, and letting my eyes adjust to the dimly lit room. It reeks of bodily fluids and God knows what else. It's about the size of the studio apartment that I lived in before my life was flipped upside down, with a couch on the back wall and a bucket of beers sitting on the coffee table in front of it. A box of off-brand tissues sits next to a trashcan in the corner. A pole with a mini stage takes up the rest of the room just in case the customer wants a private show to go along with their lap dance.

I recognize the song playing over the speakers: *Sex Metal Barbie* by In This Moment. I heard it back at the MC clubhouse a couple of times. I used to love this song and how liberating Maria Brink would make me feel, but now it brings nothing but dread. I wonder if I'll ever be able to listen to this band again without thinking about my time as a sex worker for Stanford Williams.

Shaking my hips as I walk over to the customer, I look up at him and find a familiar face. He's one of Stanford's guys, not one of the top men in the club, but he's still a member of the MC. I've seen him lingering around in the last few weeks, but he usually sticks to himself. He's always quiet and always watching. The club holds him at arm's reach which is odd to me. Something is off about him—I can feel it in my gut. I just have to push that uneasy feeling away because I've got a job to do.

"Hey, handsome," I say, sauntering to stand beside his spread knees. "Mind if I sit?"

He looks up at me and gives a single nod, sitting back against the couch. I place my hands on his shoulders and climb onto his lap, my knees resting on the side of his thighs, as I begin to softly roll my hips. I push back the vomit threatening to come up. This man is old enough to be my father, yet here he is wanting me to ride and grind on him. He's not as rough and tumble as the other members of Demon Rebirth, though, he's more clean-cut, but I still wouldn't want to meet him in an alley alone at night.

"You don't say much," I comment.

He doesn't make eye contact, just looks at my throat, almost like he's trying to avoid ogling me—as though the visual show isn't a main part of the attraction. "I could say the same about you," he finally grunts. I'm thankful I can't feel his cock hardening yet. Maybe he has issues getting it up, I don't take offense. I should thank him for not getting turned on instantly like most guys.

I shrug and lean into him, pressing our chests together. "Isn't that what I'm supposed to do? According to your president, women should be seen and not heard. I think Stanford would cut out all of the women's tongues if he didn't deem them useful sexually."

"I've been watching you," he says, and I flinch as if he slapped me. Does he know what I've been plotting? "You're not a woman who is going to sit down and smile pretty because you've been told. I know the things you've done. I know what you're capable of."

"I don't know what you're talking about," I tell him. I flip around to grind on him while facing away. I don't want him to be able to see my face. "I'm just trying to survive."

"I have an offer for you," the man says, and I almost roll my eyes.

"I'm not sucking you off for money," I tell him. "You know the rules. You bought a private dance. So why don't you just shut your grumpy mouth and enjoy it?"

To my surprise, he still doesn't feel like he's enjoying the dance at all. I'm getting no reaction behind his zipper. I look at the countdown timer in the corner of the room as the song changes to some rap music I've never heard before. I've got fifteen minutes left of this dumb lap dance.

"I don't want your mouth anywhere near me, sweetheart. I like my women a little classier," he says, leaning up to whisper in my ear. "Besides, pretty sure your *boys* would skin me alive if I tried that. And I'm not referring to Stanford."

My body freezes. "I don't know what you're talking about. I have no one."

He chuckles and leans back. "Uh huh, a girl like you doesn't have anyone. Word on the street is you've got three special someones."

I grit my teeth. "Leave them out of it. What do you want?"

"Your cooperation," he says, his breath reeking of garlic next to my ear. "I know you're trying to get some intel for your boys, but I need you to work for me. We've been trying to shut this MC down for years—"

"We?" I ask, trying to turn from his face before I gag. Would it kill the guy to pop a breath mint? They even sell them in the bathroom from a little dispenser. They only cost a quarter.

"I've got some friends in the Mafia, Miss Christina," he whispers, and I stop my sensual dance. "We need your help. And if you can get your boys to cooperate, we'll grant them immunity from all the gun and drug charges we could put against them from back when Mr. Thomas was alive. And don't you think I don't know about the murders you committed. We've got eyes everywhere, little Kitty. I just need your help putting this club to extinction. You have evidence, I'm sure of it."

My gut tells me not to trust this man. What if he's lying? I didn't even know the Mafia had any ties to Kentucky. Why the hell would they want to help us out and grant us safety from the downfall? None of it makes a lot of sense.

"Why should I believe you?" I demand. "What if you're just putting a bigger target on our backs, and I'll be known as a rat for the second time in my life? Stanford would kill me, no questions asked. He'd kill you too if he knew you were a mole in his club."

"You've just gotta have a little faith," the man answers. "Help me take out Stanford's human trafficking ring, and I'll keep your little harem out of harm's way when shit hits the fan. There's a war coming, Christina. You need to pick a side."

I glance at the clock on the wall, realizing we only have ten minutes left to figure out a plan to shut down Stanford. That's all my life has been since walking into Stanford's gang—me counting down the hours and minutes until I can figure out how to get back to my men, that is . . . if they all even want me back. If this man is lying, all our lives are on the line. I take a moment to mentally weigh the pros and cons, but I'm not sure how much more I can take from Stanford's sick games.

"Okay," I answer. "Tell me what I need to do."

CHAPTER 2

"Christina!" Stanford yells up the stairs from the foyer. "Get your tight little ass down here. We need to leave! Now!"

I muster the best nauseous face I can and spray my face with water from the spray bottle. I'm wearing a robe over my leggings and t-shirt when I leave my room to look down the stairs.

"I'm sorry," I call back. Stanford gazes at me with angry eyes. "I can't go, Stanford. I've been vomiting since breakfast."

"Fucking bitch," Stanford mutters under his breath, but I can still hear it. "You know you're supposed to be my arm candy today."

"Do you want me to vomit all over the fairgrounds?" I ask. He's got some business to attend to. To me, it just sounds like he's employing some carnies to get him more women and children to sell on the black market, which makes me want to actually vomit. "I can't go."

My body freezes as Stanford runs up the stairs two at a time to get to me, and his hand snaps out before I can jerk away. He hits me so hard across my cheek that I fall to the floor and taste blood in my mouth. I hear Sissy and Candy snicker as they come out of their rooms. I've tried to ignore them the best I can. I'm *almost* thankful that they've stuck around to keep Stanford's bed warm. I try not to imagine what would happen if they weren't here, and bile rises in my stomach thinking about Stanford forcing his way into my room.

"Fine!" Stanford says. "But don't you dare think you won't get punished for this. Maybe I'll see one of your boys tonight and have to teach him a lesson because of you."

"No!" I plead before I can stop the words. "Leave them out of this, Stanford. I came to you! You promised you would leave them alone."

Stanford laughs wickedly. "Oh, baby. Don't you know not to trust me? Such a dumb little whore you are."

He kicks me in the stomach and I curl into a ball, gritting my teeth, praying that he leaves. I glance up just in time to see Sissy lean into Stanford.

"Come on, baby," she whispers into his ear. "I'll give you a handjob on the Ferris wheel."

Stanford pinches her cheek and praises her. "That's what good girls do. Come on then. Let's go see if Hell Prevails wants to play a little game tonight. Maybe we'll have a nice trip to Lexington after the state fair . . . and go hunting for some men."

He won't find them today.

The guy that claims to be part of the Mafia gave me a crash course on the secret history of Mr. Thomas and Demon Rebirth MC. Apparently, Mr. Thomas took a cut of the sales that Stanford got from human trafficking. At one point, HPMC was trying to merge clubs with Demon Rebirth. I was promised to Stanford for a pretty penny as bribery, something to sweeten a deal, but Stanford wanted more, and that pissed off Mr. Thomas, which is why I was used to burn the daycare Demon Rebirth owned.

I use the anger that I'm feeling for Stanford as fuel I'll be adding to the fire tonight. This is the beginning of the end, and I can't wait to see our victory.

* * *

"Showtime," says the Mafia member, knocking on my door frame a couple of hours later. "You ready to end this?"

I nod and stand from the bed. I don't even take one final glance at this room that I've called my prison for the last couple of weeks . . . weeks that have felt more like years. I leave the room the same way I entered it: with nothing but the clothes on my back. Besides, Stanford liked to dress the girls under his roof in the clothes he picked out. I didn't want anything to do with the sleazy wardrobe he bought me. I wanted to burn it down, just like I was going to burn their clubhouse down tonight, just like I burned down the daycare months ago for Mr. Thomas. Everything is coming full circle, an eye for an eye since they destroyed the clubhouse of Hell Prevails. The place I was finally starting to call home.

"Ready," I tell the man. I still haven't learned his name or much about him personally. All I know is what he wants me to know. Stanford left him and three of his prospects here to guard me. The mobster has already handled the three prospects, putting some sleep agent in their beers and knocking them out for the evening. I stare daggers in their direction as we pass through the kitchen. All three men sit at the table, their heads down and dark playing cards with fancy backs scattered across the table. If you asked me, they almost look like they're not breathing at all. Maybe he actually poisoned them. I can't bring myself to care. I want to make Demon Rebirth extinct for all they've done.

The man escorts me outside where a shiny black town car awaits. He slams the door once I'm settled in the backseat, and the driver doesn't say a word. I don't ask any questions. I know my task tonight. I'm readying myself for it. I called Griff from the mobster's burner phone earlier and requested that he meet me once I'm done. I didn't tell him what I was planning because I didn't want his help. I want to do this on my own. The Mafia is planning something, and they want Demon Rebirth out of the picture. Who am I to argue with that? As the saying goes, the enemy of my enemy is my friend.

The Mafia is en route to the warehouse where the "merchandise"—kidnapped women and kids—are being held while the clubhouse burns to the ground. They have three buses on speed dial to pick up the women and children once the distractions are made. Griff will be at the Demon Rebirth clubhouse waiting to pick me up, per my instructions.

My ribs ache where Stanford kicked me, and I try to push the pain away as we drive up to the clubhouse. There's no sign of Griff yet, but I told him to give me at least fifteen minutes. Just enough time to get in and out. Nice and easy.

I climb out of the car and grab the gasoline and other supplies that I'll need and shut the trunk right before the car speeds away, its taillights shining. It's dark out, not a soul in sight. The DRMC clubhouse is on the edge of town, in a bad area known for crime, though that's most of Louisville. No one comes out here unless they're looking for trouble. I've only been to the clubhouse twice in the time that I've been under Stanford's control. The activities that go on here make the things that I saw at HPMC's clubhouse look like child's play. The moment I walked into this clubhouse, I watched Stanford put a bullet hole in some poor prospect's head while he was taking advantage of a girl who looked like she wasn't even a teenager yet.

Stanford wasn't upset over the fact that the prospect was touching an underage girl, no, he was pissed that the girl went down in value by about ten grand because she was no longer a virgin. *Sick fuck.* I wish I could set *him* on fire, but his club will have to do—for now. Maybe someday I'll get the chance.

There are ghosts in the walls of this clubhouse, and they're about to become ash.

I don't hesitate. Gas spills from the jerry can in a pungent wave.

The Mafia guy gave me three bottles of cheap vodka and an equal number of old shop rags soaked in grease. Three Molotov cocktails. I throw one through each window and light that motherfucker up, smiling as the warmth of the fire penetrates my body. When I burned down the daycare, I thought it was so Mr. Thomas could have dirt on me if I ran off and reported their club to the authorities. Now I realize I was just a pawn in his game, and he had no intention of releasing me unless it was as a bribe or payment to Stanford. He was going to trade me to Stanford like I was just an object. Burning down that daycare was the best thing I've ever done, and I smile thinking about the kids I've saved from these dangerous men. The ones I'm saving right now.

"Just like the old days," says a familiar voice behind me. I didn't even hear his bike pull into the gravel lot.

I turn around and dash to Griff, ignoring the pain in my ribs.

I launch myself at him before he has the chance to get off his bike or even cut the engine.

He wraps me tightly in his arms, placing a hand on my head and softly stroking my hair. My heart aches from the time I've been away from him. I move only a few inches away, just enough to connect my lips with his. We only kiss for a moment before Griff is shoving my helmet and leather jacket at me.

"We gotta get out of here," he says quickly, helping me onto the back of his bike once I'm dressed for the ride.

I wrap my arms around his torso and give him a squeeze to let him know I'm ready. I take one final glance over my shoulder at Stanford's club going up in flames.

* * *

My heart races as we pull down the familiar street.

Home.

The house is brightly lit, the garage door open when we pull in.

Danny's car is here, but his bike isn't sitting beside Beau's like it usually is. Griff pulls up between the car and Beau's bike.

"Danny's out with some prospects right now," Griff tells me as we close the garage behind us. "He should be back in a few hours. He'll be so happy to see you."

I can hear Beau's booming voice coming from the living room. He must be arguing with someone on the phone. I've never heard him raise his voice like this. I shrink back into Griff as Beau curses and ends his phone call, his heavy boots stomping down the hall toward us.

Griff puts his hands on my shoulders and bends down to whisper in my ear. "I'll be right here. It's okay," he says, urging me to walk farther into the house. I sort of find it funny that Griff is now trying to protect me from one of the only people I'm not afraid of in this twisted world. We both set our helmets in the mudroom before entering the kitchen.

"Where the fuck have you been, Griff?" Beau shouts, bending over to pull a beer out of the fridge. He hasn't even looked up at us. "Shit's hitting the fan and you run off without a word . . . again? If you were president and I did that, you would be tearing my ass up and making me do prospect work. You can't keep bailing on me, man. I *need* you."

"Beau," I whisper, moving closer. The words barely escape my mouth. He stands up and closes the fridge but doesn't look. Maybe he things he's just imagined my voice, like he thinks if he looks he might be disappointed at not seeing me. Or like Lot's wife, perhaps he thinks he'll be turned into a pillar of salt if he turns around. Or maybe . . . he's disappointed to see me. "Beau, say something. *Please*."

He finally looks, and it's not with the happiness I imagined being on his face. It's not the tender love that he's always given me. He doesn't open his arms for me to run into them, not like Griff did when he picked me up tonight. He doesn't take a step toward me, doesn't even crack a smile. I would take our reunion from a few months ago over this void between us. At least I saw tenderness in his eyes when he realized who I was while covered in blood by the lake. Now he's looking at me like I'm a blood stain on the carpet.

Griff clears his throat behind me. "Look who I found, Beau. Our girl is back."

I stare down at the ground and count the steps that it takes for Beau to walk over to us. He stands there silently until I look up at him.

"You left me," he says flatly. "Again."

My heart breaks. Actually, it shatters into a million pieces.

Could he really believe I would leave him like I did in high school without saying goodbye? That I would simply walk away? I thought we had gotten back on track, that he knew I was going to be his girl forever.

"I know, but I did it for us!" I plead, trying my best to smile. "I left to help you. And tonight, I helped again. I burned down their MC, and there are people releasing the women and children that he had holed up in a warehouse to sell. He was *trafficking* women and children, Beau, I couldn't sit around and do nothing! Beau, I helped—"

"You burned down their clubhouse?" he asks, voice even. Not even a touch of warmth graces his words.

I try again to smile. "I got revenge for them destroying ours."

Beau grits his teeth and turns to chuck his full bottle of beer at the wall behind him. I flinch as it shatters, beer dripping down the wall, the floor littered with broken glass. Beau has always been very even tempered—I'm not sure who this shell of a man is. He places his hands on the edge of the sink and hangs his head. I don't dare say another word as I watch his body. He's so full of tension. Why didn't Griff tell me things got this bad while I was gone?

"I've had men searching for her every damn day," Beau says, and I realize he's not talking to me, he's addressing Griff. Its like I no longer exist. "I've wasted my men's time searching for her. Put their lives on the line. Danny drank himself dumb over his heartbreak for *her*. Meanwhile, you knew where she was the entire time? You let her go to

Stanford. You were with her the other night, weren't you? You've been disappearing to see her."

Beau shifts only his head to look over at us.

"We were handling things," Griff answers, reaching down to thread our fingers together. "You don't know what she's gone through—"

"What about what *we've* gone through?" Beau shouts. "She fucking disappears in the middle of the night to play hero without saying a word, and you knew where she was while we were busting ass to rescue her."

Beau moves his attention back to me. "I've been a fucking mess since you left. Wondering if I did something wrong. Wondering if you're safe. If you're happy. If you're *alive!*"

"Beau, I'm sorry," I mumble, dropping Griff's hand and taking a hesitant step toward the raging man. "I'm fine. I'm safe. I came back. I'm here now. Please . . ."

As I take another step, my body decides to betray me and finally comes down from the adrenaline. A spike of pain stabs through my torso where Stanford kicked me in the ribs. I wrap my arm around my body like that's going to hold myself together. Griff comes up behind me, and Beau notices my face morph into pain and he's suddenly standing in front of me, finally looking panicked instead of pissed.

"What's wrong?" he asks, reaching for the kitchen chair.

I suck in a painful breath. "I think I have a cracked rib or something."

"From what?" Beau asks as Griff helps me settle into the chair.

I avoid looking at either of him. "What do you think? I took a pretty bad beating today. Got kicked in the ribs."

"That motherfuc—" Griff starts.

Beau cuts him off. "Who did this to you?"

"Stanford," Griff says through gritted teeth before lifting my shirt up to look at the damage. "Fuck, baby, your torso is turning black and blue. You've got a boot shaped bruise on you."

"Why were you that close to Stanford?" Beau demands. He goes to the freezer and comes back with a bag of frozen chicken fried rice. I shake my head at it. That's my favorite meal to cook for myself.

Griff takes the rice from Beau anyway and gently places it on a portion of my bruised skin. I flinch at the chill. Griff and I share a look, not wanting to tell Beau the details of where I've willingly been for the last month and a half.

"Griffin, so help me God," Beau says. "I swear if you tell me you let her walk into that snake's den . . ."

"Beau," I interrupt, looking up at him. "Don't be mad at Griff. It was my idea. I wanted to fight. I wanted to help."

"He's a fucking human trafficker, Christina!" Beau shouts, making me flinch away. "He could have sold you in an instant. We would have never been able to track you. You could have been shipped out of the country in a matter of hours! Were you staying in his house?"

I drop the frozen food from my ribs and stand up, trying to pull Beau's face to look at me. He turns his head from my touch, and I break when I see the tears welling in his eyes.

"Beau, I am so sorry," I whisper. "I didn't realize the damage it would have done to us. I just wanted to save the other women and children. I wanted to protect Bonnie and her babies. I wanted to prevent this from happening to anyone else. I want us to be safe."

He finally looks down at me, brushing tears from his cheeks. "I won't lose you again, Christina. I won't. If you do something like this again . . ."

"I won't, I'm here," I promise. "I'm here."

Beau closes his eyes and leans down to press his forehead to mine. "He didn't—"

I shake my head against him. "No, I never let him put a hand on me in that way. I'm still yours."

"I still want to fucking kill him," Beau seethes. "When I get my hands on him . . ."

"I've got your back, brother," Griff says, coming up behind me and placing a hand on Beau's head. "We're not going to let him win."

Beau's phone rings, but he doesn't pull away from us as he fishes it out of his jeans and answers.

"Hello?" he asks, and I can hardly hear the voice on the other end, but I make out the words 'Fayette County Jail.' "I accept the call."

CHAPTER 3

"I should let his ass sit in the drunk tank all night so he can think about what he's done," Beau mutters. Nonetheless, he grabs the keys to Dan's car. "If he's going to make dumb decisions, then he can sit and think."

"Has it been like this since—" I begin to ask.

"Since you left, yeah," Beau says, running a hand through his choppy blonde hair. It's grown out since I last saw him, almost the length it was when we dated in high school. "And the dumbass hasn't shaved since you left, so he looks like hell. He stopped taking care of himself. He's just . . . gone off the deep end, I guess."

"I didn't realize I meant that much to him," I whisper, hit with a fresh pang of guilt.

"You mean everything to the three of us, Princess," Griff says, grabbing us a snack and some water from the refrigerator.

I'm speechless.

I knew that leaving to try and end this war would hurt Beau, but I hadn't realized that Dan was that deep into what the four of us shared. I figured, eventually, Danny would get tired of me and give me up to Beau. I also didn't ever dream of the day when Griff would start calling me Princess in a sweet way, not his original menacing tone.

"Let's get to Moose's place," says Beau, nodding to the door. "We can have his wife give you a check-up, and then we'll bail out Danny . . . again."

"Let him sit a little while longer?" Griff asks with a grin. "You're a better man than me. I would let him sit there all weekend."

I roll my eyes and grab my jacket. "Come on, let's go. Moose better have some good painkillers. My side is killing me."

Sitting in the passenger seat on the ride to Moose's house, I stare out the window, finally feeling peace for the first time in months. I smile at the thought of helping save those women and children from the trauma they were living, waiting to be sold. I wish I would have been able to see them when they were rescued, but I know I still did *good*. I just hope the mobster was using his connections for good and not evil.

I pull out my phone and search the local news. There's gotta be a story about the release, right? I scroll through the news page and find nothing. Then I go to the Louisville police social media page, but again nothing.

Maybe they're just protecting the identities of the women and children. Maybe they just want to keep it private until everyone is returned to their homes. I'm sure something will break on the news in the next twenty-four hours. I just want to know that they're all okay. But . . . what if the mobsters weren't successful?

"You okay?" Beau asks, glancing over at me as we pull into the driveway at Moose's place.

"Just thinking," I answer. I slide my phone into the pocket of the leather jacket the guys got me. "Shouldn't there be something on the news about a bunch of kids being found in a warehouse?"

Beau shrugs and turns off the car. "You'd be surprised about the stuff that law enforcement and government cover up. Half the time they're the ones running the Mafia and gangs. Hell, they made a whole movie about the CIA importing cocaine. They've got ways of making even the most sinister crimes get no attention at all. And if you say anything about it, they just call you a conspiracy theorist and move on."

"The fire I set wasn't even on the news though . . ." I say. "How was that not covered? How did we not hear sirens on the way out of town?"

Griff reaches from the backseat to rub my shoulder. "It'll be okay. Right now we just need to get you checked out to make sure you're okay. Are you still feeling pain?"

I nod my head and hold my side. It throbs whenever I move my torso or don't sit *just* right.

"Let's go," Beau says, opening his door. "Looks like someone is excited to see you."

He nods his head toward the front door where I spot Rocky jumping against the screen and barking, begging to get outside to greet us. God, I missed that little scraggly dog! Moose appears a few seconds later, picking up his dog and opening the door for us as we come up the walkway.

"There's my favorite girl," Moose says, greeting me with his partially toothless grin. Rocky wiggles in his arms, trying to get down to see me. I give Moose a big hug and lean over to let Rocky kiss all over my face.

"Damn, I get a better welcome home from a dog," I tease, looking behind me at Beau. "I should've had Griff bring me here first."

"Just because you're hurt, and I missed you like crazy," Beau starts, "doesn't mean that I'm not furious with you, Christina."

My teasing smile falls, and Moose gives a stern look at Beau before letting me inside.

"Don't run her off again, boy," Moose says. "She was just trying to save our asses. You should be treating her like the queen she is. I didn't expect this behavior from you, more so from Griff."

Griff had caught Moose up over the phone before we left the

house, letting him digest the highlights of what I went through. He also explained some of the medical care I would be needing. The issue is, most of the abuse can't even be seen—it's all in my head. How long will it take me to recover from the mental pain that Stanford and Mr. Thomas have inflicted? I had constant nightmares after Mr. Thomas . . . are they going to happen again even worse than before?

"Is that my patient?" Moose's wife asks, coming out of the kitchen with a steaming mug.

"Hi, I'm Christina," I tell her, reaching out to shake her hand. She's petite and curvy, and has the sweetest smile. She's wearing a pair of scrubs with Snoopy all over them. She shakes my hand and gives me the mug.

"I'm Marie. I made you some tea," she says as I take the mug. "Come on in. I'm set up in the kitchen. Let me look you over, sweet girl."

I take one last glance at Griff and Beau, and they just nod, letting me know to go with her. They follow Moose to the other side of the bungalow and a dimly lit den where they close the door so Rocky doesn't escape and jump all over me.

"I can't do much without an X-ray machine," Marie tells me as I take a seat at the kitchen table. "But I can feel around, check over you, and give you some meds for the pain."

"Thank you for the late-night call," I say. I take a sip of the peppermint tea and set it down on a coaster nearby.

"No worries, dear," she tells me. "Why don't you lift up your shirt enough for me to check. Griff said you have some wicked bruising."

I glance at the closed den door before pulling up my shirt. She kneels down in front of me and hisses through her teeth, reaching out a hand to touch my tender flesh.

"Oh lord," she says. "That looks painful. I'm going to have to put some pressure on your ribs, okay?"

I nod and grit my teeth. The moment she applies some pressure, I gasp, but I don't say a word. It hurt worse when Stanford was kicking me over and over again. I can sit through a few minutes of a nurse checking the bruising.

"Well, it's going to get worse before it gets better," she finally says, looking up at me. "I have some pain meds I can send you home with, but I do recommend going and getting some X-rays. I don't think he broke any ribs—or maybe not more than one—but you don't want to leave this or it could heal incorrectly. There could be more damage that I can't see."

"I'll have one of the guys take me to the hospital tomorrow," I promise. "I just really need some rest, I think. It was . . . a long month and a half of minimal sleep."

"I can't even imagine what that monster did to you," she says, standing back up. I pull my shirt down and take another sip of tea. It warms me from the inside out and reminds me of Christmas sitting in front of a warm fire with a cat on my lap. Marie goes over to her pantry and pulls out some medication. "This is the good stuff. It'll knock you out tonight, but don't take it unless you're going to bed. I'll have to go back to my room and grab you some daytime pain meds."

"Um," I say, looking down at my chipped nails. "Do you—do you have a pregnancy test as well?"

She freezes in the doorway of the kitchen before turning back to me, her hand touching her lips, trying to keep her composure. "He didn't—"

I quickly shake my head, speaking in a hushed voice. "No . . . I didn't let that monster inside my body. I just missed my period this month, and I can't remember the last time I had my birth control because things got crazy in the last few months. I'm sure it's just the stress, but—"

"Better to be safe," she says. "And with the pain he inflicted . . . let me go to my bedroom and get some supplies. My niece was over a few months ago and needed a few tests as well, so I have a spare in the bathroom. You're in luck."

My heart pounds in my chest at the thought that I could be pregnant. I've been feeling nauseous, but just the sight of Stanford makes me want to vomit. But what if I *am* pregnant? The abuse he dealt me this afternoon was horrid enough to hurt a baby if I'm carrying, enough to cause a miscarriage. Beau would be heartbroken, but it might not even be his anyway, it could be Danny's or Griff's, and I can't see them being happy tied down to a baby mama.

"Here you go, sweet pea," Marie says, handing me a closed pack of tests. "Take both to be safe, a day apart. If they're positive . . . you can't have the pain meds. We'll have to get you to the hospital for extensive testing. For you and the baby."

"Okay," I say. I'm on the verge of tears. I don't think I'm ready to be a mother, but I'll do it if I have to. I quickly take the box from her and walk to the bathroom. I close the door behind me and flick on the light. My hands shake as I read the instructions. I've never had a pregnancy scare before. Beau and I used condoms when we dated in high school, and I've always been diligent about birth control.

That is—until I got distracted by three insanely hot bikers with high sex drives. I believe I stopped taking my pills shortly after the chaos of Mr. Thomas' death. As I take a seat on the toilet and try to pee, I ponder what Griff will think if I'm pregnant . . . What about Danny? Will they be furious? Will either of them think I was trying to trap them for the next eighteen years? Will Beau be happy? He's so mad about me running away without telling him my plan, he might not even want me anymore. I might have to do this all on my own if the test comes back positive. I *can't* do this on my own. My parents sure as hell won't help me out. The moment I turned eighteen and headed off to college, it was like I never existed to them.

They haven't even called to check in on me since I visited them in Florida when my life was flipped upside down.

My parents never wanted a baby. My mom was never nurturing, and my father just didn't understand how to speak to his own flesh and blood. People think that every woman is born to be a mother, that their nurturing side will come out the moment the baby leaves the womb. But I've read the news. There are dozens of cases of women losing their minds and drowning their babies or locking them in closets without proper nutrition. I would never do that, but I can't stand how society thinks a woman refusing to reproduce is the worst thing she could ever decide. I'm shocked my mother never put me up for adoption. I was mostly raised by nannies anyway.

Once I cap the test, I wash my hands and avoid looking at it. I take the hand towel and wipe my hands. I swipe the test from the counter and open the door just as Beau reaches out for the handle. I'm not quick enough at hiding the test behind my back.

"Christina . . ." he says, and for the first time today, he doesn't look furious, he looks panicked. "Did he—did they ra—"

"No!" I practically shout before lowering my voice. "God, no. Don't say it, don't think about it. No one did that. I just . . . I missed my period. It's probably nothing. Just have to be sure before I can take any pain meds."

"Baby—" he says, and I can't tell if he's using my pet name or possibly rolling the idea in his head that there might be a baby growing inside of me right now.

"I haven't looked at it yet," I fire back, trying not to cry. "Go back to your meeting, Beau."

"But—" he starts, reaching out to try and stroke my arm. I think I see hope in his eyes now that he knows Stanford didn't rape me. Beau always told me he wanted to be a dad one day, and I always knew he would make a good father, but I don't know if I want that right now. Not with all this mayhem going on.

I flinch away from him. "Don't. Go back to the den. Don't mention this to Griff. I'm going to wait with Marie until we know. Then we're going to go pick up Danny. We have other stuff to worry about."

I can tell he wants to say something, but I don't let him. I push him out of the way and go back to the kitchen. Marie is leaning against her kitchen counter and gives me a small smile when I hand her the test. She sets a timer on her watch and places the test on the counter. I pace back and forth in the kitchen, chewing at one of my nails. I almost jump out of my skin when her watch beeps, signaling that it's time.

"Do you want me to look, or you?" she asks quietly.

"You," I say, stopping in front of her, placing my hand over my ribs as they throb in pain again. "Please, I need you to look."

She nods and turns.

It feels like a million years.

"Negative," she finally breathes, relief in her voice.

"Thank fuck!" I shout. I let out a breath, all the tension leaving my body. "Can I have a glass of bourbon? Before I take the pain meds tonight."

Marie chuckles and reaches into one of the upper cabinets to pull out a glass for me. "Just don't over do it. No mixing liquor with pain meds on purpose."

I nod quickly. "I would never. I just need something to take the edge off. I don't know when or if I'll ever want a test like that to be positive. Or how that would even work with three boyfriends. Let alone three boyfriends that are in a motorcycle club. Too much danger."

She pours some Old Bardstown into my glass. "Just means the baby would be loved by more people. We're all family, Christina. We take care of our family. But don't rush it if it doesn't feel right."

"Did you and Moose ever have any kids?" I ask, taking my glass.

She shakes her head. "No. I was way too busy being a nurse, and we were always worried about the direction the club was going in under Mr. Thomas' rule. Sometimes it feels lonely, but we've got each other and that little mutt we both love so much."

"So the answer is to get a mutt of my own?" I ask her with a smile.

"I thought you already had three hot mutts?" She winks, and I nearly choke on my bourbon.

"Sometimes it feels like they're all trying to mark their territory," I say after I compose myself. "But I don't hate it."

She chuckles and hands me two bottles of pills, one for day time and the other for night. "Take these with food. If they don't help you sleep tonight, you really need to go to the hospital. I can only do so much for you in my kitchen. And don't tell the doc where you got pain meds. Those are for club emergencies, and only the club can know about my supply."

"Understood." I stand and finish my bourbon as the door to the den opens and the guys filter out. "Thank you for seeing me so late. And for taking care of me."

"No problem, sweet pea," she says, giving me the sweetest hug. "Now go get your other man out of jail before he finds himself as someone's boyfriend. And take the second test in the morning. Call me if it comes back positive, but I don't think it will."

"Ready to go?" Griff asks, coming up behind me and gently wrapping his arms around my waist.

"Yes, sir," I answer, putting the pills in my jacket pocket. "Got some meds, ready to go. Marie said they'll knock me out, so no funny business tonight, mister."

"It'll be nice just to have my Princess back home," he says. He places a kiss on my cheek before pulling away to give Marie a hug. "Thanks for looking after her."

"Anything for my boys," she says, looking up at him and patting his cheek.

"You okay?" Beau asks. I know he's not just asking about my ribs, but I really don't want to discuss the pregnancy scare more than I already have.

"I'll be fine," I tell him, noticing Marie discreetly throwing the used test into the garbage before the guys notice. "Marie gave me some bourbon for the pain."

I try not to wince when Beau's face falls a little with disappointment.

While he seemed to be hoping for a baby, I was praying that I wasn't expecting. I force my gaze from him and say my goodbyes to Moose and Rocky before heading out of their house and back into our car, my guys trailing at my heel like obedient sled dogs. Instead of getting in the passenger seat, I take the back, not wanting to be so close to Beau right now.

"Let's go get Danny," I announce over the sound of clicking seatbelts. "And then let's go home so I can finally sleep."

CHAPTER 4

Beau cracked the windows for us while he went to retrieve Danny. I'm thankful he went in instead of Griff. I really didn't want Beau to have the opportunity to grill me about the pregnancy test I took . . . that's a conversation for later—or never. Griff is sending out a mass text to club members while I stare at the doors of the jail, waiting for Danny. I don't think either of them have told Dan about my return today.

I see them emerge from the building, and it looks like Beau is tearing into Dan about his recent lifestyle change. Their voices drift into the car as they get closer, and I wait for Danny to open the back door and climb in. He doesn't notice me at first, jerking his seatbelt on and grumbling about not being able to drive his own car.

"I just bailed you out of jail for drunk driving," Beau scolds, firing up the engine. "No way in hell am I letting you drive. You're lucky they didn't take your driver's license. Next time they probably will!"

"Whatever, man," Danny says. "Just take me home so I can get fucked up and go to sleep. My buzz is gone after sitting in the tank for so long."

"I could think of something better to do," I say from my side of the car.

"No!" Beau says from the front seat. "You need rest, and I'm still pissed at you. Everyone in this car is banned from sex until I say so! We're going full chastity time! I'm turning the house into a convent."

Griff grunts out a laugh from the front seat, and I smile when Danny finally looks at me.

"Eh," I say, shrugging my shoulders. "It's okay, I'm sure the pain meds will knock me out anyway."

"Baby girl?" Dan asks, squinting his eyes like he's seeing things. "That you?"

"God, I missed hearing you call me that, Dan," I say, unbuckling my seatbelt and scooting to the middle of the backseat. "I missed you so much."

He doesn't say a word. Instead, he grabs my face and pulls me into a painful kiss. He bites and nips at my lips as I mingle my tongue with his. We kiss and kiss. All the while Beau grumbles in the front seat about how no one respects him as the new president of the club. Danny moves one of his hands down my torso, squeezing my hip, and I wince in pain.

"See! That's what you get for fooling around," Beau says. "You're going to do more damage. You're going to the hospital first thing tomorrow!"

"What happened?" Danny asks, pulling back from me and trying to figure out where the pain is.

"I got my ribs kicked this morning," I tell him. "And then I set Stanford's clubhouse on fire."

"That motherfucker kicked you in the ribs?" Danny demands, suddenly vibrating with anger. He turns his attention to my two guys in the front seat. "You killed him, right? No one hurts our girl!"

"He's still out there somewhere," Griff answers. "We'll find him and end this."

"And torture him to death," Dan adds. "That sick fuck. Selling humans and abusing women. He deserves to rot in hell. I'm sick of just sitting around and waiting."

"You're not wrong," I say, reaching out and stroking Dan's unkempt beard. "But first, let's get home and get some sleep. I missed my guys."

Dan leans in to place a soft kiss on my lips before carefully pulling me against him for the remainder of the ride to our house. The four of us are quiet as we walk into the house, and we all head straight upstairs without turning on any of the lights. Silently, we all pile into Griff's room. Griff leads me to the bathroom so I can take a shower and my medication with a bedtime snack. He joins me under the warm spray, carefully washing my bruised body. I can tell he's just as furious as Danny and Beau with what Stanford did.

"I should have gotten you out of there sooner," Griff says, taking on all the blame.

I reach up and cup my palm against his cheek. "Don't blame yourself, Griffin. You and I both know there was no talking me out of my plan."

"I just want to keep you safe, Princess," Griff says. "I have never cared about anyone other than my brothers . . . until you. You're mine, and I want to keep you safe."

"I know," I say softly, pressing my head against his tattooed chest.

I watch the water swirling down the drain. Griff's arms wrap around my torso and hold me against him until the water turns cold and we're both shivering. He shuts off the shower and steps out, wrapping a towel around his waist, before holding a towel open for me to wrap myself in. We dry our bodies and Griff surprises me by grabbing the hair dryer below the sink. I sit on the closed toilet seat while he brushes out my blonde locks and dries my hair. I smile at the assistance. Even just a small gesture means so much after everything I've been through.

We both brush our teeth at the double vanity, and he fills up a water glass and hands me my medication to take, not saying a word, just taking care of me.

"Good girl," he says, stroking his calloused fingers below my chin. The space between my legs aches at his praise for the first time in over a month. How am I even thinking about getting railed by my men when I'm in such pain? And I'm not even going to try to initiate because I know they would all tell me no, terrified of hurting me.

I smile and climb into the massive bed, Danny and Beau already in their spots, just like before I ran off. Griff joins me on my other side, and I reach below the covers to hold his hand once we're settled. It's always a tight fit in this bed, trying to sleep four, but I love feeling their bodies pressed against me in the darkness.

"I missed you guys," I say into the dark room, listening to the three of them breathing.

I feel the medication already starting to work its magic, and I close my eyes, snuggling deeper into the sheets.

I'm home. I'm safe. Finally.

* * *

Voices come from the office in the clubhouse. Muffled behind the big door. I could have sworn the clubhouse was destroyed over a month ago, yet here it is, standing in perfect condition. It's a little foggy around the edges, but it's here. I'm back at the clubhouse, and my boyfriend is in charge.

I expect to hear his sugary sweet voice on the other side of the door, but the voice is deeper, harsher. I knock on the door but don't wait for an answer. I'm their queen, I can come in whenever I want. My body freezes when I find the office filled with at least thirty children sitting on the floor, crying, fear written all over their faces. Some of them are so dirty it looks like they haven't showered in a month. The older kids are holding onto the younger ones, staring up at me with wide, terrified eyes.

"There's our highest priced whore," says a voice from the other side of the room. "She walked right into our little trap. Dumb bitch."

The moment my eyes meet Mr. Thomas', I try to back out of the door, but I'm stopped in my tracks by two bodies on either side of me. I look up to find Danny and Beau, their large hands holding onto my biceps, pulling me farther into the room. I beg for them to let me go, but when I look back, their ears are just missing. They can't hear my protests.

"Such a pretty little whore," says another voice. When the man in the chair across from Mr. Thomas turns around, I see that it's my second worst enemy, Stanford. "She'll make a perfect slave once one of us tears her down. That'll be fun, don't you think?"

Mr. Thomas chuckles. "I think my son would be the best at that. Griffin was born to degrade little whores until they learn to obey their masters."

"Please," I cry. "Please, no. Let me go. Let the kids go."

"Isn't she pretty when she cries?" Mr. Thomas asks Stanford before turning his attention back to me. "I'll make you a deal, pretty little whore. We get to keep you and free the children, or I keep the children and let you go back to your mundane little life."

I close my eyes and let the tears flow. I know this philosophy: the dilemma of pragmatism. I studied it in my short time in college. Save oneself, or save others. Everyone says they would sacrifice themselves, but when the chips are down, history says no one ever does.

"Let them go," I sob. "Keep me."

When I blink my eyes open again, the room is completely empty except for Mr. Thomas. Even Stanford has vanished. The kids are gone, like they were never there to begin with. I'm dreaming, but I can't wake myself up from this nightmare like I usually can. I try *screaming myself awake, but it's not working, I'm trapped in hell. It's like something is keeping me asleep, and I'm drowning in my fear.*

"Silly girl," Mr. Thomas coos, standing from his desk and walking around to where my feet feel like cement blocks glued to the ground. "You think you can outrun me? You think you can destroy the monsters of the world like a hero? No, you're just my son's little toy, a distraction to his friends. Just wait . . . Stanford is going to come for you again. He'll make you disappear quickly. If he doesn't kill you, he'll make a pretty penny off you."

I flinch away when Mr. Thomas reaches out to brush some hair out of my face.

My eyes squeeze shut as I begin chanting the same words over and over again in my head, begging myself to wake up.

"It's not real. I'm home. It's not real. I'm home. It's not . . ."

CHAPTER 5

I jolt awake with a gasp that shakes my body so badly that my ribs ache.

"Fuck," I say through clenched teeth. My body is soaked in sweat. I glance to either side and find the bed empty of my guys. It's sort of a relief. I'm almost embarrassed by the amount I sweat in my sleep. I blame the painkillers for that and my full eight hours of nightmares.

I shimmy out of bed and begin pulling the sheets off so I can toss them in the washing machine after breakfast. I'm starving, and I know I'm going to need to eat with the daytime pain meds. I Pick up one of the guys' discarded shirts from the floor and gingerly pull it over my head, putting my arms through the holes.

The guys' muffled voices are coming from downstairs as I cross over to the laundry room to start the sheets. I tiptoe down the stairs and freeze when I hear Beau mention the pregnancy test that I took yesterday.

"I'm telling you," he says. "She was coming out of the bathroom, and I was getting ready to go in. She had two in her hands, I think."

"But they were negative?" Danny asks. I place my back to the wall between the living room and kitchen, listening to them discuss.

"Yeah, but those tests aren't always right," Beau says. "I feel like we need to actually take her to one of those lady doctors. Make sure she's okay."

"She told you that he didn't rape her?" Griff asks, his voice sounding concerned. Beau gives a silent answer. "Do we believe that?"

"That's enough!" I say, peeling myself from my hiding spot and going to the kitchen table. "You have no right to have this discussion behind my back. We're a team, a family. No, Stanford didn't rape me! No, I'm not pregnant! You guys are making something out of nothing. The test was just a precaution to make sure that I could take pain meds. I just haven't had my period in a while. It's probably from the stress."

None of their gazes meet mine. The three of them no longer look like the badass bikers they are. They're more like scolded children who just got caught with their hands in the cookie jar. I march over to the coffee pot and pour myself a cup, adding in my creamer. The guys just stare down at the table. Griff picks at a hole in his jeans like it's the most interesting thing.

"We were just worried about you, baby girl," Danny says, speaking up first and turning around slowly to look at me. "Can't blame us for worrying about you. Your safety is our top priority."

I huff and sit my mug on the counter behind me before going over to stand in front of Danny. He looks up at me as I reach out to stroke his scraggly beard. He really needs to trim it. He's starting to look like Tom Hanks in Castaway. He could probably use a good detox as well from the amount of liquor he's been consuming.

"I know you worry about me," I say, speaking to all of them but only looking at Danny. "But I'm not the fragile little Princess that you guys think I am. Between saving your asses from Mr. Thomas that day to burning down Demon Rebirth's clubhouse . . . I think I've proven that I'm more than just your old lady. I'm your queen. I'm just as much a member of Hell Prevails as the three of you."

Danny lets his head fall, and I hold it against my chest, running my fingers through his tousled brown hair. "I missed you so much, sugar," he tells me. "Don't ever leave me again."

I hold his head against my chest, soothing his turmoil. Had I known that this is how broken my men would get . . . no, I made the right decision. I saved lives. It doesn't make the guilt any less. I left without saying a word to Beau and Danny. They thought I ran off, that I didn't care for them, that I don't love them.

"Hey," I say softly, urging Danny to look up at me. He keeps his arms wrapped around me but lifts his head. "I won't leave again. This is my home. The three of you are my home. I love you so much."

I feel his heart pounding in his chest. "You love me?"

I nod, and he stands up and kisses me breathlessly. "I love you," he says. "I . . . love you."

I chuckle against his beard. "Well, I'm glad we're on the same page. Do you love me enough to make me some breakfast so I can take more medication?"

"Scrambled eggs and toast?" he asks, pressing a kiss to my forehead, and I give him a nod. He stands from his seat and urges me to sit down, going over to the counter to bring me my mug of coffee.

When I lift my eyes to look at Griff, he gives me the sweetest smile. "It's good to have you back home, my queen."

I smirk at him, warming my hands on the mug.

* * *

"We need to do something with that bushy beard," I tell Danny. I'm laying across his bed in just a shirt and underwear, waiting for Griff's sheets to finish drying. Beau and Griff headed out after breakfast to check on the club's warehouse and to see how the rebuild is going on the clubhouse.

Danny walks around his room with a trash bag, tossing out empty bottles of bourbon, used paper plates, and some small baggies that look like they used to hold a white substance. He pauses his cleaning to glance over at me, scratching said beard.

"You're probably right," he says, scrunching up his nose. "It's getting a little itchy."

"I can help," I offer, sitting up and crossing my legs. "Save you a trip to the barber."

He gives me a smile. "Okay, let me finish cleaning up, and we'll do a little self-care after. Lord knows I need it."

I grab the battered copy of *1984* that I snagged from Beau's bookshelf and open it to the page I bookmarked, occasionally looking up to admire Danny. This might be the first time we've been alone since the cabin months ago, and it feels different. I enjoy the time we've all had together, but maybe I need to start giving my guys the individual attention they all deserve. Don't get me wrong, I love our *group activities*, but it would be nice to take things a little slower. Danny ties the garbage bag and leaves his room to take the trash to the outdoor can. Suddenly, my core heats at the thought of being alone with Dan, about that beard, how it would feel between my legs, rubbing against my thighs. The perfect friction.

I almost groan thinking about his tongue coming out to stroke my slit. It's been too long since I've gotten to feel the pleasure of my men. They've created a monster. I thought for sure that being subjected to the stuff I saw during my time with Stanford would make me never get wet again. As my hand travels down my stomach, going under my lace panties, I find that I was absolutely wrong.

I guess the lack of sex—and watching Danny being so domesticated—is enough to get me hot and needy. The front door opens again, and my heart starts beating faster as I hear Dan walk up the stairs. I get up on my knees on the bed the moment he walks back through his bedroom door.

"Dan?" I ask.

"Yes, baby girl?" he asks, coming toward the bed. He reaches out and smooths some of my hair.

"It's been so long," I start, practically pouting. "I need to be touched. It's just you and me here."

He grins. "Is my baby girl needing some relief?"

I nod my head quickly, reaching down to the hem of the oversized shirt and pulling it over my head to reveal my simple white bra. I look into Dan's eyes just in time to see the spark of arousal in them. He lets his hand trail down between my breasts and across my stomach, avoiding the bruising. I'd hardly eaten while I was gone, and it shows on my belly. I didn't have an appetite while I was in Stanford's home. I was already thin to begin with, but earlier when I looked in the mirror, I almost looked too thin.

"Let's get Mexican for lunch," Dan says, his hand trailing further south to the edge of my underwear. "Your favorite."

I give him a smile. "From Pepe's?" I ask, and he nods. "Add a margarita to that and I'm good."

"But first," he says, his hooded eyes looking at me. "You're going to sit on my face until I can't breathe. You're going to rub that sweet, tight cunt all over this beard until you cum on my face."

Dan pulls his shirt over his head and lays back between the pillows.

"Come here," he commands. "Put your hands on the headboard, sugar."

I crawl over his body and open my knees to spread my legs over his face, suddenly feeling self-conscious at his view. I go to move away, but he grabs my ass and holds me over him. I swear I hear him growl in disapproval.

"Don't you dare think about moving that pussy away from my lips," he scolds. "Let me taste you, baby. I've missed your taste."

I place my hands on the headboard like he instructed and hover

over his face, melting the moment his tongue sticks out to lap at my folds. When he sucks onto my clit, I let out a shriek and move my hips away.

"Baby girl," he scolds. "I said to sit on my face, not hover. Smother me until I can't breathe!"

Lightly sitting down on his face, he licks deeper into me, and I let out a soft moan, feeling his beard scratch against my thighs. The friction has me grinding my pussy against his face harder which earns me a pleased groan and a swift slap on my ass. I grind myself harder and harder, ignoring the pain in my ribs, knowing when I find my release, the pain will be even further from my thoughts.

"I missed you so much, Dan," I whimper, letting my eyes close and my head fall back as I continue fucking myself on his tongue. "Never let me go again. Make me remember why I should have stayed."

Before I have time to grasp what's happening, Dan swiftly lifts me from his face and has me pinned on my back. He doesn't even remove his pants all the way before he's thrusting his thick cock deep inside me.

"You're never going to leave us again," he growls, thrusting so hard it feels like he's trying to fuck some sense into me. "Never. You hear me? I was a mess with you gone, and Beau turned into an absolute asshole. We're never going to let you out of our sight again. You belong to us!"

I nod quickly, feeling myself getting wetter with every word. "I belong to you. I'm yours. Make me yours."

"Fuck," he says, looking down to where his body keeps sliding in and out of me. "Take it, baby. Take what's yours. Grip me so tight with that perfect pussy."

"Dan," I gasp, feeling myself right on the edge. "Harder, I need . . . harder."

His eyes lift to mine, and I can tell he's fighting to control himself. "You're hurt. I don't want to do any more damage to you."

"Just fuck me," I plead, lifting a hand up to pull his slicked back hair. "I'm right there."

In a flash, his eyes grow darker, and his cock pounds deeper and harder into me.

"That's it," I praise. "Right there. I'm gonna—oh fuck, Dan. I'm cumming."

"Fuck yes," he grunts, thrusting deeper once more and stopping so he can feel my walls clench around him. "Fucking squeeze that cock."

His gaze meets mine as I ride out the waves of my climax, and then I groan when I feel his cock throbbing inside me with his own release.

He gently pulls out of me and curls up on the side that's not currently throbbing in pain. I totally need to go have some X-rays run so I can get better quicker. But all of that can wait. Right now I just want to live in the moment and let everything else fade away.

"I love you," he whispers, placing one of his hands on my chest. "I wish I had said it sooner. You have no idea how many times over the last month that I kept worrying that I would never get to tell you. You're the only woman I have ever loved, Christina."

"Dan," I say, softly. I roll onto my side and place my hand on his bearded cheek. "I love you."

He lifts his hand to cover mine and closes his eyes. "Please don't leave us again. We won't survive it."

I scoot closer to him and place a kiss on his lips. I can taste myself on him, and I don't hate it. Actually, I enjoy it. "Never again."

I'm not sure how long we lie there with each other, but when I move to my back again, I cringe in pain. Dan notices—of course he notices.

"We really need to get you checked out at the hospital, baby," he says.

I roll my eyes. "I know. Can you take me? I don't want Beau there hovering and making me a nervous wreck."

After we both take a quick shower, and Danny finally trims up his beard, he grabs the keys to his car and we head downtown to the hospital. It takes us hours sitting in a waiting room, then sitting in an exam room, before I'm finally checked over. Danny stays close by until the doctor asks him to leave the room so he can ask me some questions about possible domestic abuse. I assure the doctor that my tattooed, rugged boyfriend didn't hurt me. I'm not sure he believes me.

Before he orders the X-rays, he asks if I might possibly be pregnant. I accept another pregnancy test just in case. Beau was right when I heard him talking this morning—sometimes the at-home tests aren't reliable. I really need to get back to taking my birth control properly. I'll call my pharmacy first thing Monday morning to ask for a refill.

Dan sits on the edge of the hospital bed with me and holds my hand while I wait for the results. I bite the finger nails on my free hand even though I'm sure I'm not pregnant. There's no way. I've already taken two tests on my own!

"It'll be okay," Dan says, giving my hand a squeeze.

"Easy for you to say," I mutter. "You wouldn't be the one carrying a baby the size of a bowling ball in your stomach for nine months. You're changing every single diaper if one of you knocked me up. I mean it."

"Gladly," he says with a smile. "It's the least I can do. I'll even get up with the little shit in the middle of the night when he or she is screaming."

"I'll believe that when I see it." I roll my eyes at his excitement. "Do you even want to be a father?"

He nods. "With you as the mother, absolutely yes."

"I'm just not one hundred percent ready," I admit. "I'm not ready to be a mom. Everyone I went to high school with has popped out two or more kids, but I'm not ready. I want to . . . enjoy my time with the three of you. Once all this bullshit is through with Demon Rebirth, I want to take a vacation, see the ocean or something. I want to get the hell out of Lexington for a little while."

"We could still do that with a baby, you know," he says, bumping my shoulder with his. "And with four parents, it'll be even easier. Mommy will never have to change a diaper."

I playfully shove him. "I never want to hear you call me 'mommy' again. Ew!"

A knock comes on the door, and the doctor returns, his body language unreadable.

He pushes the computer mouse to awaken it and then enters the password that reveals my chart. "Okay, it looks like your test came back negative. So I'll get you in line for the X-rays, and I'll send someone in shortly to escort you down to radiology. With all the construction here at the hospital, patients have a tendency to get lost, and that looks bad on monthly reports to the board."

"Thanks, doc!" I say, my heart beating so fast at the confirmation that I'm not pregnant.

The doctor leaves, and I almost feel bad for how relieved I am when I find Dan looking disappointed.

"Hey . . . It's okay. Besides, it's way more fun trying to make a baby, right?"

"He was just so matter-of-fact about it," Dan answers, staring daggers at the door the doctor just exited. "He needs to learn some bedside manners. What if we wanted to be pregnant? He's an inconsiderate asshat."

"I'm fine with how he delivered the news, Dan. Like ripping off a bandage," I say, placing a gentle hand on his shoulder. "And besides, what if I was? The kick to my ribs that Stanford gave me could have harmed the baby, and we wouldn't want that. Not to mention the pain meds last night."

"When you do carry our baby," Danny says softly, like it will happen someday, standing in front of me and pressing his palm to my flat stomach, "we'll keep you both safe. We'll be a family."

"Let's hope that after this there won't be any more enemies. You guys are going to turn this club around. No more sketchy business."

"No more sketchy business," Dan promises, leaning in to place a kiss on my forehead. "For our future."

I give him a smile. "For our future."

CHAPTER 6

The ER doc gave me the all clear. No broken or cracked ribs, just some nasty bruising that should go away in a couple of weeks. He said I can go about my normal life, I just have to be a little more cautious about what I do until I'm fully healed. When Beau and Griff get home, I hand Beau my discharge papers and cross my arms over my chest.

"Not pregnant, not broken," I tell him as he scans the documents with a blank face. "You, however, have a big hospital bill coming in the mail. And since I don't have a bar to tend to, I don't have money."

"Not a problem," Beau says, folding up the papers and setting them in the mail carrier on the counter. "Glad you put your big girl pants on and went to get checked out. Hope you didn't give Dan too hard of a time."

I give him a bratty smirk. "Well, I am more agreeable after getting an orgasm."

Beau's face turns from his usual light tan to bright red, and I laugh as he loses control.

"What?" he shouts, turning to where Dan was heading to the living room with a family size bag of Doritos and a Coke. "You were supposed to be taking care of her!"

"I was!" he says, holding up his hands. "But then . . . I missed her so much, man. We went easy—"

"For the most part," I add with a shrug.

Beau squeezes his eyes shut and puts a hand up to stop Dan from finishing his sentence. "Ah ah ah! I don't want to hear it!"

"Since Beau seems to not wanna play anymore . . ." I trail off, looking at Griff who just smiles and shakes his head from the recliner in the living room. "Guess more for Griff and Dan!"

"I never said I didn't want to play anymore," Beau shoots back, exasperated. "I just don't want to hurt you after everything you went through—"

"And I want to forget," I say, crossing the kitchen and getting in his face. "I want my boyfriends to make me forget that I had a lapse in judgment and left for a month. I want my boyfriends to make me forget I chose to run off and be a hero and ended up being a sex worker against my will. I want my boyfriends to fuck me and make love to me until I forget about Stanford standing over my body and kicking me. I want my boyfriends to remind me that I'm still theirs, and that they didn't give up on me. Is that too much to ask for?"

"On your knees," Beau practically whispers his command.

"What?"

"You heard him, Princess," Griff adds. He stands up and walks over beside Beau. He tosses a throw pillow onto the floor for my knees, directly in front of them. "On your knees."

I sink down to the floor, my knees thankful for the cushion. I stare up at my two boyfriends with fire in their eyes.

"God, she's beautiful," Griff whispers, placing a gentle hand on my cheek and rubbing his thumb over my bottom lip. "And she's ours."

"I'm still mad at you both," Beau says, turning his attention to Griff. "You're my brother, and you lied to me. You knew where she was the entire time."

"I know," Griff replies apologetically. "Never again."

"You're damn right," Beau says, turning his attention back to me. "You'll never leave us again, Christina."

It's not a question, it's a demand. A demand that I stick by their side, and I nod in agreement.

"Yes, Sir," I say, staring up at Beau. He's still wearing his cut, his biceps straining his T-shirt underneath. He must have worked out extra hard while I was gone, because he's bulked up a lot.

"I'm calling the shots in the bedroom tonight," he says, reaching down to grab onto my ponytail, twisting it just enough for it to sting. "I'm the leader of this MC now, and you're forever part of us, so you answer to me now. Got it?"

Beau uses my fisted ponytail to make my head nod in agreement.

"Yes, Beau," I pant, feeling myself dripping already. "I understand. I'm yours. You're in charge."

"That's a good girl," Beau praises. "Now, get that ass upstairs. When we get up there, you better be presentable and ready. Understand?"

"Yes," I answer, biting my bottom lip. Beau releases me and stands to the side, holding a hand out and pointing to the stairs. I get up from my knees and march my ass right up the stairs and into Griff's bedroom. I certainly don't need to be told twice.

The guys don't say a word as they walk up the stairs. I hear Beau's heavy boots, and I know the other two are following behind him. I can practically feel them approaching like some weird sixth sense. I quickly pull off my shirt and slide my shorts down my legs. I don't have time to remove my thong or bra before they step into the room, so I kneel down on the floor at the foot of the bed, placing my hands on my bare thighs when they walk in, palms up.

"So obedient," Beau says, and now there's some sarcasm to his tone. "Funny, when I first got home, you were bragging about getting what you wanted from Danny, but now you're on your knees for me."

I blush. I expect this kind of bravado from Griff, but Beau was always my sweetheart. The one guy who only belonged to me. It's like

Griff and Beau have switched not only their status in the MC but also how they want me in bed. I'm not complaining though . . . however, my panties are. They're working overtime trying to keep my pussy from melting all over the carpet.

Danny and Griff stand on either side of me while Beau crouches down in front.

"Look at you," he says with a smile. "Are you going to behave and listen to me now?"

"Yes," I say immediately, letting him cradle my face in his hand. "I'll do whatever you want, Beau. I promise."

"Who do you listen to tonight?" he asks.

"You."

"Who do you belong to?"

"You."

"Who is going to make you cum tonight?"

"You."

He smiles. "That's right. You don't get to cum for Griff or Danny tonight. You only cum for me, only on my dick. Got it?"

"Yes, Beau."

I'm not sure how I'm going to obey his request. I'm practically dripping for my men. I haven't had all of them at once since I returned home, and I think they know damn well how much I love having them. I guess that's my punishment for running away, and I'm willing to try and take it like a champ.

"Fuck her face," Beau says, and he doesn't have to tell Danny and Griff twice. They both unzip their jeans in a flash and shove them and their boxers down their thighs. The moment their hard shafts are out and at my eye level, I reach my hands for both of them. Griff grabs the back of my head first and shoves my mouth down on him until I gag, making it nice and sloppy just like he loves. My insides flutter at the sound of his grunting. He tugs me off his throbbing cock and pushes my face down onto Danny. I feel alive as they pass me back and forth.

I'd become so numb in the month that I was with Stanford, making myself go into a darkness so I wouldn't be fully aware of how much I missed my guys. Now, though, I love the power they give me, even when I'm submitting for them. Even when I'm gagging on their cocks.

Beau reaches forward and rips the thin material of my thong from my body, and I gasp on Danny's cock. Beau runs a finger over my desperate slit. I crack open one of my eyes to try and look at him.

"You're absolutely drenched, baby," he says, rubbing his finger back and forth. Purposely avoiding my clit. *Jerk.* "You missed this, didn't you? Three eager cocks to share my girlfriend? Our queen missed her kings, didn't she?"

Griff pushes me all the way down on Danny so all I can manage is a small nod in agreement. My eyes begin to water, but Griff lets me up before I choke.

"I missed you," I gasp, my own saliva dripping from my mouth. "I missed all of you."

"Prove it," Beau says, standing up and nodding toward the bed. "Make my brothers cum at the same time. Take all they give you, but don't you dare let that pussy climax until I'm inside."

I climb on the bed as Griff and Danny remove the rest of their clothes. All three sets of eyes track my body on the bed. Danny goes over to the bedside drawer and pulls out a bottle of lube, tossing it to Griff who catches it without taking his eyes off of me. Danny joins me on the bed, planting a heart-stopping kiss on my lips before he lies back and pulls me on top of him.

"Ride me, baby girl," he says, lining up my core with his rock-hard erection. I slam myself down on him, taking in every single inch as Danny pulls my lips to his. We moan into each other's mouths, our tongues collide, and I frantically grind my body on top of his. "That's it. So good."

I hardly notice the bed dip behind me, and I don't even flinch when Griff's lubed fingers meet my tight hole. I slow my movements and arch my back for Griff, presenting my ass for him. I don't even blush anymore at the thought of one of them playing with my ass. I know they'll take their time and make it feel good. When you have anal, you're putting so much trust in your partner to not hurt you. I know hurting me is the last thing these three men want.

"So eager," Griff remarks, slowly pushing one finger inside me, and then another. "Seems we've turned you into an eager little anal whore."

"Yes, Daddy," I say, pushing back on his fingers. "Give it to me . . . please."

"You know I can feel Danny's cock inside you like this?" Griff asks, rubbing his finger along the thin wall. Danny bucks his hips and groans against the sensation.

"Stop fucking around, man," Danny says beneath me. "You think you're teasing her, but it's just messing with me, asshole."

Griff chuckles and pushes a third finger in before moving them gently thrusting to lube my insides. "Sorry, gotta get our girl ready."

"I'm ready," I moan. It could just be the meds the doctor prescribed me, but I feel zero pain right now, just pure ecstasy. "Please give it to me, Griff!"

"You heard her," Beau says, walking along the side of the bed, watching us. "Give it to her. Our girl can handle it."

Griff removes his fingers and lines up the tip of his cock with my ass. I don't wait for him to slide in, instead, I move back, taking him inch by inch until he's deep inside me.

"Oh, fuck," he gasps, placing his hands on both of my ass cheeks and giving them a squeeze. "That's it, Princess. That's our girl. Fuck us."

I move back and forth on Danny and Griff, biting my lip and trying not to cum on the spot. They groan, and Danny squeezes my breasts in his calloused palms as Griff does the same with my ass. This should feel absolutely dirty, but I feel like a *goddess* when I fuck my boyfriends at the same time. I feel like they're worshiping my body and giving me parts of their souls no other woman has ever had before. That no other woman will ever have from them in the future. They're mine. I own them, just like they own my body.

"You're so fucking gorgeous when you take us both," Danny says, looking up at me like I'm some sort of miracle that he just can't understand. "Are you going to take all our cum?"

"Yes!" I gasp, speeding up my rhythm. "Give it to me—please."

"Where are you going to take Beau?" Griff whispers into my ear, licking along the edge of it. "Are you going to let him cum deep in that pussy, or are you going to have him tear this ass up even more?"

I let out a feral squeal, trying to push my orgasm away at Griff's dirty words. He knows damn well what his words do to me. I think I've read about edging in one of my romance books. I believe that's exactly what Beau's doing to me right now. Denying me my orgasm. I *hate* it. Ah, but at the same time . . . I *love* it. "I'm going to let him take me however he wants."

"You're damn right you will," Beau says, leaning over the bed and squeezing one of my nipples. "Tonight, we get you however we want you."

Staring at Beau, I nod my head quickly in agreement. Tears flow down my cheeks. They're not from pain, not from sadness or embarrassment. I let the tears flow because I know this is where I'm meant to be, having my body used by the three men I've fallen in love with. Letting their pleasure bring me my own pleasure. There's nowhere else I should ever be.

"I love you," I yell. I feel Griff's cock begin to throb deep in my ass. "Griff, I love you, and Danny. And Beau. Fuck, I love you so much. I'm yours, I'll never run away again. I swear!"

Danny smiles and pushes some blonde strands from my face. I close my eyes, feeling both of them release inside me, their two cocks pulsing and pulsing until they're done. Griff pulls out and collapses on the bed beside us, and I'm about ready to move off of Danny when

Beau pushes me back down against his chest. Danny wraps his tattooed arms around me, holding me in place.

"You're not done yet, baby," Beau says. "My turn."

He slaps my ass after leaning down to spit directly on my asshole, and he uses a finger to push his saliva inside.

"Left something in there for you," Griff laughs. "Should make it easier for you to slam right in."

I can practically hear Beau rolling his eyes as he spreads my cheeks open, plunging right inside my ass. Thankfully, Griff prepped me enough that it doesn't hurt when Beau takes me. I feel Danny's cock pull out as he adjusts his hips. He's still holding me in place as Beau fucks my ass deep.

Beau removes one of his hands from my ass and sticks two fingers inside my pussy, making me groan with pleasure.

"Yes," I say, my walls clamping down on Beau's fingers.

"Not yet," Beau says, removing them so I don't cum. "Not until I say so. You can cum when I cum. You know the rules."

"But can she follow them?" Griff asks, reaching over to wipe some of the tears from my eyes. "She usually listens to Daddy, but can she listen to sweet Beau?"

I bite my lip at Griff referring to himself as Daddy. I forgot how much I enjoyed that taboo little nickname. If Beau's fingers were back inside, he'd probably be able to feel me clenching even tighter.

"She's our good girl," Danny says, his voice vibrating against my ear on his chest. "Reward her already. I think she's been deprived enough."

Beau picks up his pace and shoves his fingers back inside me. He doesn't even have to wait when he tells me to cum on his fingers. It instantly happens, and I arch my back, trying to take him in deeper. I turn my head and bite Danny's chest at the intense pleasure.

"Oh, fuck!" I yell. Beau's cock throbs deep inside me. "Yes, yes, yes!"

"That's a good girl," Beau says, still cumming. "Take it all. It's all yours."

When his orgasm finally ends, he slowly pulls out of me, and I glance behind to find him still kneeling between my legs. I start to squirm under his gaze. He's looking right at the holes him and his friends just filled up, and I feel exposed. Danny keeps me held in place as Beau reaches a finger out toward me.

"Keep it in, my little whore," he almost whispers. "That's our gift to you for coming back home: our seed. And there's more where that came from."

I feel some of the cum sliding out, but Beau just smoothly pushes it back inside me, not fazed in the slightest by the fact that it's not just his, it's all three of them mixing together inside me. He pushes some of it back into my pussy, and I start shaking and moving myself up and down on his fingers.

"You're going to cum again, aren't you?" Beau whispers. "You like me playing with our pleasure like this? You want me to shove it all back, deep inside you?"

"Mmhmm," I whimper. Danny loosens his hold on me, allowing me to thrust back and forth as I please.

"Take it then, little whore," Beau says. "Get yourself off on my fingers. We're waiting. Let us hear you scream."

Danny reaches between us and rubs soft circles over my sensitive clit. Griff reaches out and wraps his strong fingers around my throat, forcing me to look at him as I grind against Danny and Beau's fingers. I pick up my pace, as does Danny, getting me to the edge, and pushing me over with a pinch to my clit, causing me to scream out my pleasure.

"That's a good girl," Griff says, letting go of my neck. I collapse on Danny's chest.

Griff and Beau climb off the bed, and I'm on the edge of sleep when I feel one of them cleaning me up. I don't have the strength to look and see who it is—I just relax even more into Danny as he casually brushes his hand over my hair, repeatedly smoothing it down. I fall asleep like that, a melted pile of bliss against Danny's chest.

CHAPTER 7

I wake up naked and alone. Again.

When I stretch out my legs and arms, I cringe at the pain. My torso hurts from my bruised ribs, my vagina and ass hurt from the rough fuck they endured last night, and my head hurts from god only knows what. I pull myself out of bed and walk to the bathroom in all of my naked glory, squeezing my thighs shut until I can make it to the toilet to relieve myself. Honestly, I probably could have slept for another two hours had my bladder not woken me up. After flushing, I wash my hands at the counter and spot a box with a note on the front.

I pick it up and see that it's Plan B, since it'll take another month for my birth control to kick in—smart.

"We're all in," says the note in sloppy handwriting that looks like it could be Beau's. *"Are you?"*

I pull my birth control packet from my drawer next to the sink, and I know I'm already over two months behind. I either need to start up a new packet and take Plan B or just throw it all in the garbage. It'll take a full cycle before the contraceptive will work properly, so the guys will need to wear condoms. I know that if that's what I want, they'll do it for me. They won't complain about wearing the condoms for a little bit, not like some men would.

It wouldn't be the end of the world if I became a mother. And after my talk with Danny, I feel much better about the possibility of them becoming fathers to our children. They're hardworking men, they wouldn't ditch me to go get fucked up with their buddies or play hours of video games while I sit in a nursery breastfeeding alone. I trust them.

Grabbing the glass next to the sink, I fill it and take two of my pain pills. Before I leave the bathroom, I throw away the birth control and backup pills. I'm all in, I guess. Whatever happens, happens, as long as I have my guys beside me. Besides, it might take a while to even conceive.

Getting dressed in some leggings and Beau's oversized HPMC hoodie that I've claimed as my own, I head downstairs to my guys who are sitting around the breakfast table. They've got a huge spread in front of them: eggs, bacon, sausage gravy, hash browns, orange juice, and a carafe of coffee. Beau's placing a platter of biscuits on the table as I join them.

"Morning, guys," I say, kissing each of them on the cheek before taking my spot at the table. I hiss as my ass hits the hard wooden chair. Between the spanking and fucking, I'm more sore than usual.

Beau leans down and places another kiss on the top of my head before taking a seat beside me. "How are you feeling?" he asks, loading up his plate.

I give him a smile as I pour some orange juice into my glass. "Sore, but happy. What's on the agenda today?"

"We've gotta run out to the warehouse for a club meeting," Griff says, munching on a piece of crispy bacon. "Luis has some surveillance footage to go over before he heads back to the hospital."

"Hospital?" I ask, scrunching my brows together. "Everything okay?"

"Bonnie had her baby this morning," Danny says. "The baby came early, so Luis has been spending his time at the hospital."

"Is Bonnie okay?" I ask, setting my glass down.

Griff nods. "She's fine, just a concerned mama. They'll make it through. They've got a whole club backing them up. Supporting them."

"Can we pick up something for them and the baby?" I ask. I feel bad that I wasn't there for my friend and her family for the last month. I hope I wasn't the reason for any stress that might have caused an early birth. I thought leaving when shit hit the fan was for the best, but the more I think about it, the more I realize how selfish I was being.

"We can do that," Beau says. "Speaking of babies, we found your birth control. Did you get it?"

The other two guys are quiet, staring down at the food on their plates. The fork and knife Danny is using to cut his biscuits and gravy makes an awful sound as it scrapes the porcelain plate. I should have known this was going to be a whole conversation this morning. That's the adult thing to do though, discuss going off your birth control and trying to have a baby.

I take a deep breath. "I did see it. I just took my pain meds. I don't need the other stuff."

You could hear a pen drop in the room before any of them speaks. I'm almost shocked when it's Griff who pipes up first.

"You mean we're going to have a baby?" he asks, and he looks scarily excited.

"It doesn't happen that quickly!" I shout, blushing. "I'm not pregnant."

"It could," Danny says with a smile. "All it takes is once . . . and I'm the only one who has spilled the gravy in you since your return so I'm ahead of the game."

"First off, ew. Never compare cum to gravy ever again," I say. "And this doesn't mean we're going to track my ovulation and all that bullshit every month! We're not tracking anything, and I'm still going to eat and drink whatever I want while I'm not pregnant. And if, *if* we get pregnant, we're not having a paternity test done to see whose baby it is. It's *ours*. I expect each of you to love it whether it looks like Beau, Danny, or Griff. We're a family, all four of us. Got it?"

I cross my arms over my chest and glare at each of them. Even Griff looks like I've given him the best gift ever. He motions me over to him and pats his hand on his thigh for me to sit.

"We'll be the best dads ever, and you'll be such a good mother," he tells me, running his hand over my flat belly.

I lean my forehead against his. "Will I still be Daddy's Princess?"

The sexiest growl comes from his throat. "You will *always* be Daddy's little Princess."

"Okay, okay," Beau says. "Enough of that. Eat up, Christina. We've got work to do, places to be."

I pull back and smile at Griff before standing up and returning to my seat. I dig into the huge breakfast Beau made and listen as they discuss some club business. Now that Danny is no longer in a drunken stupor, Beau's going to announce that Dan will be taking over as the vice president while Griff is going to be taking over the enforcer position and some of security due to Luis stepping down to treasurer since he's got a new baby. It seems like they've gotten most things situated since I've been gone.

When the guys go to shrug on their cuts, I walk over to Beau and run my hand along the President patch that wasn't there the last time I saw him. It suits him. He places his hand over mine on his chest, and I give him a soft smile.

"Congrats," I finally tell him. "I'm proud of you."

"I'm going to do what I have to to make this world safe for you and our future children, Christina," he tells me. "I promise."

"I trust you." I stand on my tippy toes to place a kiss on his lips. I grab my Converse sneakers from the floor and lace them, then shrug into my own leather jacket.

Before I follow the guys out the door, I catch sight of myself in front of the floor-length mirror. Shocked that I finally look the part of an MC's old lady, my hair is tousled, I've got my leather cut over one of their hoodies, and something on my face just screams 'don't mess with me unless you have a death wish.'

I'm their queen, and I'm back to show everyone that I'm not going anywhere, never again. I'll stand by my men and the club until the day I die. It feels like this is where I was always meant to be.

* * *

I stand in front of the MC members, shoulder to shoulder with their new president. They all stare at me as he speaks, and I try my best to keep my head held high as Beau debriefs them on club matters. I was happy to see some of the families here as well. It shows that this is no longer going to be the brutal men's club that Mr. Thomas wanted it to be. My guys are turning it around, finally. Marnie is here, holding her husband's hand. Erica is here too standing beside her husband, but I've yet to be introduced to him. Randy, the man who helped Luis dig up some dirt on Stanford, stands in the back of the club beside some of the unpatched prospects.

"As everyone knows, Luis is stepping down from his role with security and taking over as treasurer, but he'll still be helping out Griff when needed," Beau says with authority. "We're still on high alert. Stanford is MIA, as are some of his top players since their clubhouse was burned to a crisp. Always be alert and report any shady shit you see to Griff. I've selected Dan as my second in command, and I look forward to him being my vice president. You have our word that we will do our very best to get Hell Prevails out of this darkness and be stronger on the other side. We're all family. We fight for each other."

"And the traitor?" one of the newer members asks from the pole he's leaning against, nodding toward me. "We're supposed to trust your bitch? She ran out on us. What if she's working for Stanford? Reporting our every move to him? She's probably a rat."

"What did you just call her?" Griff asks, eerily calm, but I see his fists clench at his side. He's been in that guy's position before. He's told me some stories about when he was a newbie and cocky as hell. I think that's why he's such a good dominant—he's learned to put his ego in check over the years that he's grown up in the MC.

"Oh, I'm sorry," laughs the guy. "I meant your whore. She is fucking all three of you, right?"

There are some gasps from the wives in the club who cover the ears of their children. I'm appalled that this guy thinks it's okay to speak so crudely in front of children.

Before Beau or any of them can stop him, Griff darts across the floor and bashes the man's head into the support pole where it makes this bone chilling crack that rattles throughout the building.

The man falls to the ground, and I'm not sure if he's still conscious or even alive. Griff kicks him in the ribs, and I flinch, feeling the hit on my own.

"Anybody else want to question your queen's loyalty?" Griff shouts to the room. Someone's child begins to cry, and his mom holds him to her chest, shielding him from the violence. If that's the worst this child sees, I'll consider him lucky.

No one says another word, and no one looks at me any longer. Beau dismisses everyone and Griff motions two of the prospects to come over and remove the unconscious man from the warehouse. But not before he leans over and uses his pocket knife to cut off the patches from the man's cut.

Griff and another member go to a separate room to go over security business while Danny goes to have a small meeting with the prospects. Everyone else is dismissed. I head over to the door I watched Beau walk through and find an office. It's not as big as the one at the original clubhouse, but I guess he's making it work for now.

"Knock knock," I say, leaning on the doorframe.

Beau looks up from the computer and gives me a smile. "You're allowed to come in, baby."

I give him a smile and walk in, looking around at the bareness of the room. Even the desk is fairly clear. Aside from the dual screen monitors, there's just a mug of pens and a picture frame. It's the framed picture of us at prom.

"I was wondering where this went," I say, setting it back down. Honestly, after I left, I thought he might have thrown away the picture, finally done with me.

"Snooping in my room while I'm not there?" Beau asks, leaning back in his chair.

I ignore the question. "You look good behind that desk, Beau Grady. You look like you know what you're doing."

He chuckles. "I have no fucking clue what I'm doing. I feel like a fraud."

"That's okay," I tell him, coming around to stand between him and the desk. "That's what Danny is for, and Griff, and all of the other men you've got standing behind you. They clearly believe in you or else they wouldn't have chosen you to be their president."

"I never wanted this though," Beau admits, rubbing at some scruff that's coming in on his chin. "I feel like I ripped the spot away from Griff. This is what he's wanted since before I ever knew him." He taps his knuckles on the wooden desk.

I chuckle and shake my head. "Beau, I think Griff is happy for you. I think he's perfectly fine with you being in this position. Just because someone wanted something doesn't mean that it was best for them. Sometimes our personal dreams aren't meant to be."

"I guess I'm just having imposter syndrome or something. I feel like I'm wearing someone else's skin and just faking my power and knowledge."

"You'll grow into it," I tell him. "I believe in you."

"Thanks."

I prop myself up on his desk and smile wickedly at him. "I know how you can thank me. You haven't christened this office yet."

"What are you suggesting?" he teases. He knows exactly what I'm suggesting.

"I want you to fuck me on this desk, Be—"

He doesn't let me finish my sentence. He springs from his chair, and his lips crash with mine. I reach down for his pants, unbuttoning them, and yanking on the zipper. He claws at my bottoms, dragging them down my legs where they get stuck on my shoes before he gives up on them. He kneels down in front of me and spreads my legs as far as they can go before plunging his face into my pussy.

"Beau, the door's still open," I whimper, his tongue darting across my flesh.

"Don't fucking care, Christina," he says. "Give me this pussy."

I shut my mouth and spread my legs open just a little bit more. Beau would never put me at risk of anyone but him and the guys seeing me. I know as much as he's concentrating on me, he's got one ear open listening for anyone possibly barging in on us.

My fist reaches down on its own accord and grips onto his blonde hair.

"Fuck, Beau," I moan. "Your tongue feels so good."

He pulls back from my pussy, and I look at him, his chin wet. "Tell me you're mine, Christina," he commands. "Tell me you'll never leave me again, baby."

I shake my head. "Never, Beau. I'll never leave again. I've always been yours, Beau Grady. I'll always be yours."

When Beau dives back between my legs, he instantly finds my clit, sucking on it until I'm bucking my hips against his face. He knows the moment I'm about to cum, because he slides two fingers into me so he can feel them constricted by my orgasm. After I've ridden out my pleasure, he pulls his fingers from me and stands up. I bite my lip, watching him suck me off of those fingers.

"You taste so fucking sweet," he says.

"Let me taste," I whimper. Beau folds his body over me, and I pull his face down so I can clean him with my tongue. Once I can't taste myself on his chin or his dimples any longer, I move to his lips, twisting my tongue with his.

"I need inside you," he says, almost painfully. I can feel his rock hard cock pushing against me through his boxer briefs.

He doesn't have to tell me twice. Reaching between us, I pull out his shaft and line it up with my awaiting cunt. He looks up at me as he thrusts in with one push, closing his eyes as his pleasure consumes him. When he looks at me again, his eyes are more gentle. He props himself up with his left hand against the desk and runs his right down my chest and stomach, pushing my hoodie and shirt up enough to show my stomach.

"I can't wait to see this belly grow," he says, like it'll be the sexiest thing on earth. "Do you know how long I've wanted you to make me a father?"

"How long?" I ask, breathless as his thrusts become excruciatingly slow—but deep, like he's trying to cum deep inside my womb.

He rests his head against mine, his breathing ragged. "Ever since we met, baby. It's always been you. I wanted it all, the white picket fence, a dog, babies, my wife. Only with you."

"I think it's too late for a white picket fence," I tease with a laugh. "I can't see my motorcycle boyfriends being kept in suburbia with a perfectly manicured lawn."

He shakes his head. "As long as we have you, it's perfect. Now hush, and let me fill you up. I didn't get to cum in this pussy last night."

I nod my head quickly as his thrusts increase. I hear loud voices approaching. It's on the tip of my tongue to tell Beau to hurry up, but

I'm too greedy. I want him to fuck me until he's ready to be done. I place my hands on his forearms and feel the muscles tighten below the skin. He's close, and so am I.

"Give it to me, Beau," I beg, gripping his hair again. "Give it to me deep."

"Fuck!" he shouts, thrusting two more times before bottoming out inside me. I can feel his pulsing cock which has me cumming on command. "That's it, baby. Squeeze me dry. Take it all."

"Mmm," I whimper. Who knew just the thought of him knocking me up would make for such hot sex? I sure didn't. Maybe making a baby with these guys won't be as terrifying as I had originally thought.

CHAPTER 8

Once I'm cleaned up, I head over to where Griff disappeared with another member earlier. When I find him, he's alone now, staring at at least a dozen security screens. He's leaning back in a chair, his fingers interlaced behind his head. A bright smile graces his face.

"New job boring you to death yet?" I ask, coming in to look over his head at the monitors.

He doesn't even flinch. It's like he was expecting me. "Nah. Honestly, I think I like this better than I would have being the president. It has its perks."

I lean in closer and notice one of the cameras. It has the perfect view of Beau's office, stuck in the corner, looking down directly at his desk where Beau's currently clicking away on his computer. My face burns bright red, and I slap Griff on the back of the head.

"What the hell?" I demand. "Please tell me that no one else got a show."

Griff laughs and pulls me into his lap, nuzzling his face into my neck. "Nope. Other guy left about ten minutes beforehand. Let me just say, I've never been much of a voyeur, but I think you've awoken something in me."

My mood instantly softens. "You're welcome to watch whenever," I tease. Just the thought of Griff sitting in here watching me get fucked on security footage has my thighs squeezing for relief. I'm sure in a minute or so, he'll be able to feel mine and Beau's pleasure seeping through my panties and leggings.

I wrap Griff's arms tighter around me, and we both continue watching the screens. There's one that points to the lot. It shows the construction on the new clubhouse, and various other cameras show the warehouse we're currently in, and then there are five more pointed at some familiar places.

Leaning forward in Griff's lap, I notice one of them is security footage of Stanford's house.

"How'd you manage to get eyes in that hellhole?" I ask.

"Wasn't easy," he says with a shrug. "Had to get one of the prospects to risk his life installing it. He'll be getting patched in soon for his bravery."

"Any action?" I ask. "House looks quiet."

Griff shakes his head. "No one has come in or out. No cars in the driveway. We've even got eyes on the remains of their clubhouse, but nothing. It's like everyone has disappeared. I don't like it. Something is very seriously wrong."

"We need to draw them out," I suggest.

Griff tightens his hold on me. "Don't even think about it, Princess. We're not past tying you up like the good old days and hiding you away for safekeeping."

"You would enjoy that way too much," I shoot back, turning my head to place a kiss against his temple. "I just don't want to hide forever. I want to be able to walk down the street and not worry about that creepy fuck coming after me."

"We'll take care of it, Christina," Griff says. "I promise. We just have to wait for the perfect opportunity. We have to keep watching for them to make a move, and then we can finish this."

"Just promise that if there's any way I can help, you guys won't shut me out," I ask, leaning my back into Griff's chest. "We're in this fight together."

He places a kiss on my cheek. "I promise we'll do our best."

It's not a promise that they'll let me help take down Stanford and Demon Rebirth, but it's something. At this point, I understand why they'd be hesitant to let me get involved again, but we're in this because of me. It all started the moment the guys handed me that match and asked me to set a daycare on fire.

* * *

I finally get a chance to catch a ride on the back of Danny's motorcycle and check on construction of the new clubhouse about a week later. A prospect had to open a gate for us on the way in—new added security that was never needed before. The clubhouse itself is coming along, the concrete is poured, and the frame is up.

Part of me is glad that the old clubhouse was destroyed. I had too many bad memories there. Between being held captive in the basement for days, to having to shoot Mr. Thomas to save my guys, the whole place had far too dark a past. At least I don't have to go into that old office ever again or force myself to go down to the basement.

When I climb off the back of the bike, I notice a gigantic swing set connected to what looks like a miniature wooden pirate ship. That certainly wasn't there before, and it *certainly* isn't the place I would expect to see it.

"What's that for?" I ask Danny, setting my helmet on the bike.

"The kids," he says, shrugging his shoulders. "We used some of the club money to buy something for all the members' youngins to enjoy. Since we're making the club more family oriented, we thought it was a good idea. We also got a new grill for cookouts since the other one got toasted during the attack."

"Look at you guys," I say with a smirk. "Turning into family men. Who would have thought?"

Danny wraps his strong arms around my waist and takes two huge handfuls of my ass, pulling me against him. "If you would have told me six months ago that I would be in a committed relationship with a firecracker of a woman and thinking daily about putting a baby in her with my two best friends, I would have laughed in your face. Yet . . . here we are. I wouldn't change it for the world, sugar. You're my life now."

"You don't miss your life before me?" I ask. "All the women? You would trade that in for me and dirty diapers, a screaming baby at four in the morning?"

He squeezes my ass tighter, making me gasp. "Of course. I can't wait to be a father to our children. I didn't really grow up with a dad myself, but I'd love to experience it with you, Beau, and Griff. Make up for past mistakes, you know?"

I smile at him. "This is at least an eighteen year commitment, you realize that?"

He shakes his head. "No, baby, it's a lifetime commitment. Eighteen years is the kind of shit deadbeat dads say as they pound Bud Light at ten in the morning. We're going to spend our lives with you. Until our hearts stop beating."

My heart swells. I hadn't really thought that far in the future. I just assumed that eventually at least one or two of them would move on from our arrangement. Someone would get bored of sharing and want to find a wife of their own. Wife . . .

My heart starts racing. Suddenly I remember how I was supposed to marry Griff. Is that still on the table? Or am I supposed to marry Beau now that he's the president? Marrying Beau wouldn't be the worst thing to happen. In high school, I used to go on Pinterest and plan out our perfect wedding during lunch. It would be one of those cute rustic barn weddings, and I would have a pretty lace dress that I bought downtown at a boutique, with some sensible heels. We'd have mason jars for glasses—it was going to be something small and intimate. Now, I can't imagine that style of wedding at all. I can't imagine choosing.

I don't want to choose which one of them to marry . . . I want them all!

"Hey, why don't you show me around," I say, trying to stop my crushing thoughts. A wedding is the last thing we need to be thinking about right now, but so is a pregnancy.

Slipping out of Dan's arms, I let him give me a tour around the frame of the new clubhouse. He shows me where Beau's new office will be, where the service bay they're going to open is, and other rooms for members. Dan says they want to get away from the drug and gun trade and open a specialized garage for historical cars and motorcycles. After all, that's the skill they all seem to share, and there has to be a market for quality work. And they're planning on buying the adjacent lot to open a bar that they think I would enjoy taking over. I try my best to listen, but my mind is running on overdrive, thinking about the future that's coming whether I'm ready or not.

CHAPTER 9

"Anything new?" Beau asks Griff as he walks through the door around midnight. Griff ran security all evening while Beau and Danny met with some new prospects and assigned them to various jobs. I hung out with Danny for most of the day, and then he dropped me off at home so I could have some me time. But first, he made sure I locked all the doors to the house, set our home security, and that I knew where all the guns were to protect myself.

I've been sitting on the couch, snuggled up next to Beau, binge watching Sons of Anarchy. I'm wearing a pair of Griff's sweatpants, rolled up at least three times, and wearing one of my cropped tanks with it. I look like crap, but don't really care. Pretty sure I could wear a paper bag and these guys would still be all over me.

"Sons of Anarchy?" Griff asks. "Really?"

"Hey!" I protest when he reaches for the remote to turn the TV off. "I'm enjoying that show! Jax and Opie are so hot! Opie is my favorite though."

"You're going to hate season five then," Griff says.

His eyes move from mine to the sweatpants, and he smirks and sits on his recliner.

"One of the prospects heard a rumor that Stanford was sighted in LaGrange," Griff says. "I've got some guys heading to one of the bars and some local businesses trying to sniff him out. Seems like most of the store owners around there have seen an increase in motorcycles last week and are worried their quaint little town is going to be turned upside down. They said they'll report any suspicious activity to us as long as we promise not to start trouble there."

"Shouldn't be an issue," Beau says. "Just gotta lead them out of there and back to Louisville."

"Should we draw them out with a diversion?" Griff asks, looking at me with a smile. This is it, he's finally going to let me help.

I sit up a little straighter, waiting for a plan, but I guess I was too eager.

"Don't even think about it, Christina," Beau says, giving me a stern look.

I cross my arms and move away from him.

"Think about it, man," Griff says, leaning forward to rest his forearms on his knees. "If we send Christina out to Louisville, I'm sure Stanford would be out in a hot second. We could end it instantly. We know he's still hanging around, we just need to lead him out in the open. We can have eyes on her the whole time."

"Are you out of your damn mind?" Beau yells, standing up from the couch. "We just got her back. What if something goes wrong and he takes her again, kills her?"

My eyes dart over to Griff, hoping he can talk him down, but Griff is speechless. Beau puts his fist to his face . . . wiping tears away?

"Beau?" I ask, standing up and placing a tentative hand out to him.

He spins around on me, and though he's glaring, tears stream down his face.

"So help me God," Beau says. "If I lose you again, I might as well be dead myself."

My heart shatters, and I wrap my arms around his waist, pulling him into a hug. He squeezes me so tightly it's almost unbearable with my bruised ribs, but I let him, because I know it's what he needs right now.

"It's okay," I tell him, and his body shakes against mine. "I'm sorry. It was my idea to help, not Griff's. Don't be angry with him. I just want all this to be behind us."

"You don't think I want that too?" he asks, pulling away from me, his eyes bloodshot. "I hardly sleep anymore. I'm up all night wondering how I'm going to keep you safe, how I'm going to run this MC properly. I'm worried that if I close my eyes, you'll try to run off and be a hero again. I want so badly to have a happily ever after, but I don't know how to give it to you right now."

There's defeat in his voice, and it sounds like he's given up on us, just as we're on the brink of finally getting what we've always wanted.

"We'll find a way," I say, turning to look at each of my men individually. "We'll find some way."

I sit my ass back down on the couch and pull Beau back beside me, snuggling into his lap as Danny joins us and the guys brainstorm our next move. I try my best to keep my eyes open, but sleep eventually takes over, and I'm knocked out cold.

* * *

I'm alone in the woods, but I can hear a baby crying somewhere. Its cries echo around me. I walk through the woods, twigs crunching below my feet, as I make my way toward where I think the cries are coming from. I see the opening of a clearing ahead.

I've been here before.

This is the same clearing where Beau had me clean the dead man's blood off in the small pond. The clearing on the warehouse property. I never expected to see Beau again, but there he was, standing right in front of me. He's not here right now though, instead, there's a figure standing on the edge of the water holding an infant.

"Hello?" I ask, my own voice echoing to match the crying.

"You're just in time," says the voice.

I suck in a deep breath, knowing it's Mr. Thomas before he even turns around.

"I guess I should thank you for bringing me a grandchild," he says, holding a baby to his chest. I can't see its face, and I'm not sure I want to. I know this is another one of my fucked up nightmares, I just can't pull myself out of it.

"Maybe next time you can actually bring a male into the world," he chuckles. "A little boy that will take over the club when Beau is dealt with. You know he'll die, right? Stanford is coming for him. He's closer than you think."

"What are you doing with that baby?" I demand, not taking my eyes off of the swaddled infant.

"I'm going to send your daughter away," he states simply. "We only want men running the club. I could sell her to Stanford for a pretty penny though, since we couldn't bribe him with you. You'd be surprised how much a baby girl goes for on the black market."

"No," I spit, reaching desperately for the child. "Give her to me!"

"Okay," he says with a shrug. He glances at the crying infant one more time. "But you'll have to go get her."

It happens so quickly. One minute he's holding the bundled infant, and the next, he's tossing her into the water where her body makes a splash. I don't even think. I dive in. My eyes open underwater, but I can't see her through the slime and algae. It's almost absolute darkness the further I go. How deep is this lake? It feels like the depth is limitless. My hands finally collide with something, and I pull it *toward me, seeing the lifeless body. I'm not leaving her down here like a piece of trash.*

I look above me, but there's no light, my lungs scream at me, and no matter how much I kick my feet, I don't make any progress. This murky water will be my grave.

* * *

I bolt upright, gasping, my hands clawing at my throat as I try to collect oxygen.

"Fuck," Beau says, holding me up. "She's turning blue, what do we do? She's not breathing!"

Griff rushes to my side and places his hands on either side of my chest as I try to suck air into my lungs.

"Hey, hey, Princess, look at me," he says, panicked. "Breathe with me. In and out."

I take a deep breath in with Griff and let it out slowly, and I follow his lead as we continue to breathe in and out until my panic finally slides away. I know it only takes a few minutes to calm down, but it feels like an eternity.

"That's it," Griff says, softly rubbing my cheeks with his thumbs as he cradles my face in his hands. "Keep breathing for me, baby. Keep breathing. In and out, good girl."

I feel Beau relax beside me, and I try to look around for Danny, but Griff won't let me take my eyes off him.

"She's having nightmares again," I hear Danny say. He comes into my line of sight with a glass of water. I whimper at the sight and close my eyes, trying not to think about drowning.

"Look at me," Griff says sternly, and he doesn't speak again until I obey him. "It was just a nightmare. It wasn't real. Do you want to talk about it?"

I suck in a deep, shaky breath, still struggling to breathe normally.

"I was drowning," I tell them, clutching my wet shirt, the sweat pungent. "I was at the pond where you took me to clean the blood off when we first met. Your father was there. He—"

I can't get the next part out before I begin crying.

"Baby, you're okay," Danny says, sitting on my opposite side. "Take your time. We're here."

"He—he . . . Mr. Thomas was holding a crying baby. He said it was mine, and he was going to sell her to Stanford because he didn't want a granddaughter. He only wants a grandson who can take over the chapter when Stanford comes to kill Beau. I told him no! But then he tossed her in the pond and I couldn't get to her quick enough, and I couldn't swim to the surface. I was dying—"

I'm a panting mess by the time I get the whole story out. The guys hold me tightly as I sob and sniffle through the tears.

"She needs to talk to a therapist," Danny suggests. "She's been having these nightmares since she killed your dad."

"I can't see a therapist!" I yell. "I can't talk to anyone about the shit I see in my head when I close my eyes. The blood, the death, the horrible men."

"We'll figure something out, baby," Griff says, moving his hands to rub my knees. "I promise. We'll find the best therapist for you, and we'll have them sign an NDA for the club or something. We'll figure something out, don't give up just yet."

"I just . . ." I start to say, placing my hands over Griff's and squeezing. "I just want to forget. And I can't."

The guys sit up with me until four in the morning, eating junk food on the couch with the lights on, watching *The Ugly Truth*. Beau knew that it was my go-to movie when I was upset in high school, so he went up to his room to grab a copy that he had hidden away. At some point I relax enough to fall asleep again.

I wake up being spooned by Griff. His breath blows against some of my hair, tickling me. I smooth the hair back and squeeze his hand.

"Morning," he says, pulling me closer to him on the couch.

"Good morning," I reply in kind. I feel kind of silly for waking the guys up with my nightmare. I thought I was getting good at controlling the fear. "Did Beau and Danny go to bed? What time is it?"

He lifts his arm to look at his watch before placing it back around me. "Little after noon. Danny went to the warehouse to get some work done, and Beau is looking into finding someone you can talk to that's not us. Someone who can help you, someone we can trust."

I pull myself out of his embrace and sit on the edge of the couch, still feeling silly. "Maybe it's something I'll grow out of eventually."

"Baby," Griff says softly. "If I had to diagnose you, I'd say you're suffering from PTSD, and it's all my fault."

"Do *not* blame yourself . . ." I place my hand on his cheek.

"Just calling it how it is, Princess," he mumbles. "I should have let you go when Beau said so. We could have sent you to the other side of the country before shit got out of hand."

"*Stop*," I say. "I wouldn't trade you guys for anything. Yeah, my brain is a little messed up right now, but my heart isn't. I've got three men who I'm madly in love with, and who feel the same about me—I think."

He brings my hand to his mouth and places a kiss on my knuckles. "We do feel the same. I love you, Christina. You're my woman, my old lady. You chipped away at this ice cold heart and warmed it with your kindness and fearlessness. You are ours."

"I love you so much, Griffin," I say, leaning down to place my forehead against his. "I mean it."

He smiles and brushes his knuckles against my cheek. "So what does my Princess want to do today? Anything you want. You've got me all day."

My first thought is to just go up to bed and have Griff fuck the trauma out of me, but I know that's not realistic. We need to start finding more things to do, and I was just thinking how I want to start going out on dates with my boyfriends and spending individual time with each of them.

"What do you usually do when you're trying to get your mind off of something?" I ask him curiously.

"Honestly?" he asks, and I nod my head. "I usually go get tatted, but I'm not sure that would apply to you."

I perk up, my mind wheeling with possibilities. "Can we go get a tattoo? Please?"

"Um," Griff says, rubbing his hand on the back of his head like he's nervous. "Are you sure you want to do that? That's a big deal, Princess. Your first tattoo. It's a forever kind of thing."

"So I'll get it somewhere that can be covered up if I don't want it to show," I answer, shrugging my shoulders. "Don't they hurt?"

"Haha, it depends where you get it!" he answers. He sits up next to me and rubs the tattoo on his hand. "Well, certain spots hurt a lot. And some tattoos take multiple sessions and multiple hours of sitting in a chair and not moving. And then you've got a few weeks for it to fully heal."

"That's fine," I say, getting up. "I'll go get ready and we can go. Think of it as a date! Maybe see if your usual artist is available."

"If you're sure," he says, and I lean over and place a kiss on his lips.

"I'm sure. Give me fifteen minutes."

Griff pulls out his phone to shoot off a text to his tattoo artist, and I run up the stairs to put on some shorts and a T-shirt. I thought about getting a thigh tattoo during college, but I was the sweet sorority girl—not the punk or biker chick. Unless I was trying to get an infinity symbol, trashy tramp stamp, or little heart tattoo on my wrist, there was no way I would be accepted. Now I've got no one to impress but myself, and I have a feeling that Beau and Danny wouldn't mind seeing me inked up a little bit.

CHAPTER 10

I lay on a black chair that kind of looks like something you'd see at a doctors office in the back of a tattoo studio. Honestly, this place is probably cleaner than a doctor's office, which kind of shocks me. I always thought tattoo studios were supposed to be sketchy, dirty, and filled with criminal patrons.

This studio is far from it. There's a badass mural on the back wall that I learned was painted by the owner who is currently stabbing me repeatedly with needles in my thigh. The mural is watercolor horses, and it's prettier than anything I've ever seen in a museum. There's a bunch of plants throughout the studio, and it's clean and modern.

My tattoo artist is Mike, his wife is the studio piercer and about five months pregnant. She looks like a freaking goddess with her baby bump, nose piercing, long hair, and tattooed arms. She's done about twenty walk-ins since we've been here. Who knew that nipple piercings were so popular with college girls?

"You're putting in work," I say with a smile.

She laughs and starts cleaning up her work space separated from the main tattoo area by a curtain.

"My wife has seen more tits than any man I've ever met," Mike says, dipping his needle into the small container of black ink. He's just doing the outline to my tattoo today along with some shading. He says I'll probably only need two four-hour sessions because I'm sitting like a champ.

"What can I say?" she says with a smirk. "Nipples pay the bills! Especially in a college town."

Griff sits up front working from his laptop on security stuff. I don't want him to see the tattoo until Mike has most of the outline done. I want him to be surprised like Danny and Beau. They called him about an hour ago to see where we were, and he lied, telling them we're having a spa day at the nail salon next door.

"Oh, damn," says Mike's wife, coming over to check out my thigh. "That's going to be beautiful."

"Your husband is very talented," I tell her. "Taking my random ideas and putting them into one thing is no easy task. I don't know how he did it, and so quickly!"

He rubs some of the ink and sits back to admire his work so far.

"This might be one of my favorite pieces I've ever done," he says. "Thanks for trusting me with your first tattoo."

Mike listened to all the ideas I wanted to incorporate into the piece and ended up drawing out a gorgeous image in about an hour. Griff and I got some lunch a few doors down while Mike drew out the piece, and I was in love from the moment he put the stencil on my skin. It goes from my hip to my knee—go big or go home.

"Almost done," Mike says. "Just going to finish shading in the face, and then we'll bandage you up. You can come back in a month or so to get shading done on the lower half."

"Sounds good," I say. "I'm excited."

The pain wasn't as bad as I thought it would be. It just feels like someone has scratched my leg too hard. Some spots have been more tender, and I know I'm going to dread the shading on the bottom half because it's so close to my knee and bone. I know it'll be worth it in the end, though. I'll have this beautiful piece of art on my body, a piece that will represent my love for my men and everything we've been through.

After about fifteen more minutes, Mike wipes off the area and cleans me up a little before telling me I can stand and go look in the mirror. I turn my leg to check it out, and I smile at how badass the tattoo already looks even though it's only half complete. Mike has done the complete outline. The top half is of a female, half of her face 'painted' to look like a skull, and Mike made her hair look like it's whipping in the wind. She has shaded flames licking up behind her, kind of like the symbol for the MC: a skull with flames shooting out of it. Mike is pretty familiar with the club tattoos since he's one of the main guys who puts them on.

Below the girl's neck is the start of some flowers, and right below that is the outline of a motorcycle that will resemble the one Beau rides once the details are added during my next session. It's already gorgeous, and I now know why people say tattoos are addictive. I've only had it for a few minutes, and I'm already wanting another.

"Mike, this is gorgeous," I say, walking back over so he can wrap my leg in Saniderm adhesive. He goes over aftercare with me, letting me know I can remove the bandage before bed tonight and gently wash it with mild soap. Apparently, lotion is going to be my best friend for a couple of days, and I am on strict orders not to scratch it at all no matter how much it itches.

"We'll see you in a month!" Mike says after Griff hands him some cash and packs up his work computer.

"See you guys! Thanks again!" I wave to him and his wife.

Griff smiles at me as we leave the studio and approach his motorcycle. "Feel better, Princess?"

"Much!" I stand on my tiptoes to kiss him. "Maybe next time I'll get my nipples pierced."

He growls. "Nope. No one sees those perky little tits except for me, Beau, and Danny."

I laugh and pull away from him. "If you insist."

Griff ushers me out the tattoo parlor's doors with a hand on my back. He hands me my helmet before placing his over his head.

"I've got a surprise for you," he says once my helmet is fastened and I'm sitting on the back of the motorcycle. I wrap my arms around his torso, waiting for him to push back the kickstand.

"Oh, yeah?" I run one of my hands up his stomach. "What's that?"

I can see the smirk on his face as he turns to look over his shoulder and back out of the parking space. He flicks a switch by his leg that I don't remember noticing before. "You'll see, Princess."

He gives the bike a little rev, and as the RPMs go up, my seat begins vibrating. I squeal at the shock.

"What the hell is that, Griffin?" I demand.

"Got you a new toy. Don't forget to hold on tightly," he says, laughing as he accelerates forward out of the parking lot.

Once we're out of the shopping area and on some backroads that lead to our house, he accelerates more, making the seat vibrations get even more intense. It's like he sewed a vibrator into my seat. I hold on tightly to him, pressing my nails into his chest, wanting to punish him for turning me on with his bike.

He places a hand on my thigh, slowing down a little so I can hear him over the bike. "You like that, baby?"

"You're going to make me cum before we even pull in the driveway!" I scream, the wind whipping against my face. "This isn't fair!"

He chuckles and accelerates even more, gunning it down the country road toward our subdivision.

"Oh, fuck!" I scream. "Griffin!"

By the time we pull into our driveway, I'm a sweaty, panting mess. My legs shake, and my arms are limp from how hard I was holding on. He climbs off the bike first, lifting up his shirt to check the damage from my nails.

"Damn, Princess," he says, looking at the bright red marks up and down his torso. "You've got some claws."

"You deserved that, Griffin Thomas," I pant, glad that the bike is finally off and no longer vibrating.

"You didn't like your surprise?" he asks, arching a brow at me as he holds out a hand to help me dismount the motorcycle. "I stayed up a few nights ago to install it."

"Oh, trust me, I loved it," I say. "Please don't tell me Beau and Danny installed it on theirs too, though. I'm not sure I can handle that."

He shakes his head. "Nah, this is just our little secret. Maybe I wanted a little incentive for you to be my backpack more often."

"I didn't think you would stoop to bribery," I tell him, wrapping my arms around him and looking up into his beautiful smile. "Big bad Griff thinks he has to bribe his girlfriend with orgasms?"

He places a sweet kiss on my forehead. "What can I say? You're changing me." He glances at his motorcycle and grins devilishly. "Looks like you made a mess. You're lucky you look absolutely exhausted, or I would make you bend over and lick your cum off my seat."

Blushing, I hide my face against his chest. "And you know I would obey you."

He gives my butt a soft smack. "You're damn right. Go clean up. I'll take care of the bike."

"Yes, Sir," I tell him, walking on shaky legs into the house. Griff's bike might be my new favorite toy.

* * *

"When will Beau and Danny be home?" I ask Griff, leaning against the door frame of our laundry room. *Our*. It still baffles me that these are my rooms, my house now.

Griff tosses some laundry into the dryer, his muscles rippling. I might have turned off the AC earlier in an attempt to get him shirtless . . . and it worked.

"Probably not until nine," he says, tossing in a dryer sheet and hitting some buttons. "Why? You wanna go get dinner or something?"

"We could," I say, shrugging my shoulders. "We're technically still on our date night, but I was thinking of something more fun."

"And what's that, Princess?" he asks as I walk over to him. He lifts me effortlessly and sits me on top of the dryer, careful not to brush against my fresh tattoo.

I place my hands on top of his shoulders and wrap my non-tattooed leg around his hip. "I was thinking about some playtime with Daddy."

"Is that right?" Griff asks, leaning in and licking my lips before pulling back. "Does my Princess need to be put in her place again?"

"Yes, please," I say.

He tugs me off the dryer and smacks my ass. "Go to the bedroom, get the blindfold from the nightstand, and cover your eyes. Wait for me there."

"Yes, Sir," I answer. I hurry to our bedroom without another word.

I wait at the foot of the bed with the blindfold on and hear Griff come into the room. "What toys does my Princess want to play with tonight?" he asks. It's not really a question though since I know he's going to make the decision for me.

"Should I get the nipple clamps?" he asks. "You sure seemed dead set on having your nipples pinched after we left the studio earlier. Or should I just tie you up so the rope can leave the prettiest indents on your skin?"

"You could just fuck me," I suggest. Big mistake. Griff's hand wraps around my neck, gripping just enough to cut off my breath a little.

"If I just wanted to fuck you, my cock would already be in that pussy," he growls, removing his hand. "I want you begging before I even think about getting deep inside that pretty pussy."

Griff opens the trunk in front of the bed, and I try to listen closely for what he's getting out, but it's no use. There's no way I can tell what he's grabbing out of there.

"There is one thing I've dreamed about doing with you," he whispers in my ear after closing the trunk. "Have you heard of edging, Princess?"

"I think so . . . Is that kind of what Beau tried doing to me?"

"Almost! It's where your partner gets you so close to an orgasm and then backs off at the last second," he explains. "And then repeats, and repeats, and repeats."

"That doesn't sound very fun," I pout.

He chuckles. "Eventually, the partner lets you have the orgasm, and it's supposed to intensify it even more."

"I don't think anything can intensify the orgasms you guys give me," I say. "You always make me feel so good."

"Well tonight, I'd like it to feel even better," he says, rubbing nylon rope against my wrist. "What do you say, Princess? Can Daddy tie you up and make you scream for him?"

"Yes, please!" I say, holding my wrists out for him to tie together.

He directs me to the top of the bed so he can tie my wrists to the headboard and keep me from touching my clit while he plays with me how he wants.

We go over my safe word before he moves down my body, placing kisses along my breasts, my stomach, my pelvic bone, until he's at my core. I'm thrusting up, trying to get his mouth to kiss my lower lips.

"Greedy little Princess," he says, carefully moving my tatted thigh to the side and putting my other leg over his shoulder. "I'm going to have you begging in less than fifteen minutes."

I giggle. "I'm ready to beg."

He reaches up and pinches one of my nipples, making me jerk against him. Then his mouth is covering my aching core. His tongue licks out, making contact with my clit, and I start to reach for his head to push him against me when I remember he's got my hands tied.

I whimper, and he only laughs in response. "Good thing I thought ahead and restrained you. Now you have to ask for what you want."

"Just suck my clit," I beg. "Please."

He does, and then moves his hand from my breast to slide two fingers into my wet pussy. I buck my hips, trying to chase the orgasm I feel coming, and right when my thighs begin to shake, he pulls away.

I whimper.

I can practically hear the smirk on his face. "How's that feel, baby?" he asks.

"Not nice," I pout. "Why would anyone enjoy this?"

He climbs off the bed, and I hear more toys rustling. I try to remember what contents are inside, curious about what's next, but I come up empty.

"People enjoy it because it makes the orgasm that much more powerful when they finally achieve it," he says, joining me back on the bed and running his fingers over my stomach. "And for the Dom, it's just an act of submission from his pet. You're letting me give you the orgasm when I decide that you've earned it."

"Does this work on men too?" I ask, my curiosity getting the best of me.

"Oh yeah," he answers. "But don't you dare try this on me. You'll be punished. Though I bet Beau would probably enjoy it. Pay close attention, and you'll learn a thing or two."

Before I get another word out, something is placed against my clit, and I quickly realize what it is. The Hitachi wand begins vibrating, and Griff holds it against me until my hips lift off the bed and I'm panting. It doesn't take long at all.

"Oh fuck," I gasp as Griff removes it, but he doesn't turn it off.

"You're being such a good girl," Griff praises. "Daddy's going to make sure you squirt before I'm done with you."

"Daddy, please," I gasp, thrusting my hips up and down, trying to connect with the vibrator. "Please. I want to cum."

"God, you're so fucking pretty when you beg," Griff says. He leans over to kiss me hard. His tongue pushes into my mouth, and our tongues fight against each other for dominance, but in the end I let him win.

He moves back to sit between my legs, placing the wand against my clit. This time, he has to remove it instantly because my impending orgasm is a ticking time bomb. He shuts off the vibrator while waiting for my whimpering and hip thrusting to cease.

This time, instead of his mouth, fingers, or the vibrator, he places the head of his cock against my opening. I grind my hips, trying to pull it into me, but he keeps pulling it out, only letting the head pop in and back out, teasing it up and down my bare slit.

"Isn't this a tease to you as well?" I plead. He moves his head back and forth across my opening again.

"Eh, a little, but I know what's coming," he tells me. "I'm trying to teach you the same amount of patience that I have."

"I think you're just torturing me," I mutter.

He clicks on the vibrator again and inserts just the tip of his dick as he places the wand over my clit. I manage to buck my hips enough to take him in another inch or two, but I want to feel him deep inside me. I *need* to.

He removes the vibrator and pulls out. "What was that, Princess?"

"Nothing, Daddy," I say breathlessly, feeling the waves of pleasure recede again. "Nothing at all."

"That's my good girl." He finally thrusts all the way into me. His thrusts are unapologetic, his thick cock spearing into me over and over.

"Can I cum?" I pant, pulling on my restraints. "Please, Daddy. I need to cum."

He rips the blindfold from my head, and I'm met with his fiery gaze. He places kisses all over my face before pushing himself up to kneel again. He keeps pounding into me and adds the vibrator onto my clit once again. My back sweats as I try to keep the waves of my orgasm at bay. I'm not going to cum until he gives me permission. I bite my bottom lip, but he reaches up with his free hand to stop me.

"Cum for Daddy," he finally demands. He thrusts hard into me as the vibrator assaults my clit.

And he doesn't have to tell me twice!

My orgasm cascades through my body like a bucket of liquid fire. I arch my back off the bed like someone's performing an exorcism on me. Something gushes between my legs as I let my body take over, and I glance down just in time to see liquid squirting around Griff's cock and the magic wand.

"That's it, baby," Griff praises. "Keep it coming."

He pushes in and out of me, then removes and shuts off the wand. He tosses it on the bed and presses down on my lower belly. Orgasms should not last this long, but I can't stop. Just when I'm finally starting to relax, I feel his cock pulse inside me, releasing his seed deeply, and it sends me into another wave of pleasure.

"I can't stop!" I gasp, helpless as I fall victim to another mind-wracking orgasm.

"I know, baby," Griff says, looking down at me with a smile. "Give it all to me."

When I finally finish, I squirm on the bed, realizing I've soaked the sheets beneath my butt and on my sides.

"The sheets," I say, blood flooding my cheeks with embarrassment. "Sorry . . . I'll wash them and put on a new set."

Griff pulls out of me and bends down to place a kiss on my lips. "I don't think so. I'll clean up. You go shower and remove your bandage."

"You sure?" I ask.

"Yes," he says, getting off the bed and wiping his member with a tissue before pulling on some sweatpants. "I'll handle this and make us a snack. The guys should be home soon. I'm sure they're going to want to see your fresh ink. Don't forget to be careful with it in the shower. Mild soap and water."

"Okay," I say. My legs shake. I climb off the bed, avoiding the massive wet spot I've left on the sheets. "Thank you."

"You're very welcome, Princess," he says, coming over and wrapping those gorgeous tattooed arms around me. "But you know the pleasure was all mine. I love seeing you let go and trust me. It means a lot."

Griff gives me one last kiss before swatting me softly on the ass and shooing me off to the bathroom. In the shower, I make sure to be extra careful as I remove the Saniderm wrapping and wash off the blood and excess ink. I take a quick shower, not wanting to damage the tattoo.

Once I'm out and dry, I pull on some loose shorts and a T-shirt. I walk downstairs to find Griff chatting with Beau and Danny over some beers in the living room. My heart rate accelerates as I walk over to join them, unable to hide what Griff and I did today.

Danny practically chokes on his beer, his eyes wide. "What the heck?"

I blush, a dorky smile plastered on my face. I prop my leg on the coffee table, and he can't stop staring.

"What?" I ask, playing coy.

"I thought you guys went to the spa . . . ?" Beau asks, his eyes trained on my leg.

I shrug my shoulders. "Do you not like it?"

"No," Beau says, and my smile falls. "I love it. It's beautiful."

"It's not done, obviously," I say. "He still needs to finish the bottom half, but we at least got all the outlines done."

Danny comes over and kneels down in front of me to get a closer look. "That's sexy as hell, baby girl. What made you wanna do that?"

I shrug my shoulders. "I asked Griff what he does to take his mind off of his bad days, and he said he gets tattooed. Figured, why not? I am y'alls old lady now, better look the part."

"Is that—" Beau starts to say, but his voice cracks. "Is that my motorcycle?"

"Yeah," I answer. I gently run my finger along the edge of the tattoo. "I wanted the top half to sort of resemble the HPMC logo but not be in your face about it. I wanted it to be womanly, but strong."

"Just like you," Beau says, smiling at me. "I love it. Mike's work, I take it?"

I give him a nod.

"He killed it," says Danny. "Can I go with when he finishes it?"

"Sure," I say. "So where's this snack, Griff?"

"I think the boys and I can totally agree that you're the snack tonight," he says with that gorgeous smile he usually only brings out around me. I roll my eyes at him, which ends up being the wrong thing to do, because in an instant, three hungry men pounce and devour me.

Not that I'm complaining.

CHAPTER 11

Sometime in the middle of the night about two weeks later, I crawl out of bed because they're all way too hot and sweaty tonight. It's unbearable. Their body odor is repulsive tonight; it's not always a sexy fun time when you're dating three men exclusively.

I wake up still naked but in Beau's room, when I feel like someone is watching me. I flip over and find Beau leaning over me and placing a palm over my mouth. He's dressed in all black, which isn't unusual. I'm just concerned that it's still dark out, and the birds haven't even started their morning songs.

"Get dressed," he whispers, tossing some leggings and a plain black shirt at me.

"Why?" I ask groggily when he removes his hand. "It's like five in the morning, Beau. I'm tired and my body hurts."

"You wanna go set a fire with me?" he asks, his hands on his hips.

That has me sitting up in bed and pulling on the leggings sans underwear because apparently I need to do a load of laundry. With the amount of times the guys spend turning me on, it's honestly embarrassing how many often I have to change my underwear. I tug on the shirt without a bra, too excited to go with Beau to care.

"What are we burning?" I whisper, following him down the stairs to the mudroom to put our boots on, thankful he's including me in a plan.

"You'll see," he says, handing me my helmet. He picks up a back-pack that he hands me to put on my own back since we're riding the motorcycle.

My heart accelerates as the bike does, and a nervous excitement rushes over me when we get on I-64 heading toward Louisville. We fly by early morning truckers and commuters, but other than that there aren't too many people on the road just yet. Beau exits the interstate and heads down a familiar road.

Nausea settles in my stomach.

"What are we doing here?" I ask when we come to a stop in front of the strip club.

"I had a hankering for a lap dance," Beau deadpans.

"Not funny, Beau Grady," I say, swallowing my discomfort. "Why'd you bring me back here?"

Beau shuts off the bike and turns his body just enough to look at me. His face is deadly serious. "Do you know how much it burns my soul to think about you stripping for scummy men in this hell hole?" he asks. "I want to slit the throats of every man who looked at you, Christina. The only people who can look at you are me and the two men we left sleeping at home. You belong to us. And I'm going to burn this place to the ground."

"Beau," I say, placing my hand on his hip and giving it a squeeze. I start to protest, to tell him its a stupid idea that could get us caught . . . but . . . . "Burn it."

We climb off the bike and he takes the backpack from me. The two of us creep around the building. This arson won't be like my first or second—there aren't any windows making easy targets for fire bombs. We need to get inside, and I know where we store the spare key. I lift the standing ashtray we use to prop the door open when it gets too hot in the club, and sure enough, the key is still beneath it.

Last night, I heard Beau on the phone with Luis. Apparently, the strip club has also been abandoned for the last few weeks since I burned down the DRMC clubhouse. I wonder if Stanford took the other girls with him or just let them go while he's in hiding.

Carefully, I unlock the door, and Beau follows me quietly inside, down the dirty merlot carpet. We enter into the main area that holds the stage, more mirrors than really necessary, the bar, and some scattered seating. Beau dumps out the supplies on a table by the stage, and I arch my eyebrow as a hammer lands on the table.

"Just in case," Beau says. "Anything can be a weapon."

"May I?" I ask, lifting the hammer. Beau nods and squirts a pair of water bottles on the curtains around the room. They smell of gas. I guess that's an easy way to transport gasoline when you're on a bike.

I climb the stairs next to the stage, holding the hammer tightly in my right hand. The entire wall behind the stage is glass. I used to avoid looking at my reflection in these mirrors as much as possible. I didn't want to see myself in the tacky lingerie that Stanford made me and the girls wear, and I certainly didn't want to see myself dancing in front of the men who came into this club.

Now, I look back at my reflection, staring at myself with the club behind me reflected back. Beau stops pouring gasoline, and my eyes flick down where I can see him clenching his fists. It's time to end this.

I lift the hammer and slam it against the mirror. It shatters easily, just a small chunk at first and then everything.

I meet Beau by the bar and hand him the hammer. He places it in the backpack and silently slides the straps over my shoulders.

"Ready?" Beau asks, holding up a matchbook.

"Hell yeah," I say. And we burn it all down.

* * *

"Mmm," I moan, closing my eyes in pleasure. "This is so good, Beau!"

He chuckles at me from across the booth, using his fork to cut his fried egg. We decided to make a pit stop on the way home at America's diner. They are, after all, always open. Who knew destroying your enemy's property would make you so hungry?

"Forgot how much you love Denny's," he says with a smile. "Remember when we used to get up super early every Friday before school and go to the one off Nicholasville Road? You'd always overeat, but you loved it so much."

I smile. "It was my favorite part of the week. Mom hated eating anywhere that had a menu item under fifteen bucks, so my parents never brought me here. I think she was more upset about me eating fried food than she was about catching us having sex in her pool house that time."

Beau drops his fork and covers his face with his hands, shaking his head. "I forgot about that! I swear she wanted me to knock you up—even at seventeen. She just wanted a way to make sure I kept coming around, but as long as I had you, I would."

"Now look at you," I say, blowing on my coffee mug before taking a sip. "You *want* to knock me up."

He drops his hands and reaches across the sticky table for mine. "I do. As long as it's what you want too."

I blush and set down my coffee. "Honestly, I only ever thought about being a mom with *you*. I let go of that dream when we broke up. Now that I've got you back, I really want to carry your babies. That's weird, right?"

Beau's hand pulls from mine, and he slinks back in his seat, staring at my stomach through hooded eyes. "God, just the idea of you being pregnant . . ."

Our waitress comes over, lays the check on the edge of the table, and takes some of our empty plates, saving me from responding to Beau's comment. I'm still worried about whatever fallout will come from the destruction we've been raining down on Demon Rebirth lately, but I trust my guys.

"We should probably get back," I tell Beau. The sun is rising, and Griff and Danny will be up soon. "Maybe we can get back before the guys wake up and have a quickie."

Beau yanks his wallet out of his pocket and pulls out a couple bills to cover the meal. We're on his motorcycle in the blink of an eye, speeding for home.

CHAPTER 12

I'm curled up in Griff's lap as he absently runs his left hand up and down my torso. It sends electric currents down my spine and a flutter in my core, but I'm too exhausted to even try anything. It's late. Danny flips through the TV channels from the recliner. I would yell at him to just pick something, but I'm too content right now.

"Turn on the news," Beau says, coming into the living room with his phone to his ear. "Quick!"

Danny switches the channel and turns up the volume. A news reporter stands in a wooded area with caution tape strung up behind her and some officers milling about. I sit up, more alert than I've been all day. The early morning arson took a lot out of me.

"Action Twelve News First Kentucky just arrived here on the scene of a gruesome crime where a hiker, twenty-seven-year-old Taylor Parker, stumbled upon at least five mutilated bodies," the reporter deadpans into the camera. She's wearing a windbreaker with the station's logo embroidered on the chest, and her dyed blonde hair is damp with rain. "Officers aren't saying much right now, but federal authorities have been seen in the area, and FBI agents have been seen combing the area with dogs and drones. So far, no names from the deceased have been released. The mayor is expected to make an address later this evening. Stay tuned to Action Twelve News First Kentucky for more updates live." The camera pans away from the reporter to a copse of evergreen trees. There's a police canopy set up in the middle with at least two dozen people in official uniforms going about their business.

"The fuck?" Danny paces in front of the screen.

"That's the nature sanctuary!" I say pointing to the screen as they zoom out for some footage of the surrounding area. "Who did that?"

Beau quietly talks to someone before hanging up and tossing his phone on the recliner. He runs his hands through his blonde hair, and it sticks up haphazardly.

"Moose and Luis are looking into it," Beau says sullenly. "They're almost certain that it's a retaliation from Demon Rebirth. That's not the only location where bodies were found today. They were also found near Louisville, Berea, Georgetown, and as far north as Newport. They believe they're all women and children, but it's kind of hard to tell because all the bodies are burned to a crisp."

I place my hand over my mouth, trying to hold down the vomit that threatens to spill out. In the pit of my stomach, I know what is happening. It doesn't take long to confirm my fears.

He's talking with a group of officers beyond the caution tape just over the reporter's shoulder.

"I know him," I say softly. The angle isn't great, but it looks like he's one of the federal agents in charge, pointing and giving orders with a clipboard and radio in his other hand. "He . . . he . . ."

"You know him?" Griff asks. Danny pauses the TV. Thank God for new technology.

I nod quickly. All the words suddenly cascade from my mouth at once. "That's the mobster guy who was pretending to work for Stanford! He's the one who set up the plan for me to burn down Stanford's clubhouse. He was undercover in the club, and he promised that he would make sure the women and children were released from the warehouse and into protective custody."

"Who do you think he actually works for?" Danny asks the other guys.

"That's what we need to figure out," Beau answers, taking a picture of the screen with the time stamp to send off to Moose and Luis. "I feel like this entire thing has been a setup. Or maybe there's another group at play here."

"That's what it's starting to feel like," Griff adds. He scratches his beard and lets out a heavy sigh. "This is an unexpected turn of events, that's for sure."

"I don't understand," I say, shaking my head and leaning forward, my elbows on my knees. "This all started because Mr. Thomas and Stanford were trying to work together, but then Mr. Thomas backstabbed Stanford. That all makes sense! But who is this guy? Whose side is he on?"

"That's what we've got to figure out," Beau says, typing quickly on his phone. "And soon. He's probably already twenty steps ahead of us."

The TV switches to aerial coverage of the forest where all we can see are a hoard of police cars, black SUVs, white tents, and a pair of vans from the coroner's office. I hang my head, tears filling my eyes. Was it all my fault? Did I get them killed?

Or . . .

Are they . . . are they better off dead?

I throw Griff's legs off the couch and run to the bathroom.

* * *

I can't stop shaking. I lie in our bed and stare at the ceiling, my eyes unfocused. My body feels like it is made of jello. My mind is worse. I didn't know what any of them looked like, so I just keep seeing faces over and over. Burnt face. Dead faces.

I go through all the possibilities for the millionth time. None of them make sense. Something is happening, and the man from the club is somehow at the center of it. But . . . he works for the feds. Probably FBI or something.

The guys sent me to bed hours ago, but I haven't been able to sleep. I'm freaking the hell out. I look at the clock on the bedside table, and it's already four in the morning. None of them have come to bed, and I think that's making my anxiety worse. This big bed feels way too empty without my men. I know damn well if I manage to fall asleep, it'll be yet another nightmare, so fight the tiredness in my eyes, constantly tossing and turning under the sheets.

An hour passes, and I still have no answers.

The bedroom door opens a crack, and I sit up in bed to see who it is.

"You're awake," Danny says, but it's not a question. He pushes the door all the way open but doesn't enter the room.

"What's wrong?" I ask, folding my legs over each other and trying to control my limbs from shivering.

"They found him," Danny says. "Griff, Beau, and Moose tracked down that mobster you saw on TV. They've got him held for questioning."

I quickly get out of bed, pulling on a pair of Griff's discarded gym shorts and tying them tightly so they don't fall. I tuck the bottom of one of their shirts that I wore to bed into the shorts and put my hair up into a high ponytail.

"Where do you think you're going?" Danny demands.

"We're family," I tell him. "We're going to go help our guys." What I want to say is that I'm responsible, so now I have to do something to make it right. *Anything* at all to help. But I can't make the words aloud. My body refuses to obey.

He shakes his head. "Baby girl, I don't think Griff or Beau would be too happy to let you watch them rough this guy up. It's going to be bloody, to say the least."

I place my hand on his beard, stroking him softly. I try my best to calm the shaking in my voice. "Dan, when are you guys going to stop treating me like a fragile little girl and realize I'm one of you? Have I not proven that I can handle this shit? How many buildings must I burn down to prove that I'm part of this MC?"

He looks at me for a moment, trying to find a crack in my armor, but in the end, he gives up. He knows I'd do anything to keep us living and breathing—together. And he knows I'm too stubborn to sit down. I proved it the first time I burned down a building for them, I proved it when I shot Mr. Thomas to save their lives. I'll stand by them in all their battles. I have to. For everyone who has been hurt because of me—I owe them all.

"You're right," he says, leaning down to press his forehead to mine. "Let's go."

* * *

Dan and I pull up on his motorcycle to the warehouse on the edge of Fayette county. It makes me wonder if they're planning on releasing the man who said he wanted help taking out Stanford Williams or if they plan on killing him once they get some answers. I'm guessing the answer is the latter. They could bury him out here and no one would ever find the body.

Wrapping an arm over my shoulder, Dan escorts me into the building. It's shockingly silent. We walk deeper into the warehouse, and Dan knocks on a locked door with a peephole. The door swings open, releasing a distinct scream, and Griff blocks my view just as I see the man slump in a chair.

"Is he dead?" I ask, trying to look over Griff's shoulder. Griff's white shirt is covered in blood that's yet to dry, but the man in the chair is covered in even more.

Griff doesn't answer me. Instead he looks at Danny. "What's she doing here? This shit is dangerous, man! No place for a woman."

Dan holds me tighter to his chest. "She's part of this. She wants to help."

I interrupt them, standing as tall as I can. "*She* has seen a couple dead bodies, so I think *she's* capable of holding her own with club business. So, is he dead?"

"No," Beau speaks up, tossing some pliers onto the steel table beside the chair. "Just passed out. He'll be up in a little bit—sooner if we want to speed things up."

I push past Griff and hear him close the heavy door behind him, still grumbling about my safety.

"Where's Moose?" I ask, crossing my arms over my chest and trying to breathe through my mouth instead of my nose so I can't smell the repulsive, metallic stench of blood. I'm fairly certain there's vomit on his shirt as well, and it looks like he's pissed himself.

"Sent him home," Beau says, wiping some blood from the instruments they've been using. "Figured Griff and I could handle this. We have a handful of prospects outside watching things just in case. Someone else might be looking for this piece of shit right now. You should be in bed, baby."

I roll my eyes. "I couldn't sleep, Beau Grady! I've been worried sick."

He drops the rag and comes over to pull me into a hug. "Sorry, we just wanted to get to the bottom of this. Every minute counts."

I squeeze him tightly before pulling away. "We're a team, the four of us. Where you go, I go. Let me help."

"If you wish, my queen," he says, stroking his fingers across my cheek.

Griff walks by us with a sloshing bucket and proceeds to dump it all over the man, it splashes a little on Beau and I, causing me to jump back, and the man gasps. "Wakey wakey, asshole!" Griff says, dropping the bucket beside him with a clang.

The man looks around, his eyes not focusing on anything, like he has forgotten where he is. Once he realizes, he begins sobbing.

"Aw, come on now, Boris!" Beau says, slapping him across the cheek. Its a degrading hit more than one meant to cause pain. "Big Mafia man like yourself shouldn't be breaking this easy! Or are you just a fraud? Who are you really working for?"

"I swear!" the man cries. "I'm just a peon at the bottom of the Calvos family food chain!"

Griff grabs the man by his hair, yanking his head sharply backward. "And why the hell would a Mafia family from Chicago give a damn about what's happening in central Kentucky?"

"They've been watching Demon Rebirth and Hell Prevails for a couple years," he admits. "They sent me to learn some things about Demon Rebirth, to eventually steal their inventory. Take over for them. The Calvos family is far more intelligent than a motorcycle club. You goddamn gearhead morons don't know anything."

Beau slaps the man again. "Morons? What does that make the Mafia? Come on, man. We're all the same. Some of us just respect our family more. We'd never turn on ours. Yet here you are, telling us all the secrets. Are you going to sing like a little birdy for me? And what's that family of yours going to think when we send you back to Chicago with a nice little recording so they can see just how loyal you really are?"

The man whimpers.

Beau leans down to whisper in my ear, and even though it shouldn't, his voice sends a shiver down my spine and starts up an electric current. I want him so badly right now.

"Your turn," he says as his breath skirts across my cheek. "Get some answers for us."

He nods toward the table of various items: a baseball bat, hammer, scalpels, pliers, nail gun, and other items that I have no idea how to use for torture. I've never tortured anyone before, but this man deserves it. *Inventory*, he said. He meant the people. Women and children. Trafficking victims held in a warehouse, destined to be sold into slavery.

I pick up the hammer. Griff is still holding up the man's head by his wet hair.

"You remember me?" I ask the man.

The man laughs at my approach. "What do you think she's going to do to me?" he asks the rest of the room. "She's just a girl. I know how weak she is. I watched your little whore dance on stage every night."

"You son of a—" Danny grabs the Louisville Slugger and pulls it back into a swing, but I hold my hand up to stop him without saying a word. "Call her a whore one more time and see what happens. Eat shit."

I cock my head to the man. "You clearly don't know what I'm capable of, especially when I have my entire club backing me up."

I lift the hammer and slam it right down on his crotch, pulling a scream from him. I look at each of my guys—they all hiss through their teeth and look away with pain. "What? Am I doing it wrong?"

Beau shakes his head. "No, I think you got the gist of it. We usually just use the hammer to break fingers, not their manhood."

I shrug. "I'll do that too. Don't worry."

It takes a moment for the guy to stop moaning and groaning about me going straight for his balls, but as soon as he sees me lift the hammer back up to go in for round two, he starts begging me to stop.

"Who burned those bodies and left them on the hiking trail," I ask, bending over to look him in his teary eyes. "Who were they? The women and children? The fucking *inventory*?"

"Stanford's crew did it," he coughs through clenched teeth. "The bodies are some of the women and children that didn't get out of the warehouse on time."

Rage turns in my belly. "The ones you were supposed to set free? The ones I burned down a building to save?"

"Yeah," he says. It takes him a moment to catch his breath before he can speak again. "Calvos took most of them, but we didn't have enough buses. We could only take so many."

I lift the hammer again and hit him across his jaw. I doubt I'm strong enough to break it outright, but some of his teeth rattle right out of his skull and fly across the room. Blood oozes from his mouth, and I step aside as he tries to spit some of it out in my direction. I feel like at any moment, he's going to stop begging for his life and start begging for us to kill him.

"So you just left the rest of them?" I demand. The sick feeling in my stomach isn't going away. I thought hitting him, really fucking hurting him, would take some of it away.

"Are you listening?" he says awkwardly from the loss of his teeth. "We didn't have enough buses to get them out. Calvos underestimated how much inventory was being held."

"What did Calvos do with the ones that made it out?" Beau asks for me. He can see I'm starting to lose my composure.

"It's not what you think," says the almost toothless mobster. "Calvos hates pedos and traffickers. Kentucky has been a hot spot for them for a few years. Calvos is working with authorities to get them all home."

"But he doesn't give a shit that Stanford is now burning and dumping the rest of the bodies?" I ask Boris.

"Every war has casualties, little girl," Boris says as blood drips from his mouth. "You should have seen Morocco in ninety-eight. Or L.A. last year. We stacked you biker assholes three high in every grave. Get used to it."

I lift the hammer again and slam it down on his left hand, knocking against the rings on his knuckles. He screams, and I just shrug my shoulders. "Oops. It slipped. Sometimes that just happens."

"Fucking, bitch," he says through clenched teeth.

"You haven't answered all of my questions. Why does Calvos give a shit about things going on in Kentucky?" Beau demands. He crosses his arms across his chest. "He's getting in the way of us handling business."

"Because the Calvos family is looking to expand their empire, obviously. You ever hear of a turf war?" he says like we should have already known. "They're going to take over this state. You wouldn't believe the money they plan to bring in from your little pony races in the bluegrass state, whatever the fuck that even means. Stealing the inventory from Demon Rebirth was just for the set up. We plan on taking over the drugs and arms everyone has been dealing in this state as well. But first, he wants to get rid of the traffickers. They're bad for business, you know? Too many missing girl posters and the police start to care. Seems like your little club was trying to get their hands on some inventory, too. Ah, but you're the *good guys*, I forgot."

"We're trying to get out of that shit!" Beau yells. "We want nothing to do with drugs and guns. I'm trying to clean up this fucking mess of a club. And we had no clue that Mr. Thomas was trying to get into trafficking!"

The guy shrugs. "Yeah, well, Calvos always wants to make sure we don't leave any loose ends. You'll either end up dead or in police custody before this war is over. Or you and Stanford are going to kill each other and do our jobs for us."

I slam the hammer on his right hand, and his screams echo around the room's metal walls. "You fucking bitch," he seethes. "I'm giving you answers! That means you stop with the torture."

"Oops," I lie. "My bad, I guess all this talk of war makes me violent."

"Damn, she's hot when she's torturing men," Danny mutters behind me. I turn around just in time to see him readjust himself in his pants. "Let's hurry and wrap this up."

Beau gives him a nod and then turns to face me, stroking his thumb across my chin. "Baby, go wait in the office. This next part isn't going to be pretty."

I consider arguing with him, but the pungent smell of piss and blood fills my nostrils, making my decision an easy one. Danny comes up behind me and takes the hammer from my hands, then gives me a little nudge toward the door. I don't look back as I leave the room. I know they're going to kill him. I think he knows too. It's either my guys kill Boris, or the Calvos family will kill Boris for giving us answers. Either way, his life is going to end.

I remember a bad guy in a TV show saying there are good deaths and bad deaths. A shudder runs the length of my spine, and the hairs on my arms stand on end.

I go into the office at the end of the hall to wait for my men to finish up business. I can't hear a thing through the heavy steel walls. I walk over to the couch on the far wall, trying to relax while I wait. There's no telling how much longer it's going to take. I'm sure they're going to want to get some more information from the guy before they kill him.

I'm not sure how long I lie on the couch, but when I startle awake, it's completely dark. Wait—no, there's something over my eyes. A blindfold. I sit up abruptly, getting ready to remove the blindfold, but a calloused hand stops me.

"Beau?" I ask the room. "Griff? Dan?"

"It's okay," whispers Beau. "Are you going to be a good girl?"

My tongue flicks out to lick my lips, and I smile, dropping my hand to my lap. "I'll be good."

"Keep your blindfold on, baby," he says. His voice is a little farther away.

"Did you finish . . . business?" I ask. "Is everything okay now?"

"Yeah, you don't need to worry," he answers. "I just wanna play a little bit. Take the edge off."

"Okay," I whisper back.

"Take your clothes off, Princess," Griff's command, his husky voice sending shivers down my spine. I thought it was just the two of us, but my stomach flips realizing I'm in for some activities. I love when the guys work together. Beau brings his softness and sweetness, while Griff brings his domination tactics that make my toes curl. And then there's Danny, playful at times, but at other moments, he makes me feel like a goddess fit for worship.

I obey Griff, carefully pulling my top over my head without moving the blindfold. I reach behind my back to unclip the bra, allowing it to fall away. I push my pants down my hips and calves, dragging my underwear with them, where they both get caught at my ankles, causing me to struggle. One of the guys reaches out an arm to assist me, and I stand on one leg to remove my pants and undies before switching legs and taking them all the way off.

"Such a good girl," Griff whispers into my ear, pushing some of my stray baby hairs out of the way. "On your knees."

I whimper in protest, not wanting to hurt my knees on the concrete floor. I breathe a sigh of relief when my knees connect with a soft pillow, and I sit back with my bare ass against my cold thighs, waiting for my next instructions.

"We take care of our little whore," Griff says, standing beside me and lifting my chin with his hands to look up even though I can't see a thing. His thumb rubs over my lips before he plunges it inside and commands me to suck on it. "You are our whore, right?"

He doesn't remove his thumb, so I'm forced to mumble my answer with my mouth full. "I'm your whore."

He removes his thumb from my mouth and smacks my cheek softly. "Good whores know better than to talk with their mouths full. Guess we're going to have to teach you a lesson."

The sounds of zippers and denim fill my ears, and I smile as I feel the guys surround me. The anticipation is agonizing, and it has my pussy dripping.

"Open up," Griff says, grabbing the hair at the crown of my head and turning my face to the left and away from him. "Suck Danny's cock for me. He's been hard as a rock since watching you torture our little friend in the other room."

My jaw drops open, and Danny buries himself down my throat. One of his hands wraps softly around my throat while Griff urges me to take him even deeper, causing me to gag.

"Fuck, sugar," Dan mutters. He tightens his hand around my throat. "I can feel my cock deep in there."

Griff yanks my head back and turns it to the other side. I gasp for air once Dan's hand releases me, but my guys don't give me a chance to catch my bearings. Another cock slides between my lips, two hands framing my face, slowing things down a bit. I know deep in my gut that this is Beau. Griff releases my hair and smoothes it down as Beau takes control, holding my head still as he slowly slides in and out.

"You're ours forever, you know that, baby?" Beau says. "We're never going to let you go. We'd burn every motherfucker to the ground to keep you safe."

"I love you," I say when Beau pulls out to give me a moment of reprieve. "I love the three of you so much. I'm yours . . . forever."

"We love you too," Griff says, pulling my face in his direction. "And, might I say, you look so fucking delicious on your knees."

I give him a little smile before opening my mouth to lick along his shaft. He grips my hair again and forces me to take him deep. I place my hands on his thighs, but let him control the pace. After a minute or so, he pulls me off and I can feel a string of saliva from my lips to his cock. Griff releases me and wipes the drool from my lips. When his hand leaves my skin, I hear him stroking himself with the remaining saliva I left.

One of the guys urges me to stand up. Once I'm up, he leads me to the couch, and my thighs collide with one of the others who seems to be sitting in front of me. A mouth latches onto one of my nipples, and

I let my head roll back with pleasure as one of my boyfriends suck and knead my breasts.

"Straddle," Griff says from behind me. He and whoever isn't on the couch help me carefully straddle the lap of whoever was just teasing my sensitive nipples. "Good girl. Ride him. Take his cum. You're not done until you have all of our seed dripping from your pussy."

Ah, so that's what we're doing now. I give a smile as I begin lifting myself up on whoever's cock I'm on. I think it's Danny's because I can feel callouses on the hands as he helps lift me up and down. I know it's not Griff, and Beau's hands are smoother. Danny has been working with his hands since he was a teenager, tinkering with engines and working in construction.

"Danny?" I ask, leaning in to ask for a kiss.

"Damn right, sugar," he says, licking my lips teasingly. "How'd you know it was me? Because I have the nicest cock?"

I roll my eyes, even though he can't see them behind my blindfold. "This isn't a dick measuring contest, Dan. This is a 'make me cum all over that cock' scenario."

"Yes, my queen," he says breathlessly. He lifts his hips up off the couch so he can hit my g-spot. I place my hands on the cushion behind him and meet him thrust for thrust. The moment my walls begin squeezing him, he tips over the edge with me. He doesn't stop thrusting until he gets the final drop of his pleasure inside me. "Fuck, I love you so much."

"I love you too," I say, leaning forward to crush our lips together.

I squeal as someone pulls me off of Danny and lifts me into the air. Danny must move out of the way because I'm turned around and being bent over the arm of the couch, my face flat on the cushion as someone pushes their way into me with one hard thrust. He doesn't give me time to adjust, just begins slamming his hips against my ass. A swift hand slaps my right cheek, and I know damn well who is trying—going—to fuck me into oblivion.

"Daddy," I moan into the couch, just as another smack lands on my ass.

"That's my girl," Griff says proudly, placing his hands on both my shoulders to get more leverage. I turn my head to the side and bite my lip. My mind is complete mush when it comes to these guys using me for their pleasure and giving me multiple orgasms.

"Is Daddy's little whore going to cum all over Daddy's cock?" he asks, moving one of his hands to between my legs where he rubs at my sensitive clit.

"Yes, Sir," I gasp. "Please."

Griff's fingers work overtime rubbing at my clit to get me over the edge. Soon, my second orgasm crashes through my body, and Griff moves his hands to my hips to pound his pleasure into me at the same time I let go of my own.

"That's my little Princess," he grunts, slapping my ass one more time before pulling out. He lifts me up and presses soft kisses all over my neck, my cheeks, my lips. "My good girl."

I smile against his lips and squeeze my legs shut, trying to keep his and Danny's cum from slipping out. Griff and I have come so far. He's gone from the grumpy,and sometimes scary motorcycle club member to this amazing lover that gives me the best of both worlds. He can be dominant, but afterwards he's the sweetest teddy bear. He wraps me up in a warm hug and kisses my neck.

He removes the blindfold, and I notice one of them has dimmed the lights in the office so my eyes don't hurt as they adjust.

"My turn," says Beau, reaching a hand out to me. I give Griff one last kiss before taking Beau's hand and letting him pull me away.

Beau runs his hands up and down my arms and lifts me up, and I wrap my legs around his waist. He softly places me down on the couch where I had fallen asleep, and I find two pillows under my hips, holding them up in the air a bit. I let out a laugh as Beau pushes my legs from his hips.

"You know?" I start, looking at Beau but speaking to all three of them. "A girl might be getting the feeling the three of you are trying your damnedest to put a baby in her."

"You're not wrong," Griff says, using a tissue to wipe off his cock. Danny sits in the chair next to him, still with his pants off and looking at me with adoration. "And I hope the little shit looks just like his mama."

"Or her," I say, and three sets of eyes go wide. "We could have a daughter."

Beau slaps a hand over my mouth to stop me from speaking, and I laugh against it until he thrusts inside me. My laugh is cut off as my eyes roll into the back of my head from the pleasure.

"If we have a daughter," Beau says. "She's never going to date . . . ever."

Griff and Dan nod in agreement, and I just roll my eyes. Beau removes his hand from my mouth and slides it down between my breasts.

"Stop talking about our unborn children . . . and *fuck* me."

I always have to demand Beau to give me anything more than easy love making. He's always so sweet and soft in the bedroom, he never lets his natural, primal instincts take over. Don't get me wrong, I love him making love to me. Right now, however, I want the sex to be raw and addicting. I want him to fuck me into this couch until my legs are jelly and I can't move. I want the type of sex that'll prevent me from being able to pull myself onto the back of one of their bikes.

I want to get fucked hard enough that I forget everything evil in the world. All the death, the murder, the trafficking and torture.

Beau grits his teeth and presses my hips into the pillows as he fucks me harder and harder. He leans down and bites my bottom lip before licking it and then pushing his tongue into my mouth, causing me to moan against him.

"Fuck—Beau," I say, scratching my nails up his back. "Yes!"

"Take it, baby," he leans down to whisper into my ear. "Take it all, Christina. You're ours. Show me that you're ours."

I moan and press my hips up against his. "I'm going to cum, Beau, please."

Instead of moving a hand to rub my clit, Beau reaches to my breasts and squeezes each of my sensitive nipples until I'm thrashing against him. His thrusts go from rapid to slow and deep, fucking against my g-spot. I shatter against him, and he holds still, deep inside me until I stop cumming. I feel him release inside me, and as he slowly pulls out, some of his cum drips down my leg. I reach down with a shaky hand and try to push it all deep inside me, knowing it'll drive my men wild.

Three hungry sets of eyes watch me, mesmerized as I finger myself.

Griff stands and comes over to get a closer look.

"Now that we've filled that hole," he says. "I think it's time to fill up the other one too."

Danny stands up beside him, his cock already hard again in his hands, while Beau is still kneeling between my thighs.

"Flip over, Princess," Griff says with a smirk. "Give us that ass."

CHAPTER 13

I wake up startled but with the most exquisite pain in my body. It feels like every muscle I have was just worked to its limit. We're still in the office, the guys must have let me pass out after we had our fun. I have no idea how long I slept, but I feel oddly refreshed. Griff's cut covers my torso, and it looks like Beau's is covering my lower half as a make-shift blanket.

"Hey, baby," Beau says when he sees me stirring. He's sitting at his computer working on something. "Sleep well?"

Sitting up, I drape the cuts over the arm of the couch where I was just pleasantly fucked. I pull on my clothes and tiptoe over to Beau.

"Yeah, really well," I answer. "First time in a while I've been able to sleep through the night without having nightmares."

He pats his thigh for me to sit down and holds me tight against him. "You were out cold. Didn't even stir in your sleep."

"Where'd Griff and Danny go?" I ask, noticing it's just the two of us.

Beau closes out of the open tabs on his computer and shuts it down. "They're getting some things together. We got some more in-formation out of that shithead before we finally killed him. Griff is getting us a car, and Danny's working with a prospect to make some arrangements."

"Car for what arrangements?" I ask. What did I miss while I was blissfully conked out?

"We're going to Chicago to meet with this Calvos fellow," Beau says. "I want to end this war before it gets out of hand. Whether we end it by a truce, or . . ." He doesn't give another option, but I know option two won't be taken lightly.

I lean back against Beau and close my eyes. "What am I going to do while you're gone?"

His chest vibrates with his soft laughter. "You're coming with us, of course. You're part of our team. The most important piece, if we're being honest."

I roll my eyes and smile. "Yeah, yeah, you don't have to keep buttering me up. I'm already yours. So anyway, when do we leave?"

Just then, the door to the office opens, and Griff walks in. Dried blood is splattered across his white shirt in a sinister arc. "Right about now, my queen. Your chariot awaits."

* * *

It's a little after lunchtime when we finally roll into Chicago. No one had any coins, and none of us expected so many tolls, so we had to take a few backroads that added an hour to the drive.

Chicago isn't exactly what I imagined, though I can't help but lean against the windows to look up at all the tall buildings. They're gigantic skyscrapers compared to the buildings in downtown Lexington. I assume these are nothing compared to New York City, though. I'm shocked when Griff pulls our car up to a valet attendant. It has to cost an arm and a leg to valet park in downtown Chicago. The attendant opens up my door and I step out, following the guys. Griff hands him the keys and gives him a fake name: Grey Calvos.

I arch a brow at him as he slings his arm over my shoulder.

"Why'd you not give him a real name?" I whisper.

"I did," he says. "It's the name of the person we've got a meeting with. He requested we bring back the body of the traitor so they can use him as an example."

"That's why the car smelled?" I squeal. Griff ushers me into a ritzy building without answering.

People stare at us as we walk in, probably because the four of us stick out like a sore thumb in our leather boots and all black ensembles. There are women wearing tight pencil skirts with flowy blouses, men in full suits and shiny dress shoes, and a few security guards with ear pieces scattered throughout the lobby. Griff walks us to a bank of elevators like we own the place.

An empty elevator opens, and the four of us walk in. The other people who were waiting decide to pass on this one. I don't blame them. His cut rides up just enough to reveal the not-so-concealed pistol on his hip. The door closes, and Beau presses the button for the very top floor.

None of us say a word as the elevator climbs all the way to the top without stopping. When the doors open, it lets us out at a small, dark lobby. There's a brown couch sitting on one wall and two matching chairs across from it. Far from what I expected. Honestly, I thought we'd be pulling up to a warehouse or stockyard or something sketchy. I guess the Calvos Syndicate likes to keep things a little bit classier. Organized crime looks a lot different in Chicago than in Kentucky.

I jolt when a voice blares from an unseen intercom system.

"Mr. Calvos will be with you shortly, Mr. Grady," says a female voice. "Please have a seat."

I glance in the corner of the room and spot a security camera on the ceiling. They probably knew we were coming from the moment we stepped foot in the building. Hell, they probably knew before we crossed state lines. Griff plops down in one of the chairs, and Danny pulls me down to sit on his lap on the couch. Beau shakes his head at us, but sits on the chair beside Griff. No one says a word, probably afraid that whoever is watching can also hear us.

Danny keeps rubbing his hands along my legs and leaning in to kiss my neck, but I just smack him away. He needs to keep his head on straight.

"Would you stop!" I whisper. "We're literally waiting to meet a Mafia boss who could be watching us right this second. Stop teasing me!"

Danny chuckles, pushing some hair off my other shoulder. "Maybe Calvos is into watching. I know I am . . ."

"Shh!" I say, trying to squirm out of his hold.

"Would you two stop it?" Beau chides, checking his watch.

"He started it!" I yell louder than I intended.

Before Beau can scold me again, the door to the miniature lobby opens, and a man in a pinstripe suit comes out.

"Mr. Calvos is ready to see you," he says. "Follow me."

The four of us stand and follow the man through the doorway. Beau takes the lead of our group, and Griff and Danny flank me on my sides, keeping me safe between them. The man doesn't say another word, just escorts us to a wide open room with an immaculate kitchen and a huge desk in front of floor to ceiling windows. There isn't a spec of dust or dirt in sight. Everything smells of expensive oils and meticulously maintained furniture.

There's nowhere for us to sit, so we just stand around the desk, our eyes glued on the breathtaking forty-fourth-floor view.

The ping of an elevator signals someone's arrival behind us. This must be Calvos' private elevator, probably making it easier for him to get in and out of this massive skyscraper. When the doors open, out walks a man in an all black suit with a woman beside him in a blood red dress. She can't be much older than me, but she gives off an aura that says she's far classier than me and only shops at the fanciest of stores, spending tens of thousands on an outfit she'll only wear once just because she can.

I glance at my guys to see if they're giving her the same attention, but it looks like they're eyeing the man. He's handsome, but totally not my type at all, way too much of a pretty boy. He's basically the type of guy I'm sure my mother expected me to meet in college and get married and pop out kids with.

"Gentleman," he says. He doesn't shake hands. He pulls out the high-backed leather chair and takes a seat. Then, as though noticing me for the first time, he inclines an eyebrow. "Miss."

I give him a tight smile, not sure what I'm supposed to do in this situation. My mouth dries when the woman casually sits on the man's thigh like we're not even here.

"I'm Grey, and this is my wife, Arden," he says, smoothing his hand on her silk covered hip. "Your delivery has been thoroughly inspected. I appreciate you driving it all the way back to my family."

Beau gives a nod. "Of course, and thank you for meeting with us."

"So, what's this really about?" he asks, like he doesn't know.

"Don't play stupid, Grey," Griff says, crossing his arms. "You know why we're here. Your little rat told us everything."

Grey gives a sinister smile and leans back in his chair. I watch him carefully as he rubs his hand up and down his wife's thigh.

"So if you know my plan, why are you here? What's to stop me from slaughtering you right now?"

"Because we don't want to get in your way," Beau replies. He places his hands on Grey's desk and leans. "Griff's father is dead. I lead our MC now. I'm trying to get out of the illegal shit Mr. Thomas was doing with Demon Rebirth. No guns, no drugs, no trafficking."

"And what do you want me to do for you, Mr. President?" Grey asks with a hint of sarcasm. "Spare you? Take out Stanford and his gang for you? I don't do favors, Beau Grady. The Calvos family is no charity. When you make a deal here, you make it with the devil."

I feel Griff stiffen next to me. He's trying his best to not lash out and lunge across the desk to choke Grey. As much as Griff was 'bred' to be the next MC president, I think this kind of tense situation is an aspect that makes Beau the better fit. Beau is calm, but he also doesn't take shit.

Arden, the wife, leans in to whisper into her husband's ear. Grey's eyebrows pinch together at whatever she's suggesting. When she pulls away, Grey gives her a nod before turning back to us, eyeing each of us individually.

When his eyes meet mine, each of my guys take one step closer to me, trying to protect me from any possible danger. My skin crawls as Grey's eyes penetrate mine.

"Mr. Calvos," I stutter. "With all due respect, I've been around Stanford for an extended period of time. He's a monster. Mr. Thomas was also a monster, and I took him out. We've been trying to take out Stanford as well. All we want is peace. We want to be able to turn our MC around and live out our lives together—happily and safely."

Grey gives a nod. I glance over at Arden and she gives me a soft, knowing smile.

"These three are really protective of you," Grey says, cocking his head to the side. "Why is that?"

I take a deep breath. "Because they love me, and I love them."

Grey arches an eyebrow. "The four of you are together?"

"We're a family," I say, nodding. I reach out and squeeze Danny's hand. Griff wraps an arm around my shoulder, holding me close. "I'm theirs, and they're mine. We'd do anything for each other, just like I'm sure you would do for your wife."

Grey glances at his wife and lifts his hand to turn Arden's face to him. "I could never share you, amore. I would slit the throats of any man who dares lay a hand on you."

"Grey," Arden says with a ragged breath. "You know you're the only man for me."

Arden places a lingering kiss on Grey's lips. I blush at how open they are with their affection and look away for a moment. When Grey pulls away from his wife, he gives her a smile and then turns his attention back to us.

"Well, you didn't come all the way from Lexington just to make your little delivery, try a deep dish pizza, and go home. No, you came to stare the devil in his eyes. Well . . . here I am. Let's make a deal."

* * *

Arden and Grey's housekeeper brings us all glasses in their sitting room along with a bottle of top tier bourbon. It feels ironic to drink Kentucky bourbon in a swanky Chicago penthouse, but I don't complain. When I was a bartender, we only managed to get our hands on one of those bottles, and we charged eighty bucks a pour. Grey pours a gentleman's finger for each of us, including Arden and I.

"So how do you suggest we solve this issue and make the Calvos family and your little motorcycle gang happy?" Grey asks.

"It's a motorcycle *club*!" Griff and I both say at the same time. He gives me a devious smile.

"Semantics," Grey says with a flip of his hand. He takes a sip of his bourbon before resting his arm on a tall, wingback chair. Him and Arden sit in matching chairs that I could actually describe as thrones. They look like freaking royalty, but I guess in their world, they really are. "Tell me what you expect from us."

"We want you to cancel whatever plans you had to exterminate our club," Beau says. "We're pulling out of all illegal activity. We want to turn our club around and redeem our name in Lexington. We want to safely live out the rest of our lives. Too many of our brothers' lives have been taken or threatened over the years. As president, I'm asking you to call off your orders and allow us to live in peace."

"And what about Stanford and his crew?" Grey asks, swirling the neat bourbon in his crystal glass. "He's a sorry excuse of a man . . . but my plans are already in motion."

"Kill him," Griff says, like the answer is obvious. "I don't give a damn. Dismantle his club. Take over his businesses if you'd like."

"The legal part of his business," Beau adds. "In addition to you letting us go about our lives, we ask that you end all human trafficking in Kentucky. You don't get to come in and just start trading people like fucking *inventory*."

Hearing the word Boris used makes me wince. I hate it.

Grey smiles and finishes at least two hundred dollars of bourbon in one swig. He pours more into his glass before speaking. "I'll do you one better," Grey finally says, and the four of us are basically on the edge of our seats waiting for his offer. "You allow my esteemed family to take over Louisville—guns, drugs, cars, you understand, I'm sure— and we'll deal with traffickers. They're bad for business. Too many feds, and things become . . . complicated."

Arden reaches out a hand for Grey. "We despise them for other reasons as well," she says coyly. "We've been working for years taking out human traffickers in this state . . . they just keep popping up like pesky weeds."

"We try our best though," Grey adds. "And we also organize a considerable amount of fundraising to promote awareness, though I must say, a nine millimeter bullet solves more problems than a thousand dollar ticket to dinner with the mayor."

I squint my eyebrows, confused. "But the guy you sent to spy . . . he said you wanted to take up all that business."

Grey gives me a soft smile. "We cannot be completely honest with the soldiers or they'll ruin the plan. Some of them tend to get kidnapped from time to time, so we must control the narrative they tell when they inevitably talk." He gives a sharp laugh and gently swirls his bourbon around in the glass. "You did not genuinely believe that you caught one lowly soldier, knocked him around a bit, and uncovered an entire Mafia plan, did you? No, no, truly, you must be more sophisticated than that."

"So what, you fed him a bunch of lies and sent him to Kentucky for fun?" Griff asks.

"We've been watching your motorcycle *club* for years, trying to figure out the best time to act and put a stop to the human trade so we can expand our more clandestine trades. When we heard that you burned down the daycare . . . we had assumed that Mr. Thomas was trying to get out of it. But it seems like that was just a retaliation to some bad blood between him and Stanford, I assume?"

Beau nods his head. "Yes, and as I've said before, we had no clue that our previous president was trying to lead our club into that business. I'm working on fixing the mistakes."

"And you're his son?" Grey asks, looking at Griff.

He nods. "Yes, but I'm nothing like that bastard. I hope he's rotting in hell."

I reach my hand over and give Griff a reassuring squeeze. "You're nothing like him, Griffin."

Grey Calvos is silent for a moment. He's calculating options in his head, weighing out the pros and cons like a merchant counting silver coins. When he finally speaks, I think we're all shocked by the outcome.

"I'm sorry," Beau says. "Can you say that again?"

Grey chuckles, finishing his second bourbon and then pouring a third. "I said, my men will make sure Stanford and his club disappear."

"And by disappear, you mean . . . swimmin' with the fishes," I ask for clarification. As soon as the words escape my mouth, I know I've made a fool of myself. What is that line from? The Godfather? Goodfellas? Its so corny, and I know none of these Italian mobsters actually speak like that.

Grey and Auden both burst out in laughter, offering a rare glimpse beyond their pampered and gilded exteriors. It's comical for these two sophisticated mobsters to share a belly laugh, but they do. Somehow, it makes me lower my guard a little as well. I've barely touched my bourbon so far, but I relax just a notch and take a sip.

"I guess you could call it that," Grey says, wiping a tear from his eye as his laughter subsides. "But that's more of my father's style. The old ways, you know? Sicilian justice. I prefer other ways of garbage removal. I am, after all, a child of the new world. As is true with all businesses, we must modernize."

I blush with embarrassment, and Danny smirks.

"I will need some of your men to help, though," Grey says, looking at my eyes. "I cannot send that many soldiers to Kentucky without arousing certain unwanted suspicions or leaving my own base of operations vulnerable. So your club is going to help. And we're going to need a distraction as well. From what my men have told me, the four of you are great at coming up with distractions."

"Trust me," Beau says, pressing his hand over his president patch. "You have our support. We want Stanford and Demon Rebirth to pay for their crimes."

"I assure you they will," Grey answers, his voice stern. He stands from his throne. "Now, if you don't mind, Arden and I have some prior engagements this evening. I'll be in contact with you when we're ready to make our move. In the meantime, keep a low profile, and work on that distraction."

"Will do," Beau says, standing up to shake Grey's hand. "Thank you for helping us put an end to this."

"It is a pleasure to make a deal," the mobster cryptically responds, sending a shiver up my spine.

CHAPTER 14

Attending my first meeting in chapel with the guys is nerve wracking. Women aren't typically allowed to attend high level chapel meetings, but Beau made an exception for me since I'll be involved with this one. I take my place at his side in a chair he pulled up beside his just for me. Danny is on my left side, and I see Griff a few seats down on Beau's right. Luis has his laptop out to take notes, and Griff watches over his shoulder. He's still learning his job as enforcer and also training two of the other guys on security with Luis.

I haven't had the chance to meet Luis and Bonnie's new bundle of joy, and I feel awful for that because they've been so welcoming of me—even though Luis and I got off on the wrong foot. I have no hard feelings for him, and he has none for me after I almost shot him in Mr. Thomas's office. He was just trying to do his job and protect his family, just like I was trying to protect my men.

Moose lifts his head when Beau calls on him.

"Are you still ordained?" Beau asks, and I gasp at the question. Beau places a hand on my knee, rubbing softly.

"Sure am, Pres," Moose says.

"Again, Moose, I'm still Beau. No need to call me by a title," Beau says. "Calvos wants us to create a distraction. I think we can call it more of a lure. He wants us to bring Demon Rebirth out of hiding. What better way to lure them out than a club president's wedding to the woman that's destroyed his property and plans?"

The rest of the MC members murmur amongst themselves, looking between me, Beau, Danny, and Griff. They know about our relationship. It's completely out in the open now, though I doubt we could hide it if we wanted. They know that I belong to the three of these men, but I still blush at their attention.

"Am I hearing wedding bells?" Luis asks, a smile on his face. "Bonnie would love to be part of the planning."

"What do you think?" Beau asks, turning to me. "Are you up for a wedding?"

"Me?" I ask, my mouth going dry. "A pretend wedding?" The whole thing feels insane.

Beau shakes his head and strokes my cheek. "A *real* wedding, baby. We've gotta make this look as real as possible. I'm talking about an announcement in the county newspaper, a white dress, food and drinks, and wedding rings."

My heart accelerates, and my throat feels like sand dunes in the desert. All I ever wanted was to be Beau's wife, but I thought I lost the chance when I walked out and left him—not once but twice. We've talked about the option of marriage, mostly about me marrying Griff once the time came for protection, but now Beau's the president . . .

"You wanna marry me?" I ask.

Beau chuckles. "I thought I was the one to propose."

My cheeks flame. "I mean, you *still* want to marry me? After all these years? After I left—?"

"Baby," Beau says, turning his entire body toward me and getting down on his knee. "Yes, I still want to marry you. You left because you had to. I had to let you go somehow. And though I'm still mad about the second time, I know you only did it because you wanted to protect us and the club . . . it's okay."

I look over to Danny and Griff. "How do you guys feel about this?"

"You're still ours, sugar," Danny says. "We're family."

"I agree," Griff says. "You'll still be my bratty little Princess."

The other guys laugh, and I blush even more. "Fine, I get it! Okay, let's have a wedding. What's the plan? How are we going to make this work?"

* * *

When Beau said we were getting married, I thought I'd have maybe a month to prepare. I was wrong. Calvos wants the distraction in two days, so I'm currently looking for a wedding dress right off the rack. Danny's got my back, watching everyone around us like a hawk. I find it doubtful that any of the five salesladies plan on taking us out with fabric shears, but we can never be too careful.

"What about this one?" the saleswoman asks, holding out a shimmery white dress. She has five others over her arm that look just the same. I've never been one to envision what type of wedding dress I would wear. I'd be happy with just a white dress from Old Navy, but Beau insisted I pick out something nice—to make this distraction believable, or so he says. I think he really just wants a 'traditional' wedding. He's a sap like that.

"Honestly," I tell her, trying to be as polite as possible. "They all kind of look the same."

"No, this one is an a-line!" the saleswoman retorts. "The other's are mermaids."

Mermaid's, I've come to find out, are very tight. I need something I can run in if shit hits the fan—no, *when* shit hits the fan. Because that's the whole point. Our wedding is going to get attacked, and I need to be prepared for that. I need something I can put my thigh holster under without anyone seeing.

The saleslady huffs when I just stare at her like she's speaking in tongues. "How about this one? It's got a slit up the thigh and has some straps. Oh, and pockets! Every woman loves pockets."

I look at the dress for a moment and check the size, finding that it's mine. "Actually, I'll try that one."

"I'll get the fitting room ready for you!" she says, already sashaying away.

"Don't you feel like this is a little much?" I ask Danny. He escorts me back to the fitting rooms. "If the wedding is just going to get crashed and possibly end up in blood . . . Why do I need a dress?"

"Just humor us, sugar," he answers, wrapping an arm over my shoulder. "Now go try on that dress and let me see how gorgeous you look in it."

I go into the fitting room after Danny takes a peek inside to make sure no one is lying in wait, and I easily slide into the dress. It hits right at my ankles, and the moment I gaze at myself in the mirror, everything sinks in. Actually, it washes over me in a dizzying cascade.

I'm wearing a wedding dress. I'm marrying my high school sweetheart, something I never dreamed possible. The saleslady zips up the back of the dress and states how it fits me like a glove.

I can't stop staring at myself in the mirror. I look like a bride, like a wife. Is this how every woman feels when they find the dress? I thought I was supposed to struggle to find the one. I thought I was supposed to try on an obscene amount of tulle and sequins before I found the one.

The saleswoman claps behind me. "I think this is the one!"

"Will blood come out of this easily?" I deadpan, looking at the saleslady in the mirror. It's an honest question.

"Blood?" she asks.

"Nevermind," I say. "I'll take it."

"Do you want to show your friend outside?" she asks.

"Boyfriend," I correct. "I don't want him to see, it's bad luck."

"Boyfriend? You mean fiancé?"

I shake my head. "No, he's my boyfriend. My fiancé is working on decorations right now. Please unzip me."

She looks pissed that I admitted to having a boyfriend and fiancé, but it brings a smile to my face because she's passing judgment. Little does she know I have three men that I can't wait to watch me walk down the aisle and pledge my life to.

The woman unzips me quickly and tells me she'll take the dress to the front to be bagged. I smile the entire time I put my jeans and HPMC shirt on with my leather jacket. It's literally all I ever wear now. Whatever bottoms I have and a shirt or hoodie that shows I'm with the club. Part of me feels like a dainty sorority girl wearing her letters to class every day, but my letters are a little different. Sorority letters tell the world that a girl likes cheap Burnett's vodka and goes to sleep after her first orgasm—if she even has one. *My* letters say I'm a badass bitch.

When I come out, I find Danny leaning against the dressing room with a grin on his face. "You starting trouble, sugar?" he asks.

I shrug my shoulders. "It's too easy to make people uncomfortable, and it's entertaining."

"So, I don't get to see the dress yet?" he asks, lacing my fingers with his as we walk to the front of the store where our saleswoman is whispering to her co-worker and giving us a dirty look. Looks like people in the wedding industry can't appreciate a poly relationship, or any relationship that doesn't fit into their expectations of a man and wife. And they probably hate the tattoos.

"Nope," I say, popping the P. "I want all three of you to have the same experience of seeing me for the first time in my dress."

"I can't wait, baby girl," he says as we approach the cash register.

He places a kiss on my cheek before pulling out his wallet from his back pocket. "What's the damage?"

"That'll be seven hundred even, sir," the woman says, eying the patches on Danny's cut. Her voice shakes a little as she tells him the price, like she's waiting for him to argue or hold her up at gunpoint and just take the dress.

Danny hands over his credit card. Beau told us to make sure to use the card at a bridal shop just in case we're being tracked by our spending. Normally, we'd use cash to fly under the radar, but right now, we want to be seen.

"Isn't my girl going to be a beautiful bride?" Danny asks, trying to get a bigger rise out of the saleswoman.

She nods with tight lips and runs his credit card. "I'm sure her *husband* will think so."

Danny chuckles. "You're not wrong. Poor sap has wanted to marry our girl since high school. I just got lucky to come along for the ride. It'll be a wild wedding night, if you know what I mean." He winks, and the woman's face goes pale.

I bite my lip and smile at Danny, imagining how our wedding night would be if we weren't planning a possible massacre. The four of us consummating our marriage and commitment together has me practically giddy with excitement.

"I . . . don't know what you mean, sir," she says, handing back his card with a receipt for him to sign.

"That's okay," Danny fires back. "We can't all have hearts big enough to love more than one person. Takes a special human to love three gruff men like me and my boys."

She's clearly baffled as she hands over the garment bag with my dress. I take it from her and hold it close to my body so Danny can have his hands empty. He tosses his copy of the receipt in a trashcan by the door, and we both laugh, happy to be finished with the process.

* * *

We hold the wedding at our warehouse on the back roads of Lexington, the same place where we hid out months ago, and the same place where I left my guys because I was trying to protect them. It doesn't look the same as it did then, with all the cots spread out for the MC and their families to sleep. Now it looks like a bridal magazine threw up inside this once cold and dark place.

"Holy. Shit," I say, walking into the main room of the warehouse turned reception hall.

Danny lets out a long whistle beside me, looking around at what the prospects, old ladies, and MC members have put together. There are string lights crisscrossed along the ceiling, the room has chairs and tables with place settings atop black table cloths, and off to the side there's a handmade arch that we'll be taking outside along with seating for the ceremony. We figured it would be best to do the ceremony outside instead of being caged in a building. I spot Beau and Griff standing under the arch, working together to put flowers around it. It looks like they're arguing over the placement, but I can't hear them over a Wage War track booming from the speakers.

Danny takes my dress from my hands and gives me a light smack on my ass. "Go solve their little lover's quarrel. I'll put your dress in our room."

"What are you two fighting about?" I ask.

"Would you tell your fiancé that writing his own vows is the dumbest thing ever?" Griff answers, stabbing a red rose into the arch.

"You wanna write our own vows?"

He rolls his eyes at Griff and continues filling in the bare spots on the arch. "Yeah, I thought we could all actually write our own vows. *However,* I wanted us to exchange them after the wedding . . . *privately.*"

"And what do you think?" I ask Griff, crossing my arms.

"I think we should go traditional," Griff huffs.

I smirk at my big burly boyfriend. "To have and to hold, to *obey*?"

Griff stops what he's doing and turns around, lifting me off my feet. I laugh and wrap my legs around his torso.

He nips at my neck. "Yes, Princess, to obey, to serve, to cherish . . ."

"Kinda hard for her to forsake all others, dumbass," Beau says.

"True," Griff says, staring into my eyes.

"How about a compromise? We have the traditional vows during the ceremony, but we also do Beau's idea too. I like the idea of all of us being able to commit to each other in a more intimate setting. That is, as long as things go as planned, and we don't get murdered."

"We're not going to let anything happen to you, Princess," Griff says sternly, holding me a little tighter.

I lean my forehead against his. "That's what I'm worried about, one of you guys getting hurt trying to protect me."

"Well, too damn bad. We'd lay our lives down for you, Christina."

Griff sets me back on my two feet, and I hug him tightly, turning to look at Beau.

Someone clears their throat beside us, and I startle when I see Bonnie and Moose's old lady, Marie, looking at us with a sweet smile.

"Why don't you three let us finish the arch?" Bonnie suggests. "Go check and make sure everything else is to your liking. We decorated your room."

Bonnie gives me a wink before waving us away to go check out what else they've done. Beau holds my hand, and Griff wraps an arm around my shoulder as they walk me to our room in the warehouse. Since it used to be the hideout place for the whole MC, Beau redid the president's suite to fit all of us into it. They've been working on building extra rooms along the main area, but who knows if that'll be needed after the wedding. We're bracing for an attack, leading Demon Rebirth right into our safe haven. This was supposed to be the one place no one could find us. Now its going to be the site of an ambush.

Between the warehouse project and the new garage and clubhouse, Beau has kept the prospects busy, leaving the other members to help plan for the possibility of a war breaking out before the Calvos family gets here. I'm still not sure we can trust them. What if they're just setting us up to fight to the death with Demon Rebirth so that way they can take over both territories?

My train of thought is cut short when Danny opens the door to our room, blocking our path inside. I try to peer around his body, but it's no use.

"Once you walk in this room," Danny growls, his voice a sexy threat. "You're not allowed to come out until it's time to walk down the aisle."

"What about if I need food?" I ask.

"The prospects will bring us food. And we've got a bathroom. All your necessities will be met."

Danny pulls me into the room. One of the other guys closes and locks the door. There are fairy lights strung along the ceiling, creating a whimsical atmosphere at odds with the apprehension in my gut. On the dresser, a few pillar candles flicker and give off a sweet scent of cinnamon. The bed is made with white linens, but there's also some various toys lying on the nightstand with a bottle of lube. That must be Griff's doing, because I spot his favorite paddle lying there, the one that says, 'Princess.'

"What's your plan?" I ask, turning around to stare at all three of my men lined up in a row, looking delicious in their cuts, jeans, and boots. "Keep me locked up in this room until it's time to battle? Fuck me until I forget about Stanford coming for us?"

The guys exchange a knowing look.

"Maybe we're trying to knock you up before you even have a chance to walk down the aisle," Danny says, prowling toward me.

I scoff. "Good luck. I'm probably not even ovulating."

"Maybe we just want to make love to our girl, just in case these are our last days alive," Beau says softly.

I march over to him and grab the lapels of his cut, shaking him a bit. "Do. Not. Say that! None of us are going to die, Beau Grady. I can't lose any of you."

"Baby," Beau says, brushing my hair back. "We don't know that. But I swear we're going to protect you at all costs. You're our girl. You're going to be my wife. If something happens—"

"No—" I cut him off with a kiss. He deepens it, and I feel tears slide down my cheeks. He must too because he starts wiping them away before backing me up to the edge of the bed. He lifts me up by my hips and sits me on the bed. I lay back as he reaches to pull off my pants, and I lift my hips enough to allow it.

"Young lady, where are your panties?" Beau asks, pulling me to the edge of the covers.

I shrug my shoulders. "Ask Danny."

Danny and I exchange a knowing look. We may have made a small detour on the way home from the dress shop to relieve some tension. Danny let me ride him in the driver's seat until I came twice. Since our talk about the future and babies, he's been hell bent on being the one to knock me up. I'm not complaining, though. I'm kind of into this new 'breed kink' he's acquired.

Beau shakes his head, but it doesn't stop him from kneeling down and placing kisses along my thighs.

"What am I going to do with you, Christina?" he asks in between kisses.

"Marry me, spend the rest of your life with me . . ." I answer, not finishing the part where I hope his life is longer than the amount of time it takes me to walk down the aisle.

He dives in to lick a long line up my pussy, and I grab at his hair, trying to pull him away. I'm probably still dripping from the quickie in the car. Griff climbs onto the bed and positions himself behind me, pulling my hands from Beau's hair and pinning them beside me. I look up to see him shaking his head at me.

"If our president wants to eat that dripping cunt, you let him," Griff says. "Don't fight it, Princess."

I whimper and struggle a little before giving up. Griff doesn't let go of my wrists, so there's nothing I can do about Beau. Danny climbs onto the bed beside me, a knife in his hands. My eyes go wide in terror. I've heard about people having a knife kink. I've read books about it. We've never talked about it though. I trust my guys, but I'm not sure I'm ready to explore that type of kink just hours before I'm getting married and possibly dying in the process.

"Trust me, sugar?" Dan asks, holding the knife where I can see it.

"Yes," I whisper, not taking my eyes off Danny's pocket knife as it moves towards my neck. He uses his other hand to pull my shirt away from my delicate skin, and then he carefully begins cutting my shirt off with the knife.

"Hey!" I protest as it's ripped in half down the middle. "My shirt!"

"We'll get you a new one, don't worry," Danny says. He puts his knife on the nightstand and then comes back to me to pull my bra and expose my tits. He pulls at my nipples, and my torso levitates off the bed, but Beau pins my hips back down to hold me in place.

"So fucking sexy," Griff says, looking down at me. "Sexy and ours. Open your mouth."

I follow his command and stick out my tongue, swallowing when he lets his saliva drip into my mouth.

"Do that again," Beau says, lifting his head and replacing his mouth with two fingers. "She liked it. She's dripping down here."

I do as I'm told.

"Our thirsty little whore," Griff says adoringly, softly stroking my cheek. I hadn't even realized he released my wrists. I stretch both my arms back to hold onto his thighs. Griff spits onto my face, some of it meeting my tongue, but the rest makes a mess on my lips and nose. I lick around my lips trying to get his saliva and his praise. It works. "That's my good little Princess."

"Fuck me, please," I ask, wiggling my body in anticipation.

"You heard her, guys," Griff says, pulling off his cut and shirt. He tosses them onto the floor. "Let's give her what she wants."

Beau flips my body over in one fluid motion and pushes me up the bed toward Griff who is now holding his thick cock in his tattooed hand. Beau kneels on the bed behind me and thrusts inside without any warning. I turn around to look at him, finding him still half dressed, like he couldn't wait to be inside me. His hands hold my hips, keeping me in place as he pushes in and pulls out over and over again.

"Fuck, I'll never get tired of this view," Beau says. "So fucking beautiful."

He pushes my head down toward Griff's cock, and I lick the small amount of liquid from the tip before locking my lips around his shaft and humming with pleasure. Griff uses his hand to hold my hair, helping me keep a steady pace. I can't look at him from this position, but I can hear his intake of breath every time I go down a little further.

"Dan," Beau says. "Grab the lube, I'll start getting her ready for you."

"My pleasure," Dan replies. I want to make a snarky remark about how it's actually me feeling all the pleasure, but my mouth is full, and I'm not sure if I could make a coherent sentence at the moment.

The lube gets handed to Beau, and a few moments later I feel him dribble liquid over my ass. He gently pushes it around the tight ring before slowly inserting a finger into me. I start pushing back on his cock and finger, wanting to ride them to the climax I can feel just around the corner.

"That's it, baby," Beau praises. He inserts another digit, ceasing his movements so I can do what I need to in order to prepare myself for Danny. "*Fuck me.* Fuck that little ass on my fingers. I can feel that pussy tightening up even more."

"Jesus, man," Griff grunts, holding my hair a little tighter. "When did our Boy Scout learn how to talk dirty?"

Beau chuckles. "I guess you guys are rubbing off on me."

Groaning, I pop off of Griff's cock. "Would you guys stop chatting and just fuck me already?"

"Sure thing, Princess," Danny says. He lays on the bed, and Beau pulls his fingers and cock away, helping me position myself over Danny reverse cowgirl style. I gently lower myself one inch at a time, letting him stretch my ass slowly. It doesn't hurt nearly as bad as it did when we first started, but the guys still like to make sure they're well lubricated and I'm not uncomfortable. Once Danny is fully inside me, I lean back on his chest, and he wraps his hands around my torso.

"You okay?" Danny quietly asks. He leans up to press a kiss on my shoulder.

I nod and look at Beau. "Quick, get inside me, Beau Grady."

"Yes, future Mrs. Grady," he says sweetly. What he does next is anything but sweet. It's erotic the way he holds his slick shaft up against my lips and thrusts inside, filling me up. Once Beau gets situated, he starts thrusting, pushing me up and down on both cocks. I want to scream about how good they feel inside me, but we're not at home, and these rooms aren't all soundproofed. I settle for whimpering and moaning.

"How's that feel, Princess?" Griff asks, kneeling on the bed beside us.

"Good," I gasp, almost on the verge of tears from the sheer overwhelming pleasure. "So good."

It reminds me of the first time that Beau, Danny, and I hooked up in my parents' guest house. Back then, I was a scared, naïve girl who didn't know a damn thing about Beau's new world. It hasn't been a full year that I've been in their lives, but it feels like a lifetime. I've fallen for these three, and I'll fight to the death to keep them safe, just like they'll do the same for me. Just like they may have to very soon.

"I love you," I gasp as Griff reaches down to rub teasing circles on my clit.

"We love you too, Princess," Griff says.

Reaching out for his cock, I pull him closer to my mouth and lean over to wrap my lips around him. I expect Griff to grip my hair and force me all the way down, but he keeps rubbing between my legs and softly petting my hair.

"You take us so well," he says with admiration in his voice.

"And we get to do this for the rest of our lives," Beau adds with a smile. "Hope you're ready. Tonight's your last chance to run."

Danny wraps his arms around my torso, holding me tightly against him. "But we're not going to let you escape."

I laugh as best I can with Griff's cock shoved down my throat. I pop off of it to smile up at him. "Good thing I don't want to run from you guys then."

"Okay, okay," Griff says, grasping the tip of his shaft. "Would one of you fucks hurry up and cum so I can get my turn inside our future wife?"

Griff gets off the bed to just watch, and Beau picks up his pace. He pushes my legs back as Danny holds them and he pounds in and out of me. I rest my head back in the crook of Danny's neck. He whispers praises into my ear that only I can hear. Beau lets out a curse before he releases inside me and leans over to press a kiss to my lips.

"Shoo," Griff says to Beau after he lets him recover. Griff lies on the bed and motions for me to climb on top. "Get that sexy ass over here, Christina."

I scramble off of Danny, but he's not too far behind. Once I'm seated on top of Griff, Danny pushes back inside my ass. This time though, it's me controlling the pace instead of Beau. Danny places his hands on my ass, and Griff holds onto my breasts as I grind myself between the two of them.

"That's a good girl," Griff says. "So beautiful, so perfect."

My cheeks blush. "Hush. Stop praising me, I'm trying to make you cum."

Griff smiles. "Too bad I didn't bring the duck tape. I'd let you tape my mouth shut."

"Sounds like someone's more of a switch than just a dominant," Beau remarks from the chair he's sitting in. He has his boxers and T-shirt back on and a set of papers in his hands.

Griff gives him a mean glare, a glare I haven't seen in a long time. "Watch it. Just because I would give Christina whatever she wants doesn't mean I would submit."

I test the waters and reach out my tiny hand to wrap around Griff's neck. The ring he gave me presses against his skin. He gave the engagement ring back to me the day after I returned from Stanford, asking me if I'd still wear it. Beau was perfectly okay with me wearing the ring and him providing the wedding bands.

I feel Griff's cock twitch inside me, and he moves his gaze back to mine.

"What was that?" I ask, arching an eyebrow. "You won't submit to me?"

He swallows, his throat bobbing against my hand. "Nothing, mistress."

I smile widely. "I think I like you at my mercy, Griffin."

"Use me, baby," he pleads.

I toss my head back and let go completely. It doesn't take long for me to find my release between my two boyfriends, and the moment I tighten up, they react by unloading inside me at the same time. The three of us stay like that until the two of them stop twitching from the aftershocks of our shared orgasm.

Danny pulls out and walks in all his naked glory to the bathroom attached to our room in the warehouse. He comes back shortly after with a wet washcloth. I collapse on the bed next to Griff and allow Danny to clean me up.

I close my eyes, trying to get my breathing even. The bed dips beside me and I open my eyes to find Beau smiling down at me.

"We've got something to discuss with you before tomorrow," he says, rubbing my cheek softly.

"What's that?" I sit up and tuck the blanket around me.

"The guys and I came to a decision," Beau starts. "And we still need to get our marriage license. Marnie, Cam's wife, is a clerk downtown and can rush the paperwork to make it official."

"Okay . . ." I say. "Let's get the ball rolling on that."

Beau looks down at the papers and hands them to me. "We decided on our last name."

"Griff and I also want to change our last names," Danny says, sitting down in front of me. "We all want to take Grady."

"Really?" I ask, shocked. Looking down at the papers, I find they're not just the marriage certificate forms. It's a legal petition for name change for Griff and Danny as well.

"Yeah," Griff says behind me, rubbing circles on my back. "We'll have to go to the Social Security office to change our names, and there's a ton of other shit that will have to be changed too, but Marnie can process the wedding certificate. We just wanted you to know we're in this too—forever, as a family."

"But why do you wanna change your names?" I ask, glancing between Danny and Griff.

"My parents ran out on me when I was a kid," Dan says. "I'd rather not be known as a Blackford anymore. I was never attached to my last name."

"And you know why I don't want to be tied to my father anymore . . ." Griff says, making me shiver at just the thought of his shitty father. "My dad can burn in hell, and that name will die with him."

I look back at Beau. "We're all going to be a Grady?" It's what I had wanted since we were teens. I always wanted to be Mrs. Grady, Beau's wife. Never could I have imagined that things would end up like this, but my heart races, even though our world may very well be falling apart.

"If that's what you want, baby," Beau says. "You know I've always wanted you to have my last name, as caveman as that might seem."

I nod my head quickly. "Yes, I want that! I love it!"

"Guys," Danny says. "We're going to be the Grady bunch!"

I roll my eyes and wrap Beau in a hug, kissing him over and over again before moving onto Griff and Danny.

CHAPTER 15

Marnie comes into my room the morning of the wedding—AKA the day we end Stanford Williams and Demon Rebirth—holding up our marriage certificate.

"Got it, chica!" she announces. "Want me to give this to Moose for safe keeping?"

"Yes, please," I say as Bonnie and Erica work on my hair and makeup. I told the girls that there was no sense getting me done all up, just in case shit hits the fan. They wouldn't take no for an answer.

The MC spent most of yesterday thinking through worst case scenarios, escape plans, and a strategy if we need to fight. Beau and Danny also had a phone meeting with Calvos to update him and his family. Calvos said that they've been keeping an eye on things in Louisville, but it's still quiet. I try not to get excited over the possibility of my wedding being successful. Chances are slim, but there's still a chance.

Before I could call my mother and tell her about the upcoming nuptials—she texted me. One of her friends at the country club where she used to be a member saw our announcement in the local paper and called her first thing to gossip. Needless to say, my parents won't be making the trip up from Florida for their only child's wedding. But

I'm fine with it. That's two fewer people that I'll need to worry about if things escalate.

I catch a glimpse of my hair in the mirror and snap out of my thoughts. "Thank you for being here for me, ladies," I tell Bonnie and Erica as they put on the finishing touches. I've never had a group of girls supporting me. The sorority I was in was so cutthroat and back-stabby I would have never asked any of those girls to be in or attend my wedding.

"Of course, Christina!" Marnie says. "You're one of us now, and we fight for our family."

"Will the kids be okay today?" I ask Bonnie.

She nods. "I'll be keeping them safe. Luis wants us here in the safe room. He didn't want them to be sent to their grandparents. We'll have snacks, books, and plenty of room in there. I'll also have a live feed so I don't miss any of the action. If things start going off the rails, I'll call the cops."

"Good." Bonnie is still recovering from giving birth about a month ago, so there's no way she could fight alongside us, but it's nice knowing she'll still be safe in the building. "You girls strapped up?" I ask the other two.

Erica lifts her shirt a little to reveal a pistol. "Hell yeah."

Marnie raises her long skirt showing me the revolver strapped to her thigh. "Ready to fight alongside our boys and have your back if it comes to that."

"Let's hope it *doesn't* come to that," I tell them. "Fingers crossed that Calvos and his crew intercept them before they set foot on the property."

* * *

The girls left to go get into position an hour ago, leaving me alone in my room completely dolled up and panicking . . . not about the possible ambush, but over the fact that I'm getting ready to marry Beau—for real. Moose is ordained, we have the marriage certificate, we're getting married. Not only that, but I'll be committing myself to Griff and Dan as well. It's absolutely crazy. Insane! I wouldn't change it for the world—well maybe I would like to have a wedding without the threat of death.

A knock comes from outside my room, and I pull it open, finding Griff standing there in some nice pants and a button down shirt with the sleeves rolled up. His gun is strapped to his hip. He scans me up and down, and his jaw drops.

"Can I help you?" I ask, smirking at him so obviously caught off guard.

His eyes meet mine—sharp and serious. "I'll take you to Vegas right now and marry you. Holy shit, baby . . . you look . . ."

"Like a Princess?" I ask, finishing his sentence.

"Like a *queen*," he corrects. "Beau is one lucky bastard."

I lean into him, placing my hands on his chest. "So are you, Griffin, and Danny. When I speak those vows today, I'm not just promising them to Beau. You'll be my husband too."

He nods, hugging me tightly. "Can I escort you down the aisle?"

"Of course," I say, hooking my arm into his. "Lead the way."

Griff leads us out of the warehouse. We decided to have the ceremony outside since it's a nice day. We figured it wouldn't be smart to be trapped inside, what with the amount that both our motorcycle crews enjoy being pyromaniacs. Beau's got some prospects at the entrance of the property standing guard. If Stanford's goons can get through the Mafia and the prospects . . . Something has gone horribly wrong. Something no one expected.

But those thoughts leave my mind the moment Griff and I approach the aisle and I see Danny and Beau waiting for us at the end under the arch. All our members and their significant others turn and stand to look at me, but my eyes are only on the end of the aisle where my forever awaits.

I look up at Griff once more as we start moving down the aisle. He smiles, and the music begins. The intro guitar riff to *My Heart I Surrender* by I Prevail sends a bolt of electricity through my flesh.

"Here we go," he says. "Time to make this official."

Once we're at the arch, Griff claps a hand on Beau's back and places a kiss on my cheek, whispering that he loves me. I give Danny a smile before directing my attention to Moose.

As he starts speaking, I zone out completely. I can't take my eyes off of Beau and my guys. Every now and then, twigs break in the woods behind us, making the guys glance into the darkness. It's just the animals though, I tell myself, squeezing Beau's hands in mine. The Kentucky wilderness is rife with deer and squirrels. But would I be able to hear them?

Somewhere above, a crow squawks, and I nearly jump out of my skin. But other than that, everything runs smoothly. We even make it through saying our vows to each other. Danny and Griff stare into my eyes as I recite the words Moose says to all of my men, becoming their wife. I agree to cherish them, obey them, and honor them—in sickness and in health, until death do us part.

"You may now kiss your bride," Moose says and our small group claps.

Beau and I crash together, kissing like this moment will be the last time. He pulls apart and presses his forehead to mine, smiling at me.

"I love you, Mrs. Grady," he whispers. "Until the day I die."

"I love you too, husband," I tell him, holding onto the collar of his shirt. "I'm sorry we took a little detour to get to this day."

He brushes some strands of hair from my face. "I wouldn't trade it for the world, baby."

Beau and I pull apart and raise our clasped hands together as the MC cheers. We begin walking back down the aisle, and I can't believe that the entire wedding ceremony went off without a hitch. Griff never got the call from Calvos saying there was trouble—or that they succeeded. No news is good news, I tell myself, my heart slamming against my ribs. It seems like we're in the clear. We just need to move this party inside.

We stride down the aisle, and suddenly everything feels eerie, like I'm living in one of my nightmares. I expect the living corpse of Mr. Thomas to pop out and tell me that I'm sleeping, but instead, something far worse happens.

I'm looking at Beau, sweet and smiling Beau, when I hear the gunshot.

I'm not sure how many seconds pass between the bang and the bullet making contact, but it's a headshot, and blood splatters all over my face and dress. I go down to the ground with Beau, placing my hand over his face like Jacqueline Kennedy in the back of the president's convertible. The blood pools so fast on my hand that its completely covered in seconds.

All I can see is red.

"Everyone down!" someone screams from behind me. I think it's Griff, but I don't turn to see. It doesn't matter. Beau gasps, a pitiful noise, and there's nothing I can do.

"Beau!" I scream, putting pressure on the bloody spot. "Don't leave me, don't leave me! God, no!" A primal bellow issues from my lungs, a noise I could never hope to contain. My entire world shatters in my hands, my bloody hands.

I desperately search for help among the MC, but everyone is on the ground, their guns raised and pointing everywhere at once.

"Christina!" Danny yells, crawling toward me. "Come here. Come to me."

I shake my head and hold onto Beau tighter. "No, no, no. I can't leave him here. I can't leave him. No, no, no. Beau! Please!"

"Christina," Danny pleads. I can hear the tears in his voice. His heart is breaking just like mine. "Please, Princess. I need you safe. I swore to him I would keep you safe. Come on. We need to get inside."

I shake my head. I can't speak. All I can do is stare at the blood mess in my hands. My husband. My forever.

"Go," Beau gasps. "R-Run."

My body shakes. A million thoughts blaze through my mind, none of them coherent enough to make any sense. "I'm not leaving you," I finally whisper.

Someone touches my arm and I flinch, thinking it's Danny going to pull me away. Instead, I find the sympathetic eyes of Moose's wife.

"Christina, let me help," she says. She's an ER nurse, she chose to be here just in case something like this happened. "Will you let me help?"

I can barely comprehend her question. She pushes me aside, and my body doesn't resist. My muscles simply do not respond.

"Please don't let him die," I beg her, tears and Beau's blood obscuring my vision.

Moose comes over and quickly pushes me out of the way. He pulls her medical bag from under the seat she was sitting at and starts handing her supplies. Someone pulls me away, and it doesn't look like Beau's breathing.

"Look at me!" Griff growls in my face, fear and anger contorting his handsome features. "Listen closely,Christina. You're one of us, you need to fight like one of us, or we're all dead, baby. Push the tears aside, you can mourn later."

I choke down the sob that wants to escape and wipe my eyes until they're dry enough to see. I try to channel my sadness into anger. More gunshots ring out. They're deafeningly loud, and I have no idea where they're coming from or going toward.

"Christina, I need you and the wives to haul ass to the warehouse," Griff says. "Run as fast as you can, and we'll cover you. Bonnie already called the cops and paramedics, but we all know they're going to take their damn time."

Another barrage of gunfire sounds all around us.

"Do not leave that warehouse," Griff continues. "No matter what you hear out here. The prospects aren't responding, I think they've been taken out, which means it's just us against—" He stumbles over his last words, and they get lost beneath the crack of gunshots.

"Go!" he yells.

Somehow my legs obey my mind. Me and the wives immediately run for the clubhouse, our desperate race punctuated by more gunfire. They surrounded us, like they had been here all along. Erica, Marnie, and I burst through the door of the warehouse just as the latest salvo hammers into the wall. Marnie slams the emergency latch over it.

"Holy shit," Marnie says, clutching the necklace on her chest. "We're fucked."

"What should we do?" Erica asks, looking directly at me.

I don't know what to say. The way Erica and Marnie are looking at me says that they want to help, but they don't want to get in the way. I'm their queen, the president's first lady, and they want me to tell them what to do.

"I don't know," I mutter. My dress catches on something, and some of the fabric rips. I rip it free and toss the bloodstained fragment aside.

"What happened out there?" Erica asks. "One minute everything was fine, and the next . . ."

"He's going to die," I whisper, my hands shaking with fury.

"Don't say that!" Marnie scolds. "Moose and his old lady will save him. She's the best nurse out there. She's always saving our men's asses."

I shake my head. "I'm not talking about Beau. Stanford Williams . . . he's going to die. I'm going to kill him."

The sadness I felt while holding Beau's lifeless body turns into rage-filled adrenaline. I pull the pistol from my thigh holster and rack the slide to chamber a round.

"You can't go out there!" Erica screams, yanking on my left arm.

I pull away from her. "Listen to me closely . . . I'm going. I'm going to defend our men. You guys stay here. Lock the door behind me."

"But Griff said to stay inside . . ." Erica whispers.

"Griff isn't the president," I tell her. "He doesn't make that call. I'm going to go out there and protect the MC or die trying. Now get out of the way. You know what I'm capable of."

Erica might have not been there when I beat the shit out of Candy and Sissy, or the time I killed Mr. Thomas . . . but she's heard the stories. She knows I'm just unstable enough to pull off something this crazy.

She holds her hands up and backs away. "Okay. Fine."

Marnie gives me a small nod. "Give 'em hell, girl."

* * *

It's a warzone outside.

I stick close to the building, staring at the chaos. It's safe to say that the Mafia finally showed up, but Demon Rebirth also brought some friends. There are men in suits with black pistols, men wearing cuts from Demon Rebirth, and a third force from another MC. It's easy to tell each side of the war apart because HPMC all left their cuts inside. It's leather against business casual.

I try not to count the bodies on the ground. I spot Danny on the sidelines protecting Moose and his wife as they hover over Beau. Griff is in the middle of the chaos, barking orders and reloading a magazine into his pistol. Sirens sound in the distance, but I'm going to find Stanford before they get here. I need to put an end to this. I'm not going to let him live out a life behind bars. He doesn't deserve that. He will die today.

I carefully move toward the woods when I see a flicker of movement in the trees. No one in the chaos has noticed me yet, or so I hope. They're all too busy fighting each other. I'm not sure how, but I can feel it in my gut that Stanford is watching the war from the trees. He's the kind of coward who would demand to be present but never get close enough to pull a trigger himself. I slip into the woods undetected and carefully walk toward the movement I saw.

I was right. Stanford is there. He's crouched behind some trees with a rifle at his side, but he isn't aiming down the sights. A pair of binoculars are pressed to his eyes.

My heart rate increases, threatening to kill me on the spot before I ever have my revenge. I come up behind Stanford on the edge of the clearing as quietly as I can, though I don't think it matters much. The sound of gunfire drowns out all my movements. I raise my gun and level it on the back of his head, finger on the trigger.

I know how to shoot, but my hands are far from steady. I need to be closer. I take another two steps until I'm only three or four feet from him.

"You ruined my wedding, motherfucker," I growl.

Stanford startles, but instantly regains his composure. "What a pity," he says, turning to me with a smile on his face. "Good thing you've got two more husbands lined up . . . that is, unless they die today too. Looks like the odds are against you."

"Fuck you," I say. "You're done. It's over."

The sirens are closer, or I think they are, but my ears are ringing so badly I might not be hearing clearly.

"Oh, dear," Stanford says, cocking his head to the side. "It's over when I say—"

I pull the trigger. The gun fires, and Stanford drops to the ground, his face falling into the dirt. I don't stop. I upload the entire magazine into Stanford's head and chest, all fifteen rounds. When it's empty, I stand over his body, his head an unrecognizable mess of blood and pulp. As soon as the magazine runs empty, every thought in my mind races back to Beau. I need to get to him, to save him, to hold his hand and tell him everything will be alright.

I sprint out of the woods and find the whole MC kneeling on the ground with their hands on their heads. A dozen or more bodies are scattered across the lawn. Members of Demon Rebirth are in cuffs or being wrestled to the ground. Amidst all the chaos, I spot Grey Calvos. He's wearing a dark suit and speaking to a handful of police officers, obviously giving them orders and directing the entire operation.

But Grey Calvos is not the man I'm looking for. An officer comes up behind me, and whether he gives me any orders or not, I don't hear him. He kicks the back of my knees, and I tumble to the ground. The spot where Beau went down is vacant. Two ambulances are already at the front of the property with at least one more coming. The first stretcher I see is obscured by a couple paramedics hastily tending to someone.

That's when I see Beau. He's on the second stretcher. The officer behind me pulls my arms back and cuffs my wrists, swiftly knocking the unloaded pistol from my hand at the same time. He screams something in my ear, but I can't hear him. My mind is a thousand miles away. Anywhere but here. A paramedic pulls a white sheet over Beau's body and points to the ambulance, and my world disintegrates.

CHAPTER 16

I've never lost a loved one. Well, I had an aunt and uncle who died in a car accident a few years ago, but I barely knew them. I went to the funeral, looked at all the pictures of their lives decorating the church, but I didn't feel grief.

My grandparents all died either before I was born or when I was too young to understand. I'm still not certain I understand death, but I've killed enough to know that we're all mortal. No one talks about how hospitals *feel* like death. How they smell like death. How every door was wide enough to accommodate the passage of a corpse.

I sit in the ER waiting to get checked out, no longer wearing handcuffs, but I'm still a prisoner. I need to be with Beau. I need to be with my husband. Griff insisted that I go with the medics to get looked over, especially when he saw me come out of the woods splattered with blood. Other than the numbness I feel, I'm fine. I got out of the war unscathed . . . well, physically. A little kid with a very obviously broken arm won't stop staring at me. I suppose I'm a sight to see, wearing a torn wedding dress stained with splotches of dark crimson.

I'm finally inspected, poked, prodded, and then released from the ER after what feels like days of inaction but in reality is a little over four hours. I head to the front of the hospital to use a phone and find out where the hell my men are when a figure steps out of the bank of elevators on my left. My instincts take over and I shove him, following it with a quick fist that he deftly catches.

"Where the hell were you?" I whisper yell.

Grey Calvos looks down at me like an insubordinate child. He's had time to change from the dark suit he wore earlier into a lighter pinstripe one that's perfectly pressed. I wonder how many suits he travels with or if a whole semi truck full of dry cleaning just follows him around everywhere he goes. "Good to see you too, Mrs. Grady," he says with a saccharine smile.

"Where. Were. You?" I demand again, pulling him to the side for some privacy. "While my club was being slaughtered, where were you and your men? You were supposed to intercept Stanford and his men."

"He slipped through our hands, slimy little bastard," Calvos says, now sounding irritated by my confrontation. "It happens."

"It happens?" I ask, a burst of sinister laughter leaving my lips. "It happens? My husband just got shot on my wedding day, and it *happens*? We lost good men today, and it just happens? That wasn't the plan, Mr. Calvos."

"You should just count your blessings, Mrs. Grady," Calvos says. "Casualties happen in our respective lines of work. Today was a single battle. You have not seen war yet."

"And your answer to that is to bring your business to Kentucky?"

He shakes his head. "You and your men are just as dangerous as mine, believe it or not. We aren't all that dissimilar, you and I."

"Whatever," I snarl. "I've got to go visit someone. If you'll excuse me."

"I'll be seeing you," Calvos says, his dress shoes clicking on the tiled floor.

I huff and turn the opposite way. "God, I hope not."

* * *

The room is dark and empty when I enter. The only noise comes from the beep of a monitor beside the bed. I gasp. He's completely motionless. Closing the door behind me, I step further into the room until I'm standing right beside him. A white bandage covers almost all of his head except for the nasal cannula connected to an oxygen tank.

I crawl into the bed beside him, watching out for the IV in his hand, and rest my head on his chest. His heart is still beating. He's alive.

"Oh my God," I cry, wrapping my arm around his torso. "I thought I lost you again, Beau Grady."

I'm not sure how long I lie beside him, but the nurses come in occasionally to check his vitals. They don't disrupt us though, they just give me a look of pity as they check the monitors and type things into his chart. I must fall asleep at some point, because it's completely dark when I open my eyes.

Two shadows are sitting on the windowsill though, and I gasp when they move toward me.

"Shh, it's just us," Danny whispers.

I climb out of bed and wrap my arms around both of them. I haven't seen them since Griff shoved me into one of the ambulances. I thought for sure they would have been arrested. Two boyfriends in prison and one in the hospital fighting for his life . . . That's a Lifetime Channel movie in the making.

"Are you guys okay?" I ask softly, not letting them go. I look them over as best I can in the dim light. Griff has bandages over his knuckles like he had to resort to hand-to-hand combat. Danny's got a black eye and a split lip. At least they've managed to change into clean clothes. The ER eventually bagged my dress and gave me some spare scrubs to change into, not wanting me to walk around the hospital covered in blood.

"We'll be okay," Griff says. "But it's not good, Christina. We might have won today, but we lost a lot of men."

"I know," I say, pressing my head into his chest. "Who?"

"Most of the prospects," Griff says when I pull away. "Cam, Marnie's husband . . ."

"No!" I yell. "Fuck. She's probably a mess right now."

"She is," Danny says regretfully. "She's with Bonnie and Luis right now. They didn't want her to be alone."

"Luis is okay?" I ask. I don't remember seeing him in all the commotion.

"He is," Griff says. "Fucked up thing is, we didn't get Stanford. It was all for fucking nothing."

Griff turns away from me and leans into the wall, dropping his head. I gently place my hand on his back, trying to soothe the tension from him.

"I killed him . . ." I whisper.

It's like everyone in the room stops breathing for a moment. I almost wonder if I actually spoke out loud.

"What did you say?" Griff demands, turning and towering over me.

"You heard me. I killed Stanford."

Griff and Danny stare at each other incredulously.

"But I told you to stay in the warehouse—" Griff says.

"You know damn well I never listen to you, Griffin," I say, crossing my arms. "I couldn't let you fight alone. I saw him watching from the woods. I snuck up on him and put an entire magazine into his fucking head. He's probably being scavenged by coyotes now. There wasn't much left."

"You're fucking crazy," Griff says, but he smiles nonetheless, picking me up and spinning in a circle. "I love you so damn much."

"I'll let the prospects know to search the woods for his body," Danny says, pulling out his phone. "We'll take care of it. Luckily, Calvos has the local cops so far under his thumb that they don't know how to take a piss without his permission."

Danny closes himself in the bathroom to make the call, and Griff sets me back on my feet.

"How are you guys not in jail?" I ask Griffin. "Grey Calvos is the answer, isn't he?"

"Something like that," Griff answers with a shrug, putting his hands into the pocket of his hoodie. "Dude has more money than he knows what to do with. Probably bought the whole department. His guys are working with ours to get rid of the bodies. We'll be having a memorial for our fallen."

I nod my head. "Do you know what's going on with Beau?"

He sighs and rubs his temples. "The docs had to put him in a medical coma," Griff says sadly. "The bullet went through his eye and shattered some bones, but it somehow missed the important stuff. One of the surgeons said its the kind of injury he's only read about in textbooks, not something he thought he would ever see. Had Beau been an inch closer to you, it would have gotten him. He got lucky. Preposterously lucky."

"Do they know when he's going to wake up?" I ask.

"That's up to him," Griff says, wrapping an arm over my shoulder. "But we'll be here when he does. We have our family back. He's probably going to wear an eye patch for the rest of his life, so start brainstorming some pirate-themed nicknames."

I sit on the edge of Beau's bed, holding his limp hand in mine. He looks like he's peacefully sleeping, but who knows what's going on in that head of his. I hope he's not having nightmares like I do. I hope he knows we're safe.

"What do we do now?" I ask, turning to Griff.

He walks around the hospital bed to sit on the other side and places a gentle hand on Beau's chest. "We rebuild," Griff says. "Get some new prospects, finish the new clubhouse and garage, get away from all the bullshit my father tried to get us into, and try to stay out of trouble."

"Any time for a vacation in there?" I ask, squeezing Beau's hand. "I could really use a vacation after all this murder and mayhem."

Griff smiles up at me. "Anything for you, Princess."

EPILOGUE

Beau

2 Years Later

I haven't seen my vice president in hours. He's been MIA since this morning's meeting. I know he had some payroll to do for the garage before tomorrow, but I've checked the garage and none of the prospects have seen him since before lunch. I shot off a text to Christina, and she hasn't seen or heard either. She took today off from the bar, saying she needed to run some errands around town. I know she's loving her new freedom and being able to go to the store without one of us hovering or the chance of an attack.

We didn't let her out of our sight immediately, not until we had a few months of quiet around the club. Demon Rebirth is no more. Calvos made sure of it. He's checked in with me a few times over the last couple years and has even invited me out to the track for a race or two, but I've always declined. I never want to meet that mobster again in person. Just looking in his eyes and shaking his hand creeps me the fuck out.

Walking down the hall to our security room, I find Griff and a prospect looking over video surveillance. Someone broke into the garage last night and stole a few parts, but I'm sure our enforcers will find the culprit and punish him. Better than waiting for the cops to do it. We don't dabble in illegal activity anymore, but we also don't put up with thieves or criminals. We worked our asses off to get our new businesses up and running—we're not going to let anyone take from us.

"Have you guys seen or heard from Dan?" I ask, checking my watch. "I need him back in the office to go over some stuff."

"Nah," Griff says. "Haven't seen him. You know how he is when Christina isn't here. He's probably moping around somewhere close by or stalking her across town. Old habits die hard."

The prospect chuckles, and we both shoot him a glare. I don't hate the kid, but this is part of the initiation. Step one is always to make them feel like they're not part of the club.

"If you see him, tell him I'm looking," I say, pushing away from the doorframe.

I continue down the hall, looking into the open doors of the supply closets, storage, and spare rooms, but I come up empty. How hard is it to lose a six foot tall bearded biker? Just as I'm about to head back to my office, I run into Bonnie who just came in from outside with a sippy cup in one hand and a sleeping Cecilia in her other. I kind of envy her and Luis. You can bet that baby fever strikes every time I see Christina holding Cecilia, thinking about the baby we've yet to have.

"Hey, Bon," I say softly. "What's up?"

She smiles. "Hey, just need to hand her off to Daddy and refill Carlos' cup. What are you up to?"

I shove my hands into the pockets of my jeans. "Looking for Danny. Have you seen him?"

"He's outside," she says, readjusting Cecilia on her hip. "I was just talking to him. He seems upset about something, but you know him, he tries to hide it."

"I'll go check on him," I tell her, already making my way to the exit. "Thanks, Bonnie."

Pushing open the heavy bullet proof door, I immediately find him.

He's just where Bonnie said he was, sitting alone and staring off at the playground he helped build. The whole project was his idea.

"Hey, man," I say, sitting beside him on one of the picnic benches. I have to sit on his left to see him, otherwise I would have to turn ninety degrees and straddle the bench. This stupid eyepatch is still taking some getting used to. I haven't learned how to ride my bike since I got shot, but that's mostly because Christina won't let me try. She's too afraid of me getting in an accident. But I'm not sure I would pass the test again anyway. "What are you doing back here?"

He shakes his head, spinning his commitment band on his ring finger. "Just thinking."

Though I was the only one who could legally marry Christina, Griff and Dan wanted to show their commitment to her by getting bands to match mine. We're a family, and I was thrilled to see them both respect the idea of marriage as much as I do. Marriage is a serious commitment, and too many people go into it for the wrong reasons. I want ours to last a lifetime, and I believe the guys do as well. All of us having my last name makes me a little emotional, because it commits them to not only Christina, but me as their brother as well.

A few of the kids are playing on the pirate playground set Danny dreamt up, running, screaming, and climbing. Dan has trained some of the kids to call me a pirate because of my eyepatch, and I don't mind.

"What's on your mind?" I ask. I can practically hear him thinking out loud. He's in rare form today. There's a sadness in his eyes that I haven't seen in a long time.

"You think it'll ever happen?" he asks, glancing over at me. He looks defeated.

"Think what will ever happen?"

He leans down and runs his hands through his hair, tugging on the ends in frustration. "Come on, man. It's been over two years since we started trying. There's gotta be some statistic that one out of three of her husbands can put a baby in her. Right? Maybe we should see if we can go to a fertility doc. What if we're all sterile and getting our hopes up for nothing?"

Oh.

Honestly, I'm surprised too. Three of us having unprotected sex surely, one would think, would result in a pregnancy. I've watched Danny slowly become disappointed every month that Christina gets her period, not that he'll ever admit that to her. He's still the first one to go to the grocery store to buy tampons, chocolate, and carbs without her even asking.

It hasn't bothered Christina, though. She's been using her time to get more tattoos, run the bar, and finish her business degree at U.K. We couldn't be more proud.

I slap Dan on the back. "It'll be fine, man," I tell him. "Think about it. The first six months, she was under a lot of stress from all the Demon Rebirth shit and my hospitalization. She started seeing the therapist, was still having those nightmares, and still worried about something else going down. Stress isn't good for making a baby no matter how much you try."

"Well what about the rest of the time?" he asks, flailing his hands. "Come on, what are the chances of all three of us being sterile? Or all four of us."

I shrug my shoulders. "Not too big of a chance. Still possible. We agreed not to go through all that though. Christina doesn't want to know if we're fertile or not. We promised her not to obsess over it."

"I just—" he says, his entire body deflating. "I wanna be a dad so badly, Beau. I know you do too, and Griff wouldn't mind it. But I'm almost pushing forty, you and Christina are still fairly young, Griff's just entering his thirties. I don't wanna be the age of a grandpa by the time we have kids. I wanna be able to run around with them, teach them how to change oil in a car, walk my daughter down the aisle one day."

"You will," I tell him. "Just . . . be patient with her. You're not an old man yet."

One of the new prospects walks by just at that moment, a young guy fresh out of high school. "Hey boss, hey old man!"

"See!" Danny shouts. "The prospects think I'm old! I'm going to have to trade my Harley in for a three wheeler soon!"

"At least you can still ride your Harley! I'm driving around in that old Ranger until our wife gives me permission to touch my bike again, but that's beside the point." I turn and wait for him to hold my one-eyed stare. "Danny, listen to me closely. You won't be an old man when you have a baby. You need to be patient with Christina."

"You're starting to sound like a broken record, Beau," he mumbles.

"Dan!" I make him look at me again. "You're not dumb. Think logically for a moment. When's the last time you saw Christina have a sip of alcohol? Have you noticed she somehow had a stomach bug last week but none of us caught it? How about her breasts? She loves having those played with, but she hasn't let any of us near them in some time. When did you pick up her tampons last?"

His face goes blank as he mulls over the questions. I can see him trying to dispute them, but he can't.

"Holy *shit*."

I laugh. "You don't know a thing," I tell him. "I think she's trying to surprise us with the news tonight."

"You knew?" he asks. "How long?"

"I know that two weeks ago she went to her lady doc," I answer. "She went four months ago for her annual, so it wasn't a routine exam. I found the test in the trash two weeks before that, but I didn't say anything because she seemed so excited, but also . . . worried."

"You think she's afraid she'll lose the baby? Or that it was a false positive?" he asks.

"Most mothers worry. Hell, people *should* worry. And she'll keep worrying until she has the baby in her arms, nice and healthy. But we'll get to worry too. For the rest of our lives. No matter what, the baby is ours, brother. We made Christina a promise."

He nods, his eyes glistening. "Does Griff know?"

"Not sure," I tell him. "He hasn't let on anything, but he's pretty observant. I think he just wants us all to be surprised and let Christina have her moment when she's ready. You know Griff, he wants to pretend like nothing excites him."

Dan chuckles and stands up. "And here I am, not noticing any of the signs."

I pull him into a hug, clapping him on the back. "Just make sure to look shocked when she tells us."

"Of course."

* * *

When Griff, Dan, and I roll into the driveway in Danny's muscle car, Christina comes out like she always does to greet us. Her sundress hits just above her knees and swishes with her movements. In a few months, that dress won't fit over her belly. I'm sure that means she'll start wearing our hoodies and T-shirts more often just so she doesn't have to buy maternity clothes. We get out of the car, and she wraps me up in a hug as soon as I'm out of the passenger seat.

We moved out of the old neighborhood we lived in. It had too many bad memories attached to it. Instead, we built a house on the edge of downtown Lexington that resembles the cabin we used to use as a safe house. With the money from that sale and our Lexington house, we were able to build our forever home on some nice, expansive property. It's far enough from the city that we can see the stars at night but close enough that we're near our businesses and everything else we need.

She loves our cabin: five bedrooms, three baths, and an amazing kitchen that she and Danny spend time baking in when midterms and finals approach. Our master bedroom is mostly for Christina, but we all usually end up crammed into her giant bed. It's more perfect than any happily ever after I could have dreamed of.

"Hey, baby," I say, pressing a kiss to her temple.

She smiles before going over to Griff to give him his welcome home kiss, and then Danny his. I watch as he's about to burst at the seams. He doesn't say anything to her, just hugs her a little longer and smiles.

"I got you guys a gift!" Christina says, bouncing on the balls of her feet.

"Shit," Griff says, running a hand over his beard. "Did I forget our anniversary? A birthday?"

Christina rolls her eyes and skips inside the house with us following closely behind.

The whole house smells delicious, and I spot the takeout bags on the counter next to four dinner plates. She ordered from her favorite restaurant, Sutton's, the same place that catered our small commitment reception after all the shit with Demon Rebirth settled down. We didn't want to use our actual wedding day as the anniversary, so we picked a different day to celebrate our love. She likes getting Sutton's on special milestones for us.

There's a big gift bag next to the food, and Griff tries to steal a peek inside.

Christina hands him the bag, and he looks at Danny and I before reaching inside and pulling out a small leather jacket with a little plastic stick in the pocket.

"I'm pregnant," Christina announces, plucking the pregnancy test from the tiny pocket. "We're going to have a baby!"

Danny gets down on his knees in front of Christina, resting his head against her stomach and wrapping his arms around her legs. She smiles and runs her hands over his slicked back hair. He murmurs promises of love and protection against her stomach, but not loud enough for me to hear too much.

Christina reaches a hand out to me, a smile on her face, and tears brimming her eyes. It might have taken a few years, but we're finally pregnant.

"We did it," she beams. I lace my fingers with hers and place my hand on her stomach. "We're going to be parents. Just like we always wanted, Beau. Our family is growing."

I place a kiss on her forehead. "I knew we'd get there. We just took the scenic route, but we found our happy ending, baby. You're going to be the most perfect mother, Christina. And I swear I'll be the best dad I can be."

"I have no doubt," she says. "All of you will be so good to our baby."

She looks down and giggles at Danny as he presses kisses all over her belly that's not even growing yet. I know he's going to be stuck to her like glue for the next few months waiting for the baby to start moving around.

I glance over to Griff who hasn't said much since we got home. His chest isn't moving. I think he's stopped breathing. His eyes are stuck to the pregnancy test. He's still holding the little leather jacket in his hands, but he looks pale in the face.

"Griff," I say. "Snap out of it!"

"What if—" Griff starts to say, but he has to clear his throat. His eyes well with tears. "What if I'm not a good dad? What if I end up just like mine?"

Danny releases Christina and stands up to give her and Griff some room. Christina instantly moves for Griff, stroking his scruffy chin.

"Griffin Grady," Christina says softly. "You will *never* be like him. You're going to be so good with our baby. I have no doubts. If I did, I would have told you guys years ago that I didn't think it was a good thing for us to try. We're going to give this baby the best life ever. We're a team, a family full of undying love."

The tears pour from his eyes, making me tear up as well, and he wraps his arms around her. "I'll try my best no matter what, Princess."

"What if it's a girl?" she says softly.

"Oh, *God*," Griffin practically growls. "I don't want to think about that yet. Just . . . give me a few years."

"I second that!" Danny adds.

I chuckle. "I think we've got some time before we find out if it's a boy or girl, but I'm ready for whatever."

The three of us envelop Christina in a hug, surrounding her and our unborn baby with love. It was a struggle to get to this point, and it's not exactly the life I wanted for us when we were teenagers, but I wouldn't change a damn thing. I got my girl in the end, and I get to share her with two of my best friends who would follow her to the end of earth. As long as we have each other, I know our love will prevail.

End.

If you enjoyed this book, please leave a review at your favorite online retailer's website!

Enthusiastic reviews from readers like you are incredibly helpful.

Thank you!

ABOUT THE AUTHOR

Penny Crane writes books and drinks lots of coffee. She's a loving mother to a handful of cats, a passionate reader, and an espresso aficionado. She lives her best life in a cozy, secluded mountain cabin where she frequently gets lost in the view and finds herself on the trails.

She enjoys going to arcades, online shopping, and hanging out at rock shows. Catch up with her at Penny Crane's Romance on Facebook: readerlinks.com/l/1453522

Don't miss all the hot new Penny Crane releases!